The Whistling Galilean

SHAI'S JOURNEY

JENNIFER BJORK

Copyright © 2021 Jennifer Bjork.

All rights reserved. No part of this book may be used or reproduced by any means, graphic, electronic, or mechanical, including photocopying, recording, taping or by any information storage retrieval system without the written permission of the author except in the case of brief quotations embodied in critical articles and reviews.

This book is a work of religious fiction. Unless otherwise noted, the author and the publisher make no explicit guarantees as to the accuracy of the information contained in this book.

WestBow Press books may be ordered through booksellers or by contacting:

WestBow Press
A Division of Thomas Nelson & Zondervan
1663 Liberty Drive
Bloomington, IN 47403
www.westbowpress.com
844-714-3454

Because of the dynamic nature of the Internet, any web addresses or links contained in this book may have changed since publication and may no longer be valid. The views expressed in this work are solely those of the author and do not necessarily reflect the views of the publisher, and the publisher hereby disclaims any responsibility for them.

THE HOLY BIBLE, NEW INTERNATIONAL VERSION®, NIV® Copyright © 1973, 1978, 1984, 2011 by Biblica, Inc.® Used by permission. All rights reserved worldwide.

ISBN: 978-1-6642-3809-1 (sc)
ISBN: 978-1-6642-3810-7 (hc)
ISBN: 978-1-6642-3808-4 (e)

Library of Congress Control Number: 2021912871

Print information available on the last page.

WestBow Press rev. date: 09/28/2021

CONTENTS

PART 1	**LIFE BY THE SEA**	
Chapter 1	Grandfather's Gift	1
Chapter 2	A Stranger Appears	11
Chapter 3	Fishers of Men	21
Chapter 4	Holy Sabbath	33
Chapter 5	Day of Rest	43
Chapter 6	Dinner Discoveries	51
Chapter 7	The Accident	59
Chapter 8	School Session	70
Chapter 9	Yona the Fisherman	79
Chapter 10	Carmi's Tale	87
Chapter 11	Carving Time	95
Chapter 12	Battle Lines	103
Chapter 13	Payment or Punishment?	113
PART 2	**MIRACLES REVEAL**	
Chapter 14	The Paralyzed Man Walked	129
Chapter 15	The Tax Collector	146
Chapter 16	Event in the Woods	153
Chapter 17	One Unpleasant Thing	165
Chapter 18	Mountain Sermon	172
Chapter 19	The Broken Became Whole	185
Chapter 20	Stormy Seas	192
Chapter 21	The Gift of Joy	204
Chapter 22	Camping in Tents	219

Chapter 23	King of the Hill	229
Chapter 24	Bounteous Meal	243
Chapter 25	Who Was There?	256
Chapter 26	Repairs and Amends	267
Chapter 27	Sabbath Revelation	276
Chapter 28	Shai's Tale	288
Chapter 29	Yona the Elder	294
Chapter 30	Shai's Choice	307
Appendix 1	Characters, Definitions, and References	315
Appendix 2	Weights and Measures	321
Appendix 3	Images	325
Author's Note		335

Part 1

LIFE BY THE SEA

1

Grandfather's Gift

SHAI FELT IMPORTANT. HIS FATHER HAD GIVEN HIM A TASK THAT summer morning. He would be noticed by all the Galilean fishermen.

"Are you ready?"

With a nod from the old fisherman, the tan ten-year-old guided Yona the Elder's hand to his right shoulder to help the white-haired man balance. The wrinkled man was part of an important ceremony. The boy took the old man's cane in his free hand. The Elder's walking aide was useless in this environment because it would sink into the sand. Shai was its substitute.

Both of them slowly made their way past several wooden boats lined bow or front facing the forest. The gathered fishermen awaited their arrival beside the gray-blue Sea of Galilee.

The sun's warmth and the occasional cool breeze on his face filled Shai with energy. With his entire body, he wanted to romp down the soft, creamy, yellow sand. He knew he dared not do as he desired. Papa was more observant than normal today. Therefore, the obedient boy demonstrated his helpfulness at a snail's pace.

To Shai, they moved in slower than slow motion. Unfortunately,

~ 1 ~

that gave his older brother time to notice them coming. The younger boy glanced up and tensed when he heard his brother's impatient stomps approaching. Ezra joined them in several large strides.

"Here, Grandpa, I will help you get there faster. Shai is too slow." Grabbing hold of the old man's thin arm, Ezra yanked the Elder's hand off Shai's shoulder.

"Not so fast, Ezra. We are almost there," Shai protested as he tried to grab hold of the Elder.

It was in vain. Events happened too quickly. The boy watched his grandfather try to take a large step forward to catch up to the Elder's arm that Ezra had pulled away. He saw the old man tilt too far forward. Shai guessed what would happen next. He rushed forward to prevent the accident. If only he could get in front of his grandfather in time.

The younger boy flung himself in front of the old man. He noticed that Ezra seemed oblivious of the problem rapidly developing behind him.

Even though Shai tried to prevent the Elder's precarious forward tilt, he was neither big nor strong enough to shore up the man he loved. First, the wrinkled man sank to his knees. Then he collapsed. Shai was squished, pinned beneath his grandfather and nose-down in the soft sand.

He felt the weight on top of him lessen as his grandfather was lifted upward. As the pile of bones on top of him unraveled, his father's voice sounded far away through the sand packed in his right ear. "Are you alright Elder?"

Then Shai heard Ezra's muffled voice, "But he was right with me, Papa. I don't know what happened. It must have been Shai's fault."

Papa yanked Shai up by his sandy robe and shook him, "I told you to help my father to the beach, to get him there safely and on time. I am disappointed in you. You failed me."

In shock, Shai watched his father and brother bracket and guide his grandfather toward other fishing boats at the water's edge. As they walked, they wiped sand off everywhere they could reach using their free hands.

The Whistling Galilean

Discovering a mouth full of sand, Shai realized that he could not protest. Instead of following, he walked directly to the surf line. He used both hands to toss water onto his face and clear sandy grit from his eyes, ears, nose, and mouth. Once sufficiently clean, he shook sand from his clothing.

While he cleaned himself, he watched the group of fishermen form a small ring. It was only now that they paid attention to the old man. Several men beside the Elder carefully wiped sand out of his robe, hair, ears, and eyes.

The boy noticed also that no one walked over to check on him. He heard no words from anyone asking, "Are you all right, Shai?" or, "Are you hurt?" No one, especially not his father, said, "Thanks for your help." All he heard in his head was the remaining echo of disappointment and disgust in his father's tone.

Snorting, the tan-haired boy dislodged the last of the sandy snot from his nose before joining the group. He wormed his small frame into a position beside his grandfather. Looking around, he noticed that the circle contained all the active fishermen on this part of the Galilean coast and many of their sons. That in itself was impressive. That told him that his father was respected. He also noticed that many of them shook their heads in disgust when they looked toward him.

The white-haired man cleared his throat. Shai's attention turned to his grandfather beside him. The old man acknowledged him with a wink of his pale blue eyes and a nod. Those small motions told Shai everything without words. The Elder was smart and noticed things. The Elder knew exactly what had happened.

The Elder took hold of Shai's hand, giving it a loving squeeze. "Here, Shai, stand by me. I may need your shoulder again." That small act of inclusion made up for everything else that had happened earlier.

The proceedings started. Their leader spoke first. Simon, a huge man with reddish hair and a deep, gravelly voice began, "Welcome to you all. We are gathered here together this beautiful summer morning to fulfill the traditions of this guild of fishermen. May Elohim, the Lord our God, bless this gathering. May we honor Elohim in all

~ 3 ~

we say and do. Under the presence of Elohim, we acknowledge and welcome a new member as an apprentice. Yona the Younger is the father of this new member. As is our custom, the father of the apprentice-to-be speaks next. What do you say, Yona the Younger?"

His father straightened and pointed proudly to his son, "Thank you all for coming to honor my eldest son, Ezra, and to accept your role in training him to become a productive, valuable member of our community of fishermen. He has worked hard to learn the basic skills such as mending nets, making and using the cast net, and cleaning and working from my fishing boat. Under the presence of Elohim, I present to you my eldest son, Ezra, 'the helper.'"

Shai became distracted and did not hear his father's next words. Everyone knew that Ezra meant helper in Hebrew. He also knew that Ezra was rarely helpful in anything. In fact, the boy knew that his older brother left many of his own chores - as many as he could get away with - for Shai to do.

He heard his father's voice again. "…and he has progressed to the apprentice stage of our trade. Now he can work with all of you on your boats, not just on mine. Now all of you become his teachers, too, so that he can become a valuable asset to our community."

Shai knew that the eldest son was expected to enter the trade of his father. Ezra was doing just that. The younger brother did not know if his older brother even desired a different profession. He strongly suspected that Ezra was just taking the easy way out by following the path laid out by his father.

Yona's voice continued, "I am proud of him."

Shai grumbled under his breath, "No, not that."

Thankfully, he had not spoken his protest very loudly. Those were not the words he wanted to hear his father say about his brother. He really wanted his father to say those exact words in front of this group in reference to him. He was jealous and impatient. He just wanted his father to be proud of him.

When his father paused, Shai knew that the square-jawed man had overheard his middle son's growl of protest. Papa glared directly at him as if to say, *just you wait. We will talk about this later. Now*

The Whistling Galilean

behave yourself. It seemed that no one else in the group noticed the exchange.

As the younger son quietly fumed, Papa continued his praise of Ezra, ending with, "From your nods of agreement, I am glad to see that you all support his progress. Now, you need to voice your acceptance of Ezra as an apprentice in this guild."

Around the circle, each man took a turn saying the same thing. "Yes, I accept Ezra, son of Yona, as an apprentice member, and I agree to be one of many of his teachers."

It was finally Yona the Elder's turn to speak. This rite of passage was as formal as any that the fishermen performed. Even though the old man's thin, reedy voice had become higher pitched, it still commanded their attention. The Elder had once been their leader and spokesman.

Shai noticed that the men listened intently as his grandfather started, "Ezra, my grandson, I too am happy to see your progress. I too have seen you learn the skills that we rely on. I too am proud of your growth. You still have much to learn as an apprentice fisherman. I am willing to continue to be one of your teachers. My experiences and knowledge will be readily shared. I am honored to have been selected to present you with your apprenticeship gift."

The Elder released Shai's hand and reached into the pocket of his sleeve. He extracted a rectangle wrapped in linen and carefully wiped off sand.

"My hands can no longer do the fine work to prepare a fish. This special gift was made by master craftsmen. I now pass it down to you. Ezra, my grandson, in honor of your acceptance by this guild of fishermen as an apprentice member, I present you with my own fillet knife."

Shai gasped in surprise. So did many others. Yona the Elder's knife was well known and recognized by this group. The blade had been crafted out of the best steel for its task. The old man was well respected for his skilled use of this beautiful, black and silver marbled blade.

The boy trembled as he backed away into the nearby palms

encircling the beach. His mind protested words that his body could not release as he heard the gathered fishermen roundly praise Ezra.

The ten-year-old knew that his brother had worked hard. Yes, he even admitted that Ezra deserved to become an apprentice. He knew that he should have remained in the circle of acceptance to voice his words of praise, too, but he could not. He did not want the Elder see his tears. He did not want his grandfather to turn from the task of honoring his older brother.

So, instead of staying, Shai hid. He was hurt. He ached inside like something was broken.

He was also jealous - extremely so. From that dark edge of shade behind the trees and vines, mostly hidden from view, he could let his emotions roil, tumble, and then settle. He had to get them in better control before he went back out to face his father and especially his grandfather.

He tried to understand. He heard each fisherman in turn praise Ezra and describe what he could teach, although it hardly registered in his brain. Earlier that morning, Shai thought that Papa would give his favorite son something special, his own first fillet knife. After all, Papa Yona overlooked Ezra's shortcomings, tirades, fits of anger, and laziness. He even boastfully praised Ezra's deeds, even when he had seen Shai and others do the requested tasks.

Shai suddenly realized that he was not merely jealous of his brother. He was also disappointed in his father. Papa Yona could have taken him aside before the ceremony and told him about the planned gift in advance. He could have told him then that he loved Shai, too, but the boy knew his father wasn't the openly kind and loving type. Large, salty droplets continued to fall down the boy's cheeks.

He was surprised that the mandatory apprenticeship gift came from his grandfather instead of his father. Because Ezra had accepted their Galilean grandfather's beautiful, sharp fillet knife, Shai felt that the person he constantly competed against for recognition in his own family had bested him again. Since Ezra was four years older than Shai, he would probably continue to be first and best in everything.

The Whistling Galilean

That bothered the younger brother a lot. Shai needed to discover one thing that he could do better than Ezra.

He knew his brother. Yona the Elder's fillet knife could not generate warm feelings in Ezra's stone heart. It was Shai that valued that specific knife for its craftsmanship and Ezra knew it. The thin, sharp steel blade cut through fish flesh like a hot knife through butter. The primary reason that he desired that knife was because his grandfather had carved the smooth, creamy bone handle himself. Just by holding the knife, Shai felt the elderly fisherman's essence. He loved the old man so very much, even more than his own father. He coveted that specific knife because it would always be a reminder of the elder fisherman who had used it so skillfully. He wanted the knife because he knew that they had a special bond.

Eventually, Shai wandered back down and joined the edge of the group with a false smile pasted between his cheeks. As he stood watching the events on the beach, the boy wondered if his competitor would always be Papa's favorite. He knew that his bossy, know-it-all brother did not display kindness toward anyone, not even his grandfather. In Shai's opinion, Ezra only appeared to help his grandfather this morning to show off to Papa and to get Shai in trouble.

Soon the ceremony was over. Papa finally drew Shai aside "I am disappointed in you. You failed to get the Elder safely to the beach. You failed to congratulate Ezra on his accomplishments. I am taking the Elder home now. You will stay and help Ezra clean up *Ole Blue*. I am leaving him in charge."

Shai groaned, "But, Papa...."

"No excuses. This time, do as you are told."

Of all people, it was Ezra who ordered him personally to do the dirty, menial labor. In a louder than normal voice, Ezra commanded, "Isaiah, clean out the boat. If I find even a fish scale, I will make you do it again."

How dare his brown-haired brother use his full name, Isaiah? Only Shai's parents or other adults in the community called him by his given name, and only when they chastised him for doing something wrong. In using that name, Ezra imitated an adult and thus lorded power and authority over Shai.

To calm himself, Shai tugged at his light brown hair tied behind his neck. He nearly reacted in protest. He nearly erupted. If they were home alone, that is probably what would have happened. He would have engaged in another wrestling bout that he would have lost. But they were not at home.

So, Shai withstood the humiliation. He pretended as if it did not matter and as if he did not care. "Sure thing, boss."

He even managed a fake smile. He knew Ezra was just being his usual self. He knew he had been set on edge by the gift of the knife. It was better for him to consider how he could undo the gift or get back at Ezra than to vent his anger publicly right now. But that was difficult.

The ten-year-old washed out smelly fish guts from his father's wooden fishing boat, *Ole Blue*, the very boat that had taken Papa Yona and Ezra out early that morning. Meanwhile, he was well aware of Ezra stretched out on an old palm trunk openly examining and fondling his newly acquired gift.

As Shai wrung water out of the sponge, he imagined wringing that knife out of Ezra's grasp. He knew he would not, no, could not, physically do it, but the imagined visual made him feel better. Shai knew he would lose any fight with his stronger, taller, and heavier sibling, but he liked to imagine winning - just once.

Then the fourteen-year-old ordered, "Do not forget to oil the woodwork. Put the boats to bed for the day. I see Papa. Since he has returned, I am joining him and several other fishermen. I will check your work when I return. I... ahem..."

Ezra's voice cracked. He was at the age that it was lowering into the range of a man's voice. Every now and then, it slipped up into a boy's higher range. The older boy cleared his throat and tried again, "I will make you do it again, if it is not done right."

The younger brother felt like laughing at Ezra as he departed, but he did not. He had been dismissed, just like that. He felt used. He felt wrung out like dirty water from his dirty sponge. The injustice of it all!

The Whistling Galilean

With a sigh, Shai helplessly joined the other boys and young men maneuvering the wooden trunks to move three fishing boats from the water's edge up to the upper sandy beach under the coconut palms. Smooth, thick tree trunks whose branches had been removed acted as a series of rollers to help the fishermen get their heavy wooden boats in and out of the water. Once the boat advanced and the rear roller was free, Shai and three other boys carried the free log toward the upper beach where it became the forward roller.

A group of muscled teens grunted together as they strained against the lines pulling the boat forward. Other muscular teens pushed from the stern or back of the boat. Their repeated grunts created a rhythm of movement.

"Oomphhh... two... three..."

"Oomphhh... two... three..."

Once the boat started moving forward, its heavy weight generated momentum. That made it easier to keep it rolling. If it slowed down to a stop, the boat became a heavy deadweight again.

The lead teen yelled at the younger boys, "Move it, move it, move it! Get that forward roller in place - now! Keep us moving forward!"

Shai's family was part a small community of fishermen. They could not afford the cost of building a wooden dock or a stone quay to secure their boats for loading and unloading, for access to make repairs, or for protection from frequent sudden storms that swept over the Sea of Galilee. So, they developed a way to roll the boats out of the water and up the sandy beach. Nestled against the forest edge, the boats had more protection. In addition, the shade provided a nicer work environment, especially during the hot summers.

After the hard work was finished, Shai felt better. Since Ezra was away, Shai walked over to his brother's cast net hung on branches on the upper beach. Now, what could he do to get even? He looked around to make sure no one was watching. Then he leaned down and tied several knots into the net, creating a tangled ball. He smoothed the folds to make the mess he had created less noticeable. It did not even the score, but it was a start. Ezra's net would not open until he found and untied the knots.

~ 9 ~

Jennifer Bjork

Sitting in the boat with the blue hull, Shai rubbed olive oil into the worn wood decking that was gouged and scratched from hard use. He folded the clean cloth several times to protect his hands from the split wood. When he was younger, he had not been so careful. Looking at his left palm, he recollected how long it had taken one particularly painful sliver of wood to work itself out of his skin, and how hard it had been to use his middle finger during that time. He did not want to suffer through that again.

The smell of olives in the oil he applied to the boat's exposed surface made his stomach growl. He was hungry. When he finished, he would go to his private little cove to clean up for dinner.

2

A Stranger Appears

ONCE THE OILING OF *OLE BLUE* WAS COMPLETED, SHAI WALKED alone down the tree-covered sandy, dirt path toward what he liked to think was his private beach. It was a small crescent-shaped beach near the stream north of the primary fisherman's beach. Inaccessible from the main beach because of the jagged rocky outcropping, few people used it. The boy felt it was his.

Whistling bird songs, he ambled down the forest path around the craggy barrier. He was so good at repeating their songs that some songbirds flew down to a low branch over his head. He hoped to get some of them familiar with him to the point that they would land on his shoulder or, better yet, his finger when called.

As he neared the small crescent beach, he wondered if Dov was there. Maybe his best friend had arrived before him. After all, it was their favorite meeting place. Whenever either of them had free time, this was where they would go. Shai wanted to - no he needed to - unload his hurt feelings on his childhood friend. He could not express them to anyone else.

Shai whistled hopefully as he approached a small knoll between the tall reeds. Over the years, he and Dov developed specific whistles to communicate with each other. So, he whistled a sharp, hawk-like territorial sound, then stood still and listened. If Dov was near, Shai would hear his echoing whistle in response. There was no echoing whistle.

Pushing through the shrubs and reeds, he arrived at the thin, flat, tan beach. It was his refuge, his place of safety. Even though this beach did not belong to him, he felt a sense of ownership of this small, curved piece of flat sand nestled between the palms and vast sea.

Shai relaxed a bit. His shoulders lowered, and he felt the tightness in the muscles of his arms release. He had not realized that he was still tense from the morning's escapades. His face broke out into a smile.

Since his father was home and not at sea, he knew that dinner would be on time. Therefore, he had to be home before sunset. Looking up at the partially cloudy sky, he used the quality of blue and the sun angle to gauge how much time he had on his favorite beach. Today, there was enough time for a hidden swim.

When possible, Shai chose to clean off at the end of the day in the waters of the Galilee. His only other choice for bathing was to fetch water from the community well, pour it into the basin beside the house next to the garden, and wipe himself off with a soapy cloth. Washing off in the sea made him feel so much cleaner.

Shai stopped at the fallen palm trunk and shook his sandals off. He stripped off his robe and gently folded it, then placed it on the log to keep it clean.

His ears registered a rhythmic splashing. This sound was not generated by waves, especially not the gentle lapping of the late afternoon. He knew those natural sounds by heart. Today, the water only tickled the sand making a soft, gentle *shush*.

Curious, he looked up. A tall, tanned, thin man with broad shoulders waded near the shore, heading toward him. He walked slowly with his sandals slung carelessly on a curved finger. His bare feet and ankles splashed through the water. He uttered a quiet, familiar sound of enjoyment, "Ahhhh..."

The Whistling Galilean

Not many outsiders walked on this particular beach. Most people followed the beach "road," a well-trod path that curved inland, to avoid small river deltas and soft marshy muds.

Shai sat on the palm log and watched the man approach. He was not someone Shai recognized. The man left the shallow water and stopped a few paces from the boy. As the man looked into Shai's light brown eyes, the boy returned his gaze, matching the man's intensity.

Shai noticed that the stranger's eyes were unusual in color, bluish-greenish with specks of brown and black. The boy classified the stranger's eyes as hazel. As he peered into those eyes, he felt like he was being drawn into the universe. After what felt like an eternity, he shook himself loose.

In a mid-range, clear voice, the man spoke first, "Shalom, the cool water feels good."

Regaining his composure, Shai chuckled at the tall stranger. "Shalom, peace be to you, too. My tasks for the day are done. I am going to wash off."

The stranger smiled and nodded an affirmation. "I have finished mine, also. Do you mind if I join you?"

Shai felt no threat or danger from the demeanor of this man, so he agreed.

The man's smile continued to beckon him into conversation, "What is your name?"

Even though Shai normally would not talk with a strange adult, an outsider, he found himself doing just that. "I am called Shai, son of Yona. It is pronounced like saying 'I' with a 'sh' in front. My father is the fisherman, Yona. Perhaps you know him?"

"Not yet. Ah, you are named for the prophet Isaiah. He was a good man, righteous in the eyes of God."

"Yes. Our rabbi reads from his scrolls quite often. It is a hard name to live up to, so I am glad to called by the nickname, Shai. I feel more like me and not someone famous. Adults use my complete name, Isaiah, when I get into trouble or when an elder wants me to really pay attention. Otherwise, it's just Shai." Normally, the boy wasn't so chatty.

"Then I will call you Shai, too. My name is Yeshua. Your name in Hebrew means 'the salvation of the Lord.' Mine means 'Savior' or 'Anointed One.'"

"So, what should I call you?"

"Call me Yeshua. I do not have a nickname... yet." The man's thin lips curled up into another smile. His eyes twinkled like the stars.

By now, Yeshua had also removed his outer garments, folded them, and placed them on the fallen log. They remained in their tunics, thin sleeveless undergarments, and headed toward the beaconing coolness. As they walked, Shai noticed the relaxation of the man's tanned face through his thin beard and mustache.

"Last one in is a rotten egg," the man said, his long legs carrying him quickly toward the surf. His melodious laugh swept into the boy's ears.

"No!" Shai's protest faded as the ten-year-old followed as fast as his shorter legs allowed.

They entered the water at the same time. Any frustrations Shai held melted away in the cool water as it caressed him. With a deep exhale, he released all remaining tension with a barely audible, "Ahhh." He could hear Yeshua do the same.

Once their heads were out of the water, Shai asked, "Do you know how to swim?"

"No. I do not know anyone who knows how. Can you teach me?"

In secret, Shai had taught himself to swim. "Yes, but you have to keep it a secret. I taught myself by copying the motions of a swimming frog. My parents do not know and would be angry because they do not want me to drown."

"I will keep your secret." The man promised.

So, the boy showed the man the frog kick. It looked like the boy was sitting cross-legged on the ground with the soles of his feet touching. Then, he kicked out quickly into a straight-legged position. Once that was mastered, they smoothly matched their arm movements to their legs. Yeshua soon mastered this skill even though it was his first time.

This swimming stroke worked well whether the belly was

The Whistling Galilean

submerged in the water or exposed to the air. Either way, facing down or up, the frog stroke propelled them forward. Soon, they were both swimming anywhere at will, laughing and spouting water out of their mouths.

Shai happened to glance at the angle of the sun. It was approaching sunset.

Reluctantly, Shai got Yeshua's attention. "I've got to dry off and go home to dinner."

As they dried off with their robes, they continued talking. Yeshua said, "You asked me if I had met your father. I would like to meet him. I am trying to meet most of the fishermen around here. That is the reason I came to the Galilee. I have already met Andrew. He spent some time with the baptizing prophet, John. John is my cousin and I am eager to catch up with him."

The boy noticed that Yeshua knew to call their location the Galilee. Good. He must have been from nearby. "Oh, I know Andrew. He lives with his brother, Simon, in a nice stone house in Capernaum about a block from the synagogue."

"I see. I am headed in that direction."

"Your accent is a little different from ours. Where do you come from?"

"I was raised in Nazareth, to the southeast of the Galilee. People say that I am from nowhere, because Nazareth is so small and insignificant. People that I meet tease me because of my accent."

"I get teased, too. People from the south love to make fun of all of us from the province of Galilee. They think they are so much better than we are." Shai was glad that they had something in common. He already liked this playful, unusual man.

Finished dressing, Yeshua stretched his arms up, pulling his back straight. The boy copied him.

The man sat on the log facing the great blue lake. The horizon in the distance was defined by hazy brown and green hills to the west. Several small, puffy, white clouds floated in the paling sky. The dry breeze from the desert to the south had quickly dried their moist skin and tunics.

Yeshua said, "I mentioned that I am meeting the fishermen from around here. Please tell me about your father, Yona."

Shai answered thoughtfully, "He's a good fisherman. Papa Yona is part of a team of fishermen that feed our community of seven families. We pool our resources to maintain three boats. He is proud that we were able to buy them and not lease them from someone in Capernaum or Tiberias across the lake."

"That is quite an accomplishment. If you are willing, tell me something more personal about him."

"Well, just this morning he was proud to honor my older brother as an apprentice in our guild of fishermen."

"That is quite an accomplishment. How did you feel about that, Shai?"

Before the boy could stop himself, his higher-pitched voice cracked as he cut to the heart of his hurt feelings. "I felt hurt and jealous. Papa told all the gathered fishermen that he was proud of Ezra. My older brother is his favorite. He doesn't pay attention to the rest of us children. He is proud of my bratty brother, proud of the lazy pretender. That really hurt. I want him to be proud of me. I want him to like me, to respect me…to love me."

Shai could not believe that he shared these intimate thoughts with a stranger he had only just met. He usually only confided his feelings to Dov. How could he have done this?

"I'm sorry that your feelings were hurt. Not all fathers know how to show their love to their sons."

As he studied his toes wiggling in the sand, Shai nodded in agreement.

"I understand that it was Ezra's time to be honored. Your time will come. Be patient, Shai. I know that is hard to do, but I promise, it will be worth the wait."

"That's not all, Yeshua. Ezra was given my grandfather's fillet knife as his apprenticeship gift. That hurt me deeply. I wanted him to give me that knife. I'm the one in the family that loves my grandfather the most. We have a special bond. Why couldn't Papa have given Ezra something of his own instead?"

The Whistling Galilean

Shai squeezed his eyes tight and shook his head, but that did not stop the hurt. Giant tears rolled down his cheeks like the flood arriving to lift Noah's ark. He felt Yeshua's warm hand gently pat him on the back. The boy couldn't resist nestling his head into the man's comforting arms and heard him murmur, "There, there. There, there."

The droning of Yeshua's voice was like a calm balm soothing his soul. "There, there. There, there. Let me tell you a story, a tale of two sons."

With a snuffle, Shai agreed, "Alright."

"There was a man who had two sons. He went to one son and said, 'Son, go and work today on the boat.' 'I will not,' the son answered, but later he changed his mind and went. Then the father went to the other son and requested the same thing. 'I will,' the second son answered, but later he did not go."

As Shai listened, he felt Yeshua's warm, caring arm around him, and he felt comforted. He relaxed as his hurt melted away. So, this was what it felt like to have a loving father. He enjoyed the feeling and wondered if this stranger would be willing to replace his father and provide him the emotional support that he needed.

Then Yeshua pushed him upright, looked him in the eyes, and asked him, "Think, Shai, which of the two sons do you think did what his father requested?"

Shai tried hard to recollect the tale. It didn't take him long to figure out his answer. "I think it was the son who actually went and did the work on the boat, regardless of what he actually said. I think his actions spoke louder than his words."

Yeshua laughed. "That sounds like someone I just met, doesn't it?"

Shai chuckled. Sitting taller, he pointed to himself. "Yes, it does. Me. I did the work on the boat. Ezra ordered me to do it but Papa asked him to help do the work. My older brother passed his work on to me."

With that realization, Shai laughed too, a hearty, deep, stress-releasing belly laugh. He laughed even harder when Yeshua tickled his ribs. They guffawed with their whole bodies so completely that they both teetered on their log perch, almost falling off.

"Oh, that was a good one!"

After catching his breath, Yeshua shared something personal about himself. "You told me about your father. I would like to tell you about my father. He is a humble, smart, hard-working carpenter."

"Is that what you do, too?"

"Yes, I work with my hands." The man from Nazareth raised his hands, palms up, to show Shai the callouses from years of hard labor, before he continued, "I build things. I even helped my father frame and construct stone buildings, but I would rather repair things, like broken furniture. Occasionally, I do that in trade, my work for a meal."

"Sometimes my father does that, too - trading for things."

Yeshua gently stuck a foot into the soft sand and threw some sand upwards. The dry powder spread thinly in the air landing like a mist of dew. Shai was having such a good time.

"Well, I am eager to share something with you, Shai, but you must keep it a secret. The time is not yet right for anyone else to know this secret. I will reveal it to others at just the right time. Can you do that?"

"Oh, yes, I will." Shai meant every word.

"I am excited to be starting a new job. It is my destiny. For a few years, I will be a teacher. I will also be a healer. Then, I will reveal my true mission. While I do this, I hope we see each other often."

"Me, too." The youngster felt a hot flush as his cheeks blushed red under his tanned skin. He was flattered. This unusual adult seemed to enjoy his company and was sharing information with him as if speaking to another man, an equal. He discovered that he was able to readily talk to this man from Nazareth. He was not at all like other adults that Shai had met.

Shai wondered out loud, "Will you teach carpentry?"

"No. I will teach people the way our Lord Elohim desires us to live - the way of light instead of dark, of good versus bad. I will tell people about the prophesies of Israel's past prophets. I will show that the prophesies are being fulfilled."

The Whistling Galilean

"Oh, my. It sounds like you will become a rabbi."

"Some will call me by that name. Sometimes my teaching will be in a synagogue, but I will heal the broken wherever I am and wherever I go."

"Oh, that's unusual. How did you know to do this new job?"

"From my Father. I came to fulfill a prophecy, the prophecy of Isaiah."

"I do not understand." Shai was confused. Rabbi Selig often taught from the scrolls of Isaiah, but he couldn't relate what he had been taught with some sort of prophecy.

Yeshua quietly thought for a while, as if he was choosing the right words, then he explained, "Isaiah prophesied that a child will be born that will honor Elohim. He will be from the Galilee near the Jordan River."

"That is here! Is the child from here?" exclaimed Shai with excitement. With a shock, the next words squeezed out of his mouth before he could stop them. After all, it was a natural conclusion. Since this man from Nazareth was talking to him and befriending him, the child that he was, Shai obviously wondered if that special child was himself. After all, the stranger had said that he wanted to see him often. "Am I that child?"

The man from Nazareth answered gently with a quiet chuckle, "You are from this area, Shai, but the child that Isaiah spoke of was not born here. The child will be known by what he does here, what he does in and around the Sea of Galilee."

"Oh." Despite his disappointment, the boy was intrigued. He felt like he was unraveling a fishing net brought out of the sea to uncover a mysterious catch. In order to do that, he needed more information. So, he asked another question, "Are you seeking that child?"

"No, I am not. It is not anyone you know that lives around here." The man from Nazareth chuckled again. "It is I, my friend. I am the child that Isaiah spoke about. I am that great light."

Shai's eyebrows went up in surprise. "You? How do you know that you are the one?"

"I know because my Father tells me that this is so."

Jennifer Bjork

"It seems to me that your rabbi would know if you are the answer to a religious prophecy better than your carpenter father."

The tall stranger did not answer at once. Glad for the quiet, the boy tried to make sense of all that he had heard. Sitting side by side, they both watched the clouds slowly turn pink as the sun began to set over the golden hills to the west. Ribbons of green trees and orchards in the valleys provided a contrasting texture to the linear dried grass and spotted brown soil and rocks. The haze of the far mountain range began to soften from gray-brown to golden-pink.

Yeshua broke the stillness by saying softly, "Remember, this is a secret between us. I will eventually tell others, but you are the first."

"And…remember my secret swimming stroke. You are the first person I shared it with, too."

Suddenly, as if a lightning bolt had struck him from the sky, Shai realized that the sun was setting and that he had promised his mother that he would be home before dark. He hopped off of the log. "I have to go home now. We both have secrets to keep. I will keep yours."

3

Fishers of Men

"Tell me a story, Fishel," Shai encouraged as he tied knot after knot in the linen rope coiled on his lap. He sat on the fisherman's beach in the shade of a palm tree. Many other men were on the beach attending to boats or nets.

Fishel, the older teenager that his father had selected to be his teacher, grinned at him. "You should like this one."

Since Papa Yona had been Ezra's mentor, Shai had expected the same experience when it was his time to learn. He knew that his tough father was a talented fisherman and had many skills to pass on to his sons. He had looked forward to learning them. He had hoped that in spending one-on-one time with his father, they would naturally grow closer. But since he had been handed over to Fishel, he felt discarded like trash in a compost pile, stinky and rotting.

Nevertheless, Shai was grateful that Ezra had not been given the task to teach him the trade. He was grateful that Fishel was his mentor instead of the bossy brat he was related to by blood. Know-it-all Ezra was already boasting that he was a full-fledged fisherman even though he was still considered an apprentice. It would have been hard to learn anything from someone who was so self-centered.

Like most brothers, they competed over everything. As the brother smaller in stature and younger in age, Shai struggled for attention. He wanted to be better than Ezra at something. Now, he had the opportunity to become a better fisherman than Ezra, so he worked hard. He reasoned that if he could do that, then maybe Papa Yona's pride would finally shine on him.

Therefore, he was determined to learn this trade regardless of who taught him. He felt lucky. Fishel was a patient and skilled teacher. The well-muscled teen not only explained how to do things but why that way was best. The ten-year old was surprised that he actually thrived under the ruggedly handsome eighteen-year-old's undivided attention.

Fishel was entertaining, too. As the boy constructed his first cast net, he enjoyed hearing stories about big catches, Fishel, and other fishermen. Some tales were believable, and some not.

"You see, Shai," Fishel said, starting another story. "It was the biggest fish I ever saw. It was almost as long as you are tall. It had silvery sides that reflected the moonlight and a giant black eye that stared back at me through the sea."

"Did you pull it in?"

"I tried. It spun in circles, soon wrapping the cord around my hand. Then it dove deep, out of sight. I tried to pull in the monster fish with one hand. I strained with every ounce of energy I could muster, but I could not budge the monster. It was too heavy. The cord began to cut into my left arm and hand. Eventually, it made a trench in my flesh and muscle that bled profusely. We were leaving a bloody trail behind the boat. I thought I was going to die out on the Galilee."

"Since you are sitting beside me telling this story, I know that you survived. How?"

"Since my left hand was becoming useless, the only thing I could think of doing was to cut the fish free. I was lucky to have my knife by my side. I grabbed it and sawed at the cord, but the fish kept changing directions, first toward the bow, then back toward the

The Whistling Galilean

stern. The cord wouldn't stay in one place. It slid back and forth on the top rail. When I pulled against the fish with my left arm, the cord cut deeper. It was hard to cut a moving target."

Almost breathless, Shai whispered, "And then what happened?"

"My trapped hand hurt so bad. I wanted to release the tension and the weight of that mighty fish. I knew I had to cut that cord soon or I would lose my hand. If I did not cut it loose, the huge fish would take me with it into the cold, deep water. Its large black eye peered at me from beside the boat. I shivered and kept cutting… and cutting…. Linen is strong but I was persistent. As you already guessed, I eventually won the battle. The strands released. Finally, the huge fighting weight no longer hurt my arm. I felt like a huge net full of fish was lifted off my arm. I felt light and free. Now, the monster was free, too. It dove. I never saw it again."

"Is that why you always have a cloth around your left hand and forearm?"

"Yes. It covers a healing salve."

"So, is that why you have trouble using your left hand?"

"Yes, and that is why I no longer go to sea. That is the reason I have time to be your mentor."

"I'm sorry you were injured, but I'm glad you are my mentor. I hope you heal fast."

Shai's attention shifted to his own hands. He resumed tying square knots using thin, light-weight linen twine. For over two weeks, what felt like an eternity in his lifetime, he had worked linen twine into palm-sized squares with a square knot at each juncture. The net grew ever so slowly.

Circular cast nets were the key piece of gear used by the Galilean fishermen because they were so flexible. This net not only caught smaller fish used for pickling but also bait fish used to catch bigger ones. It was the smallest and most versatile net used by the Galilean fishermen. A solitary fisherman could throw it either from the shore or from a boat. It was the first net all fishermen learned how to make. This was the net that Shai tediously knotted together.

Adult fishermen could throw a seven-cubit diameter net. If his

~ 23 ~

teacher laid his own net out on the beach, just under three men could lie in a line on top of it. Each of their heads would touch the next person's feet. That was too large for a ten-year-old to handle. Therefore, he knotted a smaller training net. It had slowly grown to almost three cubits in diameter. As he got older and stronger, and as his skill in using the cast net improved, they planned to gradually increase the outer edge to make it larger.

After a while, Fishel spoke again. "It's time to look over your net."

Once a day, Shai laid the net out on the beach to make sure it was actually becoming a circle. He watched as black-haired, muscular Fishel walked around the net tugging on it here and there.

Today, he heard the teen exclaim words he yearned to hear, "Your net has reached our target dimension, nearly twice your height."

Shai saw him smile and wink, and he heard the welcome words, "This part of your cast net is finished."

"Finished! Finally!" Shai erupted from the log like a nearby ancient volcano had done centuries ago. He ran down the beach waving his arms with happiness and relief.

"No more knots! No more knots! No more knots!" Each word was accentuated with a step or jump. When he returned to his teacher's side, he wore a broad, silly grin.

Fishel chuckled at his pupil's antics. "The net looks good."

Shai felt so proud. He could not wait to show it to Papa.

After joining his teacher, stretching his lean body in the warm sand, and basking in the sun for a little while longer, he felt Fishel pat him on the arm. "Good job! Let's get back at it."

The boy felt the young man pull his shoulders and him back onto the log beside him.

With a groan, he wiped off sand. Shai said, "But...no more knots, right? I thought I was done with knots."

"I said that we had reached the dimension we needed. Now, it is time to add the weights and the cords to collapse the net around the fish to catch them. Are you ready to do something different?"

"Yes, I am," he sighed. He felt deflated and resigned but was ready for anything else but square knots.

The Whistling Galilean

Fishel explained with a laugh, "No time off for the weary fisherman."

"I know. Papa Yona says that a lot, too. Honestly, I just hope I no longer have to tie any more knots."

"You know that you will tie them forever more." Fishel grinned and shrugged with his hands facing the blue sky, which today matched the color of his eyes. "You will grow to love knots. Without strong, non-slip knots, there will be no fish for dinner."

"I know, but I cannot seem to escape them. I already dream about knots in my sleep. In my dream world, I am usually the fish swimming along, getting trapped by knots all around me. It is horrible!"

"Hmm." Fishel rummaged in his oval cloth bag, which held mending threads, needles, and other tools. The mentor pulled out the desired roll of twine. "We will finish the outside edge of your net using this waxed twine. These knots are tighter, so you will create smaller squares. This makes the edge of the entire net stronger."

"I see." Shai's voice mirrored his pout.

"Look in my bag. Hunt for the small pouch holding weights. As you tie the edge knots, you will also tie on the weights. There are three pouches in my mending bag. The smallest pouch contains the weights we want."

After hefting several small pouches, Shai dropped the requested pouch onto Fishel's robe at his feet. The young fisherman poured out rounded river stones. Each stone already had a hole naturally worn or bored near its middle for the twine to pass through.

Fishel began the next lesson. "This is how to tie the weights on as you strengthen the edge." He demonstrated the triple wraps.

Since Shai knew how close he was to having a completed cast net, his energy was renewed. Fishel watched over his shoulder as the youngster struggled to imitate what Fishel had done so easily. With a few corrections and suggestions, the lad was soon on his own making a 0.05-cubit-wide edge on his net to be measured by the width of Fishel's palm.

It was pleasant listening to the waves lapping on the shore and the peeps of shore birds looking for worms and insects. Shai discovered that he was softly whistling, trying to imitate those rapid-fire, high-pitched peeps. Occasional human grunts down the beach barged in on the natural harmonies as fishermen plied their trade.

After a while, he muttered to his mentor, now repairing his own net. "This feels like women's work. I did not think I would have to know how to sew like a woman."

"That surprised me, too, but men sew, especially fishermen. You will have to repair the sails on the boats, your nets, and sometimes your clothing. It is really important to know how to stitch things up properly. If you do not do a good job, it quickly tears or frays. Then, you will have to do it again. That's no fun. Do a good job to make it last. Sewing is not my favorite task. It's not the favorite task of most fishermen, but it is an essential skill. Did you know that your grandfather could repair canvas in the dark just by feel?"

"No. Did you ever have to do that?"

"Not yet. You are progressing well, Shai. Keep at it." Fishel stood and stretched. "Now, it is time to catch my dinner."

Fishel carried his net to the water. From the sound of feet entering the water, Shai knew his mentor had begun to fish. The first thing the boy noticed when he looked up was the young man's dark-brown hair shining with a golden glow from the sun. The broad-shouldered fisherman waded into the thigh-deep water carrying the folds of his cast net on his left arm. He gripped the center cord in his teeth and held the outer edge of the net in his right hand. After standing still to let the fish settle and return to where they had been feeding, the teen tossed or cast his net in a broad circular motion. The boy heard the *swooosh* of the net in the air. It opened into a circle, like magic, just before landing with a gentle splash. The youngster knew that the idea was to trap any fish below it as the weighted net descended and settled onto the sandy sea floor.

"Don't the fish hear the net landing?" Shai asked loudly so that Fishel could hear his question.

"Sure, but they do not know it is a net. You see, the net imitates the natural sound of a branch or a gull landing on the water."

"Oh. So, the fish do not swim away?"

The Whistling Galilean

"Not if you are good and you do not let the net make a loud smacking sound."

Everything seemed so complicated. There was so much to learn. Shai was eager to actually throw and retrieve his own net. He wanted to finally feel useful - catch fish. That desire had kept him tying those many knots.

As the boy worked, he heard the continuous *swooosh* of the net being cast and *splash* as it landed on the water's surface. By those rhythmic sounds, he could tell that the young man he had grown to admire and respect was not catching fish.

As the sounds moved farther away down the beach, Shai considered Fishel's patient attentiveness and skill, so different from Ezra's impatience, laziness, and bossiness. Shai already wished that Fishel was his brother, not Ezra.

A shout broke into his pensiveness. His mentor exclaimed, "Finally!"

The boy looked up to see the fisherman pulling the cord that went from the outside of the net near the weights up through the center. Normally, a fisherman pulled the net up with a hand-over-hand motion. Instead, his teacher pulled with his good right hand and pinned the cord to his body under his maimed left arm. The technique worked fine on land, but it might not work from a boat.

"Shai, I caught a big one! Come help."

The thin lad jumped up, dropping everything that he was holding onto Fishel's robe. He scampered eagerly down the beach, long hair trailing behind. He watched Fishel take a deep breath and dive down to the sea floor. Since he had watched fishermen before, he easily visualized him entangling the big fish in the net, pulling the net against his body, and grasping it tight. His teacher seemed to stay underwater for an eternity.

Finally, the teen's brown back appeared on the surface of the water. Shai heard the deep inhale of his breath. He watched his teacher shake his head to get the water out of his eyes. At this point, he noticed his mentor's hand clutching the net in a big ball against his belly in a two-armed hug.

Jennifer Bjork

Fishel, the net, and the student arrived at the edge of the waves at the same time.

"Pull the net out of the water."

Grunting, the son of Yona strained as he pulled the wet weight of the net. Once all of the net was on the sand away from the edge of the great blue lake, they collapsed.

"Life is good," Fishel happily exclaimed, with the entangled net and fish lying on his belly. "Ah, the life of a fisherman."

Together, they carried and drug the catch to their log under the coconut palm. Shai knew that his bronzed teacher was nude but he no longer noticed. The fisherman had left his clothes under the palm to have something dry to wear once he was through fishing. He rubbed himself with his outer garment, the fringed mantle, to dry off, then stretched that out to dry. He pulled on his thin, poncho-shaped undergarment between his legs and tucked it into a leather belt tied around his waist.

Shai could not wait to use a cast net because he would not have to wear clothes while fishing in the water, either. What a wonderful tradition! He knew that it would become one of his favorites.

They placed the baskets on the shady side of the log. As they sorted through the net, they removed some small, thin, silvery anchovies entwined in the netting and tossed them into the baskets. Fishel pawed through to the center to uncover the big fish. It was silvery, too, but it was gray-blue on the back with a white belly.

"What a beauty!" Shai exclaimed as he pulled open the top fin, the dorsal, to examine it. The fin started just behind the head and ended just in front of the forked tail. Shai had never seen such a long fin. It traveled nearly the length of the fish's body. It also had an unusual color. A yellowish glow was captured between the bluish color of the fish's back and the midnight-blue top edge of the fin.

"Beautiful," Shai admired. "What type of fish is it? Is it tasty?"

"It's a musht, or tilapia, and is it ever tasty. It has very few bones. The meat melts in your mouth if you do not overcook it. Yum! My family is going to be very happy with this catch. You take most of the small sardines home for your dinner."

~ 28 ~

The Whistling Galilean

Naturally, the man who caught the fish took most of the catch. Giving some of the daily catch to other fishermen was not just a generosity to a friend. The community took care of each other, making sure no one went without food.

As they worked over the net removing fish, Shai asked, "Do you miss going out in the boats with other fishermen?"

"Yes," Fishel nodded as he uncovered several more sardines.

"Will your arm heal? Will you be able to fish again from the boats?"

"I do not know," was Fishel's irritated answer.

Shai figured that his mentor was afraid of the answer, afraid that the answer would be *no* - so he stopped talking.

Once the fish were in baskets covered by damp seaweed, Shai whistled bird songs as he removed seaweed and other debris from the net, then tossed the debris into the trees. Finally, the net was cleaned of debris and fish. The teen and boy stood together and shook the sand off of the net. Then they laced it over some dead branches stuck into the sand on the upper beach to air dry.

When he straightened and looked down the beach, Shai was surprised to see Yeshua walking on the beach toward them. The man was followed by a bunch of little kids, about the age of Shai's younger sister, who was a seven-year-old.

"Yeshua!" Shai greeted with a wave.

Yeshua returned the greeting. "Hello, my friend. I am at work today. It looks like you are, too."

Yeshua turned and approached two other fishermen. It was the brothers, Simon and Andrew, who were casting their nets into the lake.

"Fishel, can I go see what's happening?"

"Sure, but only after we clean up our messes."

The boy quickly did as he was told.

"Remember to hang up your net to air dry. You sure do not want all that hard work to rot away."

"I know, I know ... I sure do not want to redo all those knots!"

After he hung his net, Shai wrapped the remaining thick twine onto a waxed ball. He put it and the remaining weights into Fishel's mending bag.

Fishel said with a smile, "Good job today. Thanks for your help. Now, you can go."

"Don't you want to come, too? Let's see if Simon and Andrew caught a fish as big as the one you caught."

Fishel shook his head. "Not today. It has been a good day, Shai. You have progressed well. Your father will be pleased. I must go home to start dinner."

Shai scooted down the beach in a slow trot, carrying the basket of sardines covered by damp seaweed. The giggling kids were already gathered into a small group. He saw them bent over and busily drawing pictures in the sand with their fingers.

When he arrived where the fishermen stood, he heard Yeshua talking with Simon and Andrew. He heard his new friend say, "I am am looking for good men. I am looking for responsible, respected men. I am looking for men that know how to work hard."

"We are responsible, respected, and work hard," Simon responded.

"I am looking for men that understand teamwork and lending a hand to others. I am looking for fishermen. Both of you seem to be the type of men I seek."

He saw them nodding in agreement. After all, those were words of praise. Simon was the leader of the fishing guild. Shai knew Simon had spoken the truth.

Yeshua pointed to each man in turn and said, "I select you, Simon…and you, Andrew."

Both brothers looked surprised.

The Nazarene continued, "Therefore, *come follow me, and I will make you fishers of men.*"

Confused, Shai repeated those words in his head - *fishers of men* - and wondered what kind of net they would need to catch men. This sounded much more like a game kids would play than something that adults would actually do. Was this a joke?

From his position on the beach, he could not see Yeshua's face, so he studied Simon's sun-wrinkled face framed by his reddish-brown, curly hair. Simon was the expressive one of the two brothers. He did

The Whistling Galilean

not - could not - hide his real feelings. Shai saw towering Simon look down at Yeshua in wonder and amazement, his brown eyes wide open and his bushy reddish eyebrows tilted upward.

Shai wondered what the three men had discussed before he arrived on the scene.

"Hello again, Shai." Yeshua had seen the boy and hailed the new arrival with a grin. "It looks like you have fish for dinner. I hear that your mother is a good cook."

"She is. Fishel shared his catch with me."

The Nazarene turned away from him again and beckoned the two fishermen with a wave. "Come now, Simon and Andrew. Come follow me and become fishers of men."

The former carpenter returned his gaze toward Shai. Yeshua smiled and winked at him, and said softly, "My secret work calls."

As the boy watched the bevy of kids scamper after Yeshua, he realized that the secret ministry was starting. He smiled because he knew he was keeping the Nazarene's secret.

Andrew shrugged, raising both arms at his elbows, hands toward the sky as if saying, *oh well, it is meant to be. I cannot do anything else.*

Then the fisherman turned to the boy and told him, "Shai, take my net. I feel compelled to follow this man. Please hang it up for me."

The ten-year-old accepted the net as Andrew walked past him towards Yeshua.

Simon had not moved. Shai put down his basket and struggled with Andrew's large net. He looked up in time to see Simon's broad eyebrows still raised in surprise. The giant of a man scratched his head as if wondering, *What? Wait. That sounds fishy... crazy.*

Shai watched the interaction between the two men unfold. Yeshua looked back at Simon with a grin and beckoned a second time, "Oh, come now, Simon. You know you want to come. You don't want to be left out of the biggest adventure of your life."

Shai heard the large man say gruffly, "Well, I cannot let Andrew go without me. After all, I am the eldest. I am responsible."

Without another look back, Simon dropped his net. He purposefully strode off to join his brother and Yeshua. Both men

~ 31 ~

walked away from their nets without a backward glance. Simon's net still lay in the surf zone. Shai gripped the edge of it and struggled to drag it out of the Galilee.

"I do not believe my eyes and ears. He did it," Shai whispered as he shook his head to clear his eyes. He realized that the man from Nazareth was very persuasive.

Shai watched the three men walk away into the forest. Neither fisherman had paused long enough to hang their nets up to dry. That was highly unusual. The damp sand would keep the twine moist. He knew that the brothers would really be upset if the damp net fibers became rotten and left holes for the fish to escape. Then, both fishermen would have to spend time mending them. Or, even worse, the cast nets could be carried out to sea in a higher surf.

It would take each man over a week to make a new net. The young student knew that from experience. Repairing nets meant lost time fishing. They and their families would be dependent on food from others. They wouldn't like that at all.

Shai wanted to follow, too. He wanted to run after them to join the adventure, whatever it was. He wanted to see if they would really try to catch men in nets, but he had a job to do. So, he dutifully remained to hang the two men's nets on nearby sticks to dry before he went home.

4

Holy Sabbath

THE FIRST THING SHAI AND HIS FAMILY DID ON SATURDAY morning, the Holy Sabbath, was to honor their God, Elohim. After all, they were Israelites, the chosen people. When he awoke, he heard both parents reciting blessings over their four children while he and his siblings arose and dressed in their nicest and cleanest clothes.

Papa intoned, "Praise Elohim for making our rooster know the difference between night and day and, therefore, awaking us every morning." This was a morning that the boy wished he did not have to get up before sunrise, so he was disappointed in the rooster's early rising.

He heard Mama pray, "Praise Elohim for giving sight to the blind, and for opening our eyes to see this morning." He liked that thankful prayer.

After all, the Sabbath day was not only a day to relax, but it was a holy day to honor the God of Israel. His ancestors had made an everlasting covenant, or promise, with their God to keep the Sabbath holy. That meant to remember their God in prayer and praise throughout the day. Through their example, Shai's parents taught him how to do just that.

Then he heard, "Praise Elohim for clothing the naked." A chuckle escaped Shai's lips.

Ezra stretched. "Except for Shai...."

Mama reacted immediately, "Not that again, Ezra. Hush."

The younger brother didn't particularly care if he wore clothes or not. Of course, if he ever did walk around the house naked, he would hear Mama's scream and scolding words beginning with "Isaiah!" If he went around naked now, she would be appalled.

Sometime ago, his older brother told him that Mama had a hard time keeping clothes on him when he was little. Shai suspected that Ezra actually disrobed him to get him into trouble.

It seemed that Ezra was similar to his best friend's older teenage brothers. They all tested the seriousness of the boundaries set by the parents. Which actions did their parents really care about? What could they get away with doing? What actions did their parents actually know about? What were the real limits of their parent's power?

As Shai quickly dressed, he looked around at his siblings. His family was smaller in size than many of his friends' families. Seven people lived under this one roof, including his parents, Grandpa, and himself. His siblings ranged in age from Ezra at fourteen to Simcha at five. If only Ezra belonged to another family.

They ate a light breakfast. Between bites of yogurt and nuts, Papa reminded his family that the God of Israel was their only God. That made them different from the Romans and neighboring Samarians both of whom had many gods. Elohim was the only name of God that Israelites could use out loud. Papa also reminded them that their ancestors escaped from Egypt about one thousand five hundred years ago. It was then that God told Moses to have a day of rest every week, a day dedicated to the Lord. Papa told them to always remember that this was the fourth of the Ten Commandments that the God of Israel wrote on the tablets at Mount Sinai.

Shai thought that it was special that his family observed the

The Whistling Galilean

same pattern as their God when He created the world. The Israelites believed that God created the world in six days and rested on the seventh. Not only did Shai's family rest on the seventh day also, but most of the residents around the Sea of Galilee did the same.

Even the word Sabbath came from the Hebrew word "Shabbat," meaning to detest from work. All families completed the food preparation, wood cutting, fishing, gardening, baking, and so forth so that no one would do any work on Friday night or on Saturday. Included in these tasks was bathing since that was considered work. This naturally meant an extra dose of work had to be done on Friday. Shai did not mind because it meant he had no work to do the very next day.

Those that lived in Capernaum had an additional bit of work to complete before sunset on Friday - to prepare the synagogue for Sabbath service. The closest synagogue was located in town. The synagogue was the life-blood of their faith. It was the intimate place where believers worshipped and were taught. Levites and honorable men living in town were responsible for cleaning and decorating the synagogue.

As they started their walk to Capernaum, Shai saw Mama wrap her shawl around her head. She locked arms with Grandpa to help him walk at a faster clip than normal, even with his cane. She herded her only daughter, Adi the gentle one, in front of her.

Papa Yona raced after the wandering Simcha and swung him onto his shoulders. "Your legs are too short today, Sim. You get to ride on my wide shoulders."

Simcha, or Sim the joyful, giggled when Papa tickled him on the way up. With mighty strides, his dark, wavy-haired father galloped like a horse to catch up with Mama. He strode in front of her, saying, "I'll set the pace. Keep up, everybody, or we will be late."

Ezra pushed past Shai elbowing him roughly and hissing under his breath as he disappeared up the path, "Later, runt."

Just like him, Shai thought as he regained his balance. He hurried his pace to catch and keep up with Papa.

While walking, Shai realized how much he admired his parents.

~ 35 ~

Through their actions, his mother, in particular, showed him and his siblings that it was not a burden to honor and obey God. In his eyes, they were exceptional role models. Even when he didn't always want to, he tried hard to be obedient to them and, therefore, to his God.

"Papa, did Fishel tell you that I nearly completed making my cast net?"

"Yes, he did, Shai."

"Soon, we can practice together. I am eager for you to teach me."

"Stop squirming, Sim. Shai, Fishel will continue to work with you. I am too busy fishing."

"But Papa, you taught Ezra. Don't you want to spend time with me, too?"

Shai was disappointed that there was no answer. Other families joined and surrounded them on the packed-dirt beach path. Everyone hurried toward the synagogue. He rationalized that his father failed to tell him words of encouragement because he wanted to do it in private.

It was over a two mil walk to reach Capernaum. The overhanging tree canopy kept the first part of the walk cool and pleasant. Once out of the forest, buildings came into view. Shai was always startled at the first sight of their impressive synagogue despite having seen it his whole life. To Shai, it glowed like a beacon inviting them in. Despite being the largest and tallest of all of the buildings in town, the front of the synagogue was the only smooth white stucco wall in town. Therefore, it stood apart from all other stone buildings. That wall had been lovingly smoothed and stuccoed white so that it did not look rough and undressed like the other buildings. All of the other stone buildings in and around Capernaum were built out of the black volcanic basalt rock commonly found in nearby fields.

Shai and his family joined the other people entering the one-room synagogue. He looked up as he walked under the carved wooden lintel over the door. Lovingly sculpted into the wood was a pot of the manna that God had fed the Israelites on their forty-year journey through the desert. Beside the pot in that carving was the rod with sprouted leaves depicting High Priest Aaron's rod.

The Whistling Galilean

A penetrating coolness poured over him as he walked into the synagogue. It took a moment for his eyes to adjust to the dimmer light. Several clay olive lamps positioned along the walls on small stone shelves provided limited lighting. There were four wide, cool, smoothed granite steps built along the length of all four stone walls. Families were already sitting on these steps, which also served as benches.

Shai was too young to sit with the men. He knew that Ezra would join Papa on the men's side. In order to join the men, he had to be thirteen, the age a boy became a man. Instead, he followed his mother to the women's and children's side. She settled Sim and Adi immediately in front of her. Shai settled down beside her. He knew that they had to sit quietly because Mama could quickly reach out and control any mischief-making. He used to sit in front of her and remembered her taps on his shoulder or, if necessary, a brisk knee in his back.

Once his vision adjusted, he searched the room for Dov and his other friends. He looked around the supporting columns and cautiously waved to those he recognized. He knew that he could not make a scene. This place was holy, consecrated to the Lord of Israel. He dared not take that lightly. There were so many rules governing their lives. For example, a person could not enter this room carrying a staff or wearing shoes. A person could not joke, laugh, eat, or talk within these walls.

Once the woven cloth over the door was lowered shut, the room quieted. That was the cue to begin the Sabbath service. Shai heard Mama and other mothers make *shhh* sounds at Adi, Sim, and the other little kids. The din of voices quieted. Shai soon heard only the sound of breathing.

Two men wearing plain, rough, brown robes stood in the middle of the floor beside a small wooden table. Two objects were arranged on top of the table - the seven-armed lamp, or menorah, and a parchment scroll. The sacred scroll selected for that day lay within a wooden box. Even though it was unadorned, the box represented the Ark that held the Ten Commandments given to Moses and carried with care on their journey to the promised land where the boy now lived. The actual Ark was housed within the Temple in Jerusalem.

~ 37 ~

Jennifer Bjork

Without saying a word, Rabbi Selig let his congregation know that it was time to honor God. Their teacher and spiritual leader pointed to the sky, lowered his head, and rocked his round body back and forth. He cleared his low base voice, "Ahemmm". The *emm* sound echoed off the surrounding smooth stones, which amplified the volume of the sound. It felt like being surrounded by a vocal hug.

The rabbi began the service by praying the standard prayers of thankfulness. The entire congregation - men, women, and older children - repeated each phrase after him in unison.

> "Blessed are you, O Lord of Israel, who created all things with His word. Blessed are you, O Lord of Israel, who created the world and all things in it. Blessed are you, O Lord of Israel, who gave light to the world."

The rabbi lit the seven candles in the menorah as he continued to pray alone. His long salt-and-pepper beard wobbled as he spoke.

"With great love, O Lord, you have cared for us. Our fathers trusted you and you taught them the statutes of life. Have mercy on us and teach us, also. Open and enlighten our eyes to your Law. Cause our hearts to adhere firmly to your commandments. Unite our hearts to love and respect your name, O Jehovah. You, O King of the Universe, have chosen us from among all nations and tongues that we may lovingly praise you.

> "Blessed be the Lord who, in love, chose his people, Israel. Blessed are you, O Lord our Elohim, for choosing us as your special people."

The congregation repeated the last two phrases, ending with "Amen."

Shai shifted in his seat as the rabbi slowly and reverently took hold of the two wooden ends of the rolled leather parchment and lifted the sacred scroll from the wooden box high over his head. After a short prayer, the rabbi lowered the parchment scroll to eye

The Whistling Galilean

level and unrolled it. Shai noticed the red thread hanging over the edge of the scroll. He knew that it marked the location of today's selected passage making it easier for Rabbi Selig to find. He was grateful that the search was quick because it made this long, but necessary, service shorter.

One of his friends had told him that rites and rituals became less standardized the farther from Jerusalem, where their Temple was located. The synagogue in Capernaum was days away from the Holy City. As a result of this great distance, Shai's synagogue, and others that were far away, did not conform to the same traditional service as was held in the Temple. At least his rabbi had been trained in the Holy City itself. In his synagogue, any learned man could act as the teacher and read from scrolls.

The previous prayers were spoken in Aramaic, their native spoken language. Everyone in the room understood each benediction and word of praise. Now, the rabbi switched to Hebrew, their sacred language, as he read from the sacred scroll. Hebrew was the language used by Moses as he originally wrote the sacred words dictated by God Himself.

Rabbi Selig signaled for the congregation to stand by raising his hand. When they were all on their feet to honor their God, he read the following passage, first in Hebrew, and then in Aramaic:

> *"Hear, O Israel. The Lord our Elohim, the Lord is one. Love the Lord your Elohim with all your heart and with all your soul and with all your strength. These commandments that I give you today are to be upon your hearts. Impress them on your children. Talk about them when you sit at home and when you walk along the road, when you lie down and when you get up. Tie them as symbols on your hands and bind them on your foreheads. Write them on the door frames of your houses and on your gates."*

~ 39 ~

After the passage was read, the congregation sat down. Most fishermen, farmers, and artisans only knew a smattering of Hebrew, not enough for spiritual revelation and understanding. They certainly did not have the knowledge to apply the passage to the Law that they were bound to, the Law creating the boundaries of their lives.

Therefore, the rabbi chose to lead all within the square room to an application of the passage through questions and discussion. Sometimes a distinguished visitor was invited to deliver the discourse explaining the scriptural passage.

It was common for the rabbi to start the instruction by asking a question. It was true that any man could ask a question and any man could answer a question. In this manner, the men in the room discussed the scriptural passage. They called the discussion "chewing on, or eating God's words." At the end of the service, the rabbi wanted them to know how to apply the scripture specifically to their lives.

"Who would like to start? Today's topic is this: who is responsible to teach our children about the laws and commandments Elohim gave to His Chosen People?"

A balding man stood up. Shai recognized him as the man who sold and traded olive oil in the market place. Shai heard the confidence in his voice as he said, "We know that it is your job to teach our children, Rabbi Selig, especially our young boys that are coming of age. The passage seems to be saying that it is also our job as parents. Is this true?"

The rabbi faced the man and spoke, "Yes, it is my job, but it is also the job of all of the adults in the community, especially you who are parents. Remember, scripture tells us to talk about the Lord's commandments when we sit at home, when we walk on the road, and when we are ready to lie down at night."

The ten-year-old's attention wavered as the discussion continued. He looked around the room for the girl that he thought was particularly cute, Carmi. She had pretty golden-hair. He thought that her hair was really light brown, but that she was outside so much it had been bleached blond by the sun, like his own and Fishel's. He imagined a

The Whistling Galilean

conversation with her as he saw her and studied her beautiful olive-toned face. She had freckles and a cute little nose.

He felt a sharp elbow in his side. He looked up and saw Mama shaking her head whispering, "No daydreaming about Carmi. Pay attention."

His cheeks got hot as he blushed. He had no idea his mother knew he liked Carmi. How embarrassing!

Shai tried to look alert and attentive. It was hard to sit still for so long. He heard Rabbi Selig say, "Your son will ask you, 'What is the meaning of the Laws the Lord Elohim has commanded you?' What will you tell him?"

With surprise, he immediately recognized the next voice. It came from the back of the men's group. The voice rang clear as a mellow-toned bell. It was Yeshua. He strained to see his face, but too many people were between them.

Yeshua's voice was not overly loud like that of some of the merchants who had spoken earlier, yet it still warmly filled the synagogue. He said, "The Lord Elohim brought the Israelites, who were Pharaoh's slaves, out of Egypt with a mighty hand. The Lord brought you from that far land to give you the land He promised on oath to Moses and your forefathers. Our Elohim is faithful and gave you this land upon which you now live. The Lord commanded that you obey His decrees and honor Him so that you might always prosper and live. This is what you are to teach your children."

"That is correct, stranger," Rabbi Selig commented.

There was a smattering of murmurs and nods from around the room.

"Amen." The simple single word, which meant "I totally agree with you," chorused throughout the room.

"I hope that I remember to say it that way...," a small voice muttered.

Yeshua added, "Moses also said to love the Lord Elohim and serve Him with all of our heart and all of our soul - then the Lord will send rain on your land in its season so that we may gather grain. That is from the same scroll that the rabbi read earlier."

~ 41 ~

Jennifer Bjork

"Yes," the rabbi sounded surprised. "You know the scripture well, stranger. Are you a Levite?"

Finally, the boy saw his friend, the man from Nazareth, shake his head in the negative. He was not a Levite.

"So, how do we show Elohim that we love Him?" the rabbi asked no one in particular.

As Yeshua made his way down the benches to the center of the room beside the round man, different men answered:

"Obey the commandments of Elohim."

"Honor Elohim by honoring the Sabbath."

"Teach our children our history."

"Yes, we are to obey His commandments and teach those to our children so that we can be His people," the rabbi reiterated.

Yeshua added, "Elohim is a God of love. He shows His love to you in every sunrise, with the blooming of every flower, and with all of the fish in the Galilee. He shows His love through your children. Love Elohim with all your heart and with all of your soul and with all of your strength."

Shai could not explain his deep desire to repeat Yeshua's last sentence, *Love Elohim with all of your heart...with all of your soul... with all of your strength.*

He was proud to be part of the multitude of voices pledging in unison, several times. He felt a powerful love emanate from the core of his being. It made him feel small, insignificant. He also felt included as a part of this community. He even felt that he was honoring Elohim with his small presence in the synagogue. The little hairs on his arms stood up.

Yeshua faced Shai and looked deeply into his eyes. The tall carpenter mouthed the words for him, "Yes, my friend."

5

Day of Rest

AFTER THE SERVICE, PEOPLE WANDERED HOME FOR THEIR SABBATH meals. Ezra walked up ahead with another male teen. Papa sauntered by with some other fishermen. Mama passed at a faster clip, having joined other women with their small children.

Shai waited at the trail head for Dov, his best friend from a fishing community to the south. The two boys enjoyed each other's company, usually playing games and just talking about whatever entered their minds, about anything.

They quickly began a friendly competition, a game they had invented and called "kick-the-stone." They each took turns kicking their selected smooth stone down the worn path. After ten kicks, the person who had propelled their stone the farthest won the game. It was something to do.

While his taller, dark-haired friend kicked his selected oval stone, Shai excitedly related, "I helped Fishel pull in a huge tilapia."

Shai kicked the flat gray stone with rounded edges as Dov asked, "How huge?"

"Not quite half as long as I am tall."

~ 43 ~

Jennifer Bjork

"That is big."

"I had never seen one. Have you?"

"They must be around now because my older cousin caught one, too. They sure taste good. My favorite."

"I have not tasted one…not that I know, anyway. Fishel took it home to his family."

After some time had passed, Shai asked, "Did you see Maya today?"

"She looked like a jewel - hair loose and shiny black."

"I did not see her, but I did see Carmi. Mama caught me looking. I have no idea how she knew I was looking at Carmi, but by what she said, she knows I like her. I wonder how."

"Mothers talk together just like we do."

"But I thought we were so secretive."

"I guess not."

They maneuvered their stones around a gentle bend before Shai asked, "Dov, what did you think about what the stranger said this morning in the synagogue?"

"Really? More religion? Enough for today. You know I rarely pay attention."

"He quoted scripture about loving Elohim with all of our heart, then we would get rain and grain and be blessed. Do you remember that?"

"Not really. You know scriptural knowledge does not interest me."

"I know. You like climbing, running fast, and stuff like that. I know you work to build your muscles. After all, your name means 'strength' and you take it to heart."

"You know I do. I like active things, not pondering as much as you. If you can, match this shot."

Dov's stone scooted down a smooth rut while staying on the path.

"Good shot. And you know that I like both activities. I just wondered what you thought about the man, the stranger, who quoted scripture. You see, I met him on my beach."

"Our beach," Dov corrected. "So?"

~ 44 ~

The Whistling Galilean

"What impression did you get from him?"

"Alright, I guess."

"Well, I thought that the stranger, Yeshua, described scripture in a manner that I could understand." Shai, in contrast to his best friend, did spend time pondering life, friendship, and spiritual matters. He grunted as he tried to kick his stone as far as Dov had.

The dark-haired boy teased in a fake falsetto, "Oh, no, your stone ended up in the bush. Oh, my."

"Drat. Now you have the advantage. Really, Dov, what do you think about the stranger?"

He persisted.

"Alright, I heard people say that he spoke with authority, as someone who knows what he's talking about. Now, let's change the subject."

After Dov took another good shot, Shai fetched his flat stone from under the bush with his foot. They could not use their hands in this game. "I do not have to forfeit. Here is my original stone."

"I see it. Alright, shoot from the point where it left the path - right here." Dov marked the dirt with the heel of his leather sandal.

Shai did. "Do you think he's a rabbi?"

"I do not care. Concentrate on the game. We only have two kicks left. My stone is well ahead of yours. There is no way you can catch me."

"You are right. I concede. I lose so I get to start the next game." Shai grunted as he kicked his stone down a long straight stretch of the path. Maybe he had a chance this time. "Yeshua told me that he used to be a carpenter and now he's going to be a teacher. After what I heard today, I think he will make a good one. Have you met him yet?"

"No."

"Well, I am glad I did. When I met him, he said that he was new to the Galilee and asked about fishermen in the area. He even asked about my father."

"What did you say?"

"I could not believe that I told him the truth about what I feel, stuff I normally share only with you. I told him that Papa loved Ezra more than me. I told him that Ezra gets away with lying and deceiving and getting others in trouble, me specifically."

"That reminds me, did I tell you that my father caught my older brother drunk? He could not sit for a few days. He had to dig out a new garden for my mother as punishment."

"I wish Papa would catch Ezra doing something wrong. I wonder if Ezra knows your brother."

They kicked in silence for a while. Dov kicked his stone extra hard. "Ummph." The stone slipped off the path.

Now, Shai grunted with the effort. He did not want Dov to win two games in a row. He had to kick from the edge of the path.

"What else is new?" Dov asked.

"Well, I saw the brothers, Simon and Andrew, walk off the beach with Yeshua a few days ago. I bet you did not hear that they abandoned their cast nets to follow him."

"What? No. That was foolish. This stranger, Yeshua, must be evil if he forced two good men to leave their profession and depend on hand-outs from others."

"I do not know if they still fish or not. I heard the stranger from Nazareth offer Simon the adventure of his life – to fish for men. Simon and Andrew willingly followed him off the beach. It was their choice."

Dov snorted in derision. "We will soon see how their choice turns out. I bet they regret their actions already. I hope they come to their senses again soon. They are both good fishermen. Their families need them." The taller lad concentrated on the curve before kicking his stone for the tenth and final time. "Now, beat that shot, Shai."

"That will be hard. Good shot."

His friend grunted acknowledgement.

Even though Shai's stone slithered past Dov's, it wobbled at the end and landed off of the path and under a bush. "Rats."

"I win! That's two games!" Dov shouted. He danced down the path to his victorious stone, both arms raised in the air.

The Whistling Galilean

As he positioned his own stone to start a new game, Shai felt Dov's elbow gently nudge his ribs and knew that his good friend was happy. They competed in almost everything, but it was just friendly competition. In any competition against another boy, the two good friends cheered for each other. If they couldn't be the winner, they each wanted their best friend to win. That was the how their friendship worked.

They walked on in silence kicking stone after stone and imitating birds.

Dov whispered, "Did you hear it? Did you -"

"- hear the osprey?" Shai finished for him.

They knew each other so well that they could finish each other's thoughts, especially when they were in agreement. At the same time, both ten-year-olds whistled the osprey screech as they slowed to look around for this feathered fisherman.

"See it?"

"Not yet."

"He should have caught -"

"There he is -" Shai spotted the bird of prey first and pointed with one arm as he tapped Dov on the shoulder with the other.

"- with a fish! It did catch one, just as I thought." Dov crossed his arms across his chest smugly.

"I like to watch it carry the fish in its talons -"

"- head first, aimed in the same direction that it flies." Suddenly, Dov snickered, "Maya. Ahhhh, Maya."

"Huh? The osprey reminded you of Maya?" Shai asked.

"No. She just pops into my mind unexpectedly."

"Your twin?" Shai teased.

"You know she is not." Dov retorted quickly, pushing Shai off the path. Shai's arms grabbed at the air as he tried to steady himself. Too late. He fell into the weeds. As he got up, wiping dried grass off his nice clothes, he heard Dov's raucous laughter.

Shai knew that this topic was important to both of them - girls. That was probably the strongest link of their friendship. Together, they spent considerable time discussing the merits of all of the girls

~ 47 ~

Jennifer Bjork

they knew, and after much debate, helped each other pick out a favorite potential girlfriend. The girls, of course, were not aware of their selections...yet.

"Have you talked to her yet?" Shai wondered.

"No, I just watch Maya. Ah, but I have news."

"What news?" Shai stopped in his tracks. If it was about one of the girls, then he was very interested.

"Carmi's family is hiring some local boys to help them harvest some fruit. You interested?"

"Am I! Of course, I am!"

Dov laughed so hard he appeared to have a hard time catching his breath. He faked ignorance, "Really?"

"Dov, get serious. We can both go. You know Maya will be there, too."

Dov laughed some more. "We are both going to go help. Maya's mother told my mother that both of our families are invited. In other words, both of our mothers...and me, of course...and even you... you lucky dog."

Shai barked like the hairy, four-legged creature and joyfully skipped down the path. "Oh, boy! You are the bearer of such wonderful news."

When they finally calmed down enough, Dov grinned. "What did your mother say to lead you to believe that she knows that you like Carmi?"

"She caught me looking for her and then staring at her. She told me to stop looking at Carmi, so I had to stop and act reverent."

"So, even she knows that you like Carmi, the 'girl with the cutest freckles.'"

"Stop it. You know I like her. Am I so obvious? I need to be more careful."

"Carmi probably knows that you watch her, too."

"Oh, no." Shai groaned. "I sure hope not. I try to watch her when she is not looking. If I am too obvious, I will scare her away. Seriously, Dov, do you think she knows?"

"Do not know," the taller boy replied, raising both palms upward

The Whistling Galilean

with a shrug. "When are you going to talk to her and tell her that you like her?"

"Not much opportunity - she lives in Capernaum and I hardly ever go there. Truth is, I am not brave enough. How do I even start a conversation with her?"

"Why not bore Carmi with stories about Yeshua?" With that snide remark, Dov bolted for the river and the rope swing dangling invitingly from a large tree limb.

Shai followed close behind.

"I win!" Dov shouted, touching the board first.

Dov arrived first, so he got to swing first. Shai watched his friend adjust himself on the wide board smoothed by many bottoms. Soon, it was his turn to climb onto the board. He eagerly pumped his legs. As he alternated between leaning forward with his legs bent under him and leaning backwards with his legs straight out in front of him, he shouted happily, "I am a bird! I will fly!"

A glance over at his dark-haired friend revealed that Dov was already climbing the tree. It was their tradition for the non-swinger to sit on the branch above the swing and try to tap whoever was swinging with a twig.

Shai would rather swing than climb. His personal goal was to swing so high that the swing's ropes would be horizontal to the ground and make him feel like a bird in the air. Wind rushed through his shoulder-length hair. Soon, he felt airborne and the swing seemed to just hang in the air. He felt the swing skip a beat as the tension on the rope lessened. He momentarily felt weightless. He loved the feeling of being weightless, similar to the weightlessness he felt in the water. But now, instead of a fish, he felt like a bird soaring in the sky. Leaning backwards, he felt free of the land. He willed himself to become a member of the sky.

"Yeeee-hah!" he shouted.

At this point, swing and boy were apparently ready to fall earthwards. Then the rope tightened, and the downward arc of the swing began.

As he let the swing slow naturally, Shai heard a voice call to him, "Hi Shai... oh, hi Shai-ooo..."

~ 49 ~

Jennifer Bjork

"Go away." Shai snapped back as he recognized the cracking voice of his older brother.

"Hi, Shai. Hi, Shai-ooo…"

"Quit it." Shai hated those repetitive sounds because they were spoken to tease him, to make fun of him. Ezra called to him in a sing-song mockery, treating him like a little child. He disliked anyone taunting him like that, especially Ezra. He understood that it was probably fun to say since "Hi" and his name "Shai" rhymed. People had poked fun of his name for his whole life, or, at least, as long as he could remember.

"Hi, Shai-ooo, come home now." Now Ezra mimicked Mama's higher-pitched voice.

"No!"

"Get your butt down and come home this very minute!" Ezra now added a demanding authority to his words.

Shai watched as his brother turned and reentered the forest. His taunting sing-song hung on the still air, "I will be home before you, Shai-ooo. I will tell Mama you got dirty."

"Alright!" Shai shouted toward the woods. He was angry with his older brother for taking away his pleasure and for teased him and….well, for nearly everything, especially for just being older.

"Sorry, Dov. I have to go home now."

The human voice from the tree canopy responded, "I heard."

Shai leaned forward dragging his feet in the dust to quickly stop the swing. He jumped off, gracefully falling with a forward roll as he landed.

"Show-off." Dov gently chided.

Ezra's voice took over the quiet Sabbath landscape from within the shrubbery: "Now, look what you have done! You have dirtied your clean Sabbath best. Mama's going to be furious – especially when I tell her what you just did, maggot."

Shai knew his brother would do just that. He dusted himself off as best as possible. There was no way he could beat Ezra home, so he turned back toward the tree, smiled, and waved, "Enjoyed today, buddy, see you."

The voice within the leaves responded, "Me, too. Run. You better get home quick. Damage control!"

~ 50 ~

6

Dinner Discoveries

WHEN SHAI ARRIVED HOME, THE SABBATH MEAL WAS ALREADY LAID out ready to eat. Mama Anat was disappointed in him as he had guessed she would be. She gently scolded him as Ezra strutted proudly around the house like a peacock. The older brother had won that match between the brothers, but the younger brother vowed silently to win the next.

Most of the preparation for their meal had been completed the day before because Mama Anat could not work on the Sabbath. On Friday, she prepared a vegetable stew in their cast iron pot. It still hung on a metal hook over the remaining hot coals from last night's fire. Covered with a tight lid, it had simmered for hours.

There was always lightly salted fish handy. Papa Yona was a good provider. That evening just after sunset, Mama added thin strips of fish and some greens and herbs from their garden to the stew. Shai's mouth watered as he inhaled the wonderful smells. He could hardly wait to taste the wonderfully sweet, tender carrots in the stew. That was one of his favorite flavors.

The little kids, Adi and Sim, spread woven mats on the floor.

Shai's family sat in a circle on the mats around their dinner. The center mat already held flat pita bread in a basket and the side dishes to their main meal. Today, the bread was cold. Baking was considered work, so no hot bread today. From the center mat, all food was accessible to every family member while they ate. In addition, the mats made recycling easy. After each meal, the kids carried the mats outside and shook the crumbs into the dirt for the chickens while Mama Anat swept the floor with her palm leaf broom.

Once everyone washed up at the basin beside the house, the meal began. Everyone except Grandpa Yona sat on woven mats. Grandpa sat on a low wooden stool with his back against the wall. The support helped straighten and support his curving back.

Since this was the Sabbath, Papa Yona led the family in prayer. That used to be his father's responsibility. Now it was his.

"Blessed are you, Lord of Israel, who created the fruit of the vine."

Mama Ana poured the wine for herself, Grandpa, and Papa, then poured grape juice for the children.

"Blessed are you, Lord Elohim, who created the grain in the fields."

Mama Anat uncovered the bread in the basket and tore a piece off for each person present.

"Blessed are you, Lord Elohim, who created the plants and the fish."

Mama Anat ladled the stewed fish into each of the seven wooden bowls.

"Blessed are you, Lord Elohim, who gave us His holy Sabbath as a heritage, a remembrance of creation. Thank you for your many and generous blessings."

Shai and the rest of the family eagerly responded with, "Amen."

Once God had been honored, the family began to eat. Shai tore off small pieces of bread to spoon food from the bowl into his mouth. Once soggy, he ate that piece of bread and tore off another. He also used small pieces of the bread to wipe food off of his fingers. Mama preferred bread napkins to wiping dirty fingers on clean clothing, which she would later have to wash.

The Whistling Galilean

Tonight, in addition to the stew and bread, there were two sides in bowls - tabouli or vinegar parsley salad, and a fruit mixture of pomegranates, grapes, and celery. Shai liked the mixture of sweet and sour and crunchy and smooth.

One thing unique to their family were their bowls. Each family member had a special bowl. When Mama was pregnant with each child, Papa carved a bowl out of hard olive wood for the baby. The bowl was intended to last a lifetime if it was cared for properly.

The bowl was Papa's gift to his children so that they would realize that Elohim, Father God, was their provider. Papa had received a bowl from his father, who had actually started the tradition. Yona the Elder's bowl was the least decorated with only the sun and rays radiating from it. Naturally, there was a huge fish on Papa's bowl. The carved light tan outline and detail of the fish's scales, gill, fins, and eye stood out in contrast to the beautiful deeper brown patina of his bowl.

When Shai and his siblings were each born, Papa prayed to Elohim thanking Him for the blessing of each child into his family. When they received their names, Papa carved each name on the bottom of the appropriate bowl and blessed the bowl saying, "Thanks be to the Lord of Israel for this child. May this bowl never be empty, and may my child never go hungry."

Papa told his children that they had to be ten-years-old before they could decorate their own bowl. They needed the hand skills to use a knife safely without cutting off a finger. They also needed to be old enough to know what they wanted to become as men.

As Shai held his bowl, he decided that now was the time to talk to Papa about carving it. "Papa. I have decided what I want to carve on my bowl. Since I am ten, I would like to start, with your help, of course."

A muffled sound came from Papa's full mouth, "I see."

"On one side, I want ocean waves, small fish, birds in flight, and maybe the rays of a sunset over the ocean. On the other side, I want *Ole Blue* under sail."

By now, Papa Yona had swallowed. "That is a lot of detail. Let's start with one thing."

~ 53 ~

Grandpa spoke up, "Since you want the ocean on both sides, maybe you could have the line of an undulating wave around the center of the bowl."

Papa responded, "Good idea."

Grandpa wiped his mouth with his hand. "The wavy line will separate sky from water, birds from fish. What do you think, Shai?"

"I like that idea, Grandpa."

The Elder suggested, "Every day that you have extra time on your hands, practice the design on wood from the wood pile. I know it is not the same as a round bowl, but it will help you refine your skills. It will help you figure out how deep each line should be. The main design is the deepest, of course."

Shai nodded vigorously, "Yes, that will be *Ole Blue*. Do you like that idea, Papa?"

His father just nodded as he continued eating. Shai could not understand why no enthusiasm was shown. He had hoped he would hear words like, *this will be a good project for us to work on together*, but as usual, he was disappointed.

Papa finally looked up, but his eyes focused on Ezra. "Do you still have the small carving knife I let you use on your bowl, son? I want Shai to use it for his project."

"I'll look for it, Papa."

Shai felt a surge of resentment. He bet that his older brother had lost the knife or would hide it to keep the younger from using it.

"Not to worry," Grandpa quickly pitched in. "I will loan Shai my small carving knife instead."

"Oh, thank you, Grandpa." Shai felt like jumping with joy and hugging the old man. He was going to get a knife from the man he loved after all.

"I will give it to you after dinner."

Shai grinned happily as everyone busily ate the delicious meal. The wordless togetherness was familiar and friendly until Papa cleared his throat, not once but twice. Shai noticed that everyone's attention was on his father.

"I have some serious news." His pitch was lower than normal,

The Whistling Galilean

and the words slipped into the surrounding air slowly and carefully. "Pay attention. Several of our local fishermen reported listening to a prophet baptizing on the River Jordan. They say that this man scolds the Roman ruler of our district, Herod Antipas, and boldly and loudly tells all who listen that the Roman lives in sin, in adultery. You see, it appears that Herod took his brother Phillip's wife as his own. She has even brazenly moved in with him."

Grandfather groaned, shaking his head. Shai did not understand the word *adultery*, but he did know that talking against Rome or any Roman would get the speaker flogged or something much worse. Therefore, he listened carefully.

"The fishermen are worried that Herod is displeased. He will not tolerate his subjects, that means us," Papa looked around the table at each member of the family in turn, "not tolerate us saying any words against him. He will not let anyone accuse him of doing anything wrong without getting even. Once he is angry, he may strike out at anyone. There will be brutal consequences. I do not want any of you harmed by accident. I love you all. Do not say anything bad about our rulers. Especially do not complain about them when you are near someone you do not know well. Understood?"

Shai understood the stern warning. Papa looked at him and his brother to make sure they understood the seriousness of his words. Shai nodded and, out of the corner of his eye, saw his brother do the same. He received the message and agreed to be careful. He would try. He knew he could still share anything with Dov, but not any of the other boys. He wondered if he should still play the make-believe battle game they called "Romans and Hebrews."

Papa spoke quietly to his wife, "Anat, be careful during your trips to town. Tell me what you hear in the marketplace."

"I will, my love. Thank you for sharing your concern."

"Enough of that." With a flick of his hand, it looked as if his father was trying to erase this serious topic. He leaned back, rubbing his full belly. His voice was louder now, pitch higher and free of concern, "Ahh, good meal." He burped to end the comment.

Sim giggled.

~ 55 ~

"Fishing has been good lately."

Shai heard his brother's irritating chuckle beside him. He knew that Ezra wanted attention. Recently, the first born of the family tried to act like Papa's equal, even though he was only fourteen years old. Now that he fished with Papa and other fishermen, he felt like he deserved to be treated as an adult.

His brother teased, "I heard that Fishel pulled in a large tilapia. Not big enough to swallow a man, but maybe to swallow Shai."

"You know that is not possible." Shai tried to sit taller.

Ezra teased, "So, Papa, have you ever been swallowed by a big fish?"

Grandpa Yona the Elder shook his head with a chuckle, "You know that neither one of us was ever swallowed by a big fish. You know that man was Jonah of the old scrolls."

Ezra continued in a smart-alecky tone, "Oh, of course. You are both too big for any fish to swallow."

At first, Shai thought both men would let the comment pass, but Grandpa did not, "Watch that tone young man. In this house, children respect their elders."

"Ah, but I am not a child anymore."

"You are when you act like one."

Shai could have hugged his grandfather for those words.

His older brother now sat silenced and sullen as Papa quickly rejoined the conversation, "There are big fish called whales in the Mediterranean. I have never seen one, but I hear that they are big enough to swallow any man, even me."

"No. Really Papa?" Shai could hardly believe that. The biggest fish he had ever seen was caught by Simon, the same Simon who had followed Yeshua into the woods to fish for men. That fish had been just over two cubits long. A fish big enough to swallow a man? Not possible.

"Yes, there are."

Papa Yona had been teased about his famous name, especially as a boy growing up. Grandpa told Shai he had named Papa "Yona" so that he would become a good man and a lucky fisherman. Maybe

The Whistling Galilean

Grandpa didn't do such a good thing naming him after the famous Jonah of old, the Jonah that had been swallowed by a big fish to turn his attention and obedience to God's command. Papa had to defend himself all the time.

Actually, Shai had something in common with his father. Named after the prophet Isaiah, he had always been teased about his name, too. He was not fond of the name Isaiah. That name made him feel responsible to do something important.

He was curious, so he asked, "Papa, what is the biggest fish you have ever seen?"

"Oh, about as big as you."

"Really? You saw one that was almost three cubits long?"

"Yes, I did. Several years ago we were in the deep part of the sea and caught some monster-sized fish. I did not catch this one, but I saw him swim by." Papa used his arms to show how big the fish had been.

Sim and Adi were delighted and clapped to show their appreciation.

Shai saw Papa look at Mama with a quick smile. Maybe he had enlarged that fish, making it bigger than it actually was. After all, fishermen were known for their tales of exaggeration.

"And, you, Grandpa?"

"About the same size." He, too, demonstrated how big it was with his arms as wide as he could spread them.

The two youngest clapped in delight again.

The mood changed, as it became time for dessert. Today, the mat held one of Shai's favorites - honeyed dates. Sim liked them, too, and exclaimed, "Yum!"

The family had another special tradition that Shai loved. No other family he knew had one like it. He thought that this tradition came from his mother's side of the family. Mama admitted starting this habit when she and Papa were a newly wedded couple. When one person said "yum", they continued humming the *ummm* part, keeping the sound going as long as they could before finally taking a breath. That gave everyone a chance to join in, each humming

~ 57 ~

ummm, too. Harmonies soon developed, and the pitches made by each family member became more like a song. Each person repeated the *ummm* so that sound was generated over and over. Mama Anat was especially good at harmonizing. Shai loved hearing his family's voices, from Papa's deep, resonating, drum-like voice all the way up to the little kid's high pitches.

Eventually, someone giggled - usually Simcha. Tonight, he laughed his carefree and contagious short bursts of hilarity. As usual, their humming ended in riotous laughter. It was something they enjoyed doing together. It helped knit them together as a family.

7

The Accident

SHAI HEARD THE HIGH-PITCHED SOUND OF GIRLS SQUEALING. WHEN he looked over at them from beneath the tree canopy in the orchard, he thought that they looked like colored flower beds floating in the air instead of long-haired girls scrambling for shelter behind tree trunks. Their bright summer frocks fluttered as they scurried like a nest full of birds taking flight.

"What just happened?" Shai asked his tall friend, startled.

"The girls are hiding from our missiles." Dov picked up another large dirt clod.

"It looks like they are scattering like dandelion seeds in the wind." Shai watched a moment longer, attempting to pick out Carmi's bright green tunic. "What missiles?"

"Dirt clods like this one. You must be daydreaming again. Have you been hit yet?"

Surprised, Shai's attention was drawn back to his friend from the girls. "No. Have you?"

"I ducked in time. Anyway, someone lobbed one at the girls, and you are witnessing the result."

~ 59 ~

The calm, peaceful morning had become one of chaos and bedlam. In the distance, he heard mothers calling their daughters. He also heard mothers yelling at each other wondering what was happening, just like he was.

Shai could pick out Maya's voice nearby. "Get down, Carmi. Hurry. I am holding the ladder steady." Even in her attempted calm, Dov's girl had the highest pitched, squeaky voice - like a mouse. To Shai's ears, it was annoying, but it never had been to Dov.

Shai heard charming Carmi respond in her gentle, now irritated voice, "Thanks. The stones are getting closer. How can the boys be so stupid?"

So that was where she had been, in the tree canopy. No wonder Shai had not seen her earlier. He absorbed the essence of the shorter girl with freckles as she lowered herself rung by rung. He hoped she was alright.

Then he heard Dov snort, "Maya is looking my way...finally. Watch this throw, Shai."

"What are you doing?" Shai thought his friend had gone crazy.

"Now is my chance to get her attention, show her my accuracy."

The shorter boy turned his gaze from his favorite girl to his good friend. "No, Dov. Stop!" Shai threw out his arm trying to stop his friend's drastic action.

Despite Shai's plea and attempts to stop him, Dov reared back his right arm and extended the left one, aiming in Maya's direction. With a grunt, the stone went flying from Dov's hand. Shai followed it in the air. It appeared to move in slow motion. He groaned audibly as it approached the two girls. Then, he heard the *thwack* as it landed against the tree trunk behind Maya.

He heard Maya squeal, an even higher sound than her voice, if that was even possible, and saw her look away from the trunk toward them and point, "There they are."

Shai exhaled in relief, "You missed her. That was too close."

"She noticed me." Dov stood smugly with his arms crossed over his chest, admiring the result of his throw. "I did not aim at her, stupid. I aimed for the trunk that I hit."

The Whistling Galilean

"You are usually accurate." Shai confirmed quietly, but he was confused. "Why even throw anything toward her at all?"

"To get her attention, stupid. To get her to notice me. And she did."

"Not in a good way." Shai shook his head in disgust. It was hard for him to believe that his friend was involved in this childish behavior.

Dov leaned down and picked up another dirt clod. "Here, it is your turn. You throw one."

Dropping it like a hot coal, Shai recoiled. "No. I do not want to throw anything at the girls, Dov. Someone could get hurt, maybe Carmi." Then in mid-step, he stopped backpedaling and crossed his arms over his chest to demonstrate that he was an immovable object and would not budge from his opinion.

Carmi and her family lived on an olive orchard off the Jordan River upstream of the Galilee. As he had hoped, both he and Dov were helping out. Some mothers, Dov's and Shai's, included, cut ripe grape clusters for both consumption and for wine. Carmi's family made their own wine blend that was becoming quite popular.

The two boys were working in a portion of the olive orchard next to the vineyard. They were assisting the professional pruners by stacking larger limbs on a small hand-pulled cart. Carmi's father sold this valued wood to carvers. It just so happened that both Carmi and Maya chose to work at the orchard edge also. Carmi was being taught how to prune the trees. Both boys were excited about their proximity to the girls. They considered this a good omen.

His friend used a falsetto sing-song voice to tease him. "You are missing an opportunity to talk to her."

"By hitting her with something hard? You must be crazy."

"We came here today to meet with the girls, not to be field hands. We work hard enough as it is."

"Well, you are right about that." Shai dropped his arms from his chest.

"Of course, I am. This is our chance to get close to them."

~ 61 ~

"I do want a chance to get closer to sweet Carmi...with her big brown eyes -."

"- her cute light-brown freckles," the sing-song voice replied.

"Stop it." Shai pondered out loud, "But I cannot - no, will not - be the one to hit her."

"If you do not want a dirt clod, throw this lemon." His friend placed it in his hand. "It has been on the ground. It is soft, near rotting."

Shai examined it.

"Aim for Carmi, and you are guaranteed to miss. Just do not hit Maya, please."

Dov took Shai's shoulders and physically turned him. Shai realized that he now stood perpendicular to the girls, at just the right angle to throw something at them.

"Well?" Dov stood tapping his foot impatiently. "It is now or never. Quick, do it now. She is nearly off the ladder. Soon she will be behind a tree."

"Well...." Shai was frozen. He could not make a decision.

"Now!" Dov pushed him in the middle of his back.

Shai felt propelled forward by his friend's encouragement. Before he realized what he was doing, he cocked his arm, and the lemon was on its way toward the girl that he adored from afar.

Splat! The lemon hit her head. Shai watched in horror as a spray of released juice misted the air around her.

"Ow!" a startled Carmi exclaimed. Both hands left the ladder to grab hold of her forehead. She lost her balance as she recoiled and slipped and fell to the ground.

"Oh, no, I hit her!" Shai's despair filled his own ears. His wail rose above the high- pitched shrieks from the group of girls. He stood in shock, his jaw hanging open.

"I cannot believe my eyes. Not only did you hit her, you hit her square on the head! That was the arm you used." Dov punched Shai's right bicep muscle.

"Oh, oh. Here come the mothers. Mama is moving faster than...." Shai whispered in horror.

The Whistling Galilean

The taller boy quickly turned away and broke into a run in the opposite direction from the gaggle of girls reacting like a hive of bees.

Shai raced after him. "Wait...I didn't mean to...."

The two ten-year old boys sprinted for the other side of the orchard. Shai hoped that no one noticed the direction of their retreat. They stopped behind an old lemon tree with a massive trunk, the grandfather tree.

The boys were satisfied that they were well hidden. Both boys leaned with hands on their dirt-covered knees, panting to recover their breath.

After catching his breath, Dov hissed, "Why did you follow me? Go somewhere else, anywhere. I need distance between us. When blame is assigned, and it will be, I do not want to be linked to you and your evil deed."

"Me? But it is your fault. You are the instigator. You started the rock throwing." Shai pointed his index finger at the stringy, dark-haired boy. He tried to put the blame back on his friend where he thought it belonged.

"I did not throw the first rock." Dov shrugged his shoulders, appearing to dislodge any blame. He even wiped the top of his left shoulder with the back of his right hand as if he were knocking the blame off, as if it were an undesirable bug.

Shai slumped down on the ground and rested his back against the trunk. "I bet the first small dirt clods were thrown between us boys... for an annoyance -"

"- or to pick a fight. You are right." Dov finished, sitting beside him and nodding.

"Actually, you were the first boy that I saw throw anything at the girls."

"You are right again - two for two. I did not throw a hard, sharp rock. I did not hit anyone. On the other hand, you did hit Carmi and may have hurt her."

"But it was a soft, warm lemon." Shai protested, in hopes that those characteristics made everything better.

Jennifer Bjork

"Yes. It carried with it dirt from the ground to soil her and it was nearly rotten so it probably stained her tunic. I saw it splatter. Her mother will be sooo happy with you. And Carmi squealed like a pig."

"It did." In resignation, he admitted what he had observed, also. Then, he admitted with a sigh, "She did."

Dov chuckled with the recollection of the scene. The two boys sat in the suddenly peaceful, cool shade in the middle of the small group of lemon trees. These citrus trees were surrounded and hidden by the larger orchard of olive trees with thick, gray-green, narrow leaves. On the outskirts of the orchard were grapes trained on stakes and ropes.

The small number of lemon trees were highly prized and hidden from view. The grandfather lemon tree that they both cowered behind was the original lemon tree in the Jordan River valley north of the Galilee. One of Carmi's ancestors had received a cutting from a trader from the far orient. It had flourished in the rich soil of the Jordan valley. Shai had been told that this ancient, gnarled, and bent specimen had nobly stood rooted in this very spot for several generations. Only a few select families were even familiar with this small grove. They had all pledged an oath of silence, a promise that they would neither divulge its existence nor location, especially to Romans and their network of assistants. Under Roman rule, only the very wealthy and the ruling class were allowed to grow lemon trees.

Shai wondered out loud, "Do you think she was hurt? Did you see her fall down?"

"No, Maya didn't fall down. She looked wildly around for me." Dov chuckled at the thought.

"No, idiot, Carmi. Did you see her fall down?" Shai's worried voice revealed his concern.

"I did. Didn't you?"

"No. You said she would notice me, and we would talk."

"I could not believe my eyes. You, Shai, actually hit Carmi with a rotten lemon."

"Not rotten, just small and warmed by the sun."

~ 64 ~

The Whistling Galilean

"Well, I cannot believe your accuracy." There was disbelief in his friend's voice. "Thankfully, my throw zipped by Maya. It hit the tree that I aimed for. You know I am the most accurate around. I am the one who can hit a thin tree from fifteen paces away, not you."

"True. It was just luck…bad luck. I just meant to startle her…to get her attention, not to knock her off the ladder and hurt her."

"Well, it sure knocked her off. She fell down to the ground."

"I know," Shai whispered back. "I didn't want to hurt her." His worried voice took on a higher pitch and shook a little as he leaned over and looked around the wrinkled trunk toward the scene of the accident.

"Don't even think of going back there unless you want to get blamed for it."

Shai shook his head, gesturing as he spoke, "No, I definitely don't want that."

He was confused. He was proud that Dov admired his aim, yet he had meant no harm. He was proud that today he had bested his friend's throw, yet, he really liked Carmi. He wanted her to like him back. How could he get her attention without appearing too interested, or even worse, looking like a sissy?

With a deep breath, he slowly admitted, "I didn't try to hit her. I was aiming for the tree trunk beside her." Friends, especially best friends, eventually shared the truth.

"Ah, that makes sense. You missed the tree trunk by a cubit at least." Dov crowed like a proud rooster. "I still have the better arm. My aim is still better than yours. My dirt clod just missed the core of Maya's body." Dov sighed in contentment that Shai had not bested him at all. They had both missed their mark, but Shai had missed by a greater distance.

The air in the hottest part of summer was still, motionless. Shai's agitated emotions did not help him cool down. There was not a cloud in the brilliant blue sky. Without the shade, they would have been even more miserable. He already felt sweaty, dirty, wretched, unhappy, and ashamed.

~ 65 ~

With a sigh, Shai stood, kicked a rock and muttered, "At least you didn't bean the girl you like."

Then, he heard several adult voices calling out. The sounds appeared to be headed directly toward them.

"Dov!" shouted one voice.

"Shai!" came another.

The boys looked at each other in dread. Oh, no. It was their mothers. The truth had finally floated to the surface, as it always eventually did.

Shai usually liked the sing-song voice his mother used to call him, "Sh...eye...iii!" But her tone was different now. It had an edge to it like an angry bird of prey. He feared his mother's demanding pitch and dreaded having to face her.

"Dov, where are you?" he heard Dov's mother shout. Her voice had anger in it, also.

"Shai, come here."

As they neared their sons, the intensity of their anger increased with the volume and pitch of their voices.

"Dov, come. Bring your friend Shai."

"Shai, come here this minute."

Shai looked at his guilty friend, then down at his feet and whispered, "They are close. We are really in trouble."

Dov whispered back, "We have been identified as the instigators. At least I've just been asked to bring you."

"Dov, come NOW!"

"ISAIAH! Now. Come here right now!"

"Oh, no. Mama used my full name. I am really in trouble," Shai spoke slowly, in surrender. Then he straightened and inhaled deeply as he walked out into the mottled light between the trees.

Dov joined him. They both bowed their embarrassed heads in shame and walked toward the voices of their mothers.

Both mothers stood side by side in full view facing their sons. With hands on their hips, they muttered in disgust. Shai imagined that they were planning a particularly gruesome punishment. He already felt bad for knocking the girl that he liked to the ground.

The Whistling Galilean

Shai noticed other mothers, too. This was going to be a public tirade about his bad behavior, not just a private one. With a deep sigh and downcast eyes, he continued to approach his mother, already regretting his impulsive actions. Once the two boys stood before their angry mothers, the finger wagging began.

"We saw you throw things at the girls. It was wrong."

"You hurt Carmi, Shai. You hit her on the forehead. You could have blinded her if you had hit her on the eye. You are lucky that she is okay." He saw the disappointment in his mother's eyes and felt terrible.

With an arm firmly gripped on each boy, the mothers marched their children back to the scene of their crime. The scolding continued every step of the way. To Shai, it felt like hours passed. Yes, they were wrong. Yes, it was a good thing that Carmi was not seriously injured. Yes, even though Dov had started it, Shai was guilty of following his friend's lead. Yes, he knew better.

Once the army returned to the edge of the olive orchard, Shai saw Carmi's mother carefully tending to her daughter. Carmi, her back to her parent, was seated with her damp yet wavy golden-brown hair in her mother's lap. The mother lovingly cooed while wiping Carmi's forehead and cheeks with what looked like a damp cloth.

Of course, during their march, his mother had told him, not asked him, to apologize, so he did so immediately.

"Carmi."

She sat up at the sound of his voice.

Now that he had her undivided attention, he continued, "Carmi, I am sorry that I threw a lemon - soft lemon - sorry that…I actually hit you with it." Once started, his words flowed more easily. "I did not aim it at you. I did not mean to hit you. It was not intentional. It was an accident. I'm sorry, so sorry. I hope that you are alright."

He could hear Dov apologizing to Maya but could not pay attention to his friend's words because now he had to apologize to Carmi's mother.

"I am sorry that I threw a lemon. Since it was on the ground and nearly rotten, I threw it away. That was a mistake. I realize that the citrus is valuable and we are here to help you, not cause harm. I will be glad to work longer to pay for any financial burden."

He felt relieved, a huge weight lifted from his small shoulders. He thought he had handled the apologies well. He turned to watch Dov make similar apologies to Maya's mother.

Then, Shai was shocked to see Carmi stand up and look her mother in the eye. The girl spoke in a clear voice, "Excuse me, mother. I really am alright. Only my pride was injured. It was a glancing blow. No real harm done. I was just startled and fell down. I am not hurt...really."

Now, Shai's mother bent down to examine the girl that he liked. She used both hands as well as her eyes to examine Carmi's rising red welt over her right eye. "Does this hurt, Carmi?"

Even though the cute freckled girl winced at the touch, she shrugged and said, "Not really. I have been bruised before. It is nothing permanent. The boys were just trying to get our attention... you know, Maya and me."

She looked over at Shai. Her glare was accusatory at first. He understood it to mean *Don't try anything like that again!* Then her eyes softened and her cheeks developed a reddish glow. This confused him. Did that mean she liked him?

His admiration grew as he watched her performance. She was not hurt, at least only bruised. She even came to his defense - him, the son of a fisherman! He couldn't believe his eyes. What an amazing girl!

After both penitent boys displayed more dismay and misgivings, the mothers seemed satisfied. The crowd around them dispersed to their previous tasks. Most mothers herded their girls with them, but Maya and Carmi busied themselves with the remaining basket of olive trimmings.

Carmi told their two departing mothers, "Maya and I will remain here to clean up this area. After all, it was partly our fault. Then we will rejoin you. It will not take us long at all."

"And Dov and I will be glad to help," Shai insisted.

Amazingly, that left the two boys with the two girls in an uncomfortable silence.

The Whistling Galilean

Maya broke the quiet. "Dov, you idiot. I know that you like me, but that is not the way to show it. You could have seriously injured someone. After all, you have such a powerful arm."

She reached out to touch his bicep. Shai had not seen them side by side. They really did look like twins. They had matching thin, black hair, and dark brown eyes. Even her olive complexion matched his friend's.

Shai saw his friend uncomfortably shuffle his feet in the dirt. He knew that Dov was happy that she noticed his physique, but he also knew that his friend did not want Maya to think that he was stupid. Dov could not resolve his emotions, so he just stood there, staring at the ground and muttering nonsense.

Then, Shai felt a tug on his robe. It was Carmi getting his attention, "Shai."

He turned his attention to her, looking into her beautiful brown eyes.

Her gentle voice swept over him like a wave on the Galilee, "Shai, I thought that you, of all of the boys, were smarter than that. I admired you. Now, I am not so sure what to think."

"Oh, I am smarter than that." He tried hard to sound sincere. As he studied her face, he saw the red welt on her forehead and felt deeply sorry and embarrassed. He saw the dirty splatter on her pretty green frock. He desired her friendship, admiration, and respect. He had lost it all. What could he do to earn it back?

8

School Session

EVEN THOUGH PAPA AND FISHEL WERE TEACHING SHAI A TRADE, THE trade of fishing, he also attended school to learn to be a good Jew. Since the age of ten, he joined other boys from the region in Capernaum's synagogue, sometimes several times a week.

Rotund Rabbi Selig rang a small bell. The jostling began. The bell did not begin a wrestling or boxing match. Instead, it created a race. Each boy wanted to get inside the class first. Seating was first-come first-choose. As a result, those arriving late sat in the front. The newly turned eleven-year old quickly learned that to be seen was to be called on, so he strived to remain in the back row. Knowing the desire of his students, their crafty teacher got all of his students in class on time.

"Ouch." Shai tried to be one of the first in line. He pushed against a larger, blond boy. The farm boy was too heavy for him to budge, so he slipped in line after him.

"As your best friend -" Dov tried to cut in line in front of him.

"Not today." Shai held his ground since they were nearly at the door beside the rabbi.

The Whistling Galilean

Once inside, Shai slid onto the middle stone bench since the back row was already full. He smiled at his friend as Dov sidled beside him. Rabbi Selig entered the room after the last student paraded past him, then cleared his throat. The ten-to-twelve year old boys stood quietly.

The rabbi began each class the same way - responsive answering, similar to the synagogue service. In his deep, booming voice, he asked a question, and all fifteen boys answered it in unison. There was never any discussion.

"Who created the world we live in?"
"Elohim, the Lord of Israel."
"Who chose the Israelites as His holy people?"
"Elohim, the Lord of Israel."
"Who do we obey and follow?"
"Elohim, the Lord of Israel."

The rabbi gave his star pupil, Heno, the honor to fetch a holy scroll from the small windowless room within the synagogue. This dust-free area held a repository of clay jars that contained copies of sheepskin scrolls comprising the sacred Torah. These scrolls had been protected and carefully passed down from generation to generation. On them were written the Laws, regulations governing the Jewish nation - the specifics on how to worship, celebrate holy days, and be God's special people.

"Remember that Elohim gave the original laws to Moses during the year that...."

As the rabbi droned on, Shai recalled copying Hebrew letters in the sand to learn how to read and write the Hebrew alphabet. Eventually, he learned to memorize a short phrase of scripture. The rabbi explained that repetition developed the culture of memory. He had also been taught how to treat elders with respect, how to be polite, and especially, that obedience to their many Laws was critical.

Shai wished that girls attended school. Then he would see Carmi and her adorable freckles more frequently. But girls did not attend school. Instead, they learned to become good wives and mothers. Their mothers and aunts taught them how to cook, wash, sew, weave, and preserve herbs and vegetables. He was not really interested in those tasks. Therefore, he was glad that he was a boy and not a girl.

The rabbi continued, "I will build on a holy passage that is familiar. *'Each of you must respect his mother and father....,'* which you already put to memory. This passage adds something new, a twist. Not only does Elohim tell us how He wants us Israelites, His Chosen People, to behave, but He tells us what the punishment will be if we break this rule."

Shai squirmed uncomfortably in his seat. He did not like punishments. His world was surrounded by it - from Romans, parents, Ezra, Rabbi Selig, and now, even his beloved God.

Their teacher read, *"If anyone curses his father or mother, he must be put to death."*

More boys squirmed, joining Shai. He knew that they wiggled not because their bottoms disliked like the hard, cold stone but because this was a potential death sentence. My goodness, the Lord of Israel took this very seriously.

Whenever they learned a new scriptural passage, the students repeated this scripture twenty times. The words *"must be put to death"* echoed loudly in his head as his voice repeated the passage in a whisper. Beads of sweat dripped from his forehead. Even the palms of his hand felt like damp sponges dripping on the cold stone bench underneath him.

"Gil, please define 'curses' for us."

"Rabbi, I think it means saying bad words, swearing."

"Yes, it does, but it goes deeper than that."

The rabbi continued to call on students, mainly those in the first row. Shai remained immobile and unseen. He knew his classmates did their best to provide the desired answers.

"Rabbi, maybe it also means saying bad words about our parents, not just to them."

"I guess it means wanting something evil to happen to your parents."

The Whistling Galilean

"Especially when said in anger."

This made Shai feel guilty about the anger he sometimes felt when his father punished him instead of Ezra. Even though he felt his punishment was unjust, anger was not an emotion honoring his father.

The class bully, Oz, asked an unexpected question. "Rabbi, what if we are treated unfairly and hurt physically? What if the things we say about our treatment are true?"

Shai listened intently to the Rabbi's answer: "If a parent treats you harshly, unfairly, or hurts you in anger, you are still supposed to honor them. That is hard to do but that is what our Lord Elohim desires - no, orders us to do."

Their teacher let them absorb his words before continuing, "Remember that cursing your parents means wishing them ill will. That's another way of saying that you want harm to befall them. Do you really want them to become ill or maimed, to lose the respect of their peers, or to be incapable to provide for their family? Those are strong words. Think, boys, would it not be better if you talked to your parent in private about your concern instead of swearing at them in public or gossiping about them? Maybe we -"

"Our Elohim is a God of love, not one of constant punishment."

"Who said that?" The rabbi searched the room for the owner of the interrupting voice, and Shai did as well.

Shai recognized the melodious, gentle voice with its lower, manly pitch. It had a special ring to it that resonated in his ears like no other he had ever heard. He stretched and turned to see Yeshua standing near the doorway looking directly at him. The man he had befriended acknowledged him with a nod and a wink.

He looked away because Dov poked him in the side, whispering, "Here comes the fake prophet and healer that you like so much."

"Stop it. Not now. Listen."

He looked back in time to see Yeshua meander into the center of the room like a slow-moving stream.

Rabbi Selig noticed him, too. "Shalom Yeshua. Please wait outside. You can speak to any of the boys after class."

~ 73 ~

Jennifer Bjork

The room grew curiously quiet. The man from Nazareth began to talk in that soft, melodious voice. "The rabbi is correct. Class is not over. I came to remind you about the great, unfailing love that our Lord Elohim has shown to the Israelites, to each of you in this class, and to your families. The second of the Ten Commandments that Moses received from Elohim is the one that I emphasize. I know that you are already familiar with them all. In that commandment, the Lord shows His great love to those who love Him into a thousand generations. The Lord only punishes into the third or fourth generation. Therefore, which do you think is more important to Him who sees all? Love or punishment?"

"Love," was the resounding answer from around the room.

"We already studied this topic and are on a different one. Wait outside, as I requested so that I can continue."

When the rabbi paused, Yeshua's melodious voice rang out again. "This message of love is reiterated many times throughout our history. I personally enjoy the psalms of King David. David said, 'The Lord is gracious and compassionate, slow to anger and rich in love.' David's experience has also been true for me. I hope you find that to be true, too. David also tells us that, 'The Lord's unfailing love surrounds the man who trusts Him.' That type of love sounds comforting, like being comforted by a pair of warm arms hugging you and patting your back saying, 'There, there.'"

Shai was glued to his words. It seemed Yeshua spoke directly to him, even though he was speaking to the entire class of Galilean boys. The man had even spoken his last words while looking directly at him.

Shai nodded his unspoken confirmation, *Yes, that is just what it feels like.*

"To understand unfailing love let's examine what it means to fail. Anyone want to try to explain failing?"

Since they had all experienced failure, answers came in rapid fire, one after another:

"To disappoint. Like when I fail to do a task or job well, I fail my father."

The Whistling Galilean

"To weaken. A rope on a boat can fail, give way, and downright break."

"That means it stopped functioning. To fail can mean that, too."

Yeshua continued without giving Rabbi Selig a chance to interrupt, "Smart thinking, boys. The beginning of the word unfailing, 'un,' means to do the reverse of the word to follow. Therefore, the Lord's love does not fail. It does not become deficient, does not weaken, does not disappoint, and does not stop functioning. Instead it can actually grow stronger and encourage us, give us hope. I like to concentrate on the Lord's unfailing love rather than all the 'do nots' and punishments, even though they are also true. In this day and time, we all need some hope in our lives. Don't you agree?"

"Yes." Most of the boys replied.

Shai glanced around at his classmates. Even most of the boys sitting in the back row were paying attention now, leaning forward and watching Yeshua. A few boys, like Dov, slouched and watched their toes wiggle.

This time, Shai elbowed his friend. "Psst, pay attention."

Before the eleven-year-old returned his gaze to Yeshua, he noticed that Rabbi Selig looked uncomfortable. He had been unable to get a word in edgewise. He seemed unable to interrupt Yeshua. His *ahem's* and throat clearings were of no consequence; these noises were ignored by both the boys and by Yeshua. Shai also noticed that everyone in the room failed to respond to the normal attention-getting rocking, a habit of the rabbi.

Yeshua still held the floor. "The Lord desires his chosen people, us, to not only love Him back with all of our hearts, our minds, and our souls, but to demonstrate this love toward others. There is a long list of people that we should be obligated to help through loving actions. Widows and the poor top that list, but let us first begin by extending loving care toward our own family. That can be difficult. Imagine it."

There was a pause that even the rabbi did not break. Discomfort spread throughout the room. As hard as Shai tried, he could not imagine loving Ezra and Papa as much as he loved Mama and Grandpa.

"Boys, this kind of love is demonstrated by offering goodwill in times of need. Can any of you think of an example?"

Shai surprised himself when he stood to speak, "The fishermen of the northern Galilee are doing just that. Many of you know several fishermen, Simon and Andrew are two of them, who are rarely fishing anymore. They have become Yeshua's students. As a result, the remaining fishermen like my father, Yona, are working harder to take up the slack. Less fishermen must now feed the same number of hungry mouths. I am proud of my father and of the others. We take care of other families willingly and with good cheer."

"This is a wonderful example of extending compassionate goodwill. It is an act of kindness and of mercy. It honors the Lord of Israel."

The boy behind him patted him on the back and whispered, "Way to go!"

Shai now felt embarrassed because he realized he had pointed out the actions of his parents, not of himself. He had no example of himself extending goodwill. Therefore, he sat and tried to shrink in size so as not to be so noticeable.

As he listened to Yeshua, Shai watched the rabbi try to use his round torso to physically move between the man from Nazareth and his own pupils. He was thwarted over and over by the ever-moving Yeshua. It was like watching a dance. Their steps seemed in time with the melody and pace of Yeshua's voice. Amazing - and actually, humorous.

Shai chuckled and whispered details of the dance to Dov. Dov chuckled, too. Soon the room was abuzz. Yeshua realized that the boys recognized his actions. He grinned, chuckled, and slowly walked to the side of the room, finally giving way to the rabbi.

"Ahem," Rabbi Selig interrupted with a swivel of his broad hips. "I will take over now. You have taken too much time. It is my responsibility to teach the boys, not yours. Mine."

"Yes, rabbi, you have a big responsibility." Yeshua used a gentle, non-argumentative tone. "Everyone is grateful for your time and your knowledge. As a result of growing Roman troop strength north

The Whistling Galilean

of Capernaum, I thought it important to share the message about the Lord of Israel's unfailing love. I chose to provide hope."

"That choice was not yours to make. If you allowed me to grow to know you better, I may have asked you to teach as a guest. Then I would have selected your assigned topic. This interruption was uncalled for. Under whose authority do you teach? Not Jerusalem's. Not mine. Whose?"

Yeshua slowly walked to the other side of the room. As he crossed in front of the rabbi, Shai heard the round man spat out harshly under his breath, "Who do you think you are to teach Elohim's desire to our children?"

"I do the will of my Father. He has given me that authority."

Rabbi Selig exploded, stomping his foot and pounding a fist into his other hand to accent each point. "First, you erroneously think you understand Elohim better than the great schools in Jerusalem, which I attended. That is impossible. Second, I have not given you the authority to teach in my synagogue. Go from this class, now." The rabbi turned bright red as he pointed heatedly at the open doorway.

"I will continue to do the will of my Father wherever I am." In contrast to the red-faced rabbi, Yeshua spoke calmly and slowly. He did not move a muscle.

"We will see about that!" The rabbi stomped out of the room talking loudly the whole way. "I will report your actions to Jerusalem, to the Pharisee sect in particular. You have overstepped your authority. Only the Rabbinical schools in Jerusalem have been given authority from Elohim as the Chosen Ones...."

As his voice disappeared out the door and faded with distance from the classroom, Shai and his classmates sat in confusion. Weren't they both teaching to love and honor Elohim? Weren't they both on the same side? Was class dismissed? Should they follow the rabbi?

"I am glad you all are staying to finish this lesson." Yeshua's smile and invitation to stay was genuine. It warmed the boy's heart. He had never heard Yeshua say anything disrespectful of the rabbi, or the Pharisees, or anyone, for that matter. He did not understand the undercurrent of a battle between the two men.

~ 77 ~

Jennifer Bjork

Yeshua continued speaking, putting his hands on his hips. "We were discussing the Lord's unfailing love and members of your community showing this loving goodwill in times of need. Another way for each of you to demonstrate this is to reconcile with a family member with whom you are in a battle, such as a bothersome brother or sister."

"Oh, oh." The hairs on Shai's neck rose as he recognized that this, too, was directed at himself and his relationship with his older brother.

"A loving action would be to reconcile with your brother or other relative. Reconcile is a big word that means to settle or to resolve the dispute. Can you help me with other definitions of the word 'reconcile'?"

"I think it also means to restore friendship," Heno replied eagerly

"...and harmony," added another student Shai could not see.

"That is true. It may be too much to ask you to restore your relationship in one step. Think about doing this in stages. Start by accepting one thing that is unpleasant. That small action on your part will be difficult. That is the truth. Change is hard. This acceptance of one thing may be all that is needed to break through the barrier that separates both of you. By accepting one unpleasant thing, you demonstrate that you are the bigger person. You show others that you are the mature adult in the relationship and not a silly, immature child. Can you do that?"

The room was quiet.

"Try that acceptance of one thing for several months. Then, it will become a habit to you. You will surprise yourself and others in your family. They will like the person that you are becoming. You can always return to the unpleasantness, if that is your desire."

Shai knew that these wise words applied specifically to his relationship with Ezra. Was he bold enough to take the first step? Did he want a better relationship with his older brother? He admitted that there had been enjoyable times in the past, but they were hard to remember. He would like an older brother that could advise him, protect him, help him, play with him...love him. He also realized that he did not want to disappoint Yeshua, so he resolved to try. Now he just had to pick one thing, one unpleasant horrible thing.

9

Yona the Fisherman

SEVERAL WEEKS LATER, SHAI WAS ON THE GALILEE WITH HIS FATHER. This was a morning he would never forget. The moisture in the slight breeze dampened his skin. In the early morning light, dots of white or brownish sails on the blue sea could be seen separating from the shoreline and going in different directions like dried leaves in a fall breeze.

Most of the fourteen-cubit-long wooden fishing boats on the Sea of Galilee had a double-bow design. Both ends of the boat came to a similar-shaped point. There was a wooden platform filling in the front half, the bow, where fishermen worked their nets.

Today, the usual pile of nets in the middle of Papa Yona's boat had been replaced by carefully stacked baskets holding fresh fish for sale. It was his father's turn to take the community-caught fish to the market.

Shai could not believe his good luck. He was with Papa in *Ole Blue* this morning because Ezra had not yet returned from his overnight fishing expedition with another fisherman. Shai, thrilled with the opportunity, eagerly jumped at every new task to please the experienced mariner at the stern, or rear, of the boat.

There was finally a lull in the business of loading the boat and sailing away from the beach. Once underway with a straight shot toward Capernaum, no additional sets of sail or maneuvers were needed. So, father and son relaxed and ate the snack Mama had packed for them. They had not yet had breakfast because they had left the house before sunrise.

After eating, the boy did not want to waste any time. "Papa, can we have a serious talk now?"

"Go ahead. It is smooth sailing from here."

"Does Ezra use Grandpa's fillet knife very much?"

"I have yet to see him use it. He mostly uses my old one. Why do you ask?"

"Grandpa showed me his knife many times, describing how he carefully carved the handle and attached the blade. I think it is beautiful."

"It is well made...and sharp. He selected good steel, steel that holds an edge. Did you know that my cousin in Jerusalem forged that blade himself and that it was a wedding gift to your grandfather?"

"No. Have I met your cousin?"

"Not yet. When you join us to attend Passover at the Temple, you will meet him. We usually stay at his home."

"I have not seen any other blade that has a wavy shiny silver mixed with black."

"It is a technique learned by my cousin in Damascus. Very special indeed."

"Papa, I thought that you, not Grandpa, would give Ezra his apprenticeship gift."

"I was going to. Ezra chose Grandfather's knife instead. Since the Elder did not mind, that is what we did."

Shai turned away to lean over the smooth side of the boat to drag his hand in the cool blue water. He needed a minute. So, Ezra chose the knife, probably to spite Shai, to hurt him, and to show off to others that the older boy was greatly loved. Well, even though Shai knew that his grandfather loved him, it did still hurt.

The Whistling Galilean

"Shai, is that what the hullabaloo at the apprenticeship ceremony was about? The knife? Be honest."

The boy looked back at his father and noticed that the familiar, sun-weathered face was thoughtful. "Yes, Papa. I hoped that Grandpa would present me with his knife when it is my time, but now it belongs to Ezra."

"Ahhh. Now I understand...a little jealousy and envy reared its ugly head." Papa took a sip of water from the leather flask and offered a sip to his son, as if that would make it alright.

After a sip, Shai wiped his mouth with the back of his hand, "Papa, why do you always take Ezra's side?"

"That is not true."

"It sure feels like it."

"I am sorry you feel that way." He was thoughtful again, then he cleared his voice. "Ahem. The Elder told me what really happened that morning on the beach. I did jump to a rapid conclusion and blamed you for the Elder's fall. I am sorry, Shai. I should have made amends earlier."

Wow! His father had just apologized to him. That was a first. Shai looked away so Yona would not see his tears forming. The lump in his throat almost held back the words he needed his father to hear. "Thank you, Papa. I am glad you know the truth."

"There is another truth that you need to know. I need Ezra's help right now, Shai. Andrew and Simon are rarely fishing but spending time with Yeshua from Nazareth instead. That leaves less men to feed the same number of mouths. I need you to be understanding and patient. I need you to act as a man, not a boy. Can you do that?"

Shai knew that Yeshua's gathering of followers directly affected his family but did not realize that both his father and Ezra worked so hard. He nodded his agreement. "I will try. I did not know that Ezra was needed and was helping the community catch more fish."

"Good. That is all I can ask of you. I have ignored you. I know that Fishel is a good man. He is the best replacement for my guidance that I could find. He is knowledgeable, responsible, and talented. Are you learning from him?"

~ 81 ~

Jennifer Bjork

The eleven-year-old had no idea that his father thought about any of this, especially about providing him, the invisible son, with guidance. He thought he heard a hopeful twinge in Papa Yona's voice. He nodded again in agreement. "Yes, he is a good teacher. He can also be funny. I like him and his stories. I am learning so much… but I also look forward to learning from you."

"I promise to make some time for you, Shai. Now, please pull in the sail until I say stop."

After they reset the sail, Papa continued to talk. "Fishel has so much promise. He is a hard worker, and he also needs the work. Did you know that he is supporting his family? His father died early this year."

"I knew he could no longer fish from boats and needed to be useful. I did not know that his mother, brothers, and sisters all depended on him for their livelihood."

"Yes. That is a big responsibility to fill five mouths. Fishel says that you are a quick learner, a hard worker, and are progressing well."

With a grin, Shai nodded again. He wanted his father to know his appreciation. "Thanks, Papa. I needed to hear that from you."

He was satisfied. He was amazed at the depth of their conversation. Together, they had covered most of his concerns, at least for now. He could not remember talking to his father at such length ever. He resolved to be more helpful, too.

The boy enjoyed the sunshine and warmth of the sun. He smiled as he refocused and looked around. He noticed a nearby boat aiming for the same location, Capernaum's stone quay.

"Papa," he pointed, "can we beat them?"

"Point with your chin, not your arm. I see the boat," Papa whispered.

They both watched the other boat. Both boats appeared to be the same size. To Shai, both boats seemed to be going at the same speed.

Papa grinned. "You bet we can win."

So, a silent race ensued. The race provided the youngster with a burst of adrenaline, "Go faster, Papa!"

It was a universal desire for all seamen to win these informal

The Whistling Galilean

races. Even though no one agreed openly to racing, winning these races meant having the fastest boat and the best crew.

Now that they were racing, the muscular fisherman whispered directions to Shai: "Loosen the end of the sail a bit to let it bag out and hold more wind. We need to whisper and not point so that the other boat does not figure out our plan until too late. Then, they can only react, and we gain the edge."

A light wind still blew over the Galilee. The boy adjusted the coffee-stained sail as his father desired, then leaned back to see if they passed the distant shoreline just a little faster. Satisfied, he leaned against the tall, upright pole, or mast, which held the sail. The breeze caught the tendrils of his light brown hair, so he retied the long strands tightly behind his neck with a brown cord. He did not want distractions that could make him lose the race.

Shai's muscular father steered from the stern of the boat with sure, strong hands using a long, wide plank. It had been carefully formed into the rudder for *Ole Blue*. The plank was sanded to thin the forward and trailing edges, thus smoothing its path through the water.

Shai reacted to his father's whispers by rapidly making necessary adjustments to the sail.

"Good. This is the fastest we can do right now, my joyful son."

Yona had called Shai, *my son*! Shai grinned broadly. He loved hearing those words spoken by his father. It was rare. The boy interpreted that spoken *my son* as his father's demonstration of his love rather than a mere admission of their kinship. That made Shai very happy.

He joyfully watched their progress against the other boat. They still appeared to be even. The prize was the dock space closest to the marketplace and, of course, bragging rights for the day. Time crawled like a snail - slowly. Eventually, Papa's boat forged ahead.

"Go, '*Blue*, go!" Shai urged in a whisper.

As they neared the dockside quay, Shai clearly saw the two men they raced against. He did not recognize either of them. They must have been from another of the fishing villages southward along the coast. Eventually, they gave way with a wave, turning their boat back toward the open sea.

~ 83 ~

Papa's boat had won! Shai took a victorious leap on the deck. "We won, Papa!"

He saw that Papa sported a huge smile, too. They both waved to the other fishermen, now headed for another spot. After all, it was just like a game of kick-the-stone - just friendly competition.

Docking was another busy time. At Papa's command, Shai dropped the sail, slowing the boat to a crawl. Then he tied several oblong rope balls on the outer hull of the boat, at the bow and along both sides. The rope bumpers protected the bow beam from damage in case the boat accidentally rammed into or rubbed along the unforgiving, rough stone. The bumpers also protected both sides of *Ole Blue* from rubbing against boats nestled against theirs.

Holding the bow line, Shai jumped off the boat to the stone structure and tied *Ole Blue* to a round metal circle cemented firmly in the stone. Six to eight boats tied only by their bows could fit along the quay's length. He knew what to do since he had helped Papa and Ezra before.

Once the line was secured, Shai looked around. Merchants stood in the shade of buildings, watching the boats arriving. Papa had explained that they were middle men surviving on the trade goods carried in boats like his father's. Many types of goods, not just fish, were carried by boat around the Galilee. He saw piles of tanned leather, ceramic pottery in boxes, and trunks carrying unknown goods from the lands to the south and east.

He saw the merchants send their children or servants to push carts to the boats and help the boatmen unload their wares. Shai recognized a classmate, Gil. Gil had told him that his father was the fish merchant Papa liked to use.

Therefore, Shai waved and shouted, "Shalom, Gil. Over here. We need a cart."

"Shalom, Shai. Here I come."

Shai was grateful that his classmate rapidly changed direction. Gil even helped him load the baskets onto the cart.

As they worked, Shai asked, "Any events in town you want to share?"

The Whistling Galilean

"Nothing exciting."

Meanwhile, Papa had moved the boat to open up room for another boat. This time, Yona did not raise the sail but used the wide rudder like an oar to scull *Ole Blue* away from the dock and toward a nearby beach.

When Papa returned to the quay, the boys had already nestled the baskets so they would not fall off the cart. The load of fish was so heavy that Papa had to pull it with a leather harness around his chest while Gil and Shai pushed from behind. Both boys grunted with the strain.

Capernaum's market square was located along the waterfront quay. Stone buildings surrounded the other three sides of the square. Shai was thankful that stones paved the entire market area. The square and all streets used to be dirt. In order to speed military troop movements, the Romans had unknowingly made a helpful improvement for the subjected Galileans. The stone surface reduced dust and made access easier, especially during the rain when slippery, muddy ruts used to bog down heavy carts filled with merchandise.

Gil was thrilled. "Shai, there's no line. You can be first."

Papa heard and pulled even harder to get the cart and cargo to the open doorway under the canvas beside Gil's home, the fish monger's shop. Shai helped his father uncover each basket of fish while Gil's father ensured that the fish were fresh, not spoiled.

Shai was fascinated with the process. Gil's blue-eyed father selected several specimens of fish from each basket, not just the ones on top. He went through a repetitive system - pick it up, smell it, squeeze it for firmness, and finally, look at its eyes.

"Shalom. These look good, Yona...as usual"

"Shalom. Yes, they are. We caught them last night - a good haul. As you know, this is the haul for our entire community, not just me."

"I remember, Yona, but I know you personally are an excellent fisherman. I am willing to bet that these big ones must be from *Ole Blue*." The man winked at Papa.

Shai was proud that his father was so well respected. He watched his father's back straighten. A smile snuck out one corner of his tanned mouth, exposing his chipped tooth.

As the two men weighed each basket on huge brass scales, Shai and Gil carried empty baskets beside the shop returning them to *Ole Blue*, now on the beach.

When he returned, Shai received a pat on the back from Papa, who told the fish monger, "Shai has been a great help this morning. I am glad that his mother suggested that I bring him with me. Now, he can relax in the marketplace while we discuss this transaction and other business."

10

Carmi's Tale

NOW THAT HE HAD AN OPPORTUNITY TO LOOK FOR CARMI, THERE was a spring of excitement to Shai's step. She was usually helping her mother sell fresh produce in the market square, so that is where he headed. After the accident in the orchard, she entered his thoughts even more often than before, if that was possible. He still had not contrived a way to change her mind about him.

He sauntered between stone buildings. He gently dragged his fingers along the hole-filled, volcanic basalt wall to feel it's rough texture. Unconsciously, he whistled a lilting bird tune that reflected his cheerful mood. He slowed to peer around the corner of the building into the square.

A startled "Oh!" escaped his mouth, and he stepped back quickly. Someone had arrived at that same corner at the same time he had. If he had not stopped quickly in his tracks, the two of them would have collided. He heard a high-pitched voice also exclaim surprise at the same time he did.

He glanced at the market square and saw that everyone had

~ 87 ~

turned towards their surprised shouts. The boy felt uncomfortable drawing their attention.

Suddenly, he recognized the other voice. It was Carmi, the very person for whom he searched. He had almost knocked her off her feet...again. He quickly stepped around the corner in time to see Carmi still waving an arm for balance.

"What? Who?" she exclaimed to no one in particular.

"Oops. Here, let me help you." Shai reached out quickly and grabbed the sleeve of her flailing arm to steady her.

"Where did you come from?" With the emphasis on *you*, he knew that she recognized him. As she regained her balance, she also regained her composure. The cutest girl in Capernaum quickly placed her arm back at her side. After all, touching between the sexes was not appropriate.

"Are you alright?" he asked as calmly as he could.

"Of course," she huffed back.

He exhaled with relief. "Good, I did not hurt you...again."

Her attention was drawn to the ground. She groaned, "Oh, no."

He looked down also at round blobs of yellow, then back to Carmi.

The sun-blond girl quickly lowered her large market basket to the ground. The core of yellow was exposed, now only partially covered by grapes and a delicately embroidered tan cloth. Now he saw that she was surrounded by bouncing and rolling lemons - the very lemons he had seen in her orchard.

They gasped in unison, "Oh, noooo."

She whispered with a fierce intensity, "Quick, help me pick up the lemons. The Romans cannot see them! The merchants should not see them. That would ruin everything. Please, hurry!"

Shai quickly complied with her request. Using his robe as a bag, he piled fruit into it as fast as he could.

She talked in a whisper as her hands rapidly rearranged the fruit in her basket. "Remember, only the Roman rulers or the very wealthy that work with them can afford to have lemon trees. Remember, my great-great-grandfather obtained a small tree from a caravan from

The Whistling Galilean

the orient a long time ago, before Roman rule. We have grafted more trees from that one. Now that the Romans are in control of our land, we must keep the small grove of six trees secret. The Romans could confiscate our entire orchard. We could lose everything, even our lives. It is an important secret, Shai. Please help me keep it."

"I promise I will keep your secret." Shai nodded earnestly. He knew that he could keep secrets; after all, he was keeping the one Yeshua had shared with him many months ago.

"Just grab the lemons, get the grapes last," She whispered between her teeth as if she was whistling.

He did as she directed. Once the escapees were corralled in his baggy clothing, he sat down next to her basket with his back to the market square to hide their actions from view. She looked around to ensure that no one was paying attention to them. Then she leaned over to Shai and whispered a soft, "Thank you."

Shai thought he would pass out. Her hair tickled his cheek. She smelled so fresh, light, and wonderful.

"I promise that I will keep your secret." That was all he could think of saying.

"Thank you." She wiped each beautiful yellow fruit on the inside hem of her ankle-length dress to clean off dirt, straw, and any other particles that would make the citrus appear to be less fresh and tasty. She muttered, "I hope these are still an attractive gift. My family will be so disappointed in me if they are not."

She then said to her companion in a normal tone, as if they were merely resuming a conversation, "Shai, you sure gave me a startle. What are you doing here?"

"I- I- I sailed from home," he stammered, hardly able to think.

"No, stupid. What are you doing here in Capernaum? It's not a school day."

Shai could not tell her the truth, that he had actually been looking for her. So, he lamely smiled, shrugged, and said, "I'm here selling fish with my father."

"Oh. That makes sense."

"What are you doing?" Shai wondered out loud.

~ 89 ~

"I'm taking a basket of fresh produce to Simon's house. They are celebrating tonight. Simon's mother-in-law is healed."

"Oh, I didn't know that she was ill." That was an understatement. Shai had not even known that Simon had a mother-in-law.

The two young people made eye contact. Suddenly Shai realized that they were actually talking. She was not angry with him. He didn't want to lose this incredible momentum of events, so he rapidly sputtered, "Wh- What was wrong with her?"

The cute freckled girl responded nonchalantly, now that they had hidden the lemons back under the cloth. She was relaxed as she picked up the grape clusters, dusting them off also. "Oh, the mother-in-law was burning up with a very high fever. Sponging her with damp cloths to relieve the heat and cool her down wasn't enough, so Simon sent for a traditional healer north of town."

Shai wiped off grapes, too. When he leaned closer beside her, he again was assailed by the delightful, clean, intoxicating aroma of her hair. Not wanting this moment to ever end, he bent even closer beside her, placing each small cluster of grapes with care in the basket.

"They look fine...very tasty...like you," he stammered unsure of what he was uttering.

With a little giggle, Carmi stood and shook out her curly waves with her hand. "I've got to make this delivery to Simon before something else happens."

She pointed resolutely to Simon's house, a substantial-looking stone house. It was only about sixty cubits from the synagogue and the marketplace where they stood.

"At least let me help carry the basket."

When she nodded her agreement, they carried the basket between them. Shai matched her steps, stride for stride. On the way, Carmi filled Shai in with more news.

"The traditional healer that Simon obtained used an ancient remedy. She tied an iron knife to a thorn bush with a braid of the mother-in-law's hair. She repeated that the next day. On the third day, the bush was cut down. An incantation was spoken over it as the bush

The Whistling Galilean

was burned in a fire. This process was supposed to transfer the hot fever to the bush, destroying it when it burnt up."

"That sounds like what rabbis do when they transfer sin to a Judas goat and send it out of town."

"Oh, you are right. I had not thought of that. Smart."

"Did the incantation work?"

"No. Therefore, Simon and Andrew tried several other types of cures, some more helpful than others, but none helpful enough. She grew weaker and weaker. She was wasting away. She stopped eating and seemed to be dying, so Simon brought Rabbi Selig to their house."

"I thought that all that a rabbi could do was to light a candle and pray. They are not known as healers, at least not to me."

"Well, Shai, think about what you just said. Prayer to Elohim can heal people. We are told that we can ask for healing and the Elohim can intervene."

"That becomes a miracle, yes?"

"Of course it does. Don't be stupid."

"Oh." Carmi had only just called him smart. Now, he had blundered and was stupid...again. He felt ashamed...again.

Everyone in Shai's community was relatively healthy, so he did not know much about doctors. He knew of a fisherman who had an infection, a problem with his eye. The doctor had crushed a long stick from a special plant and mixed it with water to make a salve. The injured man wore a cloth compress with that salve on his eye for days. Finally, the redness and swelling had gone away. The fisherman's vision had been restored. And now, Fishel had a healing salve on his wounded hand. That was Shai's extent of knowledge on the subject.

As they walked, Carmi continued the saga about Simon's mother-in-law. Her voice had a charming lilt to it. It was easy to listen to, like the bubbling of a spring. He really did not care what she spoke about. Shai relaxed into her voice and wished that he could listen to it all day.

"Well, you heard that a stranger from Nazareth named Yeshua, cured her, right?"

~ 91 ~

"What?"

Shai was so shocked that he immediately stopped walking. When his side of the basket stopped progressing forward, Carmi had to stop, too, or the lemons would have gone bouncing away again. She turned to face him.

"Do not stop… the fruit …. What's wrong?

"Yeshua healed her? Really? How?"

They stood there as she explained. "It was after our last Sabbath service. He was invited to Simon's house for the Sabbath meal. Yeshua discovered that their mother-in-law was ill, weak from over a week of a high fever and minimal food, and possibly near death. The stranger from Nazareth asked for permission to see her."

"And then what happened?"

"Apparently, all Yeshua did was speak to her illness. Then, he lifted her hand and helped her stand up. She was healed instantly. She was so healthy that she was able to join the Sabbath meal. The adults around Capernaum quickly spread the word that Yeshua did a healing miracle."

Shai was amazed. A part of the secret that his friend, Yeshua, had told him was now exposed and shared. He knew that his friend was already teaching about Elohim and gathering followers called disciples. Now, he had begun to heal people, too. Maybe the secret was no longer a secret. Even so, Shai decided to still keep his word and not talk about it.

Carmi wiped some dust off of her cute chin with her free hand. "The mother-in-law did not even have to remain in bed to recover her strength. Since it was evening and the sun was setting, the Sabbath was over. Therefore, she joined the other women in the household in preparing a large, festive meal. Word spread rapidly that she had been healed, so other families in the area grew hopeful that their own mother, daughter, son, father, or whatever loved one could be cured also."

"Yeshua, my friend. You did it." Shai smiled with pride.

"Yes, he did. In no time at all, a line of beds and pallets spread from Simon's house to the marketplace."

~ 92 ~

The Whistling Galilean

The boy looked around the market square trying to imagine the scene of the infirmed lying in rows. Where he stood, he saw the market square with an open side to the quay. Otherwise, two-story buildings surrounded it. Merchants lived in rooms above their shops. Colorful cloth awnings now stretched from the building walls toward the open marketplace, but probably had not been part of the night time scene as Yeshua healed one person after another under the stars.

Today, the awnings provided inviting shade next to the cool, black, basalt stone walls. The shade attracted shoppers to tables piled with items for sale. Shai was not interested in the bundles of dried herbs, baskets, and tools hanging from the rafters. His attention again focused on the girl beside him.

In a passing thought, Shai wondered why Gil had not shared this important news. It did not matter. He liked hearing about it from Carmi much better than he might have from Gil.

The freckled girl across the basket from him continued, "Yeshua went through the sufferers, blessed them, and healed every one of them. It was truly a miracle."

"I had no idea."

"Everyone in Capernaum has been talking about it."

They walked awhile in thoughtful silence. Shai was amazed that she had been talking about the very stranger he had met, the man who wanted to see him often.

Finally, he braved breaking the silence. "This Yeshua is interesting. I met him on the beach. We have even become friends." Glancing at her, he grinned. "Carmi, you are a likable person."

"Me?"

"Yes, you."

She grinned and looked at him from the corner of her eyes.

"Somehow, I am not surprised that you have become friends with the healer. My whole family was amazed to watch some of those healings. It was an incredible night. I remember thinking that even the stars over the marketplace - the one just behind us - the stars were a witness to this man's healing power."

~ 93 ~

Jennifer Bjork

By then, they were standing in front of the door to Simon's house.

"I must go in, Shai. It's been great talking to you. Anyway, I wanted to tell you why the family is celebrating. They bought this basket of expensive fruit. Lemons add a wonderful flavor to food. They are also said to have healing capabilities, not that she needs healing anymore. I am just the delivery girl."

"And a pretty one at that." He smiled broadly at her. "It has been wonderful talking to you, Carmi. I hope today makes up for my stupidity in the orchard."

"It does if…if you can keep our secret safe." She bestowed a smile on him as she spoke, her white teeth sparkling in the sunlight. He felt the back of her soft hand against his. Her final words filled his heart with joy. "Thanks for your help today."

11

Carving Time

TIME PASSED SLOWLY. THE REGULARITY OF SHAI'S LIFE RESUMED. Being one year older had not made a difference. He had not seen Dov for nearly a month. Therefore, he started a project of his choosing in his spare time. As he sped toward home from the fishermen's beach, he eagerly sought out his grandfather, Yona the Elder. Today was the day!

He sped onto the packed dirt work area in front of their one-room home, then slid to a stop. He inhaled deeply to gently awaken the wrinkled man who might still be taking his afternoon nap.

Through the slight dusty mist he had generated, he saw the Elder sitting in the afternoon sunshine with one foot propped up on the round stone fire pit. The old man was sitting on the soft, hair-filled cushion that Mama had sewn for him to soften the hardness of the wooden stool. Shai realized quickly that it would have taken the old man two trips to settle himself in that position. He understood that to mean that the old one was eager to begin, also.

Shai first heard the old man's soft chuckle, then his voice, "Well, Shai, time is wasting away."

There was a glint in those pale blue eyes. Mischief, perhaps?

"I got here as quick as I could." Shai huffed. He was almost out of breath from the long run through the woods surrounding their home.

"Are you ready? I am."

Shai was impressed. Beside the old man's thin foot sat the food bowl, the one that his father had made for him when he was a mere baby. Beside the chopping log sat Grandpa's carving knife and the sharpening stone on an oiled rag. To celebrate his eleventh year, the beloved old man was giving him the gift of his time and knowledge. Now, that was special!

It was the boy's turn to chuckle. "Oh, boy! Let's start. First, would you like some cold water?"

"Yes, I would."

Shai slipped into the house and grabbed two small gourds with handles.

"Hi, Mama, I am home."

"I heard your arrival, son."

"Today is the day we start carving."

She returned to chopping. "I know that makes you happy."

Shai went down to the well and filled the two gourds with fresh water. Returning carefully, he offered his grandfather the larger gourd. "Here you go."

"Thank you." After a long gulp, the Elder asked, "Do you want a few practice strokes first or do you want to start carving immediately?"

"I am ready to start."

"Good. Use the tip of the knife to carve a thin outline first. Remember, not too deep."

Shai and Yona the Elder had practiced for several weeks on spare wood lying in the wood pile until they had achieved the design that Shai liked best. In this design, the tip top of the boat's sail centered near one edge of the bowl. The sail would billow around the words that his father had carved in two lines:

'Isaiah - God provides.
Never empty, never hungry."

The Whistling Galilean

From there, the sail bowed out and down one side of the bowl to the boat's wooden hull. Curvy waves surrounded the hull on the water. Mountains arose on either side of the sail and mast. He planned to carve the outer skin of the bowl away to create a lighter color for the sky. Along the rim of the bowl encircling this design, he wanted to carve a twisted rope. He really liked the design, but was still unsure where to start.

"Grandpa, should I carve the circle of rope first? Or start with the sail? Or the boat hull?"

"You choose. There is no wrong answer."

Shai picked up their practice board. On it was the design. He sat down on the log beside the Elder. He studied their final design carefully by tracing his finger over it and imagining his carving strokes.

"Well, the rope takes more carving strokes. It has a twist that repeats itself. I want that part to end up in even sections. The sail takes fewer strokes, but it is the critical center of attention."

He could feel his grandfather watching his face twist up in indecision, just like that twisted rope design. Suddenly Shai decided. He knew what he wanted to do.

"Grandpa, I will do the sail first. I know I can do this."

"Wonderful. I spent the morning sharpening the carving blade, so it is very sharp, especially the tip."

"Thank you."

As he looked up into those loving eyes, he realized how lucky he was to have so many wonderful, caring people in his life - Grandpa, Mama, Papa, Fishel, Dov… He hoped to add Carmi to this list soon. He was excited at that thought.

Now, he found it hard to concentrate on the bowl. He imagined Carmi sitting across from him, eagerly watching him work. In his daydream, her praises were wonderful and plentiful.

"What are you waiting for, Shai?" Grandpa's voice interrupted his daydream.

The boy nestled the bowl between his legs to keep it stationary while he carved. His left hand found the lettering on the bottom of

~ 97 ~

the bowl. He touched the starting point above that with his finger, just as his grandfather had taught him.

Holding the carving knife in his right hand as if he was going to stab something with a downward thrust, he placed the tip of the blade beside his finger. Holding the backside of the blade with his left fingers to steady it, he rested his left pinkie finger on the bowl. Now, he was ready to begin.

Gently he pushed the blade down the curve of the half-a-cubit-diameter bowl in as straight a line as he could. He lifted the blade tip less than halfway down the curve toward the rim. He had not realized that he was holding his breath until he inhaled deeply.

"Good start." Grandfather's soothing voice calmed his nerves.

He did not want to make a mistake. This was his second big project, the cast net being the first. It did not take long to outline the open sail. He imagined it pulling the boat toward him with the wind from the stern. He was about to start on the outline of the boat when a voice from the woods suddenly captured his attention.

A friendly, familiar pitch called out, "Hello, inside."

Yeshua! It was Yeshua. Shai had not put Yeshua on his list of caring people, and he should.

"Shalom, Yeshua." The boy eagerly stood.

"Shai, what a surprise to find you here. Shalom, my friend. I had hoped to catch your father."

"He is out on *Ole Blue* fishing."

"Yes, it is a beautiful day to be on the Galilee. And this must be your grandfather. We have not met."

Out of the corner of his eye, Shai saw Grandfather struggle to stand. Yeshua covered ground quickly as he strode across the packed dirt. He patted the lad on the back as he slipped by. With a gentle hand on grandfather's shoulder, he both greeted the white-haired man and encouraged him to remain seated all at the same time.

"Yeshua, please meet Yona the Elder." Shai naturally dropped into the polite language of introductions.

"Shalom, Yona. It is a great pleasure. Shai has spoken well of you quite often. May I call you the Elder?"

The Whistling Galilean

"Shalom, Yeshua. I can say the same about you. Yes, most people call me the Elder."

Now that formalities were over, Shai asked, "What did you want with my father, Yeshua?"

"Occasionally, I need to leave a place quickly and hoped your father and his boat might help me out in the future."

The Elder responded for the Younger, "I am sure that a boat ride here or there would be no problem, especially if my son is already headed in that direction. For instance, a quick trip away from Capernaum."

Yeshua chuckled, "So, you heard about my long night at Capernaum in front of Simon's?"

"Yes, Shai reported the multiple healings."

"I heard about it from a girl I know, Carmi."

The Elder added, "And Shai repeated that tale to me. I also heard from Andrew that you had to escape to rest because you worked all night."

"That is true. That is why I need your father's help, Shai. I am afraid I am becoming popular for the wrong reason."

The Elder was interested. "Can you explain that to us?"

"Gladly. First, though, I want Shai to show me what he is carving."

The boy obliged by gleefully showing Yeshua the design carved on the practice plank. Now he had four eyes watching him carefully etch his design on the bowl.

"Very nice design, Shai. I am carving something also."

Yeshua pulled out a small carving knife and a rounded wooden object that fit snugly in the palm of his hand. "I am carving a river wren and hope to shape the wings today. Do you mind if I join you and carve while we talk?"

"I have seen carvings on furniture, but never a small sculpture like this. May I?" Shai held it to feel the shape and weight before returning it to the owner. "Nice."

So, the two men and the boy settled down for a good discussion. Shai was not surprised that his beloved relative wanted to know more about the man from Nazareth, whom Shai had befriended and trusted.

As he settled into carving, Yeshua started, "My heart goes out to those that are lame and infirm, and I cannot resist making them whole, like repairing broken furniture. In this case, it is to mend broken bodies. I really desire that they and their families listen to my words, prayers, and the intent behind my actions."

"That is understandable. There seem to be many healing prophets during these hard times of Roman occupation. Most of them have been exposed as shams, fakes, and abusers of our trust. Some say that of you. Over our history, a few prophets have had special talents for healing. You seem to be one of the later. I have heard Andrew, Simon, and John say that before their eyes, you have done what seems impossible. You have done that more than once."

Shai was impressed that his grandfather had heard so much and come to such conclusions. Now, he knew that he could talk to the Elder about Yeshua and their growing relationship. It almost felt like the Elder could replace Dov in his life.

Yeshua thanked the Elder for his kind words, "It is the one who is the power behind the healing that I desire to glorify, not myself."

"Who would that be?"

"Elohim, the Lord of Israel."

"Ah, yes. I have heard that you pray to Elohim before each healing. You are a wise man indeed, for I have been taught that only Elohim has the true power to mend bodies and hearts and minds."

"Yes, that is the truth, Elder. That is the message that I want people to remember."

"Many, perhaps not all, have already received that message. I understand that a growing number of people gather wherever you appear."

They sipped on some water. Shai was learning a lot about his friend and his grandfather. They actually were quite alike. Maybe that was the reason that Shai liked both of them.

"I am glad people want to hear my message. I have travelled around the Galilee and spoken in many synagogues, but also from hilltops, beaches, and market squares."

The Whistling Galilean

"You have been busy. You were gone a long time." Shai jumped into the conversation.

"Yes, my friend. I have missed our beach and spending time with you."

Grandfather was in serious thought. "Yeshua, the hard-working Galileans are a generous, warm-hearted, and conscientious people, not like some, especially to the south."

"I, too, have noticed that, especially about the fishermen like yourself. The cross-roads bringing trade from around the Galilee and afar exchange not just goods, but ideas. This area of Israel is unique. It has brought peoples of many cultures, intellects, experiences, and backgrounds together. I have noticed that as a result, the local Galileans like yourself, have developed a broader view about life and the world."

"I agree. When compared to those that work and live in Jerusalem, for example, we are as you describe. Those 'townspeople' in and around the Holy City think they are more intelligent and better than the rest of us. My cousin is a metalsmith 'townsman,' so I get some of that superiority from him toward me." Grandpa laughed.

Yeshua joined him, "Well, I specifically chose this location for my ministry based on the type of people the Lord of Israel is giving me to spread my message, the message that Elohim loves and provides a way for his people."

"I think that your message, Yeshua, stresses what is truly important. The message I hear from Rabbi Selig is often about the rigid, complex Hebrew Laws and about Elohim as a punisher to those that do not follow those Laws. We know that it took the rabbi's many decades, even centuries, to develop and write down the rules we live by...based on the stone tablets Moses received from Elohim himself."

Shai thought he followed their discussion, "I guess that is why I must go to school, so that I learn how to behave and not to break any of the Laws."

"Yes, Shai." both adults answered.

Yeshua added, "Yet, Elohim is so much more than what school teaches you, Shai. That is why I must speak out."

Jennifer Bjork

"I suspect that you are aware that your words are unsettling some of the powerful."

"Yes. It cannot be helped. I must speak the truth."

Grandpa grew more serious. "The news that I hear is that Rabbi Selig contacted some of the Pharisees in Jerusalem, at the Temple, through his old classmates. He accused you of being a foreign disrupter of the school in Capernaum. Beware. This particular group of Temple priests are very powerful and dangerous."

Yeshua smiled reassuringly. "At times, I have seen one of their scouts or representatives where I speak or heal. Right now, they are just curious."

"Just be careful."

Shai suspected that there was more to this conversation than he understood. There seemed to be layered messages between his grandfather and his healing friend. Despite not hearing everything, since he was working hard on outlining the boat on the bowl, the boy did hear words of warning.

Therefore, he became worried and looked at his beach friend. "Please be careful, Yeshua. I do not want any harm to come to you."

After a sip of water, Yeshua looked at Shai, "Do not worry about me, Shai. I have plenty of time for my ministry to grow."

12

Battle Lines

About a week later, Shai had just a few remaining chores around the house before sunset.

While his younger and only sister fed their ten chickens cracked corn, he ensured the birds were secure in the bamboo coop for the night. It stood against one wall of the house on a wooden frame above the bare ground.

Adi giggled as a hen pecked at the grain in her small hand. "It tickles."

His family had a few animals, chickens and a pair of goats. In addition to keeping the goat milk for their family to drink, Mama used it to make cheese and yogurt. The family hoped to obtain a second female. Growing boys were always famished.

Shai was glad that the goats were Ezra's responsibility. He wished that the billy goat would knock his brother to the ground with his tiny horns like he had walloped an unsuspecting Shai earlier that day. He thought that a bully taking care of a bully was not merely appropriate, it was just.

The youngster made sure Grandpa's cane was beside the door

ready for use. The Elder was taking his long afternoon nap in a dark corner inside the house. Shai was glad that they spent several afternoons that week carving his design on his wooden bowl. Grandpa had shown him how to sharpen the blade before he made the delicate, deep gouges. He enjoyed this project very much, probably because it let him spend time with the old man. It was also because it was a project that he had chosen.

Then, the boy went to the wood pile, a random collecting area of dried wood for various uses. There was wood for repairing their home and boat, making furniture, and cooking meals. He sorted the outer edge of the randomly tossed wood into piles of different diameters and lengths. He planned to only pull out enough wood to build the fire to cook their dinner.

Ezra arrived noisily, just in time to supervise. "Oh, good, my slave is already at work."

"Great," Shai snorted under his breath.

"Look, weakling," The elder brother selected logs by pointing to each one with a lazy toe, "I want these three big pieces as the cooking core. Get them to the pit first, runt."

As Shai dragged the first heavy piece over to the fire pit, he countered, "Bet you are too weak to carry one yourself."

Ezra yawned, stretched, and sat lazily on the large tree trunk Papa used for cutting wood to size. "There is no need. I have you to do the work for me."

So, Shai felt he had no choice. He reluctantly took one load after another, placing each piece as Ezra ordered. When he was nearly finished, he was past the frustration of being ordered around. He was fuming. He realized that a good brother would have worked with him. That way, together, they could have finished quickly and had more time to play. Ezra was not that type of brother.

As bossy Ezra sauntered over to the pit to light the cook fire, Shai noticed the fillet knife in a new leather scabbard hanging from Ezra's broad leather belt. He recognized the creamy bone hilt. Ezra gently fingered the beautiful handle when he noticed the direction of Shai's gaze and gloated, "Mine, all mine."

The Whistling Galilean

"For now. You have to earn the right to keep it." Shai wanted to say more, but he already said enough to make trouble.

That taunt made Ezra straighten and flex his biceps. "I will earn it this very minute and you know that I can. Stand up and back up your words...or take them back and apologize."

The boys warily circled each other in preparation for their battle, probably a wrestling match. Usually, Ezra attacked first. This time, Shai decided to go first. He wanted to catch his elder brother unaware and gain the advantage. At least, that was his plan.

With a growl and a step, he began his lunge. Suddenly, his father's deep voice stopped him mid-step. He went tumbling to the ground at the sharp command, "Isaiah!"

The shout of his name was quickly followed by his brother's. "Ezra! Stop it both of you. We have a guest for dinner tonight. I am disappointed in you both. We will talk about this later. Go wash up. Now!"

Shai hated to disappoint his father, especially now that they were developing a better relationship. Although he was still frustrated with Ezra, he knew that this was not the time to protest. He quickly went to wash both his hands and his face to help him cool down. For extra measure, he walked into the edge of the surrounding woods to quiet his nerves. He wanted to be on his best behavior for this mysterious dinner guest.

As he walked, he remembered Yeshua's teachings in school from just two months before. They had been about reconciling differences and settling disputes. He could not remember everything, but he did know that his beach friend had suggested breaking down the barrier by accepting one difficult thing about a family member. He knew that family member, for him, was Ezra.

Shai wanted to show Yeshua, his father, and even Ezra that he was the more mature. He did not want to disappoint the Nazarene. So, as he walked, he tried to choose something about Ezra and their relationship to accept. What was he willing to change? He could accept Ezra's bossiness, his bragging, or his laziness. Dare he accept Ezra's ownership of the coveted fillet knife made by their

Jennifer Bjork

grandfather? That would be the hardest. Since Grandpa let Shai use his own carving knife and lovingly spent time with him, maybe he could give up his desire for that very special fillet knife and accept that it now belonged to Ezra. That would be difficult!

When Shai returned home, he smelled the delightful aroma of grilled fresh fish. Each entire fish was skewered onto a sharp olive twig. Papa had angled a row of them over the hot embers and remaining flames in the fire pit. Shai watched his father drizzle a mixture of herbs in olive oil over each one. This was the boy's favorite way to prepare fish. To him, it tasted better than all of the others. It immediately brightened his mood.

Inside the one-room house, he noticed that the kids had already laid out the woven vine sitting mats. Mama placed several large bowls of food on the central mats. He could smell the fresh-baked flat bread.

Shai announced, "This looks and smells wonderful, Mama."

He looked up in time to see Papa, Ezra, and the surprise guest enter the oil-lamplit room. The boy was delighted. The guest was Yeshua.

Papa made the introductions. "Mama, I'd like you to meet the stranger from Nazareth that you have heard so much about. Yeshua, this is my beautiful bride, Anat."

He saw Mama's cheeks blush red. He could tell that she was pleased. He realized that Papa did not compliment her enough. He reminded himself to tell Papa that she would appreciate him noticing when she really looked nice, smelled good, did something caring for him…and he resolved to eventually do the same for Carmi.

Shai recognized also that Yeshua took time to really notice, then say something nice to each new person that he met, even children. When he came to Shai, he grinned. "No introductions needed here, Yona. Hello, my beach friend. It is so nice to meet the rest of your family. How are you today?"

"Much better now. Welcome to our humble home." Shai was elated that Yeshua was actually in his home. He knew that Yeshua visited many families on the north side of the Galilee. He guessed that it was their turn.

~ 106 ~

The Whistling Galilean

Yeshua offered grandfather an arm helping him to his stool, "I am glad to see you again, Elder. How are your hands today?"

Grandpa shrugged, "The usual."

Shai filled the Elder's wooden bowl as he requested. He settled cross-legged beside the old man to be in a good position to get him seconds, if he desired any. Then he filled his own bowl. His design was beginning to show. He was currently deepening the outline of the planks comprising the boat's hull.

Yeshua noticed. "You have worked on your bowl some more, Shai. I really like the way the hull of the fishing boat is developing."

Shai nodded in thanks. He felt the heat in his cheeks and knew he was blushing. Glancing at Papa, he hoped for recognition. Not tonight.

Despite that oversight, Shai was proud of his parents. On what had probably been short notice, they had quickly pulled together a nice meal. Besides the grilled fish, Mama prepared a chard salad with lentils and artichokes, and hot pita bread, of course. Everything smelled wonderfully inviting.

Papa and Yeshua talked together in low tones while Shai worked hard eating while not making eye contact with Ezra. He didn't want Ezra to ruin this special evening. He savored Yeshua's presence as much as the dinner.

As usual, Yeshua soon went to the heart of the matter. The Nazarene turned toward Mama, while placing his hand on Papa's arm, thus including the entire family in the circle that he created. His pleasant voice filled their small room drawing everyone's attention toward him. "I understand that I have created a hardship on you and your family. I have heard that you now must share more of your catch with the families of those that I have called to follow me."

Among a gathering of men or strangers, women usually did not talk. Therefore, Papa cleared his throat to prepare an answer. Shai knew that his father wrestled with the need to be polite to his guest and also to tell him the truth. "Elohim blesses us with enough fish for all of us. It is the season of plentiful fish. When winter hits, it will truly become a hardship."

~ 107 ~

"That is good to know. Therefore, I will ensure that each man has time to help provide for his family this coming winter."

Ezra let his pride speak for him. "That is not necessary, stranger. I am now a fisherman, too. I have become a dependable provider to replace those foolish men following you."

Grandfather chuckled, "I doubt that your skills can replace those of the expert Simon, Andrew, and the others."

"Oh, but I can -"

Before Ezra could finish his thought, Papa leaned forward and quickly interjected, "What is it that you need these fishermen to do for you, Yeshua? I understand that they have chosen to follow you and that they believe that you have an important message. I do not understand the role our fishermen play."

Grandfather entered the conversation. "In speaking to Yeshua, I have learned that he is driven to teach us all how to please Elohim."

From the corner of his eye, Shai noticed Yeshua nodding.

Yeshua swallowed his bite. "These men are becoming my closest friends and disciples. Eventually, they will become teachers themselves to bear the good news - Elohim, the very Lord of Israel, the creator and sustainer, is making a way for us."

Now, Ezra interrupted, "Not Simon. A teacher? Impossible!"

Shai was surprised that Ezra was even listening.

His brother continued, "I hear that you are mainly a healer, not a prophet."

"It is true that I repair deep wounds, whether they are physical and observable to you or not. Some wounds are invisible, pertaining to the heart and soul."

"Even though some call you the Nazarene physician, there is no way you could know what to heal from seeing and touching a person only once. I do not believe that is possible."

"It is only possible because I draw on the wisdom and power of Elohim through prayer and petition. I do not act on my own."

Papa spoke thoughtfully, "I want to hear more about this ministry, Yeshua. I want to hear what you believe to be true."

"I know that Elohim has a great love for His people, Israel. There

The Whistling Galilean

is a way to live that will please Him immensely. I want to show that way through words and actions. Please ask what concerns you."

Papa did. "Rabbi Selig has told us to distrust teachers that are not taught in Jerusalem like he was. He has been my rabbi my whole life, a man I know well, a man who was taught by men who interpret the ancient scrolls. The rabbi does not trust you and that concerns me. Where were you trained?"

"I was not trained in Jerusalem like the rabbi, but by my parents and other rabbis. I, too, was raised in the Hebrew faith. I obey the Ten Commandments and other laws set down by the Lord of Israel. I, too, honor the Sabbath. I have never been immoral or dishonest or treacherous. I am not a rebel. I am not a hypocrite like some of our faith, pretending to believe something that I do not. I do not accept money for my services. As you know, many of those characterize false prophets."

"That is good to hear, but you have not said what credentials you do have to teach about the Lord of Israel."

"I receive my instructions from the Lord directly, not from Jerusalem. I do not act on my own accord. Through prayer to Elohim before I speak or heal, I draw on His wisdom, His thoughts, and His words."

"In that case, Yeshua, I must take your word that you are guided by Elohim. How do I know that is true?"

Yeshua looked around the circle in the small room. Since this was a serious matter that they were discussing, Yeshua spoke quietly and with assurance. "The best way for any of you to know the truth is to open your heart to the guidance of Elohim the wise. Ask him through prayer. He will lead you to the truth if you let Him. Then, my words will ring true in your heart. Next, confirm what your heart tells you through people that you know and trust."

Grandpa spoke up, "I understand your concerns too, son. After considerable prayer and discussion, my heart tells me that Yeshua is a good man. To confirm what my heart tells me, I spoke to several men that I know well and that I trust - Simon and Andrew. They trust Yeshua so much that, as you already know, they became his primary

~ 109 ~

supporters, friends, and students. In addition, I spent more than an afternoon talking to Yeshua himself. Lastly, I listen to my grandson, Shai. All of them together confirm that this man breaking bread with us for a meal in our home indeed speaks truth about Elohim's goodness and great love."

Yeshua smiled at Grandfather, "Thank you for your kind words, Yona the Elder."

Shai was not surprised that the Elder had been so perceptive. The boy watched the Nazarene gather his father into his gaze. Shai knew that those eyes contained the depths of the stars; at least that was the way they had appeared to him, several times now.

"For confirmation, Yona, ask my new disciples, the fishermen that you know well, whether I speak the truth or am a crook, a liar, or a deceitful phony. You know that they will speak the truth to you."

Papa nodded his affirmation as he chewed.

"As the Elder suggested, speak to your son, Shai, with whom I have spent considerable time. Most of all, I hope you spend time with me to make up your own mind. Tonight is a good start."

"It is a good start. Thank you for understanding my concerns."

Shai felt good that his grandfather loved him so much that he had spent time with Yeshua to get to know him. His father seemed to be doing the same thing. He was pleased the Elder also chose to believe that Yeshua was truthful and not deceitful. Shai had recognized those qualities in Yeshua during their first meeting on the beach. Despite the flattery and attention paid to him by the Nazarene, they had discussed meaningful things. Mostly, he had felt a deep, joyful love emanate from the Nazarene, like no other. That had probably been the main attraction that bound them together. As he smiled in remembrance, the lad realized that the adults were still talking.

Grandfather was speaking, "…and I have spoken about the spies sent north by the Pharisees to squash any thought of change, dissent, or rebellion."

Ezra interjected, "A rebellion against oppressive Rome is desirable by many of us. We no longer want to be bugs under their feet to step on."

The Whistling Galilean

Grandfather spoke again, "Grandson, I for one do not desire open rebellion. Rebellion would harm many innocents. It is the Pharisees that some of us worry mostly about. As interpreters of the Hebrew Law, they can make life even tougher for us."

Papa asked, "Yeshua, are they watching you to determine if you are dangerous...if you tell the truth?"

As the Nazarene nodded in agreement, Shai jumped in, "I have spent time with Yeshua. I know him. I know his character. Trust me, Papa. Let me tell you what I think right now. Let me confirm that Yeshua speaks the truth."

"Alright Shai, please continue." Yona leaned back.

The boy felt all eyes around the table on him. He felt uncomfortable, but spoke anyway, "Yeshua has not spoken lies or stretched the truth to me. Remember when I was upset with you, Papa? It was on Ezra's apprenticeship day. That was the day that I met Yeshua. He stressed that you did love me but did not always know how to show it. I did not believe it then, but he was correct. Later that summer, you and I spent a morning sailing together in *Ole Blue* and we talked about Ezra's apprenticeship day. Your words proved Yeshua's words to be true. I know now that you do love me."

Shai was standing. He had not realized when he had stood up to speak. He was embarrassed. He had not ever shared these feelings with his family.

As he sat, he received Papa's warm smile, "I remember, son. That was an excellent example that you provided. I believe you. I promise to take time to learn more about this stranger and not judge him too soon."

Ezra was not so easily swayed. "Well, I do not trust this man's words just because he says that we should. I think that he is a false prophet and a false healer. So do some of my friends."

Yeshua responded calmly, "You do not have to depend on the opinions of your friends, Ezra. You, your father, and anyone can pray to Elohim. When you are uncertain, ask Him to break down any barriers to the truth. I pray to Elohim many times a day, asking

~ 111 ~

Him to guide my words and for strength and power to see and help those that are broken and need healing."

Ezra's answer was a curt, derisive *snort*. Shai realized that Ezra had just drawn a major battle line between the two of them. Shai knew he would have to give this difference between them some attention - later.

"Please, help yourselves to dessert. Thanks be to Elohim who created the sweetness of our meal." Mama defused the conversation by offering a bowl of dried apples with toasted sesame seeds drizzled with a little bit of honey to her houseguest.

Yeshua was the first to praise his hostess. "These are truly delicious. You are a wonderful cook. The entire meal was wonderful. Thank you. Yona, you are a lucky man."

Papa beamed. Shai realized that his mother had ended the serious discussion for the night. The boy was not surprised when Yeshua helped the little kids clean up, even making it a game. Giggles again filled the house. Even Grandpa could not escape being part of the action.

Eventually, Mama started the *hum*. Shai knew that Papa felt proud of his family and content from eating a wonderful meal. Even though he was usually too shy to sing in public or around strangers, tonight he was not bashful. He joined in with gusto adding his deep bass to the harmony. Even Yeshua added his musical voice to the group. The perfect ending, of course, was Sim's giggles of glee.

13

Payment or Punishment?

IT HAD BEEN THREE MONTHS SINCE SHAI HAD BEEN TO TOWN WITH his mother. To the boy, trips to market were adventures. But that day's trip with Mama Anat was terrifying. They carried freshly picked produce from their garden to Capernaum either for trade or for sale, whichever worked out best.

Mama twisted a cloth and placed it on top of Shai's head to form a circle. This created the flat spot on which to balance a two-cubit-tall basket, just under half of his height.

"I am ready," Shai anticipated.

She hoisted the basket holding half of the late-ripening pears and avocados onto his head. "I remember the first time you carried a basket. You learned quickly until you skipped in happiness when you learned to whistle like a wren. You went ahead but the basket did not."

Shai laughed. "Yes…and I remember that you were not happy with me."

Her musical laugh joined his. "Even though I was stern with you, and even called you Isaiah, I was laughing inside."

"I did not know that, Mama."

"There was no real harm done, and you did look so funny. That day, you were trying so hard to be a helpmate."

They both walked with flat, even strides down the well-worn, dirt path, Shai in the lead. Each of the pair balanced a basket on their head and supporting it with one hand. Mama's free hand carried the bundle of nested baskets holding bananas. Shai carried a package of seasoned, smoked fish wrapped in banana leaves.

"Mama, when can Adi help you go to market instead of me?"

"I know. Ezra and others tease you about doing women's work. Today I hope to have a heavier than normal load coming back home, so I need your help."

"I like to help you, Mama, but I just wish it was something more manly."

"You can help me pick out a new kitchen knife. Ezra broke my old favorite."

"Yes. That is definitely more manly - knives."

"In addition to the heavy flour and olive oil, I need linen yarn to weave more clothes for you and Ezra. You are both growing like weeds."

"I do feel taller."

Walking with a load balanced precariously on one's head was truly an art. Shai had learned this talent slowly. He had started with a small basket, just like he had started with a small cast net. Today, he felt like a real helper. Each time he accompanied Mama, he carried a bigger load. Now, he could walk with an even pace. He looked well ahead to pick a smooth path for his feet. He searched for ruts, large stones, wood limbs sticking out into the path, and anything in the way that might trip him.

In the quiet of the morning, he naturally took to whistling. He especially liked to whistle bird songs with Mama. She had taught him that skill and she had a wider repertoire of bird songs than anyone he knew.

"I've got a challenge for you. Warble the song of the river wren."

He had to think hard. It was a soft, three-note repetitive song. He tried a rendition.

The Whistling Galilean

"Not bad, my son. Try it in a higher pitch."

She was a patient teacher. Eventually, she trilled the wren song helping him learn it. They worked on it together. As he added it to his own repertoire, he was eager to demonstrate this new whistle to Dov.

Time passed quickly. They soon turned left onto the main road that went into Capernaum known as the Upper Galilee Road. As they left the cover of the shady trees, a multitude of bright colors, unusual smells, and a slow-moving river of people assailed his senses.

Capernaum was a busy trading center. Many traders from the southeast set up camps and tents next to this section of the road to offer their varied wares. Soft cotton cloth dyed in many colors and patterns hung from poles. Wispy material danced gracefully in the light morning breeze. Below them, rows of swords, knives, and enameled jewelry reflected the bright sunlight. Clay pots, fancy silk cloth, and foreign spices were displayed on makeshift tables.

Shai was proud of his city. It was a major crossroad, a city where roads from four large, distant cities intersected. The Romans had paved the part of the old trade route going between Damascus in the northeast to ports on the Mediterranean Sea to the west. This highway was now called the Via Maris, the "way of the sea". Trade goods arrived here from around the entire Mediterranean basin.

With a firm forearm on his back, Mama Anat hurried him along. She gently pushed him ahead of her warning him, "Walk faster."

The baskets she carried bounced against his back. He heard her low whisper, "Hurry your step, son."

He heard her hum a lilting tune under her breath to hasten their pace. Shai knew she hummed either when she was particularly happy or nervous. She was nervous now. He stuck two fingers under the twine of the wrapped fish. Raising this second arm to steady the basket, he quickened his pace. He did not know what she had seen, but he trusted her instincts.

There were so many different travelers on this road. A fancy, carved carriage with a roof carrying an important Roman dignitary passed them. It was surrounded by a group of ten marching Roman centurions. The silly red plumes on their helmets bounced with each step that they took in unison. He saw them push a small group of disheveled boys about his age out of the way with their shields.

Just then, a cloaked man gripped Shai's left shoulder with his thin dirty hand. The man grabbed at the wrapped package of fish Shai carried in his left hand. The boy tried to twist away while keeping his balance.

Instantly, Mama shouted, "Stop thief!"

Shai used all of his strength to kick backward with his left leg. He felt the man's legs buckle as he heard a *thud*. Immediately Mama pushed herself between the man and Shai while also helping her son regain his balance. Shai headed to the right, obeying her nudge.

She whispered as they picked up their pace, "Good job, son. I'm glad you are with me today. That kick will slow him down. Let's stay beside the centurions for a while."

Shai shifted the weight of the basket he carried on his head. He felt its weight begin to strain the left side of his neck.

"Bandit?" he asked.

"A thief hoping to enrich himself with what you carried."

"He obviously did not know that it contained smoked fish and not coins or jewels to make him instantly wealthy," Shai chuckled. If the man had stolen his package, the boy could imagine the thief's disappointment when he opened it.

Then he recognized a small group of rabbis from Jerusalem. They wore unusual small square black boxes on their foreheads. He had learned that these boxes actually held a tiny scroll containing two specific scriptures from the Torah. The Lord of Israel told them through Moses to keep God's word close to mind. These rabbis took that literally. Even though they looked funny wearing the phylacteries, he knew it was irreverent to think such thoughts.

He knew that rabbis were not the Pharisees that Rabbi Selig had notified. These rabbis were regulars. They travelled from town to town visiting local rabbis. This was the way Jerusalem's religious schools tried to maintain a tight control. As leaders of the Hebrew religion, their job was to ensure that local rabbis taught the religious

The Whistling Galilean

laws in the proper way. It was their job to ensure that all Hebrews lived according to God's law as recorded by Moses. These visitors never stayed in Capernaum very long.

Shai and most Galileans disliked these traveling rabbis from the south. In addition to the phylacteries, many of these visitors wore fancy robes and sometimes even jewels. Many of them acted like they were better than everyone else. Their assistants would *shoo* commoners like he and his mother off their path, as if scattering ants away from a food source. Local Galileans thought that those haughty know-it-alls were an embarrassment to the Hebrew religion.

Shai and Mama Anat joined a slow-moving line toward the marketplace.

"This is new. Why are we in line?" Mama wondered out loud.

A dusty man behind them muttered, "Romans started taxing here, too."

"Oh, my," Mama whispered under her breath just loud enough for Shai to overhear.

The eleven-year-old saw a newly built, two-walled stone booth abutting one side of the old custom house. A stone arch joined both walls making the booth both weather-proof and sturdy. About three months ago when he had joined his father selling fish in the marketplace, they had noticed stone masons working in this area but had thought nothing of it. As a result of the dusty man's comment, the boy easily concluded that Romans had fortified the custom house where the Upper Galilee Road dipped down into Capernaum for the purpose of collecting taxes.

As they got closer to the arched gateway, he recognized a local man, Levi, sitting behind a wooden table within the booth. Bent over a leather scroll, Levi wrote something detailed. Shai wondered what Levi was doing there. He saw the glint of shiny coins in a flat wooden box beside the scroll. A neat stack of additional flat wooden boxes stood on the ground next to the booth.

Next to Levi stood a muscular Roman soldier in a bright red robe. The robe looked new. The foreigner had a narrow nose that resembled a hawk. Shai wanted to whistle the osprey's shriek, but

~ 117 ~

quickly thought better of it. A line of centurions stood at attention on either side of the booth.

The man behind him covered in dust lowered a small leather trunk from his back. He shared his disgust in a low mutter, "Like all big cities, tax collectors at every city gate...greedy, greedy, greedy."

Shai whispered, "Mama, did you know this would happen today?"

"No, son. Let us rest our backs and necks since there is a delay."

Her voice sounded tight, worried. As she helped him, he noticed that her delicate yet calloused hands were shaking slightly. He could hear her nervous, low-pitched hum as they shuffled forward, pushing their baskets before them. They slowly approached the booth and table.

Shai was now on high alert and paid careful attention. He watched Levi examine merchandise carried in cloth bags on a small, two-wheeled cart. The black-turbaned merchant accompanying the cart opened each bag for Levi to examine. The merchant said, "But Levi, this is the custom house. This is where I come to verify standard measurement using your metal bars and weights. There was no cost for this service."

"That is true. The opposite side of this building facing the marketplace still handles the standard verification. As of today, this is where Rome collects taxes."

"So, what are you doing here, Levi?"

"I was appointed the tax collector. I must estimate the value of each person's merchandise carried into the city and record it on this scroll ledger with the assigned tax beside it."

"So, you work for Rome?"

Levi kept his eyes lowered, "Sire, you owe six denarii, Roman coinage only."

"What? This is an outrage!"

The loud protest brought the Roman overseer to the merchant's side. The overseer crossed his arms, making him look bigger and stronger. In a loud commanding tone, he delivered a stern message, not just to the merchant but to everyone within earshot:

The Whistling Galilean

"I am in charge here. My red robe gives me total authority over this taxation center. I have authority to obtain and guard the taxes. I have authority to deliver punishment to those who protest or refuse payment. What is your choice? Payment or punishment?"

"But there was no forewarning that we would be taxed in Capernaum."

"That is not an excuse. Pay immediately. If you refuse to pay the required tax, you will be punished. Then, you will return from where you crawled. Those are your two choices."

The merchant took a small suede pouch from his leather belt. He counted out the denarii into the Roman's outstretched palm.

"You may pass into the market. If I hear you complain again, I will flog you."

Shai could not believe this was happening. He thought he must have been dreaming. This was his Capernaum! Unfortunately, the dusty man behind him reminded him that this was very real, as he felt the man's trunk push against the back of his right leg. He heard the low droning monotone start up again, "Soldiers, soldiers everywhere. Soldiers for order. Soldiers for punishment. Soldiers for control. Soldiers for power. Soldiers for money."

He recognized an orchard man in front of them. This man worked an orchard near Carmi's. His cart was loaded with freshly picked produce - lettuce, onions, leeks, carrots, and such. Shai watched Levi and the Roman overseer walk around the cart and burrow their hands down to heft produce. Shai saw that Levi examined the produce for both quality and weight just as the fishmonger had done with Papa's catch.

Levi had conducted the standard verification for all the merchants for many years and had earned their respect and trust. Over time, Levi had become adept at quickly estimating weights and measurements. He had also learned how to settle any disputes between bargaining parties. Papa spoke highly of him and trusted him. Shai wondered what Papa would think now.

Shai watched the country man kneel before the local tax collector to plead his case. "But, Levi, I don't have enough Roman coin for my tax. I will gladly pay upon my exit."

~ 119 ~

"Payment or punishment." The overseer stood over the pleading grower.

"I do not have the coins."

With a motion of the Roman overseer's hand, two Roman centurions grabbed the man's arms and quickly led him to a newly installed, sturdy wooden post next to the tax collector's booth. The boy had not noticed it until now. He watched in disbelief as the soldiers roughly tore the gardener's robe to belt level. Then they chained his arms to the post and tore his tunic, exposing his bare back. This could not be happening!

A centurion carrying a whip approached, and with a snarl growled, "Another stupid, poor man with no money."

The Roman overseer loudly and authoritatively pronounced the man's sentence. "Four lashes for not paying his taxes. He failed to plan. He did not have sufficient Roman coin." Then he grabbed the man's face and stared intently into his eyes. "If it happens again, you'll get a double dose. I remember faces."

Astonished, Shai looked at Mama. In a shaky voice, he whispered, "Do we have enough Roman coin, Mama?"

"I hope so, son," she whispered back, wincing.

As she turned her head away from the gruesome scene, she protectively grabbed Shai and pulled him toward her. Together, they heard the first crack of the whip.

It seemed to take an eternity. Shai and his mother remained silent as meek statues with downcast heads, flinching with each blow. Shai could not shut out the sounds of the whip's cracks or of the man's screams. He wished that he could be anywhere else. He wished he was a man and could whisk his mother away from this bloody horror.

As many times as they had come to Capernaum on market day, he had never experienced anything like this. He had heard that tax collection occurred in other cities, but not here - not his home. He knew that the Romans used brutality to rule, but he had never witnessed it firsthand. He also knew it would be a long time before he could get those sounds out of his head.

Through fearful tears, Shai saw shiny black Roman sandals

The Whistling Galilean

appear right beneath his nose. The voice beside his ear demanded, "Step forward. You are next. Uncover your baskets for scrutiny."

"But, sir, we are not merchants." Shai blurted out.

Almost instantaneously, Mama spoke loudly trying hard to drown out her son's shocked, squeaky voice. "Yes, sir. We will do as you request."

She moved forward to position her body between the Roman and Shai. She pinched the boy hard to get his attention. "Here son, let me help you."

Two soldiers were motioned forward to carry their baskets to the tax collector's table. One of them whisked off the protective cloth coverings and dropped them in the dirt. Even their baskets succumbed to Levi's evaluating eyes.

Mama maintained a position between the boy and the overseer as she greeted the new tax collector, "Shalom, Levi."

Shai saw the sadness in Levi's eyes as the local man rifled through their belongings. Thankfully, Mama had enough denarii for their new admission-to-market tax. The boy tried not to notice several tears fall down her checks as she paid the tax collector the precious meager coins.

As they loaded their baskets back on their heads, Shai heard Mama's whisper, "Stay close, son. We do not know what else to expect today."

The two unremarkable, grateful peasants hurried away from the custom house and into the marketplace. Like prey from predators, they quickly scurried into the open market near the synagogue, blending with others for protection. Many growers sold fresh produce from small carts in this market square. Growers that arrived early positioned their carts in the best locations. Others had to find open areas along the roadways.

Shai was still shaking. He was angry and scared at the same time. He knew one orchard grower that would not be selling produce that day. He could not understand why the Romans were so stubborn, unbending, and vicious.

The full marketplace was no longer a safe, familiar place, but was a place of refuge, a place to hide. Mama led him to her favorite vendor. The merchant handled a large variety of goods and offered her favorable trades, good for them both. Despite the fact that her voice still trembled with fear from the experience with Levi, neither Mama Anat nor the merchant spoke of the Romans or of taxes.

Shai closely followed his mother's brown dress from vendor to vendor. She had worn a fringed, pale blue sash today to make it easier for him to find her if they got separated by the crowds of people. In addition, their baskets had streamers of short blue threads, again making it easier to recognize.

What he had previously enjoyed as a happy, familiar place now felt like a thin scab over something that was dangerous and ugly. Today, he felt defeated, helpless, and poor. Maybe his older brother was right. Maybe rebellion was necessary. He just wanted to hurry to the safety of his home with Mama.

His mother bartered with a general merchandise vendor in Greek, the language of trade. The flogging scene replayed in his head over and over, so Shai had trouble paying attention to anything else. He did not understand very much Greek, but he knew that she wanted him to listen, so he tried to be obedient. He had to learn some Greek since it was the common language spoken for bartering despite the person's actual heritage, origin, and home language.

The boy watched his mother balance several kitchen knives in her knowing hand before she had him do the same. She told the merchant the specific qualities for which she was looking. The merchant did the same as he evaluated her produce and baskets.

"This knife has the best heft in my hand. What do you think, Shai?" She was clearly trying hard to include her son in the manly part of the day.

Since his mother knew which knife she liked best, he deferred to her. After all, she was the one who would actually use it. But he did appreciate her openly asking his opinion, as if it really mattered.

He spoke his first words since the flogging. "I like it best, too."

After completing their transaction, Shai helped Mama Anat add cloth, sewing needles, the selected kitchen knife, and some coins

The Whistling Galilean

to a small basket. He noticed that her hands still shook slightly. Apparently, she had been as afraid as he had been.

Mama told her son that their next stop was the olive oil merchant to refill their clay pot. She turned to her son with an attempt at a smile. "Shai, you have been a big help today. Take a break. Go look for Carmi. Stay next to her stall. I will meet you there. I am eager to get home today."

"I am, too."

Shai then found himself in search of Carmi's friendly freckles. As he snaked his way toward her family's normal location, he knew he badly wanted to talk to her, to warn her, and to ensure her safety.

Suddenly, he heard a soft voice. "Hi, stranger. Shopping with your mother?"

It was Carmi! She had spotted him first.

He grunted looking down at his feet, "Yes."

He looked up into her sparkling brown eyes, when he heard her gentle voice, "I repeat, it's good to see you. Is anything wrong, Shai?"

She spoke in a matter-of-fact tone, as if they met and talked every day. That was far from true. They had not seen each other since she delivered the basket of fruit to Simon's house. Therefore, this market morning presented an opportunity. He wanted to make the best of it.

He stammered, "I - I - I'm glad to see you, Carmi."

It was difficult for him to start a conversation with her. He felt self-conscious. After some other niceties, it was like the dam broke, and his words gushed out just like water. He could not believe his ears. "You brighten my day like sunshine on a cloudy morning. You are like a breath of clean air after a wind storm. You are like desirable, round, yellow orbs of citrus -"

"Hush. You have kept the secret, right?"

"Yes. You know I did," Shai whispered. He could not help but smile at her reddened cheeks. His words of praise must have embarrassed her.

"Good." She batted her eyes as she commented on his appearance, "You look worried. Has something upset you?"

~ 123 ~

He wanted to warn her. He wanted to share the danger that he had experienced earlier that morning. He did not know how to do it gently, so he just started in a conspiring whisper, "Today, the Romans started collecting taxes at the city gate they just built. Your neighbor did not have enough coins to pay. They are punishing us for being poor. That is wrong. What they did is cruel." Shai was now on a roll, releasing all his fear and anger in a single burst. Unfortunately, his voice grew louder with every word.

"Hush. Shhh. Hush," she shushed.

Carmi put a finger up to his lips. Shai nearly fainted. She had touched his lips, the part of the body that he would use to kiss her!

She continued, unaware of the effect of her actions on the boy. "You do not know who is listening. There are spies everywhere."

He dropped his voice to a whisper and quickly looked around. "You are right. Sorry, but I am so upset."

"I can tell. What happened?"

"Your neighbor did not have enough denarii. He offered to pay on his way out of town, but the Roman overseer said no. They whipped him at a post next to the custom house."

"Oh, no! That is terrible!" she hissed. "No wonder you are upset."

They looked into each other's eyes with the knowing sadness of an oppressed people, survivors in their own land.

"But it gets worse. They even looked through our two baskets. They made Mama pay taxes, too. We were lucky to have the appropriate coins."

"Oh, my goodness. I am so sorry. I do not understand. You are just a family, not a wealthy merchant. Did she expect to have to pay taxes today?"

"No."

"I am glad she had enough Roman coin."

"Me, too. Carmi, I am so afraid for your family. You grow and sell produce for a living. Please carry some Roman denarius with you, maybe wrapped in your cloth hem. I could not stand it if you were punished."

The Whistling Galilean

"The Romans caught my mother and I off-guard today, too. We were lucky to have enough denarius. I will warn my father."

"Good. Oh, Carmi, I will do anything to keep you safe."

That is when Mama Anat appeared. "Sorry to interrupt. Carmi, you look wonderful. Shai is right. You and your family take great care."

"Thank you. We will. You take care, also."

Time between the two young ones had passed quickly. Mama balanced the heavy basket on her head and handed Shai the one with the flour and dried goods.

As Mama coiled the cloth on his head and helped him balance his basket, Shai spoke to Carmi. He meant every one of his final words to the girl he adored, "Take care, Carmi."

Part 2

MIRACLES REVEAL

14

The Paralyzed Man Walked

ON THIS WINTER DAY, SHAI EARNED HIS FIRST SALARY BY MENDING nets for the oldest fisherman in their guild, older than the Elder. Like Grandpa Yona, the hands and fingers of this shriveled legend were swollen and arthritic from years of use and exposure to the elements, especially cold temperatures. Shai felt useful because today he added money to their family coffers.

His friend, Dov, sat beside him on the worn, smooth rocks of the beach in sight of Capernaum's massive stone quay. They had not spent time together for over three months - too long.

Fishel taught a small group of boys how to repair a large trammel net. As instructed, the boys cut and loosely hung different widths and lengths of twine cords on their leather belts.

Their mentor explained, "By taking this step, your mending will actually go faster. When you find a rip in the net, you have what you need close at hand, hanging from your belt. You will not have to go and find the right twine, cut it, return to the net, and rediscover the tear. You are actually saving time."

Dov elbowed Shai and grunted, "Glad for that. I would rather be fishing than this women's work."

For the next step, they followed instructions from the old man: after all, it was his trammel net, and he had used and repaired it for more decades than Shai knew. This large four-cubit-high net was actually three nets in one. Two larger mesh nets were attached to and sandwiched a net of much finer mesh. The junctures between them sometimes tore loose.

The respected elder's last words to the group, as he made his way slowly to the shade, were, "Check where the nets join. If you discover any tears or repairs, stitch them shut with the medium-sized twine. Look for any large rips in the nets themselves. Use the small twine on the smaller net in the middle."

Fishel half carried the bent old fisherman to his napping spot. "Do not worry. I will check their work. We will do a good job for you."

When the older teen returned, he walked from boy to boy, going over the junctures with his good right hand. He showed one boy, "A large thrashing fish trying to jump free from the net tore this area. I wonder how big it was."

Since his mentor was beside him, Shai asked, "Do you think it was as big as your monster fish?"

"Not sure, maybe. I cannot tell if it was the sharp fin or teeth that did this damage."

Shai noticed Fishel's left hand. It was no longer wrapped in a cloth covered with a healing salve. "Your hand looks much better now. Can you fish from a boat?"

"Not yet, but soon. Keep up that good stitch."

After a friendly pat on the back, he moved on. This gave Shai an opportunity to catch up with Dov.

Shai asked, "We get a dinar today for our three hours of work. I get to keep ten percent of that. Can you keep the same?"

"Yes. Our fathers must have had a group meeting."

The Whistling Galilean

They both laughed at the thought.

"What will you do with the coins you earn, Dov?"

"I want a good carving knife. All I use now is a hand-me-down from my brother, which I will hand down to a younger brother."

"Yikes. I am grateful that Grandpa is letting me have his small but good and sharp carving knife. Have you seen Maya? I really mean, have you talked to her?"

"A few times, but not enough."

"I still feel bad for beaning Carmi. I am thinking of getting something nice for her with my earnings."

"You are too young for that. You might not even like her when you get older. Take care of yourself first. No one else will."

Shai doubted that he would ever not like Carmi. Maybe his best friend was just being selfish...or maybe he was wise. A good carving knife is an excellent tool with which to make gifts.

"A few weeks ago, I went to market with Mama. Have you seen the Romans in Capernaum collecting taxes? Scary, brutal."

"The phrase 'payment or punishment' spread like wildfire through the Galilee. We heard it before we went, so they did not catch us unaware. We went with denarii in hand."

"We were there on the first day they collected taxes. There was no notice or warning, they just started. You see, I saw a man flogged for lacking his tax money. I felt so helpless. I want to prevent that kind of harm from falling on Mama...or Carmi. Instead of a gift, maybe I will save some denarii to pay the dreaded taxes and give some to Carmi."

"How gallant of you. Shai, you are too young to accept that kind of responsibility. That is the job of our fathers. You are too weak to fight back. I have a plan. I am building up my muscles so that I can win battles and free myself from Roman rule." Dov showed off his growing bicep. "See?"

Just like his friend - muscles, muscles, muscles.

Shai and his best friend had nearly finished the repairs on their half of the net. Shai realized that he had to speak louder for Dov to hear him. There was an increasing noise from a growing group of travelers along the road. As he turned to look, he was surprised to see a stream of people heading into Capernaum. Several of them walked using crutches. There was a man with an injured arm wrapped in a cloth.

Shai knew that the tall stranger he had befriended on the beach only seven months ago taught in many towns and villages around the Sea of Galilee. Occasionally, he heard a lesson delivered from near the quay. That was a good location because there was room for a crowd to gather.

Since Yeshua continued to heal many types of physical ailments, his friend now had a nickname - the Nazarene physician. The boy looked forward to seeing him again and teasing him.

"I hear that the false prophet that you like is back in town. He is just like burping up the taste of a rotten egg," Dov responded to Shai's wonderment.

The intentional shock value of Dov's words worked. Shai scrunched his face, stood, and made a fist ready for battle.

Dov did not respond accordingly. With a cough, he snickered, "Yeshua, Yeshua, Yeshua. Is that all you can talk about anymore?"

"You know that's not true." Shai felt his face redden with his growing irritation.

"Look, my friend, do not follow that man Yeshua. He fools a lot of people. I hope that he has not fooled you into thinking he is a miracle-worker or a prophet."

Eleven-year-old Shai breathed deeply, hoping to subdue his sudden urge to punch Dov in the nose. Instead, he responded with a slew of words, like steam arising from boiling water. "Look at the people on the road for yourself. The ones seeking him are real people needing real healing. If Yeshua was faking, I do not think they would seek him anymore. They would go to someone else."

"That is your belief."

"Simon, Andrew, and other fishermen still follow him. They believe him. They are level-headed, hard-working fishermen like our fathers."

"Simon? Level-headed?"

The Whistling Galilean

"Alright, Simon is hot-tempered. But I have found that Yeshua says just the right things to me, exactly what I need and when I need to hear them. It is almost like he can read my mind. You should get to know him."

"Just be careful, Shai. You are so naive."

"Suit yourself. He's got to be in Capernaum. I am going to welcome him back from his travels. Come with me, Dov. Maybe we'll even see the girls."

Dov shook his head. "Not today, Shai. Not if it's about Yeshua and not the girls."

Dov and Shai were usually inseparable. Shai tried not to look disappointed. He shrugged, acting as if he did not care, said his goodbyes, and walked away. Alone, he climbed the bank and disappeared into the crowd. It hurt that his best friend was not eager to go with him. Did Dov not want to be his best friend anymore?

As his eager anticipation grew with the growing size of the crowd, Shai's pace quickened, and just as quickly, his anger and hurt were replaced with excitement. Eventually, he fell in line behind a group of rabbis from Judea. They wore the little black phylacteries on their foreheads. Those boxes and their accent told Shai that they were from Jerusalem. Despite their accent, he understood what they said.

"Just watch," said the tall one.

"No, try to trap him into saying something against the Law," ordered a short older man with a white, bushy beard.

"Remember, we are here to gather evidence that he is indeed a trouble maker, that he is a false prophet."

Shai remembered his father's warning to keep his mouth shut. He realized that he stood in front of Simon's mother-in-law's house. There were so many people crowded around it that even with his slight size, he could not wiggle to the front door. The crowd quietly listened, so Shai could easily overhear the voice of Yeshua already teaching those within the domicile.

The eleven-year-old knew Simon's house from previous visits with his father. He remembered a window beside the outside stairs going up to the roof. Trying to become as thin as a parchment scroll,

~ 133 ~

he slipped his slender frame between person after person, going slowly, upward step by step.

Finally, he reached the window and peered inside. A large number of people, mostly men, were jammed into one room. The teacher from Nazareth was standing just outside the door leading to the courtyard. Today, he was wearing clean, pure white clothing. Most people's clothing was earth-to-cream-colored, matching the dirt that had been used as a dye. The teacher was easily seen. It appeared to Shai that his friend was a light amidst the gathering.

The teacher was surrounded by people of all ages, from young to gray-haired. There was even a child seated cross-legged beside him. Shai wished he was that child.

Yeshua's familiar voice rang out clear as a bell, even to Shai observing from outside the house. His favorite teacher seemed to effortlessly project his words to each person. By their rapt attention, he knew that the Nazarene was able to make each person feel a direct connection. Everywhere he looked, both around the room and the stairs where he stood, he saw concentrated gazes of people paying close attention to Yeshua's every word.

The Nazarene spoke in Aramaic, the local language, except when he quoted from the ancient scrolls of the prophets. Like Rabbi Selig, he switched to Hebrew, the language in which the ancient words had been written in order to quote them exactly. Then he would switch back to Aramaic again to paraphrase and offer an in-depth explanation.

On his tip-toes, Shai noticed the Jerusalem rabbis he had followed. They had been admitted into the room and were seated in places of honor on a solitary bench in the shade beside the doorway. Most people sat on the floor.

Shai wondered how they had even gotten in. He guessed that people just naturally made way for the holy ones, venerating their position. He watched the group of Judeans nod in unison as Yeshua quoted a scriptural passage. Shai assumed they recognized that the Nazarene quoted it correctly.

The Whistling Galilean

Suddenly there was a commotion on the street. Shai awkwardly turned his head to glimpse four young men carrying a mat holding another man. They tried to approach the doorway.

Shai recognized the young man on the mat. It was Alter, a young man born in Capernaum and unable to walk or even crawl since birth. He was totally paralyzed from the waist down. Family and friends of the family carried him around town to let him sit in the sunshine, have a conversation with locals passing by, or eat a meal with a friend. Sometimes he would be given some handiwork, something he could do with his hands and feel useful.

With shouts, the group tried to enter the house, "Pardon us, excuse us. Please let us through to the Nazarene physician."

Their words let Shai know they wanted Yeshua to heal their friend. To many Galileans, the Nazarene had a reputation as a true healer, not a sham.

The group of five could not enter the front door because of the thick crowd.

One man in that crowd growled at them, "Stop pushing. We were here first."

One of the men with Alter pled, "Please let us through. We must see Yeshua."

Another stranger in the crowd shushed, "Hush, keep quiet so that we can hear."

No one budged an inch. Either they did not want to miss the "event" - anything that the teacher said or did - or maybe they, too, needed a loved one to be healed.

He overheard one of the four men say, "It is impossible to get in this way."

"We have got to get Alter to Yeshua. He is the only one with the healing power." said another friend.

Since they now stood directly below the stairway, Shai pointed out to one of the men, "Unless you become a sirocco wind blowing the crowd away, you could always try the roof."

One of the four friends muttered, "The roof. Of course. Why didn't I think of that?"

~ 135 ~

Another said, "Let's try it."

Since most houses in and around the Galilee had flat roofs used as open-air living extensions to their home, this was a probable solution to their access problem. Some roofs even had a stairway down into an internal courtyard.

Trying to be helpful, Shai provided more information. "There is no way inside the house or inner courtyard from the roof."

The friends were persistent, "We have to try."

People gathered on the stairs were more polite than those around the doorway and moved to make room for the procession carrying the man on the pallet. The four men carried the paralytic as carefully as possible up the stairs. After all, they dared not flip their friend off his support and down to the roadway below. They wanted to heal him, not harm him.

Shai led them up the stairs to the roof. Once on the roof, the four friends laid the mat on the thick, mud-paved surface and examined their surroundings.

The one wearing a striped robe knelt down, speaking to his friend, "Do not worry, Alter. We will find a way in."

Alter recognized Shai and said, "Shalom, Shai. Thank you for your help."

The friends were searching for the location of Yeshua's voice. The largest friend stepped over the cubit-high wall or balustrade encircling the roof onto the less substantial partial roof over the gallery surrounding the courtyard. Shai followed this friend and listened to his mutterings, "...got to take advantage of this tremendous opportunity...must be a way in...maybe over...."

Then, excitedly, the man waved his friends over and whispered, "Here. Yeshua is below me. He is beside the doorway leading to the courtyard."

As Shai had already told them, there was no stairway down into the inner courtyard. A narrow, thin tile roof had been built surrounding the courtyard to provide shade and shelter from harsh weather. When it rained, extended family members could remain dry while reaching the various apartments of the house.

The Whistling Galilean

The man in the striped robe put a friendly hand on Shai's shoulder. "You are right so far, young lad. Even though the Nazarene physician is right below us, we cannot reach him. We must!"

The larger friend said, "Well, young lad, can you get us an ax? I know how to get Alter to Yeshua."

"I know what you're thinking," responded his friend quickly. "Good idea. If not around, through! If not an ax, a shovel will do."

"Why? What are you going to do?" the boy fearfully asked.

He was surprised when an ax appeared from the stairway. Men on the stairs had been listening, too. As if by magic, the sharp tool floated from hand to hand to be passed on up to the men on the roof.

"It is now or never," said one of them.

The man with the ax used the tool to pull a tile from the thin mud and wooden beams.

"No! Stop!" Shai's frantic words had no effect.

Now, Alter's friends busily used their bare hands to ply up other tiles. These were hastily but carefully piled to one side.

With a shout, the man with the ax cut through the mud-covered woven branches between the roof beams for water proofing. "Look out below."

"Stop! What are you doing?" Shai croaked in panic. He tried to pull the large man with the ax away, but he was not strong enough. In fact, he did not even slow the man's swing.

"Stop!" The brother below, Andrew, had heard the ruckus above him. Andrew walked into the inner courtyard and looked up to see what the men were up to. He ordered loudly from below, "This is our home. You are destroying the roof."

His words had no effect. With only a few more strikes, a hole opened. Many hands frantically pulled the loosened material to the side. The eleven-year old could not believe that these men just dug a hole in Simon's roof.

In shock, his mouth was wide enough to suck in a fly. Coughing to dislodge it, Shai realized he did not want to be considered a participant in this destruction, so he backed away.

It took a few minutes to recover from swallowing the fly. Then,

Shai's curiosity overcame his fear. He approached the new hole and saw dust and small splinters of twigs float down onto the floor below. He hoped no one would be hurt. An expectant silence hung over the crowd.

Shai saw a mother show a young boy how to cover his face. "Protect your eyes and nose, son. Cover them with your robe, like this."

He noticed Yeshua protect his head with a forearm as he gazed upward. The noisy activity on the roof had disrupted his discourse.

One of Alter's friends hurriedly ordered another, "Tear your robe."

"We need to lower Alter through the hole," another friend caught on and explained.

"Look, the boy has rope twine hanging on his belt," another friend said pointing at Shai. "Please, let us use your ropes. We need them to lower Alter to the Nazareth physician. We believe he can be healed."

The youngster protectively covered his belt with his hands, "I need these to mend nets."

He knew that if the men really wanted the hemp mending lines, they were big and strong enough to just take them. And, as he looked into Alter's pleading eyes, he could no longer say no. Yeshua's instruction in the classroom to help those in need slipped silently through his mind.

He nodded to Alter. "In that case, you can have them. Here, take them."

Now that the damage to the roof was complete, Shai wanted to help. He pulled strand after strand of the twisted cord from his belt and handed them to one friend after another. Quickly, the four friends tied the cords together to make them thicker and longer. Meanwhile, one of their robes was torn into strips with a knife. The combination of rope and cloth strips was enough to tie the paralytic to his pallet.

The boy plopped down on the roof with his head over the courtyard edge to watch. With Yeshua in his sights, he realized

The Whistling Galilean

that by choosing to damage another man's house, these men really believed that the man in white below could truly heal their friend. He had to watch.

Each of Alter's four friends grunted as they lifted the paralyzed man on the pallet carefully over the hole.

"Ready, Alter?" one man said.

"Oh, yes...since birth."

Shai watched their hand-over-hand motions as they slowly lowered the paralyzed man feet first into the gallery below. Voices beneath him grew louder as what looked like a wrapped parcel appeared over their heads.

"What is that?"

"Here it comes. We better make a space for it on the ground or one of us will get hurt."

Shai saw several people move out of the way.

"I recognize the mat and the man," said another man. "It's the paralyzed Alter. I can help from down here. Anyone want to join me?"

Shai watched several men appear under the hole and reach up toward the immobile man hanging in the air. They steadied him to keep him from spinning. Shai knew that their strength, combined with those above made the job of lowering Alter easier. Alter's worthless feet finally touched the ground.

One of the men who had orchestrated the help from below greeted the paralytic, "Shalom, Alter. May we offer assistance?"

"Yes. My friends above you and I would be most grateful."

So, two of the men laid the cripple in front of Yeshua, untied him, and helped him settle more comfortably on the mat pallet. Shai heard Alter's friends on the roof thank the men down below for their kindness now that their friend lay at Yeshua's feet.

The murmuring crowd grew quiet as the man in white knelt in front of Alter and looked into his face. The first words that the boy heard the healer calmly and tenderly say to the paralytic man were, "Take heart. *Be of good cheer.*"

Really? After all of that hard work, those were the words that his older friend chose to offer? Then, Shai thought that maybe Yeshua

~ 139 ~

knew he must first relax the hopeful man on the mat. Maybe he knew that he must set him at ease after that harrowing experience of being lowered through a hole in a roof.

Then Yeshua said, "*Son, your sins are forgiven*. With Elohim, there is no past or future, only the present. Therefore, your sins already have been forgiven, friend."

The boy on the roof did not understand. Most people in the room also shook their heads in confusion. All of the locals knew that Alter was born unable to move his legs. Any sins that he had committed had not caused his paralysis. The Nazarene had been around Galilee long enough to know this, also.

Shai saw the rabbinical scribes, the Judean teachers of the law, huddle their heads together, whispering. Since Yeshua's words had stilled all speech, their whispers hissed like vipers in the room and were loud enough for everyone to hear.

"This man speaks blasphemy. He thinks he is Elohim? Only Elohim can forgive sins, and only through us and our efforts."

"All Jews know that sin can only be forgiven through appropriate blood sacrifices."

"He has to be a false prophet or crazy. Anyone who thinks that they have the same power and authority as Elohim, the Lord of Israel, is crazy!"

"Crazy dangerous, you mean."

"Perhaps a crazy, dangerous zealot."

On the roof, the hum of a different conversation was underway. Alter's large friend, the man who had used the ax, knelt beside Shai. Together, they spoke in whispers.

The friend said, "That is not good. These men are here to prove that Yeshua is a danger to those in authority."

"I do not understand."

"It appears that these strangers have an agenda. They want to prove Yeshua wrong."

"Why? He teaches about love and hope. I have not heard him speak of rebelling against anyone."

"Not specifically. He is becoming well-known, popular, and

The Whistling Galilean

draws a large following. I think that scares these men from the south. I think they fear losing control of us."

"Control?"

"Yes, boy. They control us through their many-layered, detailed Law about how to live our lives."

"But the Torah is from Elohim."

"Yes, originally so, but there are so many new laws that have been added, layered upon the original ones. The result of non-obedience is very serious - expulsion from the Hebrew family of faith...or even death."

"I did not know that."

"You will learn. Their system of continuous correction uses fear, sort of like the Romans. What if there is another way? What if their interpretation is wrong? Can they make mistakes?"

Shai wiped dirt off of his chin. "I cannot follow all of this. I did hear them call Yeshua dangerous and crazy. That is not true."

"Yeshua is smart, not crazy, but his ideas may be dangerous. I have heard him point out that some rabbis do not practice what they preach. Those words can make powerful enemies."

It appeared that the Nazarene heard the words of both groups. He turned his gaze from the roof and responded only to the Judean scribes, *"Why are you thinking evil things in your hearts? Which is easier: to say to the paralytic, 'Your sins are forgiven,' or to say, 'Get up, take your mat, and walk'?"*

He waited for an answer. There was none. Not one visiting rabbi uttered a word.

The friend on the roof whispered quietly to Shai, "Both forgiving sins and healing a paralytic are impossible for a man to do."

Having already joined them, Alter's friend in the striped robe whispered, "True, but neither is impossible to Elohim. I wonder what the rabbis would say to that."

Shai, sandwiched between the two friends, saw the Nazarene nod in recognition of the whispered words spoken above his head. He also noticed that the visitors remained stoically still and silent.

Yeshua looked directly at the gathered dignitaries from the south

~ 141 ~

and said, *"But so that you may know that the Son of Man has the authority on earth to forgive sins...."*

The witnesses below and above the roof gasped in unison. Shai on the roof heard this reaction as he, too, gasped in astonishment at what he thought he had heard his adult friend say. He knew that only God could forgive sins. Had his healer friend from Nazareth just made himself equal to God? The boy was confused and wanted to speak to Yeshua alone.

The rabbis could only mutter, *"...blasphemy, blasphemy, blasphemy...."*

Shai also noticed that during these conversations, Alter continued to stare trustfully up into the eyes of the man that he and his friends believed would heal him.

From the roof, the youngster had a clear, unobstructed view of both Alter and the man in white who knelt before the cripple. Yeshua smiled as he reached out and touched Alter's shoulder. Then he stated clearly and with authority, *"Get up, take your mat, and go home."*

There was another hush, so quiet that Shai heard a bead drop to the floor below and roll. It only took a few seconds for the eager man on the pallet to react. Alter rolled slowly onto his side, pushed himself up with his arms to a shaky kneeling position. He took the hand of one of the men who had helped him to the ground and pulled himself up with his strong arms to a wobbly standing position.

His large friend on the roof cried, "Yes. He stands."

In front of all of the people in the room, Alter reached out for Yeshua's arm and took a step. In his whole life, he had never stood or taken a step on his own.

Altogether, as if one organism, the crowd exhaled a satisfied, "Aaah...!"

After a few more hesitant steps, Alter walked off of his mat, the pallet that had been his home for years. He turned, bent down, and rolled it up.

The expectant crowd below murmured, "Oh, my! Impossible."

"It's a miracle!" Shai echoed the sentiment from the roof.

His large friend shouted down, "Alter, you are healed!"

The Whistling Galilean

Another friend sobbed, falling to his knees, "The paralyzed is walking. Yeshua did it. Thanks be to Elohim!"

When Alter stood with his mat in hand, Shai saw the former paralytic's tears flowing down his cheeks. Alter spoke, his voice cracked and filled with emotion, "Thank you."

The boy saw Alter straighten and try his best to stand tall in front of the Nazarene physician. With a sniff, Alter whispered haltingly "I...I am...standing."

"You have walked, Alter. I know you as a paralytic. I am a witness to this. Thank you, Yeshua," the man who had helped from below spoke, amazement in his voice.

Alter continued to look into the Nazarene physician's eyes. "You blessed me. It is beyond what I deserve."

Then, Shai watched Alter turn and walk shakily through a rapidly parting crowd out of the doorway. Shai pushed up from his belly, stepped over the balustrade, and joined Alter's friends in rushing down the steps. From his vantage point, Shai saw Alter walk out of the doorway onto the street. Alter walked into the sunlight for the first time in his life. Even though he walked on still unsteady legs, he walked. He stopped at the eave post and grabbed hold of it for momentary balance.

The large friend turned and hugged Shai, "Thank you for your help today."

The amazed youngster watched the four friends join Alter, lending a hand and arm. Together, they walked down the roadway. Their laughter and happy voices trailed behind them.

Shai slipped inside the room and went directly to Yeshua. "You did it. I saw you heal Alter."

"Yes, my friend. I am glad you were here to help. We will meet at our beach and talk later. More needs to unfold today."

Shai understood that his friend's work was not done. He backed away and watched. Eventually, in hushed voices, those that remained began to talk to each other.

Shai said, "I have never seen anything like this. Praise the Lord!"

"He walks, Alter walks!" one woman outside the doorway wailed.

~ 143 ~

Jennifer Bjork

Someone inside the room spoke softly, "We have seen a remarkable miracle."

"He has to be the Messiah."

Many people wiped tears from misty eyes. They knew Alter. He was one of their own.

A solitary voice began singing a song of praise to God,

> *Praise the Lord, O my soul; all my inmost being,*
> *praise His holy name. Praise the Lord, O my soul,*
> *and forget not all His benefits - who forgives your*
> *sins and heals all your diseases...."*
> (Psalm 103)

Shai knew the song, so he joined many other voices. During the song of thanks and praise, he saw his beach friend place his hands together before his face and bow his head. He knew Yeshua was in prayer.

The singing boy saw that not one of the foreign rabbis had moved from the bench. They did not lead this humble song of praise. They did not even join in the singing, and it could not be because they failed to remember the words.

Shai was confused, again. They were supposed to be the religious mentors of the people, examples of righteous behavior. They should have been the ones leading praises to God.

With a farewell yank on Yeshua's sleeve, Shai left the room, "See you later."

The boy rushed away from Simon's house, chasing after Alter. He could not stop thinking. The visiting rabbis were supposed to be the holy ones chosen by God. They were supposed to lead God's chosen people, Israel. Today, it had not felt that way.

His smaller legs caught up with slow-moving Alter and his adult friends. He squirmed in front of the joyful man, "Alter, I am so glad to see you walk!"

"Thank you for your help, Shai." Alter was ecstatic, beyond happy. "I knew he could heal me if he so desired. I am lucky to

The Whistling Galilean

have such persistent friends. Our prayers were answered today. My mother will probably faint when I walk in the door."

Alter laughed as his joy bubbled over. Shai joined the laughter. He had never heard a happier sound, not even his from his brother, Sim.

15

The Tax Collector

SUDDENLY, SHAI FELT TWO PALMS IN THE CENTER OF HIS BACK. He was shoved hard, so hard that he fell and sprawled on his hands and knees on the stone roadway in front of the synagogue.

"Ow," he sputtered, turning onto his bottom to see who had pushed him.

He groaned at the danger hulking before him. The largest muscular farm boy was bracketed by two others. All stood in similar poses, hands on hips and scowls on lips. Oz, the boy in the middle, was undoubtedly the ring leader, as usual. One of the others was a total surprise. It was Dov.

Today, Shai and his fellow students were dismissed from school earlier than usual. Once Rabbi Selig gave the word, most of the pupils bolted out of the door into the warming sunshine of early spring and scattered in the wind like dandelion seeds.

Since he had some extra time, Shai was eager to play until it was time to do his chores. He had been looking for Dov because he hoped to play the kick-the-stone game on their way home. He also needed to test whether they were really friends.

The Whistling Galilean

His former best friend stood partially hidden by Oz. This was the first time he had ever seen Dov and Oz together. Shai knew he had no chance of winning a lopsided fight...unless his friend joined him.

Looking straight at his taller friend, Shai forced a nonchalant smile and stood. "Dov, I was looking for you. Let's walk home together."

In effect, he laid everything on the line and forced his friend to pick sides - either his or the muscular bully's. If his taller buddy walked over to him, they were still on good terms.

"Dov is with me today," Oz gruffly responded before Shai's long-time friend even had a chance to make a decision and respond.

The farm boy spat on the ground and defiantly stuck his thick arm out, blocking Dov's path forward in case he even desired to join Shai. That posturing basically drew a line in the sand, telling Dov - s*tay here and go no farther.*

"Dov can speak for himself." Shai busily dusted himself off. He noticed that his right knee was scraped and bleeding.

"Go home, mama's boy," Oz continued to speak for the group of three. "We don't want anything to do with you."

At that point, the shadow of Rabbi Selig's rounded frame covered two of the trio. He cleared his throat loudly, "Ahem. Can I help you boys? I have a brilliant idea. We will go back inside and review our latest scripture together."

Upon hearing that suggestion, the boys scattered.

"Nope!" As Oz left, he stomped his foot loudly. Shai thought that the bully was showing his disappointment that the fight he had started had been squashed like a bug on the roadway.

"Thank you, Rabbi, but I too must go." Shai left with his usual politeness.

As he walked away, he wondered why Dov had not lingered. Why did his friend rush off? Why did Dov appear to side with the bully, Oz, his enemy? Ever since he could remember, Oz had not liked Shai and went out of his way to bully him. He could not remember anything that he personally had done to start the feud, but he could not wait until he had a growth spurt so he could really fight back and end the larger boy's torment.

Before he got very far down the road, he heard the gentle voice of Carmi. Then he saw her giggling with another girl. They both were headed toward him. He quickly wondered how to react to his favorite girl in front of her friend. He needed time to figure something out.

In an instant, she was in front of him. Her freckled cheeks smiled at him. "Hi Shai. This is a nice surprise." She quickly turned to her companion, "Go on without me. I will meet you at the olive merchant's shop."

Then she turned her total attention to Shai. He wiped off his tunic as she examined him from head to toe. Under her studious gaze, he felt like a piece of merchandise for purchase instead of a budding friend. He reddened with embarrassment.

"What happened to your knee?" She sounded concerned.

"Just rough play with the boys." He shrugged it off.

He did not tell his favorite girl the truth. He did not want her to think he was a weakling, a push-over, even though that had been his lot in life just minutes ago.

"Let me help you clean up at the well. It is only a short walk down the road. Besides, we can talk as we walk."

So, they did. Shai quickly recounted his morning, leaving out the part with Oz.

Now that they were talking, he felt bolder. "Carmi. I want to give you a coin from the money I earned more than a month ago. Before you say no, I want you to have it for your protection. Since I cannot help you through that dreaded gate and customs house, I want you to have this token just in case...to get yourself out of a bind. If that Roman overseer wants a denarius for tax and you are short, use this coin."

Shai had carried the denarius in his tunic pouch all this time in hopes of seeing her. Now, as he proudly presented it to her, it felt small and insignificant.

"But, Shai, your family needs it -"

He interrupted, "They get the rest of my earnings. This one is for you. I do not want any harm to come to you."

The Whistling Galilean

The eleven-year-old peered hopefully at her while pleading inwardly with all of his heart. He did not have to wait long for her response.

"Alright. I accept your generosity. Thank you for being so thoughtful and caring. I am really touched."

He was thrilled. It was an appropriate gift after all. She carefully used a cloth to wipe the blood from his scraped knee. This turned out to be a very special day - the day he gave a gift to the girl he liked. He knew he could not stay with her forever, so they said goodbye, and he continued home.

He felt lighter than air as he walked. He was not sure that his feet even touched the ground. He felt so proud and knew that he must have grown a minimum of the length of his baby finger. He was so blissful that he did not notice the crowd around the customs house.

Then he noticed Yeshua standing next to Levi in front of the doorway. Shai was startled at first, afraid that the Nazarene had to pay a tax for something, but then he saw that they were merely talking. The Roman overseer was not in sight.

Shai saw Levi roll up the open scroll before him on the table. The tax collector placed it on top of a box filled with coins. At his request, a soldier standing nearby lifted the box, coins, and scroll. He was joined by a second centurion. Together, they marched their haul into an inner room of the stone customs house. After they entered, Shai saw the Roman overseer in his red cloak just inside the doorway leaning over something.

The curious young Galilean sauntered over to where the two men remained in conversation. He stopped to watch.

"...and I am staying at Simon's mother-in-law's house," Yeshua was speaking.

"Yes, I know the house well." Levi gave Yeshua his undivided attention. His body leaned forward in rapt eagerness.

There was a lull in Levi's work. No one was currently passing into Capernaum by boat, on foot, or in a carriage. Therefore, Levi had time for small talk.

"Follow me." Yeshua told Levi.

"What?" Shay's surprised high-pitched voice cracked and interrupted their conversation before the tax collector had a chance to respond.

That drew Yeshua's attention. "Shalom, Shai. Not now. Please, give us some time to finish."

Shai backed away a few steps to show that he understood. He knew the Nazarene's impossible acts, so he knew he wanted to stay and respectfully watch.

The tall teacher repeated, "Follow me, Levi-Matthew, for I know your full name."

This time Levi responded, "Me?"

Shai saw Yeshua nod in agreement. Levi looked baffled, mouth gaping open as if he were eating. Then, the man seemed to bury his head in a scroll as if reading something essential. Yeshua waited patiently.

Shai hoped that he had misunderstood what the Nazarene physician had said, but knew that he had not misunderstood. The Nazarene had said *"Follow me"* twice. About seven months before, the boy had witnessed Yeshua call Simon and the other fishermen with similar words.

Inwardly, Shai wished, *Please, Yeshua, not the tax collector. He cannot be worthy.*

As he wondered, he watched Levi seem to busy himself with work. The black-haired man dusted the clean wooden table and piled the remaining coins, clinking them together in an empty box. His hands were trembling and seemed to need something to do. While apparently working, the tax collector frequently rubbed his beard. He laced his smooth fingers through the wiry hair. Shai knew many men that did those same actions when deep in thought.

Levi finally responded, again asking, "Me? Now?"

"Yes you. Follow me. Now." Yeshua pointed to the space beside himself on the opposite side of the table from Levi.

Shai observed the eye contact between the publican and his beach friend. From experience, Shai knew it was impossible for anyone to refuse Yeshua when looking into the universe within

The Whistling Galilean

the teacher's hazel eyes. Levi was locked into that gaze. Shai was astonished to see wetness pool in Levi's dark brown eyes and stream down his cheeks.

Shai heard the publican whisper, "Thank you for accepting me."

Yeshua touched his shoulder, "Come."

Shai watched Levi push the scroll and box of coins that remained on the table away from him and heard him mutter, "Finished. It is over."

Then Levi actually smiled as he wiped his hands on the dust rag and threw it in on the ground. He walked around the table toward Yeshua. The dazed boy saw Levi's brown eyes crinkle. He looked unusual - happy.

This process seemed to be a repeat of what the boy had witnessed on the beach when Simon and Andrew dropped their nets to follow the Nazarene when bidden. Yeshua had even used the same words, *"Follow me."* To the eleven-year-old, the most amazing thing of all was that Levi had responded in exactly the same way as Simon and Andrew. It did not take these three men very long to drop their work and follow as requested.

As Levi distanced himself from the customs house, Shai saw a traveler in a dusty brownish robe spit toward the tax collector, "You greedy man. You work for Rome now. You work against us."

A man near Shai growled, "Levi, are you getting rich off of the sweat of my brow, too?"

Shai knew Levi had recently changed careers from a respected keeper of the standards to a hired official of Rome, a hated collector of taxes for the sole benefit of their oppressors. It seemed to Shai that local men, like Levi, were traitors and by doing Rome's bidding, they worked against the Galileans, his own people. Obviously, other people thought the same thing.

Today, Shai observed Levi change careers again. He wondered if Levi could so easily stop working as a tax collector, or if the Roman overseer would catch him and flog him.

Now, Levi was being called to become a disciple or student, following a man that some people called a prophet - maybe even the

~ 151 ~

Jennifer Bjork

hoped-for Messiah. Shai watched the tax collector rush after Yeshua, in full stride toward town and the quay. This sight reminded Shai of an eager puppy dog following behind his master.

The boy bet that Levi was grateful. Tax collectors and their families were banned from the synagogue. Maybe now, they would be admitted back among the community of the Hebrew faith.

As the lad, too, headed for home, he felt disgusted, shocked, and confused. He failed to understand the actions of the man he admired. He was disappointed in Yeshua's choice of followers and badly wanted to speak to his adult friend about this.

How could Yeshua consider Levi on the same level as the respected Simon and Andrew? Or other fishermen that had been called to follow this adult teacher? Shai could not understand Yeshua inviting Levi to follow him, too.

16

Event in the Woods

NOT LONG AFTER THE CALLING OF LEVI, SHAI WAS IN THE FOREST collecting firewood. Specifically, he was in the wood southeast of his house looking for downed tree limbs. He sought wood around the diameter of his forearm. He either broke or cut each piece to about the same length, approximately the length between his fingertip to his shoulder. This was an easy length to bundle and carry. His job was important because firewood was essential for cooking food, boiling water, and keeping warm at night since it was still winter.

As usual, he whistled while he worked. He had already collected half of what he needed. He used a large downed tree trunk as his table. Placing a collected branch on this sturdy trunk and steadying it with his left foot, he swung hard with this small but sharp ax - *thump*. Then he smoothed this piece of firewood by removing any small branches - *whish, whish, whish*.

Soon, rhythmic sounds filled the woods around him - *grunt, thump, whish, whish, whish*.

He enjoyed generating rhythms and bird warbles. He wasn't as good as Mama Anat at creating words to the rhythms and sounds - not yet. He secretly hoped that one day he and Mama would make up songs together.

It did not take long to generate a pile of firewood. He tossed the cut pieces onto one of two piles: the pile of long, skinny, branchless sticks or the pile of stubbier, thicker lumber.

He took a break from cutting to tie each pile together. He already had several bundles. By putting similar diameters and lengths together, it was easier to bundle and would be easier to carry on his back and shoulder. When he got home, the wood could be used immediately since it was already presorted. He had learned this trick from his father as a labor-saving device. Papa Yona had shared the philosophy behind this - *Why do something twice when you can do it only once?* - He liked that premise. It made a lot of sense.

As Shai worked, he wasn't thinking of anything in particular. He just enjoyed the late winter woods. His nostrils filled with fresh, earthy smells as bright green leaves of wild bulbs pushed their way out of winter dormancy and up through the soil. With buds of new green foliage springing out in some of the trees, he felt renewed. It was a sunny day, and he was not in school.

Suddenly, he heard a familiar whistle. Dov was nearby. Maybe now was the time to sort out their relationship. So, Shai carefully placed his ax next to the pile of wood, cupped his hands around his mouth, and screeched like a hawk.

Almost immediately, he heard the familiar return whistle and a, "Hi Shai-ooo."

"You." Shai answered frostily as the taller boy appeared from behind a tree trunk.

Dov acted as if nothing was wrong and responded cheerily, "What a surprise! What are you doing in the woods?"

"Collecting firewood, traitor."

Shai watched Dov's reaction. He had never accused his friend of anything before, but he felt that it was justified.

"Why the harsh accusation?"

"You know why. You remember the last time that we stood this close. It was in Capernaum...."

The Whistling Galilean

Dov just looked up at the sky, as if he were trying to recollect.

"...after school a few weeks ago." Shai reminded him.

Now, Dov looked down at his feet. As he scuffed the ground with the toe of his sandal, he responded, "Alright. I remember the day after school when Oz shoved you down. It probably seemed that I was siding with him against you. That's why you called me a traitor. That is not the truth."

"Oh, really? That is hard to believe."

"How can you even think that about me? We are best friends."

"Or were. You did not then and have not since then done or said anything to make me think otherwise. You have not explained nor apologized."

"You're right, Shai. But, in my defense, I didn't really side with Oz. I was just getting to know Abram, the other farm boy with Oz, before he pushed you to the ground. This all happened behind your back, so you did not see what I was doing."

"That is correct. I did not see you before Oz pushed me, but I do not believe your words. Why didn't you tell me that earlier? Now, it sounds like something you made up." Shai knew his friend and knew that he was not telling the whole story.

"I guess I felt bad and didn't know what to say."

Shai watched and waited, not wanting to let Dov off so easily. After all, Shai had been wounded, both physically and emotionally.

As they stood there, he heard the impatient *tap, tap, tap* of his own toes against a fallen limb. Shai had not realized he was nervous. He surprised himself. He had never spoken this boldly to anyone before. He had not realized that he had that strength of backbone. He was proud of himself for standing his ground yet he did not want to lose Dov as a friend.

Finally, Dov broke the silence between them. "Look, Shai, I just wanted to ask Abram about Maya. I didn't get a chance to say anything to you after you landed on the ground, if you remember. Oz took over, then Rabbi Selig interrupted."

"And later? Your actions and your silence during all of this time

~ 155 ~

have really hurt my feelings. That is not the way that a best friend behaves."

"I'm sorry I didn't say anything earlier to make you understand that I still value you as a friend."

"Good. If you are not part of Oz's hooligans, then we can test a friendship."

"Test?"

"Yes. I do accept your apology. I know it wasn't easy."

Shai hoped that his acceptance was not too naive or simplistic. He badly wanted Dov's apology to be honest and from the heart. Shai hated confrontations. He would rather dismiss this debate than keep it going for additional weeks.

So, Shai took a deep breath to shake it off, smiled, and asked Dov, "What are you doing in the woods?"

"Hunting," the taller boy grinned widely as he held up his homemade sling shot, which he dangled lazily from the fingers of his left hand.

"What are you hunting?"

"Nothing in particular. Small birds or rodents, either would be fine. I just want to bring something home to add to the cook pot for supper, something to make my father proud of my skill."

"I heard that your family slaughtered a young goat a week ago."

"They did. I just want my father to recognize that I have become a good hunter."

"Oh, I see. I understand that because I feel the same way. I want Papa Yona to be proud of my skills, too. I've got my sling shot, too. See?"

Like most boys his age, he always had his sling shot with him. He pulled it out of his belt, letting the leather strap unwind from the soft leather triangle shaped to hold the stones.

"Even though I am not as good as you are, I would like to help you hunt. Stalking prey is way more fun that collecting downed wood. Can I join you?" Shai asked.

"Of course, let's join forces, but I get to take the meat home."

"Agreed."

The Whistling Galilean

As they walked, Shai asked, "So, did the farm boy help you out with getting closer to Maya?"

"Not really. I haven't seen Maya since then. I just want to know if she is alright. Mainly I want to know if she still likes me."

"I understand. I feel the same way about Carmi."

"I know. How is she?"

"Just beautiful - I mean, fine."

They chuckled together as they thought about their favorite girls. It felt good to be doing something together again. Shai had missed this togetherness.

Dov uttered a low, soft whistle, "Hush. I think I hear something."

They stood at the edge of a clearing in the forest, a small meadow. They had hunted together before, so they did not need to talk. Every now and then, one of them warbled like a songbird or cooed like a dove in hopes to draw a bird down from the tree canopy to a visible branch.

One of Shai's chirps resulted in a feathery echo. Little by little, the sound approached them, so the boys moved slowly and silently into a back-to-back position in hopes of covering a larger visual field.

Suddenly, his friend let out a breathy, hardly audible, "I see it."

In one motion, Dov stepped forward, and in seconds, he had quickly set the stone into his sling shot's leather harness, whipped it around, and released the missile in the direction of the bird.

Shai heard a *thump* as he looked in the direction in which the stone had traveled. It wasn't the sound of a stone hitting a hard, wooden tree trunk. It was the sound of something softer.

"Got it!" Dov exclaimed excitedly as he sprinted over to the feathery pile on the ground. It was under a bare tree with rough, dark gray bark traveling in vertical, uneven lines upward.

Just a few steps behind, Shai caught up and joined him in looking down at the bird. "Good shot."

"Thanks."

Both boys hooked their sling shots back into their belts. Shai bent down and watched the hunter beside him scoop up the unmoving lump of tannish-gray feathers using both of his hands.

Dov explained, "I don't know if this dove is dead or just stunned. I better cut its head off just to make sure it is dead."

He put the bird on his leg while he searched his belt. "I forgot. I didn't sharpen my knife last night, so I left it at home. Do you have a knife with you?"

"No, but I have an ax back by my pile of wood. Follow me."

They stood and walked single file. Shai felt like Yeshua collecting disciples. He wondered how many disciples his friend had gathered so far. Shai had not seen him since the Levi incident.

As they approached Shai's bundles of wood, he saw a man bent over them.

"Shalom," Shai hailed the stranger. "Can I help you?"

"Shalom." The man stood and faced him.

"Yeshua, what a nice surprise. I was just thinking about you. It is good to see you."

"You generated a good pile of wood, Shai. I'll help you collect some more, if you would like."

"That would be a help. I would like that. Besides, I want to talk to you."

The Nazarene turned to Shai's friend. "Shalom, Dov. What have you been hunting?"

Dov straightened, proudly holding up the bird in his hands. "Shalom. I've got a dove for the stew pot. It may only be stunned now, so we need Shai's ax to kill it."

"May I see the bird?" Yeshua asked.

Dov handed it to him, waiting for the expected response - "Good shot," "You've got a heavy adult," "Your father will be proud of your talent," or something like that.

Instead, the man from Nazareth unexpectedly leaned over the dove, saying, "And you, too, are a creature of Elohim our Creator." Then he breathed on the dove. The feathered animal sat upright in the man's palms, shook its head, and stretched its wings.

"I must have just stunned it."

In less than a second, the dove flew away from Yeshua's open hand.

The Whistling Galilean

"Noooo!" Dov ran after the gray-brown medium-sized bird. He leapt up as high as he could stretching out his arms. He tried to grab it in mid-air in vain. He even yelled after it hopefully, "Come back!"

When he stopped running, Dov turned and stomped back toward the Nazarene physician.

In anger, the hunter gestured wildly, "You let my bird go! Why did you release it? It was for my supper, for my mother's stew pot."

Yeshua spoke calmly and softly, "Think before you take a life, Dov. All creatures were made by our Creator. You already have sufficient food - vegetables, goat meat, and fish - for your supper. You are not starving. This dove was a parent and providing for a family of young. Today, what was really the greater need? Your pride?"

Dov did not want to hear any more words. Before Yeshua could finish his question, Shai watched his tall, black-haired friend turn on his heel and stomp away in frustration from the adult beside him. The fuming boy was obviously in no mood for a parable, a paradox, and especially not a lecture from this Nazarene.

Shai had never before seen Dov really angry. As his friend retreated through the forest, Shai heard Dov's angry movements. Twigs snapped as they were ripped from a shrub. Tree trunks were thumped as a mad foot kicked them. Worst of all was the long trail of expletives. The swear words grew fainter as Dov put distance between himself and the duo remaining by the pile of wood.

Shai just stood there, not knowing what to do. As usual, he had conflicting emotions. He felt sorry for his friend. He knew his friend was too angry to talk to right now, so he decided not to follow. He let him go in hopes of catching up with him later, after Dov had calmed down. He was also embarrassed that his friend became so angry. He was also amazed that Yeshua chose to heal a bird...or did he?

Shai turned away from the departed Dov to face Yeshua. He started to explain Dov's behavior. "He's my best friend."

"Yes, he is," the Nazarene interrupted. "I'm sorry that his pride in showing off his skill to his family became his main goal. It became a barrier to Dov's understanding and appreciation of Elohim's creation.

~ 159 ~

Your friend's anger at me will take a while to calm. Maybe later you can talk to him friend-to-friend. Maybe that will keep his anger from smoldering into something worse. Dov will not listen to me in the near future. His quick burst of anger reminds me of Simon's outbursts. At least once Simon releases his anger, it is done with. I'm not sure that is true of Dov."

"Yeshua, I do not think words will make things better."

"You are correct, my young friend. Today we will let him calm down. Ah, but best friends have a special way of communicating. Friends have disagreements from time to time, but eventually they are less important than their friendship. The tight attraction you both have includes things you enjoy doing together. It should also include having similar innermost desires. A friend's heart is open and accepting, even when there is discord. Give it time, Shai. You will know when it is time to talk to Dov."

Shai knew his beach friend was right.

Yeshua continued, "Let me help you find some firewood. We can talk while we work together. Ask me what you would like."

The tall man began his search, occasionally bending to pick up a piece of dead wood. Shai realized that he was now the puppy dog following the master. They worked side by side in silence.

Eventually, the younger asked, "What just happened, Yeshua? Was the dove just stunned and reawakened, or did you just breathe life into a dead bird?"

The former carpenter answered, "A dove returned to his family. I know that I told you that part of my job is to mend the broken?"

"I remember you saying that."

"It all started with mending furniture as I learned carpentry from my father. Then, I found that I could mend broken wings or injured animals. Now, I want to repair injured, sick, and hurting people. My real desire is not just to heal their physical bodies but to mend broken souls and hearts yearning for Elohim but with no knowledge or ability to reach Him."

"You did heal Simon's mother-in-law from her high fever. I heard about that from Carmi, a girl I know in town...and I saw you heal

The Whistling Galilean

Alter, the paralyzed young man lowered through Simon's roof. I have also heard of other people that you healed from sickness."

"In each case, I pray for the power to heal. Elohim gave me that power, so it was His power and strength that actually did each healing, Shai. I want you to understand that it is nothing that I did on my own."

They collected more sticks in friendly silence. After a while, Yeshua broke the silence between them with a *coo* that sounded just like a dove. Shai whistled a different bird song. They took turns enjoying this whistling game of imitating the forest birds. The Nazarene was good at this game, much better than Dov and even better than his mother. To the boy's ears, the healer's imitations sounded like the real bird, not imitations at all.

Finally Shai felt that it was time to ask about what was really troubling his heart. He wanted to talk to this healer and preacher about Levi. So, he tapped Yeshua on the shoulder, and asked, "Can I ask something that bothers me, troubles me?"

"Of course, you can. We are alone now. Ask me whatever troubles you, and we will talk, man-to-man."

They sat on a downed tree.

"Ask what you want to know."

Thoughts rambled out of the boy's mouth. "Why call Levi? He treated my mother so badly. No one likes tax collectors. By your selection, people will think less of you, Yeshua."

The Nazarene tried to provide understanding and peace. "Think back. Was it Levi or the Roman overseer or the soldiers that treated your family roughly? Was it just fear that made you twist the story to fit your desired image?"

In the quiet of the fall woods, Shai recalled the events. Yeshua was right. It was his fear, especially of the lashing that he witnessed. Levi had only done his job as required. He had spoken no harsh words.

"You do not have to agree with the thoughts of those around you, Shai. Maybe it is only gossip that you hear. Do you want to believe and communicate gossip? You know that is wrong."

~ 161 ~

Yeshua was right again. The boy could misunderstand so easily. He resolved to learn patience. In the future, he wanted to know a more complete story. He disliked gossips and did not want to become one.

"Ouch. I did not behave well."

"Time and patience can be good allies."

"So, why did you call the tax collector to follow you?"

"I have called many men, Shai. I have the twelve that I am personally teaching. They are a varied group. Let me give you a comparison. Remember the carpenter that I once was? As a carpenter, I needed a variety of tools, not just a single type. In order to make a mere table top, I needed an ax, a hammer, and a wedge to split a rough board from a log. I also needed a saw to cut smooth edges. Then, I used a plane to smooth the wood. Do you get the idea?"

"Yes, I do."

"As a teacher, I need a variety of men with different backgrounds and skills to help spread my message. Some of these disciples are bold but need taming. Most tell the truth but may need to learn truths about themselves. Some are leaders but need to learn that all men have valuable insights. Some are very intelligent but others are not. Some are respected, some are not. Some are wealthy, some are not. Do you see that I am trying to build a human tool box?"

"I think so, Yeshua. I recognized a few traits you mentioned in the men that I grew up around. But what about Levi?"

"You are right that tax collectors are a hated group. All of the men I call or befriend have faults, my young friend, just like you. For example, you are too quick to judge. You are also young and naïve, eager to please. Shall I go?"

"No, please don't."

"Despite your faults, I like you. We are friends, are we not?"

"Yes, we are. You are right. I am not perfect." With a chuckle, Shai asked, "Yeshua, what about me drew you into friendship with me?"

"That is an excellent question. Listen and remember my answer. You have a big heart, and you love the Lord Elohim with

The Whistling Galilean

all of it. That is the main reason we were drawn together. Other personality traits that I enjoy are your joyful nature, eagerness to learn, and willingness to question. Since then, I have learned about your graceful ability to change. I ask you to remember those characteristics."

Shai blushed with pride. That was high praise. He loved that Yeshua did not feel the need to point out all of his flaws but instead gushed with kindness.

"I will try to remember those kind words, Yeshua. I am not perfect but I haven't become a traitor to my people like Levi."

"Matthew is not the worst of my followers, Shai. Remember, even the imperfect can be loved by Elohim. Even sinners can be forgiven."

"Matthew?"

"Oh, Levi-Matthew dropped the Hebrew part of his name, 'Levi,' so we all call him by Matthew."

"Alright, I am listening." Shai understood the idea that Elohim forgave sin through blood sacrifices.

"Matthew is intelligent but was broken in spirit. You and many others do not have the complete story and are judging based on one aspect only. Matthew was hired by the Roman power to become a tax collector. He had the skills and respect that they needed. He was forced to do so. His wife and family were threatened with rape, separation, and even death. Do not be so quick to judge when you do not know the whole story. The disciples helped Matthew hide his family away from Roman eyes. Remember, once he was a respected customs house official."

"I forgot that part. Papa Yona respected him. I did not know what the Romans did. I, too, judged based on the gossip." Shai apologized meekly.

"Shai, you have watched people gather around the quay when I taught near that spot in Capernaum. I have seen you among the listeners. The customs house is a stone's throw away, so Matthew listened, too. Did you know that?"

"No."

~ 163 ~

Jennifer Bjork

"He was already developing an open, receptive heart and was ready for a change." Yeshua pat him on the shoulder as he stood and stretched. "Do not be so hard on yourself. At least you are willing to realize some mistakes and try to correct them. That is a good start."

Shai joined him, stretched, and picked up a bundle of wood. "Thank you for explaining. I have been troubled."

Yeshua picked up another bundle of wood. "You are growing up, maturing. I am proud of you. We will continue to meet and talk, my young friend. Just know that people who want to think less of me by my selection of friends and students will do so. By my selection, I invite many types of people to listen, to learn, and to follow. I invite the imperfect, the sinners of the world, to join me."

They left the forest whistling bird songs.

17

One Unpleasant Thing

LIFE RESUMED ITS NORMAL ROUTINES - GOING TO SCHOOL, TRAINING to become a fisherman, eating, sleeping and...dreaming about Carmi. He liked the last activity best.

Today, before the spring rains arrived, Shai had to finish a particular chore. Papa gave both Shai and Ezra the task of reapplying mud plaster to the outer surface of the walls of their house to keep it dry inside. Shai dreaded that they had to do this together, as a team.

First, as a delaying tactic, he helpfully carried his mother's loom outside. He knew that his parents valued the loom greatly. Most of their blankets and clothing were made from the cloth Mama wove.

The slight woman stepped outside beside him. "You selected a great spot, Shai. I will enjoy the warm sun on my arms as I work the loom. Even better, you situated it out of the breeze."

She liked to weave and was good at it. He knew she needed to be out of the wind. Once the loom was set up and she started weaving, there were always many spools of thread dangling from beneath the working surface of the loom. Any wind, even light puffs, could wrap these lightweight bunches and tangle the threads into a huge, unruly knot that would be very difficult to separate. Therefore, he had placed the wooden frame near the front wall beside the door and in the good light.

"What are you weaving today, Mama?"

"Something special for your father. Don't say anything, please. I want it to be a surprise."

"He will like anything, if it is made by you. I see spots of that pretty cardinal red color that Papa and I like. You have made quite a bit of cloth already."

The olive skin on her face crinkled into a grin as she put down her open basket of thread and situated her three-legged stool to just the right spot before the loom. She began to hum as her strong fingers attached and dangled some new spools of cream through light brown to the threads already becoming cloth.

"Son, you and Ezra need to start plastering, or you will not finish the wall today. You can work with your older brother. You can do this." She gave his arm a loving squeeze, then pushed him away encouraging him to go and get started.

He had no more excuses to dally, so he walked to the back of the house. The north wall was exposed to winds and squalls funneled from the high mountains into the Sea of Galilee. The stucco base of that wall had become so eroded that the woven branches of the framework were exposed. As he surveyed the area, he noticed the pile of tools that Papa had accumulated for this task.

That was when Ezra appeared from the woods. "There's my slave. Now we can get started."

Nothing seemed to have changed between them.

"Papa told me where to get the dirt. Grab the shovel and bucket. Follow me."

The command, "follow me", reminded Shai of how Yeshua called his disciples from their work. That made Shai's arm hairs rise as his stubborn streak set in. He would not *follow* Ezra. He did not even like his older sibling.

"I don't see you carrying anything," Shai grumbled crossing his

The Whistling Galilean

arms over his chest. His feet took root in the packed dirt surrounding the house.

"Don't need to. I've got you." The words trailed behind Ezra's muscular frame, which was already moving into the woods.

The larger brother stopped when he realized that his smaller slave was not obediently behind him, so he ordered in a loud command, "Come. Now."

Different words produced a different result. Shai knew they had to finish the wall before his father returned from his day fishing. He knew his mother wanted him to work with "His Bossiness," so he grudgingly went after the teenager.

The older brother supervised every step of the way. He told the younger what to do and how to do it. Shai did the actual work, of course. He piled dirt into two buckets, carried it back to the house, and dumped the dirt beside the wood. After several trips, he went to the well and brought water. At some point, the younger boy ceased listening to Ezra's commentary and orders. The words coming out of his brother's mouth washed over him like water over a duck's back.

Back at the house and ready to start, Ezra actually did something. He stirred water into a half bucket of mud to show his slave the desired consistency required for the gooey glob, the thickness that would stick to the wall and not slide off.

Shai was sure that Papa had carefully taught his brother these tricks and assumed that they would be taught to him in the same manner. Like the cast net, it was not exactly so.

Ezra grabbed a handful of the mud and slung it against the lower wall with a *thud*. He used his hands and fingers to spread the reddish-gray goo into the exposed wooden framework.

"Do not leave any pockets of air, maggot."

Ezra even grabbed a thin twig and pushed mud into areas that his fingers could not reach.

On his knees, Shai copied "His Bossiness," mixing mud and throwing it against the wall with satisfying *thuds*. That felt good, and it sounded good, like his fist was connecting to something bigger.

~ 167 ~

Jennifer Bjork

His lips curved into a smirk. His imagination helped to defuse his brother's commentary.

Once they both had a section of wall covered with fresh mud, Ezra said, "Now watch this."

He poured some water into another bucket and used the coarse brush to smooth out his handiwork. "A little bit of water smooths out the plaster. Papa wants a smooth but slightly rough texture. Too much water on the brush, and the patch will slump off, got it?"

Shai tried. It took several tries to get the right consistency. When he didn't get it right, he had to reapply mud. As he worked into the quiet of the afternoon, he could hear Mama's hums waft occasionally around the corner of the house. It was a calming balm to his soul.

Eventually, Ezra stood, stretched, and walked to the forest edge to survey their work. Shai sneaked a glance over to see Ezra slip out of the top of his tunic and roll it up around his waist. His brother redid the belt to keep the tunic from slipping off entirely. Then, his brother flexed his tanned back muscles, arms, and chest. Shai figured the fifteen-year-old was just being a showoff and nearly said so.

Ezra spoke first. His tone was soft, like two people sharing a secret. "I think I have a girlfriend."

"What?"

That was a such a surprise! Shai knew nothing about Ezra's likes and dislikes.

"A girlfriend. She is a farm girl. No one else knows."

What should he say? He knew how to talk to Dov about girls because they did it all of the time, but he had no idea how to have a civil conversation with his brother.

"Did you hear me?"

Shai turned toward the voice and saw Ezra peering at him intently. He knew he had to respond unless he wanted to be punched in the arm, or something worse.

So, he offered the first word he could think of, "Nice."

Ezra looked strangely content. "She has a nice figure, large breasts, and a huge smile, even though there is a gap between her teeth."

The Whistling Galilean

Really? His brother was speaking to him about girls? This was so unexpected. It was definitely a first. Shai had been wondering about squishable breasts but would never think of talking about them.

"Where did you meet her?" He still had no idea what to say or comment on.

"Capernaum near the fish market."

Warning signs flashed in Shai's brain. That was near Carmi's sales location.

"Have you two talked?" he managed to squeeze out.

"Yes, several times. She is the oldest of many girls. One of her sisters is the girl you like, Carmi."

"No!" Now, Shai was worried. This must have been the reason Ezra brought up the topic of girls.

"Yes. Both are nice girls, don't you agree? Who knew that we would like sisters? This is great because if Papa wants to arrange a marriage to unite our two families, you know, fishermen and farmers, he doesn't need to wait until you grow up. He can marry me to Rachel."

"Oh, no," Shai muttered under his breath as he quickly turned his head away.

He did not want Ezra to see his expression and know how much he really cared about Carmi. He returned to mudding the wall with a vengeance under his brother's watchful eyes. He heard his brother's snicker as he worked alone.

Thud... pat... pat... pat....

He needed to talk to Carmi about this. Did she even have an older sister named Rachel? Was her older sister even talking to his older brother? Maybe Ezra had made this up to irritate Shai. That was very possible.

Thud... pat... pat... pat....

If only he and his brother got along, were friends again, then he wouldn't have to worry about such things. He remembered that as little kids they had been friends. They had always competed, but they had played together, wrestled, laughed, and raced everywhere.

Ezra had taught him to skip flat stones on calm water. What had happened to change that?

Ezra had become a teenager. That was what happened. He became a surly, frustrating brat. Shai wondered if he would become such a horrible person when he became a teenager. Did that automatically happen to everyone? Even Dov's older brother had become an impossible, lazy slob. He sure hoped that would not happen to him. His instinct told him that Carmi would not like that type of person.

Thud... pat... pat... pat....

His mind was swirling from one topic to another like a sirocco wind in the desert bouncing from one sand dune to the next. He remembered Yeshua teaching his school class last summer. The lesson had been about God's unfailing love. Shai recalled that, when the teacher asked, Shai himself had provided an example of unselfish love. Shai had recounted that his father and the fishermen he knew took care of their community with tenderness and caring.

Then, Yeshua had challenged the boys to demonstrate that love through their own actions, for example by reconciling with a family member to settle and resolve a dispute. He remembered feeling Yeshua's eyes boring into him. He felt it all over again, even though the Nazarene wasn't present.

He knew that Yeshua had selected that topic because Shai had been upset with Ezra, as usual. He knew that it was up to him to demonstrate that he was the bigger person. Ezra would not take that step. It was up to him to take the first step in breaking down the barrier between them. It was up to him to accept one unpleasant thing - that was Yeshua's exact challenge.

Just a few weeks before, Yeshua had praised him. The teacher was proud of the youngster for displaying progress and maturity toward adulthood. He deeply desired to accept and meet the Nazarene's challenge.

Thud... pat... pat... pat....

Over the last few months, Shai had given this a lot of thought. He had even selected the unpleasant thing he would try to accept. He just had not done anything about it.

The Whistling Galilean

The younger brother looked over at the teen that he lived with. The enemy within his family leaned against a tree trunk, hands crossed behind his neck. He looked relaxed and at ease. He had talked about his girlfriend, maybe even was thinking about her right now. Therefore, this might be the best time to take that first step.

Shai stood and stretched out his stiffening back. He had been bent over the lower wall for a long time. The sun had lowered in the sky. Papa would be home soon. He had to act now.

He took a big, calming breath and slowly walked over to Ezra. Shai did not wait for an order. Instead, he made an announcement, "I'll go get some water so that we can wash up."

As he picked up the water bucket, he continued speaking, "Ezra, you know that I have been jealous that Grandpa gave you his prized possession, the beautiful handmade fillet knife."

Ezra just nodded in agreement.

The youngster's tummy was tight with nervousness but he bravely continued despite feeling that he would throw up. "Grandpa gave me his small carving knife, and we worked on my food bowl together. His gift to you does not hurt as bad anymore. I know you worked hard to become a fisherman. You earned that fillet knife. I accept that it is rightfully yours."

There, he had said it. It had been hard to do, extremely difficult. And he had done it.

Now, it was Ezra's turn to be surprised. "Oh? How grand of you. So, if I choose to toss it in the deepest part of the Galilee, you will not care?"

"Of course, I will care if you throw it away. After all, it was Grandpa's favorite knife. If you choose not to keep the knife anymore, I hope that you offer it to me first to keep it in the family...but it is rightfully yours."

18

Mountain Sermon

As Shai and Dov met in front of the synagogue after their departure from school, a large crowd of people who had been walking northwest quickly surrounded them. Shai was instantly distracted from Dov because he knew Yeshua would be the only reason for such a diverse, purposeful group.

The taller boy yanked on Shai's sleeve. "Come on, let's go. You said you wanted to play."

That was true. It had been Shai's intent to spend some time with Dov. He had hoped to mend the distance between them. Unfortunately, Shai now felt drawn in two different directions. He was unsure of which to select because they were both important to him.

He wanted to follow the crowd toward the Nazarene physician. After all, the man was doing what he had said he would - actively teaching and healing wherever he could. News of his movements and activities spread quickly through word of mouth. Yeshua was popular. Large crowds from many areas gathered expectantly whenever they heard that he was near. They traveled from the southern province of

The Whistling Galilean

Judea and even Jerusalem, from Syria to the north, and even from Jordan in the east.

As crowds appeared, pushing and shoving for the cure of a friend or loved one, Shai had heard that his healing friend managed to distract these unruly masses to escape into the hills. More than once, the boy had seen him get into a boat with a fisherman and sail out into the Sea of Galilee. Shai's father and *Ole Blue* had even helped the healer escape a few times.

With a shake of his head, Shai responded, "Wait."

He needed time to think, to decide.

A young man leading a woman riding on a donkey gently pushed the lad aside so they could pass, "Excuse me."

The man holding the donkey's harness proudly announced to all around, "We're following the healer. We want him to bless our unborn child."

Even though Shai already suspected Dov's refusal, he said, "Let's follow the crowd. You may witness your first miracle. It may change your mind. Chicken?"

"You know miracles are impossible, Shai. No, I am going to play with someone else if you don't come with me. I want to relax and have fun before my parents find me and put me to work. I will not follow you. You follow me," Dov urged.

Shai stood his ground, "No, not today, Dov. You come with me."

There, he had made his decision. That wasn't so hard, was it?

With a disgusted shake of his head, the taller boy's response flowed in like a stormy tide, "Shai, he has suckered you in. Do not believe everything you hear. It's a waste of time. Why listen to a sham when you can come play with me instead? We have so much fun together."

"Yeshua is not a sham," Shai defended the teacher, the man that he knew well. "Other rabbis listen to him. He explains life and relationships better than anyone I've ever heard. His words pierce my heart like arrows of truth. I want to learn from him. For me, it's not like going to school. Come with me. I want to spend time with you, too. After all, I think you are still my best friend...aren't you?"

~ 173 ~

Following this question, his companion looked down at his feet, then in a mocking childish tone, sang, "Yeshua...Yeshua...Yeshua.... But it is you, Shai, that are pulling away from me. You are choosing him over me - me, your friend whom you have known your whole life."

"I want both of you in my life. There is no competition, silly. You are my playmate friend who confides to me wonders about our girls. He is my teacher friend who confides to me truths about myself and recommends ways to become a good man."

"Don't you see that who you choose to spend time with is your friend?"

"Don't you see that the events happening around us right now are not ordinary? They are special, even spectacular. These events only occur once in a lifetime. I don't want to miss any of it. I told you that I witnessed a miracle, the healing of the paralytic man, Alter. Now, even you see Alter walk everywhere instead of being carried on a pallet. He is proof of Yeshua's miraculous healing powers. So, please come with me. Then we won't be going separate ways. That would restore our friendship."

"No. You have already made your choice and tried to defend it."

The taller boy turned away, and Shai watched Dov stride away, even when he held out a beckoning arm and begged, "Stay!"

Shai felt abandoned. His best friend had chosen to walk away from him. That hurt. That hurt deep down. Despite being surrounded by people, Shai felt lonely. He felt like he had stepped over a cliff and was falling headfirst into a dark unknown, an abyss. He already missed their togetherness and wordless communication. He realized that Dov rarely sat beside him in school anymore, and now, if they ceased playing together, what was left of their relationship?

Through his despair and disappointment, the youngster found a bright beacon of hope on which to cling. He realized that he had made his choice. Suddenly, he felt a sense of relief. It was his choice to seek his heart in his quest for emotional growth. He was not a blind follower. He recognized that he was a seeker, a thoughtful

The Whistling Galilean

one. He was not a mere muscle-builder concentrating on escaping responsibility.

So, he turned in the opposite direction and followed the curious crowd. He walked with them almost a Roman mil. Along the way, the boy listened to the many dialects and intonations around him. Some people spoke words, some grunted or clucked, and others hummed, like Mama. Different tones of voice and speech patterns sounded to him like a musical score. They generated a growing excitement that was contagious. They pulled him along as if he floated in a gently moving stream of sound.

An old, gnarly man bent over a wooden cane came into his field of view. The ancient white-haired man walked very slowly, gripping the cane tightly in two bony hands. His spine arched over like a doorway. The boy tried gingerly to move around the elder. Just then, a rush of young adults sped through, bumping both of them. This caused the old man to tilt and almost fall into Shai.

After a grunt to clear his throat, the man spoke in a language that the lad did not recognize. Shai smiled at the ancient man, helped him regain his balance, and nodded as if he had understood. Then, he realized that a girl in light-green was on the elder's other side doing the same thing. As she peered around the elder's inward-curving chest, Shai recognized the glint in her brown eyes - Carmi!

They grinned at each other as they left the old man. They naturally fell into the same pace and progressed side by side along with the crowd.

He spoke first, "I didn't know that you listened to Yeshua."

"Remember, I've known he was special ever since he healed Simon's mother-in-law and all those other people that night in Capernaum."

"I forgot about that. Can you spend the afternoon following Yeshua? Do your parents know that you are here instead of the marketplace?"

"Family members and I spend time not only listening to Yeshua but watching the Nazarene heal. My mother knows where I am."

Jennifer Bjork

"Good. In that case, I am glad good fortune has brought us together in this huge throng of people."

"Shai, my father is not aware that I am here. He's in the orchard. Mother and I are keeping this secret from him because he had not witnessed what we have. What about your parents?"

"They both know how I feel. Neither has told me not to spend time with Yeshua."

"I'm glad. Isn't the Nazarene physician incredible? He may be the one."

Shai had no idea that Carmi believed so strongly that Yeshua was indeed incredibly special. It was a surprise to discover someone besides his grandfather with whom he could discuss spiritual matters. She was more than an ample replacement for Dov as his favorite companion. And she must have felt the same way because they progressed contentedly, now making small talk to pass the time.

Their destination was a hillside shaped like a natural bowl near Bethsaida. It was called the "amphitheater" because sound readily carried from one side to the other. This hillside was used for important announcements to the people and for performances including singing, dancing, and plays. The amphitheater was amazing because everyone sitting along the treeless hills and within the grassy bowl could hear every word spoken by a speaker or singer. The performer did not have to yell or scream, only project in a loud voice.

Sunshine warmed Shai's shoulders as he and Carmi settled in a spot overlooking his beautiful Galilee. He loved feeling so alive on this early summer day. The bright sunlight sparkled off of the calm blue waters and made him squint. Best of all, he was with the lovely, delightful, freckled Carmi.

He thought, *What a nice turn of events. One friend departs and another arrives to take his place.*

Yeshua appeared near the bottom of the amphitheater surrounded by several of his close followers. As the noisy crowd began to quiet, Shai recognized Simon and Andrew standing behind the teacher. He even noticed Matthew, the former tax collector, hovering nearby,

The Whistling Galilean

and was surprised that he didn't feel disappointed in that selection anymore.

The tall Nazarene knelt in prayer. The crowd hushed to stillness. Then Yeshua sat facing the crowd below him.

Adjusting his light beige robe, he spoke in a clear, calm, distinct, almost musical tone, "Today I challenge you to act in a manner that pleases Elohim, the Lord of Israel. It is a wonderful way to honor the Lord. Today I will share with you eight blessings, eight ways to please Elohim. The first one is: *Blessed are the poor in spirit, for theirs is the Kingdom of Heaven.* Blessed are the poor in spirit, for theirs is the Kingdom of Heaven."

Shai noticed that his friend used repetition to help his listeners remember, just like Rabbi Selig did in school. Yeshua paused for effect. During the lull, Shai thought, *So the poor, those without possessions or food, can go to Heaven.*

Then, Yeshua defined the term *blessed*: "By blessed, I mean to be happy, to be content. To be blessed invokes divine care. It is a gift from Elohim. Let your spirit soar with inner joy. To be blessed means 'congratulations, for you have achieved ultimate well-being.' Blessed are the poor in spirit…."

Naturally, as he continued, Yeshua's explanation took an unexpected twist, "By this I do not mean that you are living in poverty, that you are destitute. That may be true, but I am speaking about your inner being, your spirit. Being poor in spirit means that you are brokenhearted, that you feel hurt, low, and small. It means that your heart is impoverished. It means that you are ill-equipped and insufficient. Usually that is because you do not have Elohim by your side. You are without the Lord of Israel."

Many in the audience looked as confused as Shai felt. But the boy noticed that others displayed large smiles and even nodded in agreement.

"Your ultimate well-being depends on you. If you are poor in spirit, you are truly sorry for your wrongs, for your sins. You act in a humble and unpretentious manner. You are not proud and self-sufficient. You recognize that you need and desire Elohim. We all

~ 177 ~

need Elohim. Believe me, the Lord of Israel is pleased that you need Him. Elohim Himself blesses and cares for you by inviting you into the Kingdom of Heaven.

"Let me describe the opposite way to live, the way that Elohim dislikes. He dislikes it when you are full of pride, are haughty, and do not need help from anyone, especially from the Lord. When you are self-sufficient, you only depend on your own actions. Your behavior shows that you do not need even the Lord.

"You may be wealthy and powerful, or you may be a poor tradesman. Remember, we are speaking about the condition of your heart, your spirit, and not your economic status. If you think you can do everything yourself, you are not recognizing and loving your creator. Without a humble heart attitude, you will not enter the Kingdom of Heaven. Therefore, you will not have eternal life with the Lord.

"Blessed are the poor in spirit, for theirs is the Kingdom of Heaven. Eternal life with Elohim is a gift, not a reward that you can earn. The Lord of Israel wants you to recognize Him as powerful, faithful, and dependable. He never expects you to do everything on your own. He is always there when you need Him.

"I depend on Him, too. Just before speaking to you, I prayed to Lord Elohim, asking Him for the right words to speak. I depend on Him to help me give proper examples. Just this morning, I asked Him to remove barriers to your understanding of and desire for Him.

"In sum, the first character trait that I want you to learn is to humbly depend on the Lord of Israel. I repeat, humbly depend on Elohim."

In that moment, Shai understood that everything was from Elohim. Shai was blessed by the gift of joy, the gift of the warm sunshine on his back, the gift of the clean air that he inhaled, the gift of his family, and the gift of Carmi sitting beside him. Elohim had blessed him greatly.

The lad wished that Dov had heard the words spoken from the mouth of the teacher in this amphitheater. He wished his friend's anger would sizzle out and become just embers. He wished his

The Whistling Galilean

long-time pal could forgive. Shai would pray for that. He now felt that his friend had a broken heart and tried to be self-sufficient. He felt that he had just lost his best friend. Maybe he had lost him entirely.

By now Yeshua had moved onto another topic, another character trait. Deep in thought, Shai had already missed some of the Nazarene's sermon, but as he paid attention again, he heard the amazing adult say, *"Blessed are those who mourn, for they will be comforted.* Blessed are those who mourn. You who are in mourning are grieving tearfully. If you are grieving, you are distressed and are expressing deep and weeping sorrow. You feel dreadfully lonely, even when surrounded by other people, even people you love. Your heart is empty spiritually. You feel brokenhearted, alienated, friendless, isolated, and detached.

"Maybe your thoughts or actions have created a barrier between you and the Lord. Maybe this barrier was something that you did, such as gossiped bad news about a friend, or coveted someone else's prized possession, or desired another man's wife, or let a widow and her family go hungry. Elohim is perfect and sinless and cannot be in the presence of imperfection.

"How can imperfect men and women, all of you, approach your perfect Lord? First, you must make amends with Elohim. Remember, the Lord of Israel loves you. By admitting your mistakes, or omissions, you can be forgiven. Show that you depend on Elohim because only our Creator provides the real comfort that you need. He can heal your heart, fill the hurtful empty void, and replace it with serene peace, joy, and comfort. It is up to you to make the first move."

As the boy listened, he watched the crowd of people around the hillside. Yeshua spoke in Aramaic. He wondered how people in the amphitheater who only knew a different language could understand the speaker's words. Somehow, language did not seem to be a barrier to their listening, enjoyment, and learning.

If most people were like himself, they did not understand everything Yeshua said anyway. Shai hoped he could understand and remember one thing from today's sermon. Based on the reactions of people around him, they understood something. Many people nodded or murmured as they agreed with one of Yeshua's points. Many people smiled in relaxed joy just listening to him. Carmi appeared to be content and relaxed by his side, so maybe she was one of the latter.

She must have felt his gaze because she looked over and smiled at him, "This is so special, Shai. It delights me to be here listening to how to please Elohim with you beside me."

Those were Shai's exact thoughts. After hearing her words, all other words spoken became fuzzy noises to his ears. All his brain could register was, *she likes me.*

He tightly grasped that thought, *she likes me.* He examined her cute face and figure while she concentrated on Yeshua's words.

Eventually, another nugget of Yeshua's truths broke through his blissful daydreams to touch his heart. The man in tan told the crowd below him the seventh character for right living - peaceful living, *"Blessed are the peacemakers, for they will be called the sons of God."*

In rapid response, he heard a rising grumble of men's voices behind him. He turned to see that a small group of young, disheveled men wearing very dusty robes seemed to be disappointed in the speaker. He heard them talk amongst themselves in Aramaic. Their dialect told the boy that they were local Galileans.

"... but we must fight against Rome, not make peace."

"They treat us like their slaves. Didn't Moses free slaves like us from Egypt?"

"Yes, and we can do it again under a new, strong king. I thought that this man, Yeshua, was worthy to be our new king."

"I thought so, too, but we need a warrior king."

"I agree. We need a leader who is strong, knows military strategy, and can unite us in rebellion."

"That is my desire, too. We do not want a king who only desires peace. That changes nothing."

"I can't listen to this pacifist. I am driven to throw off the yoke of Roman oppression...."

The boy watched as three of the men worked their way through

The Whistling Galilean

the crowd to leave the amphitheater. Carmi pulled on his sleeve. "Listen to Yeshua, Shai. Ignore the crowd."

This wonderful girl had reacted as his mother would have. With confusion swirling in his brain, Shai tried to return his concentration to Yeshua. He hoped to understand what the teacher from Nazareth really meant. He understood and sympathized with the dissenters, but the speaker on the rock always had another spin to his tale. Maybe there was something else to consider.

The Nazarene was saying, "The opposite of peace is war, hostility, and even anger. To be at peace means to agree, to be in harmony with, to be untroubled, and even to be friendly. Peacemakers are pacifists, people who promote peace. They are also mediators and intermediaries helping to find a path to peace and calm harmony. You see, wars between nations are just magnified arguments between individual people. As a result, arguments between any of you is not a good thing. It should be avoided wherever possible. An argument can grow into a feud. A feud can grow into tribal warfare. That is not what Elohim desires.

"The first step to reduce arguments is to stop gossiping. Freely discuss and praise the good things people do. Do not share with others the wrongs you think people have done to you. Don't talk unkindly about anyone. Instead, look for the good in people. If you have to speak about someone, speak about the good deeds that they do and the good traits that they display.

"As a mediator or intercessor, did you know that you can pray for someone else? You can ask the Lord Elohim to heal a friend. You can ask for wisdom to resolve a neighbor's problem. You can ask for protection of a loved one from harm. Prayers are effective, and they do work. Look for the good that you can do. Not only can you pray for someone else, you can also help them with your direct actions. You can provide food, clothing, shelter, work, or a listening ear.

"Be a peacemaker. Help someone that you know. By reducing arguments and by looking for the good in others, you will be called a son or daughter of Elohim. Peace is always healthier than anger.

~ 181 ~

Remember, Elohim's peace is an incredibly deep calmness and joy in your heart. Let the peace of the Lord rule in your hearts."

Shai thought about his best friend, Dov. He really liked having a best friend, a person to confide in, to play with, and to share good times with. Dov had been his best friend for years, for his whole life. Shai really didn't want that close friendship to come to an end. Therefore, he needed to be the intermediary. He needed to take the first step...again. He needed to pray for his friend. He would ask Elohim to open Dov's heart so that his friend could receive Elohim's promised peace and understanding.

It seemed to him that the relationship he had built with Yeshua was the cause of Dov's distress. There had been no wedge in their friendship before the Nazarene appeared. This healer and peacemaker seemed to be driving them apart. Shai knew that it was not an intentional action by the healer. He knew their strife was based on the differing perceptions and emotions of each boy towards Yeshua and his teachings. Their interpretations seemed to be quite different. This had to be the wedge in their friendship.

Or...maybe the real issue was jealousy. After all, Shai had developed a close relationship with the man from Nazareth. Was Dov jealous of that and therefore of Yeshua? Relationships with people were not a competition or game like kick-the-stone. There wasn't just one winner.

Shai still wanted Dov to be his best friend but the younger boy realized that he wanted - no, needed - Yeshua in his life even more than he needed his friend. He admired the man, respected him, and believed in what he taught. For example, today this incredible teacher could have rallied the crowd to fight Rome, but he didn't even mention their oppressors. Instead, he spoke about the condition of their hearts and their relationship to Elohim.

Shai had grown to love the man teaching them today. He had included Yeshua in his heart as his family.

If only his friend would listen to Yeshua's words. He, too, could learn the truths about goodness that were taught. If his long-time companion could learn from this new teacher, maybe Dov would

The Whistling Galilean

grow to respect and listen to Yeshua, too. Then, maybe, they could remain good friends.

Yeshua was still speaking, "...there is more we can agree about than we disagree about. For example, I think we all agree that we want our children to have better lives than our own...that we want to belong to a loving family...that we want to be respected for who we are and what we do...that we want to accomplish something helpful that matters, that makes a difference."

Shai realized that he could hear no further murmurs of disagreement. The few remaining young rebels behind him were quiet. He turned to see interested listeners. A few remaining disheveled men must have had a change in heart. From personal experience, he knew that Yeshua could use just the right words and turns of phrases to get his point across.

The boy also remembered that the Nazarene had prayed first. Therefore, Shai concluded that this speaker relied on Elohim to provide just those right words. Yeshua had even admitted that very thing at the beginning of his talk.

The man at the bottom of the slope of the amphitheater continued his discourse. "We each desire someone to love us. Love contains elements of respect, trust, admiration, faithfulness...."

When the man in tan spoke about wanting someone to love him, Shai immediately thought of the girl beside him, not his parents. Well, he did want her to be his girlfriend. After all, he was eleven and a half years old, old enough for a girlfriend. Right now, he could not imagine anyone other than Carmi taking that role in his life.

He moved his hand to pat the top of hers. She looked at him, into his eyes. Her gaze melted his heart. He felt her hand move and was disappointed until he felt her warm, soft fingers link through his. They were holding hands!

Yeshua interrupted his thoughts again, speaking with the authority of truth, "The Lord Elohim loves us, each of us. He loves us unconditionally. He desires unity among all who believe in Him. He desires a bond of peace because we have Him to depend on. Peacemakers bring people to Elohim, to the Lord's special peace throughout our hearts. When you say 'Shalom,' you are saying 'Peace be to you.' Do you really mean it? Or, are you just saying it because it is a common saying, a tradition? Elohim wants you to mean it."

Shai was elated that he was on the mountainside on this particular afternoon. He was ecstatic that he and Carmi had met for this shared experience. As usual, he felt that his teacher had spoken, at least part of the time, directly to him.

As Yeshua finished his sermon, he said, "Today, I gave you eight characteristics for you to display to the best of your ability. I repeat those eight characteristics:

1. "Be poor in spirit, humble before the Lord of Israel.
2. "Be mournful, grieve and repent over your sin.
3. "Be meek, seek Elohim's way and not your own.
4. "Be hungry for righteousness, show moral excellence and justice.
5. "Be merciful, show compassion and leniency.
6. "Be pure in heart, repent your sins to Elohim.
7. "Be a peacemaker, live in harmony with Elohim and your neighbors.
8. "Be a follower of Elohim, love the Lord without reservation.

"If you can display these characteristics in your daily living, Elohim will bless you. Start with one at a time. That will please Elohim. Your progress will be blessed. In displaying these characteristics, you will be blessed with the gifts of comfort, restful peace, loving joy, forgiveness, and mercy. You will be called sons and daughters of Elohim. Blessings to you all."

Shai had already accepted Yeshua's challenge to accept one unpleasant thing about his brother. He would take another step, praying for Dov. Shai was certain that he was destined to follow Yeshua as his mentor and friend, regardless of the consequences, especially with Carmi by his side like she was now.

19

The Broken Became Whole

SADLY, SHAI HAD TO SAY FAREWELL TO CARMI BEFORE THEY LEFT the amphitheater. She was in a hurry to return to the marketplace to relieve her mother and older sister, Rachel. On their way out, Shai had asked about her siblings. Carmi was surprised that Shai's older brother was interested in Rachel. Before parting, they both quickly admitted that this twist created a problem to their own budding relationship.

Once he headed down the hillside alone, the boy's mind whirled with powerful mixed emotions. He felt glad to have witnessed the enormous, peaceful, joyful gathering of people. He felt amazed that each person seemed to learn something of value. He felt grateful to have learned more about his adult friend's mission. He was joyful that he had spent so much time with Carmi, even holding her cute, soft hand. On the other hand, he was disappointed that Dov had not joined him and felt abandoned by his former best friend.

Jennifer Bjork

Today, Shai had witnessed a small miracle of sorts. It was miraculous that so many people remained calm and attentive for so long. That should have been enough, but he, like many around him, desired more, something on a grand, epic scale.

Shai admired this humble teacher who acted out what he taught. Many people could not understand why Shai wanted to emulate Yeshua; after all, the boy already had a father, a well-respected, dependable, leader in their community. Shai also had a respected and well-liked mentor, Fishel, teaching him his future profession. Even though Papa Yona and Fishel were wonderful examples to follow into manhood, it was Yeshua who had replaced them in Shai's scale of importance. Yeshua was teaching him how to be the type of person he wanted to become.

As Shai walked down the mountainside in chain step with the person in front of him, he was deep in thought about the roles of a father. The concept of Elohim as his spiritual father was a radically new idea to him. After all, the boy felt insignificant, imperfect, and worthless compared to Yeshua, but especially to the Lord, the magnificent creator of the universe. Yet, the Nazarene had told him that Elohim was his father, too, even pushing his index finger into the boy's chest over his heart to hammer the point home. It just didn't seem right. Shai was not worthy. How could the powerful God of Israel love him regardless of what he did or how he acted? Understanding a love that big and inclusive and forgiving was impossible to understand when it became personal, when it meant his holy God loved small, insignificant, imperfect Shai.

The sound of a bell brought Shai's mind back to his surroundings. His thoughts rushed in free fall as if they slid down from the clouds. He recognized the tone of the bell's ring. It was the warning bell used by a leper. Shai was immediately shocked to hear that sound among all of these people. Immediately, fear grabbed him and stopped him in mid-step. His eyes searched wildly for the source of the sound.

Then, he heard the thin raspy voice carefully say, "Unclean. Unclean."

The Whistling Galilean

The bell rang again. Shai's searching eyes finally saw the leper in front of him and to his left. The first thing that he noticed was the hushed crowd surrounding a tall pile of black rocks. The unclean bent man had been corralled and was pressed against the basalt.

Many individuals near the boy had not been paying attention to their surroundings either. Three men in front of him rapidly backed away from the leper, pushing the smaller boy out of their way in their fearful retreat. Shai was rammed into a woman holding the hands of two young children, and knocked one child loose from her frantic grasp. The resultant wailing cry assailed his ears and added to the terror of the moment.

"Unclean, unclean…." That small, raspy voice could still be heard over the crowd's reaction only because Shai's ears were listening for it.

It was all happening so quickly. Shai tried to escape backwards away from the voice. A young woman beside him shrieked as she fell. Two men stepped on her before she could circle herself into a protective ball. Shai bent over to help her up.

The immediacy of the terror slowed as people backed into a safer zone. Groaning in unison from the horror presented before them, the crowd continued to back away, now at a slower pace, from that gnarly old man ringing the bell. The immediate gut reactions subsided, and people adjusted themselves to form a wide circle around the rocks.

In the newly formed clearing, Shai saw that the leper was a man hunched over his cane. He held the bell up against his chest in a dirty, rag-wrapped hand. He was not wearing any clothing. Instead, dirty rags were wrapped around almost every inch of his body. Uncombed hair stuck out from underneath a ragged hood on his head like weeds in a field. The hood covered most of his dirt-covered face.

This was the closest that Shai had ever been to a person with leprous skin. From his safe distance away, he gazed with fearful curiosity. He tried to get a good look at the man's face. When he did, he rapidly swore under his breath, "Oh, my God!"

Part of the leper's cheek had been eaten away by the disease. Shai felt nauseous. As the diseased man turned to face him, the boy

Jennifer Bjork

saw how misshapen the leper had become. What used to be a man was also missing a nose.

The boy quickly muttered a fervent, urgent prayer under his breath, "I pray to you, my Lord Elohim, that I never get leprosy. I do not want to live in lonely isolation. I do not want to be separated from my family. I would miss them terribly. I do not want to become like this leper before me. Please, Elohim, not me."

Shai shuddered at the image of himself as a leper. He could not imagine living without the contact of his family. If he had that wasting-away disease, only other brave lepers could touch him. That meant no relationship with Carmi.

He muttered, "Please, Elohim, not me."

There was no cure for that dreaded disease that ate away the flesh. Shai tried to ward off the horrible disease by placing his forearms in parallel in front of his face, palms out.

He heard a man, perhaps an elder or rabbi, accuse the leper, "You should not be here. Go away. You are unclean."

The leper was surrounded and could not possibly go anywhere.

"Why are you here among the people? You know it is against the Hebrew law."

The raspy voice emanated from the rags, "Walking to my mountain forest home…separated from you without this skin disease."

"You saw all of these people. Why try to walk through them?"

"Returning from seashore foraging for food. You were in amphitheater. It was safe. You erupted from the bowl like ants from a mound…. Now hide here."

It was at that point that the boy saw Yeshua moving through the crowd and approaching them. The contrast between the two men was striking. Yeshua wore a clean, tan tunic and a brown robe. The leper was covered in dirty gray rags. Yeshua walked upright, straight, and unbent. The leper was bent in a curve like a young willow branch. Yeshua strode with a muscular, powerful strength looking straight before him. The leper leaned against the rocks for support with downcast eyes looking at his rag-covered feet, embarrassed to be seen at all in public.

The Whistling Galilean

Shai had been taught that leprosy was easily transmitted by contact. Either directly touching the skin or contact with the bloody, weepy fluid on the rags with which a leper was wrapped could transmit the disease. When those with the skin disease were away from their colony, they had to carry and ring a bell to protect the healthy. The sound of the bell warned people away from their very presence.

According to the Israelites, lepers were considered ceremonially unclean and could not come into a town or be in close contact with people. Hebrews had to undergo a ritual cleaning to be able to go to synagogue even after just being in the same vicinity of a leper. Therefore, all of the Israelites in this crowd would have to undergo that ritual cleaning before going into the synagogue on the Sabbath.

By now, everyone had moved away from the gnarly shape. Shai watched Yeshua walk straight toward the wrapped shape of a former man. Now, the Nazarene and the leper were both surrounded by people in the human-created clearing. The speaker from the amphitheater was the only person who didn't seem to be afraid.

Amazingly, the leper limped forward a few steps, moaning in pain with each one. After his slow approach on the wrapped stubs of his feet, the leper knelt with difficulty before the Nazarene physician. The boy heard him say softly in his raspy voice, "Lord, I came to hear you today. If you are willing, you can make me clean."

Then Yeshua did something shocking. He reached out his hand and touched the shoulder of the leper.

"NO!" Shai yelled immediately. "Get away, Yeshua, get away."

The man in tan did not avert his eyes from the leper toward the boy's voice. He did not step away. Instead, he concentrated on the leper. With his other hand, he reached over and held the wrapped hand holding the bell.

The healer said with quiet yet certain power, *"I am willing. Be clean!"*

Before the boy's astonished eyes, the leper straightened his body. As the man's cowl fell away from his face, Shai gasped sharply in shock, "Ohhhh!"

The leper's cheek and nose were now intact. They had been instantly healed. They were perfect. There was not even a pockmark visible.

The leper slowly straightened until he was standing tall to match Yeshua. Shoulders that were bent inwards slowly straightened. The surrounding crowd inhaled sharply as if one organism.

The youngster heard a ripping sound as the man's hands and feet tore out of the rags. The arm in a sling pushed outward, five perfect fingers stretching toward the Nazarene physician. Even ten toes pushed out of the rags binding his feet and gratefully wiggled in the dusty grass. The man touched his own face in amazement.

Shai heard a *thump* as the man's cane hit the ground. The man wiped tears away from his cheeks with fingers that had fingernails.

Then Shai heard the *clang* as the man intentionally dropped his bell. He was no longer a leper and did not need the bell any longer. He had been cured this very instant. The miracle that Shai had desired earlier occurred right before his eyes.

The startled - no, shocked - boy heard the man whisper, "Oh, thank you, Lord. Thank you, Lord." The man continued to repeat the heartfelt praise in whispers between huge sobs. Even his voice seemed smoother than it had been before.

Yeshua took off his robe and placed it on the former leper's shoulders. He covered his own mouth with his hand for privacy and whispered something quietly into the healed man's ear. Shai couldn't hear what was whispered, but he did hear the astonished gasps of people in the crowd.

"The leper is healed."

"Instantly."

"It cannot be. There is no cure."

"It's a miracle!"

"He did it with a mere touch of his hand."

"No, it was his words that healed him."

"Oh, Lord Elohim! How can this be?"

A man a few steps away whispered to his friend, "Yeshua healed another leper over a week ago. I witnessed that healing, too."

The Whistling Galilean

"He's got to be the Messiah, the one we've been waiting for," a woman near Shai sobbed in whispers.

The boy knew that he had seen a miracle. It could not have been anything less. The clearing shrank as the crowd around the healer moved forward in eagerness. Shai noticed Simon and Andrew next to Yeshua. They were soon out of Shai's view, surrounded, nearly smothered by many people wanting to be healed, too.

Shai wanted to stay but knew he could not. He had to go home. A dazed Shai made his way to his favorite beach where he stared at the horizon of the Sea of Galilee and the distant shores of the mountains. No mere man could have done what he had just seen. No mere man could cure leprosy. But Yeshua did heal that leper! Yeshua cured the leper with the mere touch of his hand and several spoken words. Shai had just witnessed that impossible event - no miracle.

The stranger he had met on this protected cove nearly a year ago now drew huge crowds to merely hear him speak. He was listened to, revered, and adored. The carpenter who had told him about his new career as a teacher had done that and much more. The man from little, insignificant Nazareth, who mended furniture had become a powerful healer and teacher indeed.

Shai wondered out loud, "O, my Lord Elohim. Who is this Yeshua?"

20

Stormy Seas

After dinner, Papa asked his two older sons to follow him to the fisherman's beach. "I want both of you to fish with me tonight. Fishel will join us. I know that this is your first night-time out on the boat, Shai. It will be a different experience for you. Ezra, I am relying on you and Fishel to explain and demonstrate what to do with the nets. Shai can already help me set the sails."

Shai was so excited. His father trusted him. His father recognized his skills and readiness. The nearly twelve-year-old jutted his jaw out in determination. He wanted to prove his father was right about him.

When they reached the busy beach, the first greeting came from Fishel. "Shalom, Shai. Lend a hand."

Shai returned the smile and hand wave. "It is so good to see you fishing again. You must be so happy."

"Yes, I am fully restored as a fisherman…finally. It took so long. It feels wonderful to be useful again and feed my own family."

Papa interrupted with an announcement to his group. "I have already ensured that the nets and other gear are aboard and ready. Let's get her in the water."

The Whistling Galilean

The eager youngster helped the gathered group of younger teens transfer the wooden trunks used to roll Papa's boat down the beach. Fishel and Ezra joined Papa to push *Ole Blue* on the rollers toward and into the water.

"Shai, hop aboard with me and handle the sails. We need to move out of the breaking waves to deeper, calmer waters. Quick."

Shai complied. As he expertly set the sail, he noticed that Simon's boat departed also. It was unusual to see Simon with the fishermen. Many other fishermen were already in the water or preparing to depart.

He heard Simon's penetrating voice order the fishermen remaining on the beach, "Now, leave now! All of you. As we discussed, no boats can be left on the beach."

The boy did not understand the urgency. He watched the remaining fishermen quickly move their boats into the water. Not all of them took time to gather needed fishing gear. Curious. Some rowed, some sailed. Shai was not surprised that all of the fishermen quickly did as Simon requested. After all, Simon was their trusted, respected leader. Soon, the beach was deserted.

Once the sail was set, the boy had time to look over the now-empty beach, one of his favorite spots. He had gazed at this stretch of sand from the vantage point of the water fewer times than he had fingers. It looked so serene and peaceful. He noticed a few people trickle onto the beach. They did not appear to be fishermen.

Shai felt Fishel's gentle elbow in the ribs. "The beach emptied as Simon ordered. You know Simon. *Simon says, we do.*"

The boy chuckled. Yes, he had witnessed that more than a few times. He felt included tonight. It felt good.

"Your hand must be functioning much better."

"Watch this." Fishel made a fist with it. It was not pretty or perfect, as the fingers still could not curl into his palm. This was probably as good as his recovery would get.

"Now, feel it." This time, the older teen took hold of two of Shai's fingers and squeezed hard. Shai didn't feel pressure from the outer fingers as a group, but he did feel the knuckles against the palm.

~ 193 ~

Jennifer Bjork

"That is so much stronger. You have worked hard. It shows."

As he released Shai's hand, his mentor just nodded and grinned.

Soon, there was a crowd gathered on the very spot from which they had sailed. Since the gathering arrived from the direction of Capernaum, Shai concluded that they were following the Nazarene physician. He scanned the beach for his tall friend. Soon, people on the beach did the same. They dispersed over the entire sandy surface seeking the incredible healer.

"There goes another group of Yeshua followers. My friends and I call them all 'the blind following the blind.'" Ezra pointed and laughed at those on the beach. Then he busied himself with a piece of gear.

It was a good thing that Ezra had moved away. Shai knew that his older brother's words were meant to rile him into doing something stupid that would remove him from consideration on future fishing trips. The younger boy wasn't about to let that happen, so he did not react at all. He maintained a stony composure that would mock the dead.

Sound carried well over water. Between adjustments to the sail, the boy in the boat watched the beach people search in vain. He even overheard bits of the louder comments.

"...did he go? Where?" a bearded man wondered.

"...in one of the boats," another man pointed.

"I think I see him!" a young woman jumped up and down to improve her vision.

That got the crowd churning like a hungry school of fish. Some even waded into the water, not caring about getting their clothes wet. One man helped another out of the water when his soaked, heavy robe pulled him under.

"Heal my daughter, Yeshua. Please heal her!" a rounded woman screamed.

The boy heard the urgency in their voices. He felt the ache in their hearts from disappointment. On this night, he doubted any one of them would get the miracle they each desired.

The beach soon became a small white crescent as the boat moved

The Whistling Galilean

farther away from shore, and the people became mere black dots. Shai heard the plaintive wail of a large, hopeful, determined, united group of a people toward the departing fishing boats, "Yeshua, come back. Yeshua, come back. Yeshua, we need you...."

Then it grew quiet, so Shai turned his gaze toward his older brother. Ezra and Fishel were laying out the long net. Without talking to each other, they both started with the top of the net. Ezra tied it to the bow cleat on the deck. Next, they laid it on the deck between the bow and the mast, straightening it as they went. After laying the net back on top of itself, they repeated the process of straightening it on the deck in the opposite direction, and over lapping itself. When they had finished laying the net on the deck, it lay in loose coils, ready to unfurl into the Galilee without any tangles. They were ready for a night of fishing.

Shai enjoyed sailing in *Ole Blue* under a full moon. It reflected enough light for him to see what his hands needed to do. He helped coil ropes and stack the baskets to hold their catch behind the mast. Finally, he stood by the mast feeling *Old Blue* react to the pulse of the swells. Papa's fishing boat rose bow first, then leveled out. Ultimately, the bow fell, and the stern rose. It was a subtle, gentle movement. He heard the *whosh* of the wooden hull propelled through the black sea during every downward glide.

Moonlight glinted on the tops of the swells and made what looked like a path straight toward him. Even though there were puffs of clouds in the sky, there were several openings through which stars glittered and sparkled. The sea breeze felt wonderful and smelled fresh. Shai was grateful to be included in this adventure.

Meanwhile, Simon sailed over toward Papa, and the two fishing boats sailed side by side. Shai's attention turned to Simon's white-hulled boat when the giant of a man hailed his father, "How goes it tonight, Yona?"

"It is a good night. I am blessed to have two of my sons with me tonight. Fishel has joined us, so we should do well. And you?"

"We are escaping the hoard tonight, as you probably noticed. Yeshua is aboard. After days of teaching and healing, the master is exhausted."

~ 195 ~

Shai blurted out, "Shalom, Yeshua, it is I, Shai."

When he made out which shape was his beach friend, Shai waved and made eye contact with him. The Nazarene stood in his light robe with a hand on the mast to steady himself in the gentle, undulating motions of the sea. Even from a distance, Shai recognized the healer, and in the moonlight, he saw what he interpreted as a smile. The boats were close enough that Shai noticed that the man looked tired. His shoulders hunched toward the deck. *Exhausted* was the perfect word for his appearance. Yeshua seemed to only have enough energy for a minimal wave.

The boy knew that now was not a time for conversation. So, he busied himself with Papa's boat again. His glances toward Simon's boat showed him when Andrew helped Yeshua to the stern of Simon's boat. He saw Andrew help the teacher onto a cushion.

That is when Papa turned *Ole Blue* into the wind to slow it down. When its wooden hull slowed to a glide, Shai furled the large sail, curling it in one continuous fold against the mast - back and forth, back and forth. He tied the rope with a special knot that Fishel had taught him. He couldn't remember the name. With a rapid yank on the tail of that knot, the sail could be released immediately to fill with air and get them underway in an emergency.

He was constantly being taught tricks to prepare him for any event at sea. Usually the event came at a crucial, unexpected, and inconvenient time.

Meanwhile, Ezra and Fishel worked side by side. In a steady, smooth stream, they lowered the net into the sea. Now, the boy's mentor provided a commentary about how and why they did what they did. The youngster tried hard to pay attention. He was so impressed watching his brother actually working that he missed some of his mentor's explanations. He was shocked to see his brother work smoothly with Fishel.

Fishel was the obvious leader of this team. Ezra was the helper. Shai had never seen his brother in these roles - worker, team member, helper. Those characteristics were unexpected.

As both fishermen lowered the net, Simon moved his boat. He

The Whistling Galilean

drifted next to *Ole Blue* on the opposite side of the net, now actively fishing. Not waiting for a word from anyone, Shai put the rope bumpers between the two boats to keep them from rubbing wood against wood. While doing this, he heard the fisherman with the reddish beard speak to Papa in a hushed tone, "...many healings tonight. The master fell asleep quickly. We do not want to awaken him, so we will not fish tonight."

Yona matched his hushed voice. "Who else is aboard with you?"

"My brother, Andrew, of course, and Mark, a new young disciple, and Matthew, the former tax collector, and a few others you have not met."

"We will continue to fish here all night. Hang around us, if you would like."

Now that the net was set, it was time to drift and wait.

Shai slipped to the stern where his father rested. "How long do we wait, Papa?"

"I watch the small glass floats at the top of the net. When I see them dip and jerk, I know that fish are getting trapped in the net. When the jerking slows down, it is time to pull the net in. I'll ask someone else to watch when I get tired. Are you interested?"

"Oh yes, Papa."

"Alright. You will be next."

Shai was thrilled. He was fishing with his father. He sat beside Papa Yona and just enjoyed the experience. With the weight of the net out of the boat, he noticed that *Ole Blue* floated higher in the water. The water surface was now well below the edge of the boat where he leaned over - about one and a half cubits below.

"Papa, does Ezra always work this hard when he is with you?"

"Of course, I do." Ezra interjected before his father could say anything. He plopped down beside Shai.

Papa concurred, "Yes, he does. That's what an apprentice fisherman does."

"You do not work beside me when we are supposed to be a team. Why not?" Shai accused his brother.

"I do, too."

~ 197 ~

"Liar. Just the other day -"

Papa interrupted, "Stop bickering, you two. That's enough. Do not be a tattletale, Shai."

Shai was even ready to argue with his father when Papa reached across to tap him on the shoulder, "I will discover the truth soon enough."

If looks counted for anything, his father's face contained the threat of great disappointment with a twinge of loving understanding. Then his father returned to his relaxed position in the stern of the boat, leaving the brothers together. Neither brother spoke for a long time.

Finally, Shai broke the frosty silence using a quiet voice, just for the two of them to hear. "You should know that I found out from Carmi that she does have an older sister named Rachel."

"So, you chose not to believe me?" Ezra mocked the sound of astonishment.

"Yes. You lie a lot. You just lied to Papa about working with me."

Ezra shrugged. "Little brothers will never understand the advantage of being the elder."

"I understand enough. You think that being the oldest means that you can be bossy and lazy. You think it means that you are entitled to not having to be nice or helpful. Since you became a teenager, you have lorded the fact that you are stronger, taller, wiser, better, have more experience - everything over me. Why?"

The gentle breeze had been building into a stronger wind. Shai's cheeks felt the difference. As the wind grew more powerful, waves started to rise on the Galilee, replacing gentle undulating swells in every direction he looked.

The younger boy grew concerned. He asked in a loud voice, "Is this dangerous, Papa?"

"Not yet."

As Shai watched the waves build, Papa called out in a loud voice, "Time to pull in the net. Fishel. Ezra."

Both fishermen had already reacted and were heaving it in. Using the rudder as a sculling oar, Papa kept the net on the leeward

The Whistling Galilean

side of the boat, the side away from the wind. Shai noticed that all of the weight caused the leeward side of the boat to slide deeper into the water. He wondered if the sea would soon begin to pour into the boat.

"Papa, are we in danger of sinking?"

"No. Hush now, Shai. We are busy."

Papa sculled the boat with the rudder to keep it as steady as he could. Fishel was on one side of the net and Ezra, the other. Each were double fisting the net grabbing whatever they could. Together, they yanked upward, dropping the net beside them and reaching over the side again for more handfuls.

"Shai, pull the net already in *Blue* at their feet toward the mast, sort out tangles and fish later. Just clear the deck. Hurry it up!" Papa had to yell this command over the growling howl of the wind.

The youngster pulled with all of his might. Every now and then one of his hands would grab not just net but something silvery that wiggled - a fish. It startled him, "Uuugh!"

He glanced around at the white caps on the huge waves. He noticed that Simon's boat had already untied from Papa's. It was bobbing a safe distance away.

Finally, the net was totally in the boat. That is when the rain began. Horizontal rain pellets blew into his eyes. There was barely any sideboard left. Shai was sure that his father's boat would be swamped, fill with water, and sink. He looked around to see if the other fishing boats were still visible and had the same problem. When the waves allowed, he could still make out Simon's white hull, but no other boat was visible in this heavy rain squall.

He wrapped both arms around the mast of *Ole Blue*. He was joined by Ezra. Fishel went to the stern to help Yona keep their bow steady in the now-breaking waves. It took four arms of two strong men.

As he hugged the mast, praying for deliverance, his grandfather's description of these sudden squalls came to mind. The Galilee sat in a basin surrounded by mountains. Grandpa had explained that the wind funneled through narrow mountain passes. This increased its speed. Both the velocity and force of the wind grew more powerful as it passed over the water. In real life, it was scarier than Grandpa had made it sound. Shai was afraid.

As they were thrown up, down, and around, Shai remembered being in such a storm once before. He had been on the beach, not in a boat. That storm had developed in about twenty minutes. Like it had during his experience on the beach, this wind rapidly grew into a furious squall.

The high pitch of the gale-force winds across the mast made it hard to think. Waves grew in height and worked into lines of white caps as their tips curled and sea foam blew off of them. Sea foam blew into the boat. Shai squeezed his eyes into mere slits.

Suddenly, the storm stopped. The wind ceased blowing, and the water of the Galilee became as flat as glass. Clouds immediately dissipated. Moonlight glowed on the nearly calm water's surface as it had before the storm. They had survived.

Dazed, the boy wiped his eyes to look at the three fishermen in *Ole Blue*. He was surprised to see the same astonishment on their faces as he felt. Fishel's mouth gaped wide open, and Ezra's eyes were as big as his food bowl. Papa muttered, repeating, "I do not believe it...not believe...no."

"Was this storm abnormal?" Shai's shaky voice asked no one in particular.

After clearing his throat, Papa answered as calmly as possible, "We get these storms occasionally, son, but they never stop so quickly. Large waves never become none at all immediately. That part was unusual."

His father walked around the boat, checking the siding and mast. As he passed by, he spoke to those in the boat with him, "Thanks for your help, Fishel. It took two of us tonight.

"Ezra, you stepped up to help just when needed. Good job.

"You, too, Shai. We needed you tonight."

Then his father waved both arms overhead and hailed the nearby boats. "We are fine. And you? Everybody alright? Injuries?"

The Whistling Galilean

Responses filtered to them from across the calm water. Shai was grateful that no one had been hurt.

Simon spoke out, "That was a scary, bad blow, Yona."

Fishel whispered, "Scary? Simon has seen a lot of storms. That one must have been especially bad for him to be afraid."

Ezra snorted, "Simon? He's never afraid of anything."

Shai watched as Fishel drummed the fingers of his good hand on the inside of the wooden hull. He heard the more experienced mentor ponder out loud, "Maybe Simon wasn't afraid for himself... after all, he is an experienced boater. Maybe his concern was to keep his teacher comfortable and safe."

Shai agreed with that assessment. His attention was diverted from their conversation when he heard the brothers arguing in the white-hulled boat.

Andrew accused, "You awakened Yeshua. Why, Simon? We were doing fine."

Simon defended, "I just wanted him to be ready to move if we needed to maneuver."

"Yes, but you asked, 'Teacher, don't you care if we drown?' That was a stupid question. Of course, he cares about us."

"Thanks for your confidence in me, Andrew." Now, Simon was being sarcastic.

Shai whispered to Fishel, "Do you think that Simon wished Yeshua would do something about the storm... or the people in the boat during the storm?"

"Who cares?" Ezra hissed.

"So, what happened, Andrew?" Shai impatiently yelled across the waves.

Andrew cupped his hands to yell his answer, "Yeshua arose from his sleep and looked around. He raised one hand and said to the raging winds, *'Quiet! Be still!'* That is the moment that the wind actually stopped blowing and the seas immediately became completely calm. Just like that."

Simon grunted agreement, then asked the other fishermen, "We have been seamen all of our lives. I have never seen a storm diffuse,

~ 201 ~

break apart, or disappear instantly like this one did. I have never seen anything like this instant calming of a raging storm in full gale. Have any of you?"

Shai heard a unison of *no's* while looking at the three others in his boat. He heard Fishel add his *no* to the others. Papa just shook his head in disbelief. So, his father had never seen anything like it either. There was no reaction from his older brother, now sitting alone on the bow. Now Shai was eager to ask his grandfather about his experiences with storms.

"Yeshua just said three words and the storm quit?" the boy asked the men in the nearby boat.

"Yes, young lad, our master spoke and stopped the winds with his words. That is what I saw and believe happened. I have no other explanation that fits." Simon concluded.

By this point in time, the white-hulled boat had drifted closer to *Ole Blue*. Shai watched Yeshua approach the side of his boat and circle his hand to include the men in Simon's boat. He heard the master teacher speak, "Now, that you have discussed what happened, I ask you of little faith, why were you so afraid? You witnessed the wind and the waves answer to my command. Who do you believe I am?"

Papa interrupted, "We must get home. There are many chores before bed. We may even have some fish in the net that need to be transferred to the baskets. Shai, set the sails again."

"Wait, Papa. I need to know the answer."

Fishel and Ezra set to untangling the net, putting the fish in the baskets, and cleaning up their gear.

"Unfurl the sail, Shai. We head for home. Now!"

The frustrated boy pulled the end of the cloth sail away from the mast. Carefully stepping through the netting on deck, he worked himself toward the stern of *Ole Blue* pulling the line attached to the foot of the sail tight as he went. Other boats were already underway. He saw the white hull eventually follow them as he busied himself helping the teens untangling the net and the remaining ropes. If he had answered Yeshua's question tonight, what would he have said?

The Whistling Galilean

On their way home, he had time to wonder about Yeshua. He had witnessed the tall man perform impossible, miraculous healings. Those healings were instantaneous, also, like tonight's storm. Tonight, he had heard from men he trusted, respected, and known his entire life that this same Nazarene had controlled a natural event. Stopping gale-force winds instantaneously was also impossible. Yeshua had demonstrated to those on the water that he could control nature.

Shai wondered out loud, "Who is he? He cannot be a man like us. If he isn't, who is he?"

21

The Gift of Joy

SHAI JOINED HIS MOTHER ON MARKET DAY AGAIN. DESPITE WHISTLING bird songs with her and occasionally seeing Carmi, Shai now dreaded these days in Capernaum. The Romans still collected taxes to the marketplace, requiring only their coin of the realm. They had hired a new tax collector after Levi had left. The boy feared and disliked going to town. He hated admitting this fear to himself, but it was true.

Finally at home at the end of a day in town, Shai and Mama unloaded the baskets together, both grateful that their day had been uneventful.

"It's nearly time for our evening meal, son. You were up early this hot summer morning."

"I beat the rooster, Mama."

"Then you were the rooster this morning… and you were like a donkey, too."

He brayed like the gray beast of burden they did not own. As they chuckled, he imitated a donkey stomp in fake disgust. He knew that she enjoyed his humor.

The Whistling Galilean

"I was grateful that the Romans were not a bother today. They now recognize us as some of the Galilean poor and no longer concentrate on examining our baskets," Mama said.

"I never thought that I would be grateful to be poor, but I am."

"Me, too. I will need you to help train Adi to carry the baskets. You are twelve now. That makes Adi nine-years-old, almost ten. Can I count on you?"

Shai had forgotten that his sister would soon be old enough to replace him as Mama's helper, just like Shai had done for Ezra. He looked forward to that day. "I'll be glad to help."

"I know you can hardly wait. Soon, women will do women's work."

"I am glad about that, but maybe a man should go with you on market day. Capernaum has become a dangerous place to visit."

"I thought the new tax collector would be a problem for us. He is merely their obedient servant. We have not heard of anyone being flogged for a while." She pulled a wrapped bundle from a basket. "I can finish the rest of this, son. Go clean up and relax for a while, but be home before dark."

Shai promised to obey and quickly headed for the nearby marshy creek, an inlet to the Galilee. There was calm water and a flat, hard-packed delta to walk on. He wanted to digest the many events of late. Most of the events included Yeshua, such as the healing of the leper and the immediate calming of the storm on the Galilee.

Obviously, the Nazarene physician had a special power. He had told Shai that his power came from Elohim. Could Shai obtain that power, too? Grandfather had not been well lately and had taken to sleeping even more than usual. Could Shai heal the old man he loved?

Once the whistling youngster arrived at the calm embayment, he noticed the man he had just been thinking about sitting on a rock under a willow. He seemed to be staring at his feet stretched out into the cool water. He was wiggling his toes.

The man looked up as the boy approached. "Why, hello. I have been waiting for you."

~ 205 ~

Jennifer Bjork

"Shalom Yeshua. You are just the person I was thinking about. I want to talk to you, also."

They both grinned at each other.

"I am surprised that you are here. You have been so busy. What have you been doing?" The twelve-year old asked as he sat down on the adjacent rock.

"Relaxing. Resting my tired feet."

"Resting from what? It doesn't seem like teaching is hard work. Not like carpentry or stonework or fishing. How can it make you so tired?"

"Teaching is not hard physical work, but it is hard mental work. In this case, it is also hard spiritual work. I just gave my followers some of my power, my spirit. I sent them off to not only teach, but to heal. There is too much work for one man to do anymore. This has made me tired, so I am resting."

"Oh, I see."

Shai did not really understand. He did understand being tired and needing rest. He did understand that teaching could be mentally draining because, at times, learning made him tired. But he did not understand the sharing of power part at all.

"Are you saying that you shared with them your ability to perform healing miracles?"

"Yes, I did."

Shai nodded, trying to appear wise to his friend. He had no clue how Yeshua had performed these miracles and what powerful spirit he was talking about. Maybe Shai had that power, too. Maybe he just wasn't old enough yet to discover it.

"Yeshua, how do you heal people? You are not a physician or an herbalist. What do you do?"

"First, I examine the person's heart."

"Did the leper you healed on the mountainside by Bethsaida have a broken heart?"

"No, he did not. He had a strong, willing, trusting heart. He believed that I could heal him. His trust and belief in me helped me heal him."

The Whistling Galilean

"And Alter, the paralyzed man lowered to you in Simon's mother-in-law's house?"

"He, too, believed in me. His friends had complete faith that I not only could, but that I would, heal their friend. You were there and saw the result."

"Yes, Alter rose and walked."

The Nazarene splashed his feet in the shallow water. "Shai, the people that need me, that trust me, have the faith to be healed. Remember, I pray first for the power to heal. It is Elohim that provides that healing power. It is Elohim that heals."

"Can I use Elohim's power to heal, too?"

"I just gave some of my healing power to my disciples. If it is Elohim's desire for you to heal, Shai, we will both learn that through prayer. Right now, you need to finish growing into an adult. Do you have someone you would like healed?"

"Yes, I do. Grandfather has not been well lately."

"He is special to you. I am sure that you are aware that he is reaching the end of his years with you. You will miss him greatly when he does die. I will visit him if you would like."

"I know you have many demands on you. He enjoys you and would enjoy a visit."

"Wonderful, I will swing by the house in a few days."

After they sat in silence for several minutes, the inquisitive boy pondered, "I don't understand so many things. How do you select the men whom you are teaching?"

"We have discussed this already. I hope you remember that Elohim selects my disciples. I rely on the Lord's guidance through my prayers. We desire that the varied backgrounds and personalities of the twelve disciples demonstrate that I willingly teach everyone, even those that are disliked, feared, rebellious, or dishonest. I am here for the young and the old, men and women, rich and poor, popular and outcast, and even the master and the slave. Matthew, the former Levi, was unhappy. He disliked what he was doing. He hungered for my words as you do, so when I provided an opportunity for him to make a change in his life, he jumped on it like a cat on a mouse."

~ 207 ~

Shai mumbled, "Oh, I remember now."

The man beside him continued to splash his toes. As the tall man talked, the twelve-year-old removed his sandals, too. Now, they both freely splashed making rhythms with their feet.

"Yeshua, I have something serious to ask you."

Yeshua stretched and faced the boy, giving Shai his complete attention. "I am listening."

"I went to Capernaum with Mama today. I heard whispers of dissent against Rome in the marketplace. I agree with the dissenters. I, too, hate living under Roman rule. They are so savage, so brutal. Many people want you to lead a revolt against Rome. Why don't you speak out against Rome?"

"I dislike tyranny and men who rule through fear. I do speak out, young one. I teach, and through my actions, I show another way to live. My message is of caring and love and justice and honesty. My message is for men to be peaceful, not to fight through rebellion and war. You heard my talk in the amphitheater that day you sat with Carmi. You know my message, Shai."

The boy was surprised. "I didn't know you saw us there together. There were so many people in that bowl of the valley." He felt his checks redden. "I really like her, Yeshua. Did you know that we even held hands?"

"I do know that you like her so much that her mere presence takes over your thoughts."

"That is true. She is so easy to be with..." Shai's deep exhale exuded contentment.

After another pause, Yeshua interrupted the boy's thoughts with a glance from the corner of a crinkled, grinning eye, bringing them back to his point. "You know my message about peace."

"Well, many present that day did agree with you. I heard your words, but I do not understand how peace can remove this horrible Roman rule."

"Evil men do much harm. It hurts me to see it and the pain it causes to innocent people. But I cannot be the type of ruler some

The Whistling Galilean

people desire. Trust me, Shai, love will triumph. Pray that you will see that truth. I do."

"I will try."

"Your family and community demonstrate a loving way to live. They provide food to others in need outside of your community, even to me and my disciples and their families. I am glad you have that example in your life."

"Are you saying that Elohim blesses those that help others?"

"Yes, I am."

"Well, am I correct to conclude that the men and families that follow you are blessed directly by learning about Elohim and indirectly by families like mine?"

"That is true. Very wise, Shai."

The twelve-year-old hardly ever heard those words and was pleased that he wasn't wrong, again.

Yeshua redirected their discussion to something of great importance. "Have you accepted my challenge to reconcile with a family member? Have you accepted one unpleasant thing about Ezra?"

"Yes, I did. I told him that I am no longer jealous that he was presented with Grandfather's fillet knife. Occasionally, I still am. I now have two gifts: time with Grandpa and his own wood carving knife. I no longer covet the fillet knife like I did when we first met. It may have worked."

"It sounds like you are breaking down that barrier with your brother. Are you both friends again?"

"Not yet."

"Then do not stop trying. You may have to continue to be the adult, the mediator. Have you thought of a second unpleasant thing to accept?"

"Another? No." Shai was shocked at the thought.

"One worked well for you. Why not another?"

Their splashing feet kicked the water higher and higher as Shai chewed on these thoughts.

Yeshua let him digest before adding, "We all live according to

~ 209 ~

the choices we make. The men who follow me as disciples all freely made that choice – a life following Elohim. They chose the life of hope, joy, peace, and love."

Yeshua continued, "Did you know that you, too, have that same free choice? You may not realize that you choose every day to love and obey Elohim, the Creator of the universe. He loves you very much and desires your love and obedience. Do you speak to Him daily?"

"Every day?"

"Yes. Even I choose to love and obey Elohim with every step I take and every breath that I inhale. You can make that your choice, too."

"Well…I am not consistent like you are."

He enjoyed talking to Yeshua about things of the heart that disturbed him. Shai had so much to learn about so many things. Amazingly, there had always been a satisfactory enlightening. Over the year and a half that they had been friends, he had become comfortable with the deeply personal conversations he had with this tall Nazarene.

The topic of prayer made him felt uncomfortable, so Shai shifted his seat on the hard rock. Something troubled him. Now, he felt unsure, embarrassed, and insufficient. He decided to speak about that. "I really do not know how to pray to the holy Lord of Israel."

"First, praise and thank the holy Lord. Use your own words, but listen to your parents pray over a meal or Rabbi Selig start a Sabbath service. Their words might help you start your own prayers. Then, tell Elohim what is on your heart - what troubles you, mistakes you have made, and gladness that you have shared. Do not go to Elohim merely to ask for His help. Develop a relationship with Him, just like you have with me."

"But it has been easy with you. I can see you and your expressions. The Lord is invisible."

"You may not see Him, but you should feel Him in your heart, as you feel me and my love toward you."

"I do. I will try. It seems so easy for you."

The Whistling Galilean

"I treat Elohim as my father and share with Him constantly. It is a strong relationship, the most important in my life, Shai. He is my guide, my compass, and my sustainer. You have already started the wonderful relationship that you seek with Elohim by sharing these concerns openly with me. Do not try to keep your thoughts hidden from Him."

Shai nodded his acknowledgement and hoped that he could do as Yeshua described. He felt that he had to take the first big stride, again. As he scratched his neck, he decided that the next time he prayed, he would pretend Elohim was just behind a tree trunk or out of view. He also decided to start each prayer by sharing one good deed he had done or experienced. Shai hoped that would help.

The boy was still troubled. "Yeshua, I find it difficult to speak up and support you. Two people are problems for me. Specifically, Ezra, who can easily beat me up, and my former best friend, Dov, who seems to have abandoned me. Neither one of them believe you are worthy of even having followers. Ezra calls your followers "*the blind*" because he considers you blind, also."

"I understand that it is not an easy path to choose, Shai. I appreciate your honesty. I myself cannot imagine choosing any other way. Living to please Elohim and seeking his great love is the only path for me, regardless of the consequences."

"If I choose to seek Elohim with all of my being like you do… do I have to leave my family to follow you, too? Do I need to do so right now? Are you going to ask me to follow you, too?"

With a small chuckle, the man answered, "No, Shai. I am already working with the twelve men chosen for me. I teach and train these disciples constantly. They, too, sometimes have doubts and misgivings. You, my friend, are still a boy. You still need your family just as they need you. When the time is right, you will find your voice."

With relief, Shai exhaled a satisfied, "That's good. In that case, I, too, choose to be like you and follow and obey Elohim."

Upon further reflection, Shai asked another concern, "Yeshua, you said the disciples are becoming your good friends. Will they replace me?"

"No, it definitely does not mean that." Yeshua chuckled softly again. "You, my first Galilean friend, will always be my friend, my close friend, even when we are apart."

"Good."

Shai felt satisfied as they sat and splashed in the shady, shallow pool.

The man reached into his belt pouch and pulled out a palm-sized object, then handed it to the boy. "Do you remember this?"

"Yes. It is the bird carving you were working on with Grandpa and I." Shai turned it over and over in his palm, "It looks finished."

"It is."

"It is beautiful, Yeshua. The feathers you carved are so lifelike, and the eyes are perfectly placed. I see an unusual hole between the two halves of its beak."

Yeshua took the rounded songbird and pointed. "Do you see the second hole just under the tail? Look here."

The boy leaned over the man's hand to see where he pointed. "Yes."

As Shai looked up into those sparkling hazel eyes, Yeshua told him, "The holes are connected. It was difficult, but I bored a hole all the way through the bird without damaging it. This little palm-sized river warbler is a whistle. Cover the tail with your lips and blow, like this."

The sound of a soft warble slipped out of the wooden bird's beak.

"That is incredible!" Shai jumped off of the rock in excitement. "Wonderful! Can I try it?"

Yeshua handed it back, "Of course, my friend."

Shai blew. The carving warbled. He blew and warbled some more. He was thrilled. He noticed that the whistle produced higher or lower pitches depending on how hard he blew.

"This is fun. It is different than whistling, yet it sounds like a bird. Maybe, it is even closer to the bird's warble than our whistling."

After some more puffs through the carved bird's carefully

The Whistling Galilean

crafted hole, the boy felt Yeshua's warm hand on his shoulder. "Shai, I made it for you."

"What?" Shai distrusted his ears, so questioned the speaker with his eyes.

"I want you to have this whistle. I call this carved bird *Joy* for one of your best characteristics, joy and exuberance."

"For me?"

"Yes. Look at me, Shai." The master craftsman waited for the pre-teen to settle and focus. "The Creator filled you with joy. As you grow to trust Him, He will overflow your heart so that you may overflow with that joy and share it with others. That is His desire. That is my desire, as well."

Shai became pensive as he fingered his new gift. "Thank you, Yeshua. This is the greatest treasure."

"The whistle is a reminder of the great gift from Elohim to me - you. It is a reminder of our friendship, and my appreciation and love for you." Yeshua let that sink in. "Don't tell anyone that I made it for you. Keep it a secret between us. Soon there will be long periods of time that I must travel away from the Galilee. I will miss you. I want you to have something with which to remember me. Like the bird you are holding, my love for you remains with you always."

"Oh, my goodness. Handmade by your hands. It is so special. I treasure it already and will keep your secret...again."

Shai looked at the realistic bird whistle in his hands. He considered this gift as precious as his food bowl carved by Papa. How could he show his appreciation? He had nothing to give in return. He thought hard.

Before long, their combined splashes united into a patterned rhythm. His giggles soon became full-on laughter in response to Yeshua's laughter and contentment. The boy accentuated his laughter with a big splash of water.

"Shai. Joyful, gentle people are very special. Surround yourself with them when you are able."

With a wiggly stretch, Shai held his arms high in the air. "Aah... that feels good."

Jennifer Bjork

Yeshua stood and stretched, too. "I enjoy being around you. You are a special person in my life. You bring me joy and relaxation."

"Really? I am glad."

"Yes, really."

Shai announced, "Yeshua, I know what to share with you. I have nothing of value to give you, but I know many games. Do you know how to skip a stone on the water?"

"Why don't you teach me now."

Leaving their sandals behind, they walked farther up the stream, the younger boy leading the tall man. The shade provided along the riverbed was comfortably cool. They both warbled like birds as they walked in the water of the shallow stream. Occasionally, Shai pulled out his new gift. Instead of whistling with his lips, he blew a warble with *Joy.*

Not far upstream, sandy muddy sediment changed to sand and smooth pebbles.

"Here is where we select our stones." The young lad tried to emulate Fishel's patient manner as he taught his adult friend. "This part is important, critical, so pay attention. The stone needs to be smooth, thin, and flat."

They both bent over and searched with their hands, hefting one rock after another. The man asked with his eyes as he showed his shorter companion the stone in his hand.

"No. That one is too big."

A further search revealed one that was acceptable.

"You selected a good one. See how thin it is? Here, hold it and feel the nice, even weight."

Yeshua tossed it up and down in his calloused hand to feel its weight. "I see."

They both collected twelve smooth stones. Then they walked together out through the marsh reeds toward the open water. The water was shallow in the inlet, so they had to wade on the soft bottom sand well away from the shore where the water deepened to calf deep along Shai's legs.

"This is a good place to skip stones. See how calm and flat the water is? No waves."

The Whistling Galilean

"Yes, I do. Now what?" The relaxed healer smiled and seemed to be enjoying himself.

"You balance the bottom flat of the stone on your middle finger. Put your index or pointing finger on one end. Lightly hold the top flat with your thumb...like this." The boy demonstrated as the man watched.

"Good." Like Fishel did with him, he complimented his neophyte pupil as he provided the instructions.

"Now, throw side arm, putting a twist on the stone at the last minute with your index finger...like this."

In the demonstration, the stone skipped on top of the surface of the flat water three times before sinking.

"That wasn't my best throw. I have gotten up to six skips. Anyway, the idea is to have the flat part of the thrown stone remain flat or parallel with the water. You probably need to bend over so that your hand is closer to water level."

He waited patiently for his companion to throw a stone. The Nazarene selected a smaller stone and threw. It skipped four times.

"Good throw. You got more skips than I did - beginner's luck." With a click of his tongue, he challenged, "Watch out. My turn...I'm going to try to beat four skips."

The two friends spent time tossing stones, matching skip for skip. They walked back up the river, laughing and chatting, to rearm. The young Galilean was so intent on their activity and good time together that he did not notice the group of boys waiting to join in. When he did notice, he recognized the twins from Capernaum.

Gil called out first, "Hi, Shai-ooo."

Even Dov appeared out of the reeds. With a mere nod of acknowledgement, the taller boy announced, "I haven't played skip-the-stone for a long time. Did you tell Yeshua that this is not just a way to pass time? It is a serious competition. I challenge anyone to beat my best throw."

Before Shai could respond, the man from Nazareth smiled directly at the new arrivals. "Why don't you boys join us? I accept your challenge, Dov."

~ 215 ~

They eagerly waded out to form an even line.

The competition began with Yeshua's words, "Okay, Dov, show us your best throw."

Dov pursed his lips and furrowed his forehead in concentration. Then he threw his stone.

Yeshua congratulated him, "Five skips. Can anyone beat that?"

They all took turns throwing. Soon, Shai matched Dov with five skips, "Yes! We are tied."

Gil reached six skips. Time passed quickly. Sounds of grunts and the rhythmic *splish* of the stone bouncing off the calm water punctuated the paling sunlight.

Before they knew it, Yeshua had tied Gil's best throw. Then, Yeshua announced, "Everyone gets one more throw. It is time to go home."

One by one, the boys tried and failed. That left Shai, Dov, and Yeshua with a turn to throw their stone.

"You go first, Shai," Dov said.

Shai wanted to have a good showing, but by now, he did not care how many skips his throw generated. The afternoon had been fabulous already.

Together, they counted the bounces of Shai's stone off the water, "One... two... three... four... five... six."

"Good toss. You matched Gil and I." Yeshua commented.

"Watch this one, Shai. I saved my best stone for last." In front of his desired audience, Dov heaved with all of his might.

Again, they counted the skips in unison, "One...two...three...four...five...six...seven."

"I win!" Dov raised both arms in victory. "I am the best!"

As he strutted away from those remaining in the water, he shouted back over his shoulder, "You should always side with me, Shai, not losers."

Shai watched the obviously prideful Dov depart. He realized that their friendship was broken. It was unrepairable. For months he had been preparing himself emotionally for this very moment. He was surprised that he no longer felt wounded or hurt. He realized

The Whistling Galilean

that emotionally, he had connected with Carmi, Grandfather, and especially with Yeshua. Even his brother, Ezra, was softening. Today with Dov, he had a surprising revelation. His feelings of friendship were replaced by lack of respect and distance – even disgust.

The other boys said their farewells with friendly waves and headed into the forest.

Shai looked over at Yeshua. "I will remember what you said about surrounding myself with joyful people."

"Good."

"I enjoyed this joyful afternoon with you. I will really treasure the bird whistle like I treasure your friendship and kindness. I will call her the same name you gave it, *Joy*. This hand-carved whistle will always remind me of you. Thank you."

"The whistle is a gift of loving gratitude, from me to you. Remember, Shai, you are the joyful person in my life. I will reveal another secret to you - you are Elohim's gift to me."

"Really?"

"Yes. The Lord knew I would need times of unbridled joy."

"Oh, my. Yeshua, you are so kind. I trust you, believe in you, like no one else in my life. I treasure you more than your gift to me."

"I treasure you, too, Shai."

The pre-teen knew it was late. As much as he hated that their time together had to end, the twelve-year-old was happy to depart with the loving words, *I treasure you* ringing in his ears. He lingered at the edge of the marsh with a sigh of contentment. From that location, he watched his adult friend hefting his final stone.

The man from Nazareth reared back his hand and threw hard with a twisting sidearm. The stone skipped - six... seven... eight... nine... ten... eleven... twelve times - before it sank. Shai had never seen a toss like that!

He heard his friend's contented chuckle.

He watched Yeshua remain in the water with a bowed head. His words floated out over the water skyward: "I thank you, Father, Lord of Heaven and earth, for the blessing of another day healing and teaching. I praise you because you hide the important things from the wise, those that should know and be in your service. They do not listen to my words. They do not repent of their evil plots. They make their laws more important than following and honoring you. But you, O Father, do reveal important things to children - enjoyment of your glorious creation, enjoyment of new skills, enjoyment of each other...but especially just feelings of pure joy. Joy is from you. Yes, Father, for this is your good pleasure, as it is mine. Thank you for the blessing of Shai in my life."

22

Camping in Tents

"Timber!"

"Look out below."

"Here comes another one."

Shai joined the young voices around him in the palm grove as he sawed a palm branch from the tree he had climbed. He loved this time of year. After the long, hot, virtually rainless summer, Shai's energy had wilted with the drying leaves on the trees. Now it was early fall, time for some early rains. As the temperatures cooled, his energy rekindled. This was the time of year that everyone took a week-long vacation together. They went to the countryside and camped in canvas tents known as Sukkoth, or booths.

They were climbing trees now, but for days, he and other boys had energetically gathered and cut downed tree limbs for tent supports and cooking fires. Naturally, there had been games associated with their tasks, like occasional sword fights with the poles and sticks they collected.

What he really enjoyed was doing something different - different from learning to become a Jew in school, learning to become a

~ 219 ~

Jennifer Bjork

fisherman, honoring the Lord in the synagogue on the Sabbath, and doing the many chores around the house that were necessary to stay clean, healthy, and fed. Chores included gathering water at the well, chopping wood for the cooking fire, weeding the family garden, patching the stucco walls and roof with fresh mud, and feeding the community animals. It wasn't a boring life, just a life full of routines.

During the week before their vacation, sailmakers sewed left over pieces of canvas to create the sleeping shelters. Fishermen dried fish, wrapped them in clean banana leaves, and packed them into baskets. Women wrapped together various crops they had grown and herbs they had dried. Men supervised the careful piling of all the gear, poles, and food onto donkey-pulled carts.

Poor Mama Anat! As usual, it was the women and girls that worked the hardest. Of course, they gathered their food by harvesting ripened crops and picking ripened fruit. Since this Hebrew festival was to give the Lord thanks for the bounteous crops, the women hand-picked the best of all they had grown. With special care, they separated the largest and the most perfect produce as an offering to the Lord.

Even the palm leaves that Shai and other twelve-year-old boys were cutting from the trees for use in the holy festival could not have any insect or wind damage.

Shai liked climbing trees. His lean, lithe-body easily walked up a bent palm tree to cut ripe coconuts or bananas and, of course, some palm leaves. He used two tools, a knife and a climbing strap. The ankle-wide circular strap was tied loosely in a single large loop around the tree trunk and his body. His father had loaned him his special knife with a saw-tooth edge on one side. This sharp knife with a hole in the handle was tied to his belt by a long cord as a precaution. If he dropped this tool, it could seriously injure anyone below him.

As his bare feet curved around the trunk, he leaned forward and slid the loose circular leather strap upward. He moved like an inchworm. His back straightened while he slid the strap upward. Then it curved while he leaned back, tightening the strap around

~ 220 ~

The Whistling Galilean

the trunk. This held his body in place. Then, as he walked his feet up the trunk, his back straightened out again. Once the strap was shoulder-high on the trunk, he leaned backward against the strap to hold himself in place.

The scroll-thin breeze on his skin felt wonderful. The rough palm bark on his feet made him feel alive. He enjoyed the sight of emerald-blue Galilee and the purplish-brown halo of mountains surrounding it. He enjoyed hearing excited voices up and down the beach as men and boys prepared for the feast, parade, and their daily living in the countryside.

Unfortunately, there was a fly in the ointment. The commands from his older brother Ezra sapped the joy out of the air. This job should have been fun, but it wasn't. "King" Ezra shouted orders at him in a constant tirade. As usual, since he was the oldest, Papa had given Ezra command of this operation. He was the boss, and Shai, his slave worker - again.

Despite the thawing of their relationship in private within the immediate family, in public, Ezra was his same bossy self.

Therefore, Ezra lorded his position of authority over Shai, yelling at the top of his lungs, "Shai, raise the strap."

"I just did." The pitch of Shai's voice floated down in a dull monotone.

"Good, now, lean back against the strap."

"I already have. Just look up."

"Lean and walk your feet upward."

"I'm already on the next step. You forget that I've picked coconuts with Fishel."

"Papa left me in charge, so you have to listen to me."

The younger already knew what to do because he had cut occasional fruit during his training with Fishel. The two of them had enjoyed drinking sweet coconut milk and drying the copra coconut meat under a fine mesh cheesecloth. Therefore, he felt that he didn't need Ezra to tell him what to do, but, as usual, Ezra refused to listen to him or to acknowledge that he had acquired some skills.

So, to pass the time, the twelve-year-old mostly shut up and

Jennifer Bjork

imagined doing the job with beautiful Carmi standing below him with arms outstretched upwards to him, as if she was ready to embrace him, only him. He imagined that it was she and not Ezra who caught the dates from the date palms, coconuts from the coconut palms, bananas from the banana palms, and new, healthy, bug-free, palm fronds from each type of tree for the festival. It was her joyful voice of encouragement and not Ezra's curt commands that he imagined ringing in his ears.

*Ah, yes. One day...*he thought hopefully.

Eventually, the family and the community were ready. The afternoon before the festival parade and solemn ritual, everyone took what they needed to the Sukkoth gathering spots where they would spend the next week. The men and donkeys had already toted several loads to the hillside. This was the last load to carry - the perishables, water, and people that could not walk that far on their own.

Now, families walked together in groups. Shai's family combined with two other adjacent families. Ezra and Papa walked with the owner of the donkey pulling their cart. Grandpa rode on the cart carrying the tents, cook pots, fire logs, and produce. Shai walked beside him to keep him company, and Mama followed behind with the other women and children.

They headed directly toward the community's designated area in the countryside past the orchards. This area was surrounded by hills. It was rocky and too far from wells or streams to have been plowed into an agricultural area. It was relatively flat and treeless. Positioned at the edge of a mountainous area, this location was still considered to be wild.

As they walked, Shai and the beloved old man in the cart talked.

"This is my first time riding in the cart. It is a rougher journey than walking, jars my back." Grandpa's voice bounced as if someone was pounding his back as he spoke.

Shai tried to add a positive note. "Our campsite is just behind that big rock over there, the same spot as last year. I am glad you will be with us."

~ 222 ~

The Whistling Galilean

"I wouldn't miss the opportunity to thank Elohim for a good year. The feast is worth the trip. The night sky is incredible."

"I am grateful Yeshua stopped by to see you. I noticed that your cough is gone."

"Yes, his cheer and warm hand did make me feel better."

Ezra dropped back to match Shai stride for stride.

Grandpa welcomed him. "Glad to see you with the family, grandson 'Number One'."

Shai had never heard the Elder address his brother by that nickname. That was new. He sure did not want to be called "Number Two."

Ezra patted Elder's knee. "For now, Elder. Got your knife with me to fillet Papa's big fish for the feast tomorrow. See?"

"Number One" pushed aside his robe to expose the sheathed knife hanging on his belt. At that instant, Shai felt a strong pang of jealousy. He had not seen it or thought about it for months. It was a fabulous knife. He realized he still desired it.

Grandpa smiled, "Oh, good. I am glad that you will represent us - me - in doing that important carving task. Did you sharpen her?"

"You know I did, just as you taught me."

So, Grandpa spent time with Ezra, too. That was interesting. Shai was not aware that Ezra wanted to spend any time with family. Well, it was alright, as long as the two of them did not compete for the old man's attention…like they were doing now.

Shai fingered his own belt and slipped out the carved bird *Joy*. He blew a few notes on the hand-crafted whistle. It wasn't exactly a replacement for the knife, but it did improve his mood.

Grandpa finally noticed. "That sounds just like a bird. How did you whistle like that?"

Shai grinned, showing him the carved bird. "Blow in the tail and the bird tweets. Try it."

Grandpa complied, then examined the carved bird. "It is beautiful and sounds gleeful. Where did you find something so special?"

That was when Papa interrupted. "We have arrived. Ezra and Shai, I need your help to set up the tent."

~ 223 ~

Shai quickly retrieved the whistle and slipped it back under his belt. "Alright, Papa. I am ready."

The lad helped his father and "Number One" dig the fire pit and set up two tents. This hard, dusty work involved the entire family. Papa selected two tent sites on the edge of a hill slope. This provided an area for the little ones to safely play.

Mama naturally led the family in song to make the tasks go faster. Each song had a working rhythm that guided particular tasks - removing rocks from the sleeping areas, carrying baskets, pounding tent pegs, stretching canvas, and so forth.

Shai enjoyed working together as a family. The two smaller kids helped Mama lay out bedrolls for sleeping. She organized her small helpers as they covered the baskets of food, cook pots, and gourds.

He watched his father's muscles ripple under tanned skin as he worked. He was a man's man - hardened by years of physical work. The twelve-year-old's desire was that he would become a muscular man like his father. In addition, he hoped to be handsome for Carmi, of course.

By their touches, grins, and teasing, he saw that it was Mama that softened Papa. She fostered humor and manners. He hoped and dreamed that, maybe one day, he and Carmi would act in that same caring, tender, playfully teasing, and loving way as his parents.

After a quick meal, it was time to look at the stars. From past experience, he knew that they would do the same thing every night of the week. Before bed, his family walked to the top of the hill.

Tonight, Shai and Papa helped Grandpa up the shallow, well-traveled slope. The boy sat beside his grandfather on some tufts of grass. There were no torches or lights to diminish the stars. He stared in amazement at the multitude of twinkling lights in the dark night sky. Just like on *Ole Blue*, Papa showed them stars that the mariners used for navigation. This time, Mama and Adi could also learn about the orbs in the darkened sky. Grandpa described several of them, too.

Once back inside the tent shared with Ezra and Grandpa, Shai found it hard to sleep. Even though he was tired, he was excited to be sleeping in a tent. It was different than sleeping inside his home. He

The Whistling Galilean

imagined wild, fierce animals in the hills beyond them. He imagined fighting them off to protect Carmi. These dreams didn't help him sleep at all.

The next day after their morning blessings, his family put on clean clothes and walked toward the orchard. Most of the palm fronds were already placed in neat piles. Shai grabbed enough for his family. Without instruction, everyone lined the orchard path and held a selected palm frond or poplar branch.

Under gently waving branches, the priests arrived with great fan-fare. He heard the plaintive wail of the ram's horns grow louder and therefore closer. Finally, he could see the trumpeters clad in white robes. Boys who were to enter the priesthood carried clay pots of smoking incense. Shai spotted a friend from school, Heno, but couldn't catch his eye. He imagined how proud Heno's parents were to have their son participating in this important ceremony.

Several bearded Levite priests followed. They wore richly embroidered robes. Gold threads glimmered as the sunlight captured their movements.

Then came the shepherds walking beside a small portion of the priests' herd of goats. All of the yearling goats selected as a fragrant sacrificial offering to the Lord could have no blemishes, just like the fruit and vegetables gathered earlier. Only the most perfect were offered to their most perfect Lord.

Everyone closed in behind the shepherds to join this community-wide parade. People around Shai joyfully waved their fronds or branches, saying,

"Bless Hosanna in the highest."

"Thanks be to the Lord of Israel."

They walked slowly and gathered at the base of another hill where an altar had been erected in front of an elaborate tent. Trumpeters, incense carriers, and robed priests gathered at the top of that hill.

The head priest, a rabbi that Shai didn't recognize, said the prayers for the community:

Jennifer Bjork

"O, holy Lord of Israel, we are gathered to thank
you. You have been generous to your chosen
people. It is you that have blessed your people with
a bountiful crop of fruit and vegetables. It is you that
have blessed your people with a bountiful amount
of fish. It is you that have blessed your people with
a bountiful crop of yearling goats. You are the one
who provides for and cares for your people. O, holy
Lord of Israel, we thank you."

By lot, Shai's community had been selected as the first to offer
their blemish-free and best produce. Mama Anat gave Papa Yona
the selected greens and fruit representing the best from her garden.
Papa already held a package of fresh fish he had recently caught. He
joined the other men approaching the altar area.

A group of Levite priests stood downhill from the altar to receive
the sacrificial offerings from the people's harvest. Each Levite
examined the offering, then passed it up the line of priests toward
the altar. Once the offerings were received, the head priest prayed,
thanking Elohim, their God, for His provision and asking Him to
receive their best in thanks for His blessing and care.

The priests burned selected handfuls of grain, olive oil, and
their secret mixture of incense along with the offerings. As they did
so, they reminded the Israelites, all standing attentively below this
altar area:

"You are to live in booths, or tents, for seven days
so that you and your descendants remember that
the Lord of Israel brought you out of Egypt. During
the forty years of wandering in the desert, the Lord
provided manna for food. The Lord of Israel did
not let you starve and die. The Lord's spokesman,
Moses, led you to the land that He promised to you.
Thank you, Lord, for this gift of productive land in
Canaan."

The Whistling Galilean

The piercing sound of the ram's horns ended the religious ceremony. This series of reverent acts would be repeated for seven days, allowing Israelites from all communities surrounding the northern Sea of Galilee to give the best portion of their bounteous harvest back to the Lord their God.

Now it was time to eat! Families returned to their own community fire pits. Shai's elders held up handfuls of crops that had been grown and fish that had been caught thanking the Lord for His faithful provision. He was surprised to see Simon and Andrew standing with the community leaders.

The gathered Galilean Hebrews enjoyed a day of feasting and of rest...almost. Even though the women cooked, they were together in a group - giggling, talking, and laughing as they moved around the fire pits. Their many hands seemed to easily prepare a feast.

For everyone else, it was truly a day of rest. Shai heard the men laugh as they, too, talked. They drank wine made from fermented juice from grapes. He would be able to join them next year when he had reached manhood. Now, he was too young for that, so he drank plain grape juice.

To his surprise, he saw Ezra standing next to Grandpa, who was seated on a stool. Then he remembered their discussion from yesterday afternoon. Ezra and several unknown fishermen stood at a table holding baskets of large intact fish, heads on. The smaller fish were already skewered, sticks angled over the cooking fire. Fishel seemed to be supervising the cooking of those fish.

What he saw next truly surprised him. At the table, Ezra used Yona the Elder's famous fillet knife to expertly cut the meat from the bone, leaving a mere skeleton, head and tail behind. He had no idea when his brother had become so skilled.

Then, an evil thought crossed his mind: *It must be the fillet knife, not his brother.* The knife must have known how to separate the fleshy meat from the bony skeleton based on years, no decades, of use in his skilled grandfather's hands. It couldn't possibly be because Ezra had actually learned to become what appeared to be an expert filleter. No, not Ezra.

~ 227 ~

Jennifer Bjork

The boy returned to the tent where he and his younger siblings grabbed their carved bowls from the tent site. Whenever he held or used the bowl, he thought of two people. His father had made the wooden bowl with his name *Isaiah* etched on the bottom, asking Elohim never to let Shai go hungry. Thanks to the guidance and help from his grandfather, his bowl now held the carved outline and details of *Ole Blue*, his father's fishing boat. Eventually, the boy would add more, but this was sufficient for now.

He joined the line of people revolving around the fire pit. Mama made him responsible for helping the youngest, Simcha. Mama and his sister, Adi, made another pair of helpmates. He was thankful that Ezra was still at the carving table.

With guidance from Shai, Simcha filled his bowl with a green salad, a hummus salad, and some pickled vegetables. Hummus consisted of ground up chickpeas with lemon juice, garlic, and spices. Of course, they grabbed hot pita bread to help them eat the salads. They joined the rest of his family minus Ezra and Grandpa. The five of them sat on their usual woven pads, now placed in front of their tent, and rejoiced together for the good harvest.

The feast was spectacular. There was a greater variety of food than he normally ate for one meal. Once they finished the salads, Shai led Sim back to the fire pit. He put several lamb kebobs, a real treat, and some fire-grilled sea bass from Fishel in both of their bowls.

When they finished with the meat, the two boys returned for dessert. Shai chose a generous piece of baklava and several figs. Sim's portions were smaller, but he was content with them. Baklava consisted of thin strips of dough layered with nuts and a syrupy honey-and-date mixture. The sweet baklava was a real treat. It took a lot of preparation time, a labor that Mama rarely had. Since Sim wasn't interested in a pomegranate for later, Shai grabbed only one.

Mama relieved Shai of all duties. On this holy feast day, he had no more chores, and he could wander as he desired. He promised he would return to their tent before sunset.

23

King of the Hill

BUUURRRP.

My goodness. The loud sound erupting from Shai's stomach could have woken the dead. Ah, but the taste of baklava lingering in his mouth was delightful.

So, he continued to wander, observing other families or groups of friends at their Sukkoth gathering. Everyone was contentedly relaxed. Some young boys played some sort of game near their tent.

Despite his meander, he purposely searched for two people - Carmi and either Simon or Andrew. He had no idea where the delightful Carmi would be. He thought that he could easily find Simon with the men from his fishing village, so he had headed there first. He wanted to hear about recent events with Yeshua. Neither disciple was nearby.

So, he sauntered into one of the agricultural camps looking specifically for Carmi. He moved slowly, contentedly, letting his bulging belly digest the huge amount of food that he had just eaten. It was a warm, fall afternoon with no responsibilities.

Suddenly, a group of boys surrounded him. They were picking teams for a game of 'king-of-the-hill." They ranged in age from about ten to fourteen. Since they were mostly from farms, many seemed to be big for their age. A blond-haired boy, about Shai's same size, asked Shai to join them. At first, he refused because he hoped for another activity - spending time with the enchanting Carmi, but the boy was persistent.

"The more the better," the blond boy urged. "Join my team, please."

"Well…"

"Come on. We can team together. We are nearly the same size. We can become friends."

After considerably more persuasion, Shai agreed, "Alright. I am Shai."

"I am Tam."

With that, he decided to postpone his search for Carmi until later. After all, they had six more days in this rocky spot. He had only played "king-of-the-hill" once in his life. The prospect to make a new friend and play this challenging game was too enticing to turn down.

The "hill" the boys decided to conquer was the same hill that Shai's family camped on. For their game, they chose a different, more challenging slope of that same hill. This northern side was far more rugged, steep, and rocky. Merely to safely climb to the top looked difficult.

Once several teams of four had grouped together, one of the older boys with reddish hair took the leadership role and described the rules of the game. He explained, "All team members have to stand side by side on the top of the hill to win. Once a player reaches the really steep and hazardous climb, they are safe from being hindered by another person."

Shai looked up at the hill where their leader pointed, observing the steep terrain their leader described.

Another player asked, "By hindering, do you mean holding onto a player from another team or wrestling them down to the ground?"

The red-head said, "Both. No hitting, punching, kicking, or otherwise physically hurting another team member is allowable. Does everybody understand that? This is supposed to be fun. After all, it is only a game."

The Whistling Galilean

A small boy asked timidly, "Why can we even touch another player? Why don't we just race up the hill?"

The leader answered, "If you can slow down an opposite team member from reaching the top, your team may gain an advantage. Actually, you only need to slow down one person on the team because every team member must be on top of the hill to win. Remember that if only three of the four team members of your team reach the top, your team has not won the game. Your entire team must reach the top of the hill to win. Do you understand?"

"Yes." The small boy nodded uncomfortably.

"You must all agree that this game is just for fun. We don't want anyone to get hurt. Agreed?"

Shai and most of the boys readily answered, "Right."

With a groan, Shai recognized Oz, the bully from school, standing with another team. It appeared that the hand-selected group of older, muscular boys could easily climb the hill. He also noticed that not one person on that team nodded or said "Right."

Oz had a wide chest, back, and shoulders. He was older than Shai by a year or two. Unfortunately, Oz noticed Shai. The slender boy watched the farm bully gather his teammates around him and point toward Shai while giving the order, "I am playing to win...no matter what! Do you all understand what that means?"

The other three boys on his team grunted and nodded in agreement.

What Oz did not verbalize bothered Shai the most. From previous experience, Shai knew Oz would break the rules of any game to win. That worried him greatly and he thought of dropping out.

Maybe this was not such a good idea after all. Maybe he should just quit the game, especially since it included Oz. Most of the time, he was able to avoid the school bully. Thankfully, their paths only met at school.

Shai urgently yanked on Tam's sleeve. "I cannot stay. I must go!"

Tam pleaded, "You must stay. If you leave, we only have three on our team and cannot play."

Shai felt bad for the group that surrounded him – blond Tam, a

~ 231 ~

Jennifer Bjork

gangly boy who claimed to be very fast, and a freckled boy. He was afraid that he couldn't avoid Oz and his team.

The red-headed leader drew a line in the sand and explained, "Team members can be in a group or spread out. Everyone must be behind the line to start the game."

Teams huddled to discuss their strategy. As Shai sought a way to gracefully withdraw, his team decided that strength in numbers would win. They planned to run as fast as they could as a group. Since they were all about the same size and weight, they assumed that they could scamper at about the same speed.

The leader whistled, and the scramble up the hill began. Now, it was too late for Shai to bow out.

So far, so good, he thought as they raced to the rock field at the base of the hill. They were one of the first groups to arrive. Now, they slowed to pick their way around the larger rocks. The members of his group were still within easy shouting distance.

He could tell they were going uphill because he was breathing harder. Then he felt a hand on his ankle yank him backward. He toppled to the ground and rolled until he bounced against two stout legs. He looked up at their owner and shut his eyes tightly in hopes that the owner would magically disappear.

"Got you!" Oz gloated with a sneer. "This is too easy."

"Okay, you've slowed me down." Shai stood up and shrugged.

"I'm not finished with you. You will not climb that hill, Isaiah." Oz was the only boy in school who used Shai's full given name and not his nickname, acting like an adult giving Shai a reprimand.

"Go. You have an advantage."

"I give the orders around here. Hush!"

The stronger boy grabbed Shai's left arm trying to twist it behind his back.

"Ow! Let me go."

"Kneel before me, Isaiah!" Oz put the exclamation mark on the end of that sentence with a spit.

Shai felt a warm glob of saliva trickle down his cheek. When he reached up with his right hand to wipe it off, he felt a thump against

The Whistling Galilean

his overly full stomach. Oz had hit him, hard! He quickly covered his face and ears with his arms and hands.

"Stop it!" Shai swung back with his right fist. It was a quick reflex and barely connected with Oz's shoulder.

That enraged the aggressor. With a swift kick, he bellowed, "Take that whimp!"

His sidewinder landed on Shai's exposed butt. That should have been enough, but it wasn't. In a sudden fury as if a startled snake striking, the farm boy kicked again...and again. His kicks became more and more forceful as the muscular boy probed for vulnerabilities.

"Ow! Stop!" Shai dropped to his knees and quickly rolled into a ball. His panicked eyes wildly searched from under a protective arm for an escape...or help.

How could he stop Oz? He moved his left hand under himself so that he could push up and run, but he was too late. Oz jumped and landed with his heels right on top of Shai's ribcage. Shai felt his right ribcage crack and give way. The sharp pain shocked him. He no longer wanted to move.

"Take that, wimp! I said, don't move!"

Shai did not move a muscle.

Then, he felt a gentle tap from one of Oz's feet and heard, "Good little bitty Isaiah. Now, you just lay there. I will be the King-of-the-hill today. Then, you will have to bow down to me."

The injured boy just lay still as a piece of marble. He was grateful that the bully moved onward, disappearing toward the hill. His ribs and insides hurt terribly. It hurt to even take a breath. He had to concentrate on doing just that. He discovered that he could only inhale short, shallow gulps of air. With a shock, he realized that if he could not breathe, he would die.

He knew that his team had no chance of winning. He realized that he had not seen any of them since the attack started. He knew he was hurt - no, he was seriously injured. He knew there was no way he could continue this game. He knew he could not even crawl to the top of the hill.

He rolled over slowly. Something was wrong with his insides. They felt soft and gooey. He felt nauseous, so he rolled back onto his side and violently threw up. That action hurt so bad he wished for death to end it. His breath came out in short wheezes. The pain on his right side was worse than anywhere else. He knew that he needed help. He hoped a team member would find him and get help.

That was when he heard, "What a surprise. Look what the cat coughed up - a fur ball."

Shai recognized the sound of Dov's voice. His former best friend seemed unaware of his discomfort. He needed a rescuer, someone to get help, not someone to make fun of him.

"Dov. Help," whispered Shai in a voice just louder than the breeze.

"Enough acting, Shai. Let's go play 'Judeans and Romans.' We've got left over palm branches as shields and all sorts of sticks for swords. Naturally, I will be one of the heroic Judeans, not the despised Roman legionnaires. You want to join me?" Through Dov's insistent chatter, Shai knew that his friend was oblivious of the situation even though his own body lay in a heap by the taller boy's feet. He felt Dov grab his arm and try to pull him upright.

"STOP!!" Shai shouted with great effort. "Owwww," he groaned in total agony gathering himself again in a protective ball. "Owwww. Pain is real."

Dov looked down at him, clearly not knowing what to do next. "Oh, I am sorry. What can I do?"

"Get Mama."

After minimal directions, Dov disappeared.

Shai just lay there. He hurt worse than he ever had in his life. He wasn't sure he even wanted to try to continue to breathe anymore.

Tam showed up next. "Hey, get up. Let's go. We're behind, but maybe we can catch up."

"No... can't... hurt."

Finally, he heard Mama's voice, "Shai. It's Mama. I am here."

Led by Dov, Mama Anat scurried to him with several other women. They surrounded him as she gently and carefully probed

The Whistling Galilean

him with her hands. His groaning responses let her know where the worst pain was located.

As she tended to him, he looked around for Oz. Shai finally saw the bully. He and his teammates were on the hill. Oz was not climbing. Apparently, he was watching what was happening around Shai.

The injured boy heard cloth tear, and before he knew it, the cloth was wound tight around his ribcage, pinning his right arm to his torso like a dead man. Was he dying? Together, three women carried him slowly. Step by painful step, they got him inside his tent.

Once inside, he was made as comfortable as possible. The women placed multiple robes under the sleeping mats to soften where he lay on the ground.

Before Mama disappeared from the tent, Shai could read her concerned terror. Little lines radiated from the sides of her eyes as if she squinted in the sun. As she left, she muttered, "I'll make a broth. Herbs will make you better."

Mama Anat was a woman known and respected for her herbal knowledge. He knew he was in good hands. With nothing to do but lay there and hope the throbbing ache would go away, he started to doze off.

She reentered the tent with a cheery, "I am back now, son. Let me help you raise your head a bit more."

Some additional padding was added under his head and neck. He could smell lemon in an otherwise stinky smelling, steamy broth. His mother hummed while she slowly spooned the hot, bitter broth into him sip by sip. He could decode her hums - this one was from nervousness and worry.

The broth didn't taste good but he had no choice in the matter, so he didn't complain. It made him sleepier than he was already.

Later that afternoon when he awoke, he discovered Ezra sitting by his side. 'His bossiness' usually hung out with his own friends, not Shai. Once Ezra saw that the injured boy was awake, he leaned over and whispered a question.

Ezra did not ask how Shai was, or if he needed anything. Instead,

~ 235 ~

he asked the unexpected, "Who did this to you. I'll get to him and give him what he deserves."

In surprise, the younger boy saw his older brother hold up a balled fist to emphasize his intention. He was not only surprised but shocked that his brother was willing to come to his defense.

"Just name him. Who did this to you?"

Shai shook his head in the negative, "I must have fallen."

"And given yourself several broken ribs? And bruises all over your body? I doubt it. I know you too well. I never saw you fall out of a tree as a youngster. No...someone beat up on you and I intend to find out who."

Shai was shocked that his older brother seemed to really care about him.

"Are you alright? Mama said your injuries are serious."

"She knows best." All Shai could do was whisper.

"Can I get you anything? Water?"

"No, thanks."

Ezra sat with him for a little longer to keep him company. Then, patting him on the head, he left, saying, "Sorry you got hurt, buddy. I will be back."

That was weird. Maybe everything is happening in a dream, and I will wake up uninjured, Shai thought. After trying a few deep breaths, he knew that wasn't the case. *Maybe Mama's medicinal broth is making me hallucinate about Ezra.* Before he could confirm or refute this thought, he drifted back to sleep.

Whenever he awoke, a family member was there. The most frequent, of course, was Mama. She either fed him spoonfuls of a healthy vegetable-chicken broth or sips of the bitter medicine. His sister often visited to chatter about her friends and offer him sips of water. Grandpa took his daily afternoon naps with Shai. They would chat and it was nicely distracting to hear his gentle snoring. Even his older brother visited several times daily.

The first evening, and several other times, his father carried him outside to relieve himself. That was usually followed by Mama closing the tent cloth door to give him a sponge bath. That was

The Whistling Galilean

embarrassing. She had not bathed him since he was a little boy, perhaps two to three years old.

He lost track of how long he was there in the tent. When awake, he often wished he had chosen differently on that fateful morning. He wished he had not played "king-of-the-hill" and instead continued to look for Carmi. The cute, freckled girl would have been a pleasant distraction to pass that day and the whole week. If only he could go back and change events of the past.

During one of his waking times, he was surprised by a visit from his blond teammate Tam. "Do you want to know who won the game?"

"Of course." Shai didn't really care but was a polite captive.

"Do you remember the little boy with the blue sash?"

"The timid one?"

"Yes. He, his two older brothers and one of their friends were a team. They won."

"Hard to believe. How?"

"Even though the timid boy wasn't very fast or strong, his brothers were. With the help of his brothers lifting him over obstacles and carrying him piggy back, he stayed out of trouble. They made it to the top first. He sat on the shoulders of one of his brothers. When I saw him, his arms were raised in triumph. It was a great sight to see."

"Surprise." That was an understatement.

"We all were. Most of the other teams took too much time trying to hinder each other. That slowed down their own effort to get to the top."

"Oz's team?"

"Yes. I know one of his friends. I thought they had a chance. He and his team spent so much time trying to hinder others that they got way behind. I hear they even injured a few of the boys. Were you one of them?"

"Did not see." Shai lied.

"You will find this interesting. Oz tried to scale the sheer cliff instead of climbing the cracks like the rest of us. Show-off! Well, he fell and broke his leg. Surprised?"

"Yes." Shai wanted to laugh, but that would hurt too badly, so he swallowed the huge guffaw. He couldn't resist a grin and a slight nod of acknowledgment. A little chuckle did escape.

The karma of the universe was good. Oz had caused hurt and was hurt in return. He had no idea if the Lord of Israel was aware of what had happened that day. Since both he and Oz were Hebrews, Elohim's chosen people, he doubted the Lord took sides. The boy in the tent had prayed daily to Elohim, not for revenge, but for healing.

Another surprise visitor was the freckled Carmi. "Shai. I have been worried about you. I heard from my sister, Rachel, that you were hurt. I had to see you myself. Are you alright?"

Shai was delighted by the sight of her. "Better now...Mama's broth. Up soon."

"You look pale, and your face is drawn in pain. Your eyes tell me that your words lie. You look like you will be in bed for a while." She reached out and patted his arm. "Is there something that I can do for you?"

She waited patiently for his response. He tried to think of something to keep her in the tent with him. She brought with her the faint scent of fresh flowers.

Finally, he looked at the gourd beside him and whispered, "Water, please."

She knelt and lifted it to his lips. That was when Shai noticed that Mama was also in the tent. Naturally, she would not let Carmi be with Shai in a tent unchaperoned.

Mama stepped forward. "Let me help. I'll lift his head a little bit."

As they both fed him sips of refreshing water, Mama felt his forehead. "You feel warm, son."

Looking at Carmi, she said, "I know Shai is glad to see you, but let's not tax his strength right now."

So, Carmi stepped back, and with a wave, she left the tent.

During another of his waking times, he was surprised by another visitor - Yeshua. At first Shai recognized his voice outside the tent. Then, he saw the hand at the cloth entryway.

The Whistling Galilean

The Nazarene stooped and peered in, "Shai, could you manage to have a visitor?"

"Yes...come in."

So, Yeshua sat down cross-legged beside him. He didn't discuss what he'd been doing or tell a story with a moral. Instead, his guest asked Shai how he got injured. In short bursts, Shai told his visitor the rough details but not who had caused him harm. Yeshua listened without interruption as if he had no other care in the world.

When Shai finished recounting the events, the Nazarene commented, "I'm sorry that you were injured. Shai, do you trust me?"

"Yes."

"Do you believe that I can heal?"

"Yes...I am a witness."

The carpenter-teacher-healer peered into the youngster's eyes. "You saw me return a man with leprous skin to wholeness. That man had traveled a long way because he believed I could heal him, remember?"

Shai nodded.

"You also watched me tell Alter, the man paralyzed from birth, to roll up his mat and walk. You were on the roof as his trusting friends lowered him through a hole in Simon's roof, remember?"

With difficulty, Shai nodded again.

"There have been many others that I have mended and healed. You have heard about many of them."

The boy finally spoke, "Miracles...like no other."

Yeshua waited patiently. The boy looked into Yeshua's hazel eyes. Within was a deep pool of loving care, both seen and sensed.

Finally the boy said, "I believe...you healed...all."

The Nazarene continued to wait.

"It hurts...to breathe."

"Do you want to be healed?"

"Yes." He had no idea why he had not thought of that himself. It took him awhile because breathing was still difficult. "I believe. You have power. Heal me."

The Nazarene knelt beside the boy on the pallet and prayed, "O, dear Father in Heaven, please give me the power to heal my friend, Shai. He has injured ribs and more injuries deep inside his body. Please, Father, provide the power to heal using my hands and show my friend that it is your power that heals. I give you all of the glory. Amen."

"Amen," the boy on the padded mat whispered, trying to be helpful.

"Let me pray - O Lord...use Yeshua...to heal me...I believe... your power."

Yeshua added, "Amen."

Even through the tight cloth wrapping, Shai felt Yeshua place both of his hands on him, one on either side of his thinning rib cage.

The popular man of miracles spoke the words, "Be whole again, my friend."

Almost instantaneously, Shai felt a growing warmth coming from the man's widespread, calloused hands into the core of his body. His forehead and palms broke out in a sweat as his temperature grew. He suddenly felt dizzy - not nauseous, but as if he was spinning around rapidly.

He heard himself gasp several times as his heartbeat increased. He could hear the blood pulse in the thinness of his temples near his ears. At the same time, he felt pressure against his bindings. He was not sure if it was Yeshua applying pressure from the outside or something pushing from the inside to realign his bones and organs.

Then, he felt as if he floated atop the Galilee. That is the point that his vision blurred, and there was a roaring in his ears.

When he came to, Yeshua had removed his hands from around his ribcage. The healer was standing and looking at him, mouth crooked into a big grin, "I wanted you to hear this part, Shai. 'Thank you, Father, for the power to heal my friend. Amen.'"

Shai was incredulous. "I am healed?"

"Yes, it is complete. Like Alter, you can get up and roll up your mat and walk away from the tent."

Shai inhaled. It did not hurt. The boy felt his body cooling. He slowly savored another inhale, then just as slowly exhaled. It felt

~ 240 ~

The Whistling Galilean

so good to breathe without pain. As he took in air, his stretched ribs no longer ached. The bindings around him still provided some restriction to a full breath.

Yeshua turned toward the doorway of the tent. "I cannot stay any longer, but as soon as I heard that you were injured, I had to come."

"I am so glad that you did. Thank you. I believe in you and the power you draw on."

The tall man nodded in acknowledgement. "I need to travel throughout the Galilee for a while. I will be gone from Capernaum. I will see you on the beach in the spring, my friend."

With a slight wave, he was gone.

Shai tried to sit up. His ribs and arm were still bound tightly together, so he was still nearly immobile.

He called out, "Mama, Mama. Come help."

She immediately stuck her head in the door, "Yes, my son? Are you alright?"

"Yes, I feel better. Please come unwrap me."

"Well, it is time to take a look."

As a precaution, Mama had kept his arm wrapped against his ribs, but not as tightly as at first. She unwrapped him gingerly, then probed gently with her fingers.

"Shai, I cannot feel the separation between your cracked ribs. They are healing well, faster than I thought they would. Does it hurt when I press here?"

"No, Mama."

"Can you breathe deeper?"

She watched him take deep breaths without a grimace.

"That is good, my son. Does it hurt to breathe?"

"No."

"Your breathing is deeper and sounds much better, not as raspy. Your expression no longer shows that you are in pain. Do you hurt anywhere?"

"No."

"I am so glad. You'll stay in bed for the rest of the day as a precaution. Tomorrow, we'll take a walk together."

~ 241 ~

"I would like to take a walk today. It would feel good to stretch everything out and use my muscles. How long has it been?"

"Four days." As she tidied up around him, she asked, "Did you have a good visit with Yeshua?"

"Yes, Mama. After a prayer to Elohim for the power to heal me, he laid his hands on me. I feel so much better. I think your broth and his healing power did the trick. I feel totally well again."

She embraced his head with both of her hands and kissed his forehead, "Praise the Lord of Israel."

She held him close. The loving clucks under her breath reminded him of the sound that a mother hen makes to her young. Both her hands took turns smoothing the back of his hair. With a relieved sigh, she left the tent.

Shai was so grateful not to be in constant pain. Thankful, he prayed, "Lord of Creation. Thank you for hearing my prayers. Thank you for sending Yeshua and providing him with the power to heal me, even me."

He knew that his ribs and insides were now completely healed because he felt uninjured. He felt energetic, healthy, well, and content. His parents and others were amazed that his healing was so rapid and complete. It usually took his type of injury over six weeks to heal. It took longer than that if there were internal complications. Naturally, Papa heaped praises on Mama's herbal brew and tender care. The son openly praised his mother, too. After all, under her care, he had improved.

He also was openly grateful for the Nazarene physician's willing words of power. He knew that his adult friend had everything to do with his rapid, miraculous recovery. Others noticed that, also.

24

Bounteous Meal

SIX MONTHS PASSED. IT WAS SPRING AGAIN. TODAY SHAI FISHED WITH his father. It was just the two of them in *Ole Blue*.

Instead of fishing, Ezra stayed home to repair the roof. His older brother did not mind that muddy task; in fact, he volunteered for it. Shai knew that "Number One" wanted the girl next door to notice his muscles and broad shoulders. Now, they even talked about girls together. In private, there had been a nice thaw in their relationship. Fishel wasn't available to fish with Papa either. It was his turn to take community fish to market.

Even though Shai's injuries had been healed in an instant, it took the twelve-and-a-half year-old a while to gain back his strength and energy. This was going to be the first time that he threw his cast net from a boat. He was eager to show his father that he had mastered that skill. He still desired his father to consider him a useful member of the family.

There was quickly a problem. The boat, unlike the land, was a floating, unsteady surface. It ever-so-gently rocked back and forth with his movements, making it difficult to throw a good cast. During

~ 243 ~

his first attempt, he lost his balance and fell backwards, landing on his bottom with a *thump* onto the hard, unforgiving wood.

He was embarrassed. "Let me try again."

He got back up, gathered the net in folds over his left arm, and placed the central gathering string in his teeth. *Ready.* He still felt unsteady. Maybe he should lean against the mast this time. He tried just that. As a result, the net only made it to the sideboards and lay half in and half out of the boat.

"Rats. This is harder than it looks."

After regathering the net, he decided that for his third try, he would lean against the sideboard. This time, he whacked his arm against the hard wood. "Ow."

The net crumpled miserably around his feet. When he glanced at his father, he knew the muscular man he emulated had seen all of his attempts. He assumed Papa Yona thought his son was clumsy and totally lacking that specific skill. This day wasn't turning out at all as he had imagined.

Groaning, Shai organized his net and tried again. This time, he was luckier. At least this time the net landed in the water. Unfortunately, it wadded in a pile and was not flatly spread out over the surface of the water as desired.

After some more frustrating attempts, he threw down his net in disgust. He wished he could just walk away and disappear from this scene, but there was nowhere to go. He was surrounded by water on a small, bobbing, wooden island. He was stuck in the boat. Embarrassed, frustrated, and angry at himself, he sat down, making a loud *thump*. He wished he could become a statue and never have to move again.

During all of these attempts, Shai had tried to show off his skillfulness. Occasionally, as Shai regrouped, he saw Papa Yona toss his net, resulting in a beautiful cast. Shai was so intent on what he was doing that he never really paid close attention to his father's technique. Therefore, as the morning progressed, learned nothing at all.

When he heard Papa swallow his chuckle, he felt even worse. He heard the older fisherman say patiently, "Son, watch me. Fishel says

The Whistling Galilean

that you are good with your cast net, but throwing it from a boat is a new skill. Do not expect to be an expert on your first toss. The first step on a boat is to learn to distribute your weight evenly."

Shai was ashamed of himself. He had regressed to learning again. He was not proudly catching the biggest fish of the day as he had hoped.

So, he watched Papa plant his feet, each an equal distance from the center keel line of the boat. Then he tossed his net. The boat hardly moved at all when his arms and the net swooshed out over the side.

His father smiled down at him, "Steady is as steady does, my son. Now, you try."

Papa had called him, *my son* again. He wasn't disappointed. This could still turn into a good day.

It took many attempts for Shai to figure out the right weight distribution, but he eventually did. Once the result of his throw was an open net gently floating atop the sea, he adjusted his technique. He tried tossing the cast net to match the rhythm of the gentle undulations of the sea. It helped. By keeping his lower body still and turning at his waist like his father demonstrated, his throwing action hardly rocked the boat anymore.

Finally, he achieved the same result as casting from the beach. His net again spread into a nice circle as it landed on the blue sea. He no longer lost his balance or had to grab onto something firm like the mast to keep himself from falling down.

His father noticed, too. "Good toss. I think you've got the technique."

They fished together, Shai on the stern side of the mast, and Papa on the bow. The boat was in shallow, clear water so he could see the schools of fish swimming near the boat. Their plan was to cast their nets over the school. Some fish would naturally scatter away from the falling net. Some would be caught.

Eventually, Papa moved to the back of the boat and sculled it using the long rudder attached to the stern. Papa used the rudder to push against the water and move the boat forward. He rocked the

~ 245 ~

rudder from side to side with a twisting motion like mixing powder into a paste by moving the wooden spoon back and forth instead of stirring around and around.

Papa was a master at sculling. He could maneuver the boat anywhere just using the rudder. Today, he taught Shai how to scull, too. Then, they took turns casting and sculling.

Shai laughed. "Papa, I am really enjoying today...even if we don't catch many fish."

Papa laughed his deep belly laugh. "Oh, Shai. I am enjoying today, too. Now that you are twelve and a half, we need to do this more often."

As the boat slowly floated forward, the younger fisherman cast his net at a small school of silvery fish. He let the weights sink, then pulled the net up over the side of the boat as fast as he could.

Excitedly, his voice squeaked with his laughter. "Finally! These two-foots are the biggest catch today."

"Good job."

Papa beamed and guffawed deeply. He was happy. Papa patted him on the shoulder while peering into Shai's net. He was proud of Shai. Oh, what a great day! After such a horrible start, the boy had caught the biggest fish after all.

They, like most fishermen, started their day just after sunrise, so they had already been fishing for hours. At mid-morning, they took a break to eat the snack Mama packed for them in the glow of the early morning oil lamp. As he unwrapped the cloth in the basket, Shai discovered barley loaves, salted anchovy fish, kale and carrots, and even some dates. These left-overs from last night's dinner tasted even better in the fresh air while floating on the Sea of Galilee.

Some people considered these small, flat barley loaves as food for the poor, those who couldn't afford to purchase white bread. He did not care. Shai enjoyed the flavor and texture of the grainy barley and was grateful that the barley harvest had begun. Even though these yeast loaves were small in size, fitting comfortably in a man's palm, Mama could make them soft, not hard as rocks like some he had eaten.

The Whistling Galilean

He especially liked barley loaves with cheese, but the salted fish provided a good contrast too. The silvery fish that he ate were small, the size of an adult's finger. There was a whole fishing industry that harvested millions of them in the southern Galilee and either salted or pickled them. The boy liked them pickled best.

As they ate, Shai gazed at the cloudless sky, grateful that the spring rains were over. By now, they had moved near the beach beside Capernaum's stone quay. Shai noticed streams of people walking from Capernaum eastward. There was only one town in that direction, Bethsaida or "Fisher town."

It was nearly Passover. Therefore, the number of people using the roadways had nearly tripled because of the additional pilgrims on their way to Jerusalem. There was still only one reason that he could think of to explain the gathering of large groups of people - Yeshua. Shai had neither seen the Nazarene physician nor heard that he had returned from his travels throughout the region.

They floated resting and digesting.

The father asked his son, "How's school going?"

"Okay, I guess. It's not my favorite thing to do, but I do know that it is necessary."

"Good. Rabbi Selig tells me that your mind wanders a lot and that sometimes you can't answer his questions. Why is that?"

This was the first time that he had heard that Papa received reports from the rabbi about him. He wasn't sure how to answer, so he just said, "I don't know."

"I think I do. Girls."

"What?" The youngster was shocked. He knew he blushed. How did Papa know that his mind wandered because he was thinking about girls?

"Which girl is it?"

"A daughter of an orchard family, Carmi." Shai had never spoken to his father like this.

"Mama tells me that it's the cute girl with freckles, the one whose family has the grove of olive trees."

~ 247 ~

Shai should have known that Mama and Papa shared what they heard and knew about their children.

"Well," Papa continued, "you are over twelve, so it is natural for you to be noticing girls in a different way." He chuckled, "My boy is becoming a man."

"So? Yes, I am. What's wrong with that?" Shai was sarcastically sullen.

"Not a thing is wrong. I'm just speaking about your body physically changing from a boy into a man. Your voice is beginning to change, to lower. You are getting taller. Other parts of your body are changing, too. I see that you even have some peach fuzz above your lip. That means that you are thinking about girls and maybe even wondering about sex. Am I right?"

Shai blushed. He couldn't lie to his father. "Well...yes, that is true."

"If you ever want to talk about it, I'm available. You'll learn more accurately from me than from your friends, who don't really know. You can confide in me about anything. I will keep our conversations in confidence."

"Thanks, Papa. I don't have any questions right now." Shai felt uncomfortable and hoped that they could change the subject.

Then Papa stood and stretched. "The fish take a nap at midday. Let's stop, too."

Papa sculled *Blue* onto the nearest beach and settled for a nap in the shade while Shai bounded over to the road in search of information.

Shortly, he returned to his father, shaking the fisherman when he arrived. He was full of news. "Papa, don't sleep now. I've heard that the crowd on the road is drawn to our friend, Yeshua. Let's follow. We haven't seen the healer in months. He'll be glad to see me doing so well, after all, he did heal me."

"With assistance from Mama...and Elohim." Papa sat up and stretched. "Alright, Shai."

They tied *Ole* Blue by the bow to a large tree. Before leaving, Shai grabbed the cloth holding the remains from their snack. After

The Whistling Galilean

all, he was growing taller and always seemed to be hungry. These days, it was hard to entirely fill his belly.

Father and son walked side by side, pushed forward by the thickening crowd. They crossed the Jordan River and headed toward the desert hills. Recent early spring rains had greened up the grass and created a soft carpet to sit upon. People gathered on the lush grass of the plain above the river and even up the hillside alive with wildflowers of many colors. It was a beautiful vision, as if the colorful groups of people were brightly colored garden beds. Shai knew that Mama Anat would enjoy this sight and made a mental note to tell her about it.

Soon the boy saw his tall adult friend walking among the people. He saw the familiar short-cropped beard and light tan robe move from group to group. His adult friend talked and healed as he went.

Papa spied Fishel and some other fishermen. "Let's join them." He pointed and grabbed Shai's shoulder with his strong hand. Pulled through the crowd, the boy felt like the fish in his net from earlier that day.

After handshakes and "Shalom's," Shai's father sat down, joining the small group. Shai didn't want to sit this far away. He felt antsy and paced back and forth. Finally, he asked, "Papa, do you mind if I get closer to Yeshua?"

"Go. Look around, then come back and sit with me."

He quickly agreed, then walked toward the man in tan who had now reached the hillside and was sitting down. As he began to teach, the boy stepped carefully around seated groups of people. He had never seen this many people before, not even in the amphitheater near Capernaum.

Most people were strangers, probably pilgrims traveling to Jerusalem for Passover. He greeted the few he recognized. Suddenly wondering if Carmi was in this crowd, he looked for her blondish braids. No luck so far.

He went up the hillside toward the master teacher. Looking back toward his father, he realized how large the grassy valley was. The brothers, Simon and Andrew, were with the other disciples. They

~ 249 ~

nodded to him in recognition. Andrew motioned him to sit down, so he did.

Yeshua was talking about the Kingdom of Heaven in his clear, musical voice that carried over this vast multitude covering it like a thin, light, comforting blanket. He compared God's kingdom to a net lowered down into the lake that catches all kinds of fish. Shai knew that he was directing this part of his talk to families of fishermen like himself, so he listened with interest.

The Nazarene gestured with his arms like a fisherman pulling in a net, "When the net is full, the fishermen pull it up on the shore."

He was describing the large trammel nets that were used by groups of fishermen on the Galilee. It took four to six fishermen to use those. They had to work as a team. One team carried one end of the net into the water by boat, creating a circular path with the net. The boat ended up right where they started on the shore. Then, the team in the boat joined the team on the shore. Together they hauled in the wet, heavy, fifty-cubit-long net onto the beach. It took a lot of strength, especially if they had captured a lot of fish.

Yeshua continued, "Then they sit down and collect the good fish in baskets, but throw the bad away."

Yes, that was just what the fishermen did.

"This is how it will be at the end of the age. The angels will come and separate the wicked from the righteous and throw them into the fiery furnace, where there will be weeping and gnashing of teeth."

"Oh, no," Shai thought to himself, *gnashing of teeth...fiery furnace...I wonder if Oz is considered wicked.*

The Nazarene explained that this separation of the wicked from the righteous would be the work of the Lord of Israel.

The lad could not recall hearing Yeshua speaking about this "end of the age" before. Did that term mean in a few years, or when the Romans were overthrown, or when? Whenever that time was, it sounded very scary.

Then, Shai heard grumbling around him. He thought people were concerned about the "end of the age" but it was about hunger. Shai realized that he was hungry, too. Many people around him

The Whistling Galilean

talked about missing their midday meal. Today, they chose to listen to Yeshua rather than eat. Therefore, many people had not eaten for a long time.

The sun sat lower in the sky. Shai knew he should return to his father. They should sail home now, or Mama would worry about them.

A man next to him asked, "This is a remote place. Where can we buy food?"

A mother with two young children muttered, "We have not eaten all day. We are so hungry."

A woman with large loop earrings spoke up, "Evening and sunset approaches, where can we eat and sleep?"

A voice in the distance asked loudly, "Should we return to Bethsaida and obtain food? My children are hungry. It has been eight hours since we have eaten."

Shai looked up at Yeshua. If Shai had heard these complaints, so had the teacher. The boy knew the disciple speaking to Yeshua only by sight. He knew that this young man was from this part of the Galilee region, so he should know where to purchase food.

The disciple asked in a voice loud enough for Shai to hear, "I know of no place to buy that much food at this time of day."

As the disciples and Yeshua talked, the crowd hushed to stillness. Shai and everyone else wanted to hear what they said. What would be their response to the problem?

Another disciple wore a striped robe and was counting coins held in a black money pouch that Shai had seen constantly at his waist. As the man in the striped robe counted the coins, the first disciple said to Yeshua, "Eight months' wages would not buy enough bread for each person in this valley to have a bite!"

The disciple in the striped robe added, "Are we to go and spend that much on bread and give it to the people to eat? We don't have that kind of money."

As was often his pattern, instead of answering the disciple's question, the Nazarene asked another question to the group of twelve, "How many loaves do you have? Go and see."

~ 251 ~

Jennifer Bjork

The disciples dispersed, asking people if they had any food with them. Most people shook their heads saying, "No food."

Andrew saw Shai. "Do you have any food with you?"

"Yes, as a matter of fact, I do." He unwrapped his small package and showed it to Andrew. "I have two small fish and five small barley loaves. I planned on eating them while listening to Yeshua."

Andrew quickly reported the findings of the group to their tall teacher. The tall man requested, "Bring them here to me. The people do not need to go away. You give them something to eat."

Yeshua then looked directly at Shai who peered up at the master teacher from below. "Shalom, Shai. You look well. Come here, my friend. Are you willing to share your fish and bread?"

How had the popular teacher and healer known that he was the one who had the loaves and fish? Had he heard Shai's reply to Andrew's question?

The boy obediently stood and took his small cloth bundle of food to the Nazarene. "Yes, of course you can have them."

As he unwrapped the cloth covering his leftovers, he looked down the hillside at the huge crowd. He felt small and insignificant. He knew that what he offered was not enough to feed the large crowd. But his friend had asked, so he offered it anyway. "Here, take all that I have."

"Thank you, Shai. You will see that your gift to me is of great value. Even though you believe that it isn't, you will see that it is sufficient, that you are sufficient. You have a good heart that honors our Lord today."

The Nazarene directed everyone to gather together on the grass in groups of fifties and hundreds for a meal. As they did as commanded, he took the meager loaves and fishes from his young friend's hand.

Then, as head of household, he blessed their meal. He took the five barley loaves and two fish and raised the food above his head toward the heavens.

"Blessed are you, Jehovah our God, who causes bread to come from the earth and fish from the sea. Thank you, O Lord Elohim, for this blessing to feed us."

The Whistling Galilean

Then he broke the loaves and the fish into pieces. He gave some pieces of each to his twelve followers who had found some small wicker baskets to carry the food to the gathered people. Then, his followers passed down into the crowd and gave each group of people some of the nourishment.

Shai watched in amazement as the people accepted more and more food from the willow wicker baskets. The multitude ate...and ate some more as they listened to the masterful teacher.

"These barley loaves are delicious. They are so soft," a man near Shai commented.

The lad responded, "Yes, my mother bakes them. I find them tasty, too."

The boy watched the disciples distributing the food carefully. Every time one of the twelve turned to another group of people, they seemed to offer them a full basket of food. The disciples did not pick up any other baskets of food along the way. They only used the same basket that they each started with, the one with the small pieces of Shai's meager two fish and five barley loaves. Incredible!

Andrew passed by a second time, "Have you eaten yet, Shai?"

"Yes, thank you."

"Have some more. There seems to be enough for seconds."

So, he did. How much had he eaten by now? He had devoured four barley loaves and at least seven sardines, more fish than he had originally provided. How could that be?

Now, he noticed that the people around him were satisfied. He heard their content sighs. He did not hear anyone mumble about being hungry. Like him, they seemed to have eaten enough to feel full.

Now that he was no longer hungry, he became curious. How many people was Yeshua feeding? He estimated by counting the groups of people in the manner that Fishel had taught him to count fish or birds or just about anything. There were roughly one hundred groups of fifty men...that was about five thousand men.

The women and children were in their own groups. By Jewish tradition, when they ate in public, they had to be separate from

~ 253 ~

the men. There were as many women and children as men, maybe more. That meant adding five thousand women and children to the five thousand men. His meager remains were feeding around ten thousand people. It had all started from two fish and five barley loaves. That was impossible!

He looked up at the former carpenter in wonder...in awe.

Yeshua looked down at the boy and winked as he continued his discourse, "You will find that the Lord provides. His timing is perfect. Believe in the one Elohim has sent."

A heavy-set man seated below the boy eagerly turned and told him, "My rabbi just taught us about the promise of a true Shepherd. He read from the scroll of prophet Ezekiel who reported that when the promised one came, the desert would be a rich pasture where the sheep would gather and feed. Today may be the day that Ezekiel prophesied. I feel like one of his sheep today."

Before Shai could respond thoughtfully, the man's companion scratched his rounded belly, saying, "Yes, I know that passage, too. This man, Yeshua, may be the prophet that Moses talked about."

He could feel the excitement build in the people surrounding him. Just then, the Nazarene's voice attracted Shai's attention again. The master told his students, "Gather the pieces left over. Let nothing be wasted."

Andrew asked for the lad's help. As the man and boy passed through the crowd closest to Yeshua picking up the fallen leftovers, the boy overheard more of the people's comments. He could feel their excitement as if lightning was in the air around them.

"...just performed another miracle. He must be the king who is to come."

"...the one foretold by the early prophets."

"...the Messiah who would become the King of the Jews."

He pulled on Andrew's sleeve. "I have a question. Do the people think Yeshua is the foretold Messiah? Do you?"

In a low, conspiratorial voice, Andrew responded carefully, "We have wondered about that ourselves. He is indeed a miracle-worker. He is a teacher with much scriptural knowledge. Yeshua carefully

The Whistling Galilean

anchors his words with the prophets of old, yet introduces new twists, interpretations, and concepts that ring true."

An older man spoke up, "Very near here, several years ago, I heard John the Baptist ask this very teacher from Nazareth if he was the 'one' or whether he should expect another."

"And, what did the Nazarene say?"

"Nothing."

"What do you think?" Andrew asked the old man.

"I hope and pray that he is the Coming One, the Messiah, our yearned-for King."

"I do, too." Andrew nodded in agreement and straightened.

Andrew and Shai had turned away and taken a few steps, when they heard a strong voice next to them announce, "Let's make him our king now!"

Andrew pulled Shai toward him. "Come with me. This could become dangerous. Yeshua says it is not yet his time."

Andrew motioned to the other disciples and they approached their tall teacher. They placed twelve basketfuls heaped with broken pieces of bread and fish at his feet. Impossible. They had collected more leftovers than even the meager starting amount of food, Shai's two fish and five barley loaves. Now there were twelve heaping basketfuls of edible fish and bread.

Yeshua grabbed Shai's shoulders with his powerful hands, "You look wonderful, Shai. I am glad. There are troublemakers stirring up the crowd. It is time for us to depart. Go find your father and slip on home. Tell your mother that I miss her cooking."

Shai responded, "I am glad you are back. Papa may be searching for me. I have stayed with you too long, so he may be upset with me."

The Nazarene patted him on the back, "No, he will not be disappointed in you. Not today. He saw your gift to me, to Elohim, and to the people. Today, he is proud of you. Thank you, my friend, you are truly a gift to me in more ways than you know."

~ 255 ~

25

Who Was There?

SHAI EAGERLY SCOOTED DOWNHILL TOWARD HIS FATHER. SOME groups were in no hurry since they had just finished an ample meal, so the boy was forced to slow to their pace instead of running fast as he so badly desired.

The balding man beside him spoke first, "I thought I would have trouble finding something to eat tonight."

Shai felt trapped, surrounded by the crowd, so he politely conversed, exploring his own feelings to a man he did not know and would probably never see again. "He certainly satisfied my hunger. He fed so many."

"Yes, the Nazarene physician drew a large crowd today."

"He seems to do that wherever he goes. I just wish those ahead of us would walk faster. I am trying to reunite with my father."

Shai knew his Papa would return to *Ole Blue*, so that was his destination. He just hoped that his father would wait for him and not sail immediately home.

"Good fortune to you, lad. I hope you find your father. I came alone today. My wife and three grandchildren stayed in Bethsaida,

The Whistling Galilean

so I am in no hurry since Yeshua multiplied the loaves and fishes to feed us all."

The bald man patted his full belly to demonstrate his contentment. He even pulled three barley loaves from where they had been sequestered within his large robe, and said, "See, I am even taking my grandchildren a gift from this magic healer from Nazareth. He has shown us another miracle."

"I agree."

"Ah, but only the real Messiah can perform real miracles." Another man added.

"How do you know that?"

"I studied under a rabbi in Jerusalem. Surely, this is the very prophet about whom Isaiah speaks. He must be the expected one who has now come into the world."

"He certainly has everyone wondering who he is, me included."

"But the one that we expect will become our king. I cannot imagine that a lowly carpenter from poor, small, insignificant Nazareth could become our king."

"Why not?" Shai jumped to Yeshua's defense. "The Lord of Israel can bring the Messiah in any form He desires…and from any location."

"Some of my brethren, other students, do not agree with me. They think that this Yeshua is a false prophet, a dangerous man that will lead a revolt against the Temple and leaders of our faith."

"How can a gentle carpenter who speaks of peace and love be dangerous? How can a man who demonstrates caring by healing our wounds and feeding our hunger be a rebel? I do not understand those conclusions." Even though Shai felt comfortable defending his adult friend, this conversation was beginning to upset him.

The people immediately behind the lad had another angle of thought going, "…our leader-warrior-king will lead us to overthrow Rome. He must."

"I, too, would follow that kind of leader."

"Let's find Yeshua and entice him to be our leader now!"

"Let's go find him now."

~ 257 ~

Jennifer Bjork

Shai turned to face them. These three men were young yet older than Ezra. Their faces each showed their determination to make Yeshua their leader by force. The eyebrows of the man in the middle were pulled together so tightly that the two united as one wild, hairy, black line. Another jutted out his chin so that his short beard pointed before him like a sword. The three men turned around and fought their way back up the hill against the mass heading down. They talked as they walked, attracting a growing group of impatient frustration headed straight toward the place where Yeshua had preached.

A thin woman who suddenly appeared beside Shai asked him, "How was all this food they fed us possible? I only saw twelve baskets of food to start with, didn't you?"

"Yes, and the baskets were not full."

"Did the men handing out the food have it hidden in their sleeves?"

"No, I watched carefully. Even if they had a few hidden loaves, they could not have produced enough to feed all of us."

"Oh, I saw you up there. You must be the boy who gave the Nazarene the fish and loaves?"

Shai quickly ducked his head and wiggled forward. He slithered past tight groups and headed downhill and across the Jordan River as fast as he dared. He wanted to remain anonymous. When he was finally able, he jogged. He did not look back, not even once.

Finally, Shai arrived on the road beside the beach. He saw his father standing by *Ole Blue*. Papa seemed to be scanning the crowd on the road. The boy tore forward waving, "Here I am...over here, Papa!"

"Finally. You made it back safely. I was worried."

"I am sorry. I meant to come straight back to you, but Andrew involved me in discussion and then...."

"I recognized you up there with Yeshua giving him our bread and fish. Am I correct?"

Shai nodded, "Yes, Papa. I'm sorry I didn't come back. You saw that I had to stay."

~ 258 ~

The Whistling Galilean

"Yes, you did, son. At least you were within my view. I am proud of you for helping."

Shai felt a rush of emotions. He was relieved that his father saw his involvement and understood. He was grateful that the man he respected was not angry and had waited for him to return. Most of all, he felt his father's love and pride. This moment felt warm, wonderful...he rushed to the elder fisherman and hugged him tightly, "Oh, Papa, I love you so much."

"I love you too, son."

A surprised Shai felt two familiar, muscular arms engulf his body. This was the first show of public love he had ever received from his father, and he did not want it to end.

But, it did. Papa gently pushed his son away. He spoke quietly, "Shai, we must return home now."

"I know, Papa. Mama will be worried because we are very late. I will help us be quick."

As they approached the bow of the boat, Papa explained, "You and I are taking Simon, Andrew, and two of the others with us in *Blue*. Fishel already left with another crew of fishermen and several additional disciples. Let's depart quickly before the crowd looking for Yeshua discovers that they are here and make it impossible."

Shai tossed the bow line to Andrew and scrambled ungracefully over the side. He was the last aboard. His father was already at the helm; after all, it was his boat. Simon always needed something important to do, so he handled the sail. Andrew, the younger brother, moved about the boat helping to get underway. He also pointed out where the other disciples should sit and made them comfortable. They were not seamen, so they were not used to being aboard fishing boats.

Andrew finally plopped down beside the lad. "Phew, what a day. I am tired. What an incredible day. Thank you for the fish and loaves. Your gift was the basis of the miracle today, the multiplication of those very fish and loaves."

Shai was proud, yet embarrassed. He was glad that he was not stingy. He was glad that he did not offer just a portion of his remaining food. He was glad to have given it all.

~ 259 ~

Jennifer Bjork

Yet, he was humble also. "You are welcome. I was glad to do it. It was such a small gift. I wish it had been more."

"It was sufficient. It was enough. It was just what Yeshua desired."

"Where is Yeshua? Aren't you and Simon usually by his side?" Shai immediately wondered if his tall friend was alright. He had witnessed potential danger. It lurked underfoot in the form of the eager mob surging uphill to make him their warrior-king.

"Yes, we are usually right beside him. This time, Yeshua asked us to go on ahead by boat. So here we are with you. The master went up the mountainside to pray alone. He does that sometimes. It refreshes him. Simon told your father to sail deep into the Galilee to disappear from sight by land. He hoped that would disappoint the crowd so that they would disperse. Then we can return and pick Yeshua up at the quay."

"Oh, no. Then we are not heading immediately home to Mama. She will worry even more."

"Don't worry, Shai. It was your father's choice. He willingly undertook this task. He saw you help Yeshua and he wants to do the same. He understood the necessity. We are grateful. Simon's boat is being repaired and was not available. We needed another boat with an experienced team of seamen. We respect and trust your father."

"In that case, we are both glad to help today."

Shai was proud of his father. He was respected, trusted, and willing to aide Yeshua, too. He had finally judged the Nazarene and made that choice.

So, they started their journey under a gentle breeze and clear sky. Shai watched the first stars of the night appear. He also saw some lights to the north, probably candles or olive lamps along the shore. He did not envy his father tonight. It was not easy to sail a group of very experienced seamen, like Simon and Andrew.

Shortly, the wind blew stronger gusts. It was easy to sail in a steady wind, even if it blew hard. Gusts were tricky. Papa steered masterfully and Simon wordlessly adjusted the sail to match the boat's point of sail. Shai was glad to have the two brothers aboard.

~ 260 ~

The Whistling Galilean

Since he had already experienced several heavy blows on the Galilee, he did not trust his level of experience to handle these growing gusts alone.

Papa loudly explained, "Pay attention, now. This feels like a rising sirocco wind. It is from the south and feels dry as the desert sands from where it came. Now, we are turning the boat to return to Capernaum to pick up Yeshua. The boat will react differently with the winds pushing from behind us. It is expected."

They had already spent several hours at sea. With the gusty wind from the stern, Andrew and Shai stayed busy. They readjusted the weight in the boat by moving the men to different locations. They tried to make them comfortable by padding the hard wooden flooring of the boat. They relocated nets and coils of rope and fiber bumpers to soften their seats.

The wind continued to strengthen. Rough seas churned into tall, wind-driven waves. Wind blew the wave tops into a frothy, misty haze. It was nearly impossible to see the approaching land. It took all of their attention to sail toward occasional glimpses of the distant glow from olive lamps lining the quay in Capernaum. It took all of the strength of the three seamen and the boy to maintain their course.

Suddenly, Simon shouted, "I see him on the quay."

Simon's eyesight must have been excellent. Shai could not make out any figure. He tried squinting but that did not help.

It was the dark of night. The moonlight previously guiding them was gone, diffused in the misty haze. What remained was an eerie, diffused gray surrounding them from all directions. It was disorienting, disturbing, and unsettling to Shai. He was glad to have the experienced adults in the boat with him. He was glad he did not have to face this alone.

As the wind howled in a fury, *Ole Blue* was thrown to-and-fro like it was in a boxing match with the tall, white-capped waves. He had to hold onto more than one part of the boat. He saw the terror in the eyes of the non-seamen aboard being tossed around like wheat separated from the shaft on a threshing floor.

Then, he saw waves break over the stern of the boat. The boy

~ 261 ~

Jennifer Bjork

immediately heard a tearing sound as the fluky wind struck the main sail with a particularly hard blow. The taut cloth gave way. It ripped near the top along the grain of the fabric.

Papa yelled over the flapping sound to Simon with an unusual urgency, "Lower the sail! Now!"

"I am on it!" The boy saw Simon quickly kneel beside the mast with knees sandwiching it and gripping firmly for balance. Simon braced his shoulder against that thick, strong pole. Then he yelled as loudly as he could, "I'm ready!"

"Now, Simon!" Papa yelled, and the sail was quickly lowered into the boat. Shai saw what was happening and quickly grabbed a rope. He wrapped the cloth in a bundle and tied it securely to keep it from tearing any further.

Andrew yelled, "I've got two oars ready. Take one, Simon."

As he grabbed an oar, Simon explained to anyone who wanted to listen, "We have to row the rest of the way, men. It will be alright."

Occasional waves lapped over the side of the boat. Unasked, Shai began bailing the water out of the boat using a gourd. The gourd was loosely tied to the bottom of the mast to keep it from blowing overboard.

He gritted his teeth and prayed, "O, Lord of Israel, please be with us tonight and use your magnificent power to keep us safe."

Shai could not tell if they still aimed toward the quay or not. He worried that Papa's boat would ram into that hard stone and crunch into a splintered pile of debris. He didn't want anyone to be hurt. His eyes strained to make out something, anything. Then, he saw a ghost-like shape of a man on the water. It did not appear that the ghost was in a boat or on the quay. It appeared to be on the water. To the boy, that was what it looked like.

Shai shouted and pointed, "What is that?"

Simon peered in the direction Shai pointed, "I see it, too."

Andrew added, "So do I. It is getting closer."

The men in the boat shifted their positions. Some kneeled to look over the side of the boat. Shai knew that they wanted to see this strange apparition, too.

~ 262 ~

The Whistling Galilean

One of the men commented, "It can't be a ghost. It must be just misty rain billowing to appear like a ghost. Ghosts are not real."

Simon explained, "It is a mariner's superstition that the appearance of spirits at night brings disaster. None of us wants disaster and death. We must be sure."

Now, it was Papa's worried voice that entered Shai's ears, "I cannot make it out, Shai. What is it, Simon? Can you make it out, Andrew? Look hard. Be sure that it is not the stone quay."

Shai observed aloud, "I think I see the apparition waving at us. It can't be the quay, Papa."

"Yona, I do not hear waves bouncing off the hard stone quay," Simon's voice was an audible portrait of a calm leader of men. "but I think I recognize the distinctive height, tan robe, and long dark hair of Yeshua."

Andrew added, "Now we are only about four cubits away from the apparition. I, too, think that I recognize Yeshua. I can even make out his short beard. It is not the quay, Yona."

A man in the boat whispered, "He appears to be merely standing there...on the water."

Simon and Andrew kept rowing to stabilize *Ole Blue*. Papa remained in the stern sculling with all of his strength. The wave height had dropped considerably, and the winds had lessened. It was still difficult to aim the boat toward the man-like shape on the water.

As they approached, Shai gasped, "It is Yeshua...standing on the water."

Other men in the boat gasped as they recognized him, also.

Then they all heard a voice emanating from the shape of Yeshua using the master teacher's voice that said, "Take courage! It is I. Do not be afraid."

Simon's pride at being the first and the best and the strongest got the better of him. He bellowed across the water, pointing at the man on the water, "I know you, Yeshua. I knew it all along."

Andrew muttered, "No, you didn't."

Simon ignored his brother saying to Yeshua, "Prove it to me. If it is you, tell me to come to you on the water."

~ 263 ~

Jennifer Bjork

Shai moved toward his father in the stern of the boat. He thought out loud what everyone in the boat was thinking, "That is ridiculous. Everyone knows that people, even fishermen, can't walk on water."

The apparition that was Yeshua said, "Alright, Simon. Come to me."

Did Yeshua just call Simon's bluff? Shai wondered and watched the red-haired fisherman.

Simon did not hesitate. He puffed out his chest and tossed a leg over the side of the boat. Without removing his gaze from Yeshua's eyes, the redhead slid down onto the water's surface. He clung there holding onto the side of the boat. Gazing directly at Yeshua's apparition, he released the boat with one hand.

Shai whispered, "Simon is standing on the water, just like Yeshua. Why isn't he sinking into the water?"

Simon, still gazing at Yeshua, heard the boy and answered, "I believe that Yeshua wants me to come to him. I believe, so I do not sink. Watch."

Simon released his second hand and took a deep breath. From inside the boat, Shai watched intently. Simon lifted his right leg and thrust it forward, planting his right heel atop the water. He did the same with his left foot. Shai watched Simon take step after step on the surface of the water toward Yeshua.

The boy whispered again, not wanting to disturb what appeared to be happening before his very eyes, "Simon is walking on water."

Papa whispered back, "I see that, son. I do not understand what my eyes are watching."

A gust of wind moved across the boat toward the two men on the water. As it hit Simon, the man took his eyes away from the Nazarene and looked in the direction of the wind. He then looked at Andrew and the other people in the boat.

As he did, Shai was amazed to see the huge fisherman's feet submerge underwater. They were followed by his ankles.

Simon quickly looked down at his feet. "Oh, no! I cannot swim."

When he glanced back at the boat, his eyes were wide open and rounded. His mouth was wide open, too. He was not just afraid. The huge man was terrified!

~ 264 ~

The Whistling Galilean

The seaman had walked so far. He was so close to Yeshua, who was standing on the Sea of Galilee, unmoving with an outstretched hand held out toward Simon. All Simon needed to do was to take one more step, just one, to reach the Nazarene.

Shai groaned, "He is sinking."

Out of the corner of his eye, the boy saw Andrew straighten, put his hands on his hips, and shake his head at his brother, "Serves you right, Simon. Bragging again."

Brothers. Even as men, they were still competing. Shai quickly wondered if it would always be that way between himself and Ezra.

Simon, in a panic, looked back at the healer. By now, he had sunk to his thighs. Shai watched him lean towards Yeshua. The healing physician took him by the hand and helped him up. Simon took several baby steps to reach the surface. Now, the disciple who claimed to believe actually stood next to the man from Nazareth. The student held his master's outstretched hand, the one that had been offered like a carrot dangling on a stick to a horse.

The Nazarene chuckled and said to Simon, "Oh, you of little faith, why did you doubt me?"

Shai watched his tall friend pat the fisherman on the back as if to say, *Well done.* Then he watched them both walk on the surface of the water together towards *Ole Blue*, as if they were taking a restful Sabbath stroll together. As soon as they climbed into the boat, the wind died down and the seas calmed.

All the boy could whisper was a prolonged, "Ooooh...my Lord."

Shai had been in a boat on the Sea of Galilee at the very moment that Yeshua and Simon had walked on these same waters. He would never see his Galilee in the same way again.

Simon finally spoke, "Today we have seen two miracles back to back. First, we participated in serving the multiplied fish and loaves to feed a large gathering of hungry people interested in listening to our master. Second, Yeshua and I walked on the water, side by side. Over the last year and a half, our master and teacher has shown us his unusual powers. He revealed to us that he is not just the good man that we've grown to love. He is not just a rabbi, a teacher who

~ 265 ~

Jennifer Bjork

knows scripture and the law. He is not just an amazing healer doing miracle after miracle. He also demonstrated power over nature by instantly calming a storm. He is not merely a prophet like John the Baptist telling us to repent, the end is near. No human could have done what he has done over the last few years. Today, this minute, a curtain was raised from my eyes, our eyes. It was like we were blind and now we can see."

Shai listened intently. As he looked around, he noticed that every man in the boat hung onto every word that Simon spoke, even his father.

Now, Simon knelt before Yeshua. The other disciples followed his example. The fisherman gazed up at his master and spoke in adoration, "We now know that you have to be the one. You are the only one who can be our Messiah. Truly you, Yeshua, are the son of God, the Messiah."

26

Repairs and Amends

Papa reminded Shai, "Enter the house quietly and don't wake up your brothers and sister."

It was dark, the still before dawn. It had been an extremely long night, but they had finally arrived home. The lad was exhausted and gratefully slipped onto his mat. Soon, he was sound asleep.

He and Papa slept much later than usual. It was past mid-morning when he finally arose. Mama did not mind that he did not beat the rooster. The two fishermen had maybe five hours of sleep before they returned to the fisherman's beach to clean up, collect any salvageable fish, and repair the boat.

Papa lit a small fire on the beach. He used an old worn pot to heat up sap from a conifer tree. Then he soaked rags in the sap and tamped them into gaps between the boat timbers using an unsharpened, broken knife blade. The sap would harden as it dried, acting like a filler glue. The pieces of rag were flexible like the timbers. Together, they both contracted when dried out in the sun or expanded when in cool water. It took a few hours for Papa to patiently teach Shai how to stop the leaks in his old boat.

Jennifer Bjork

An unspoken, close connection had developed between them. Yesterday, Papa had expressed an open love and pride in Shai. Now that it had been expressed, it could never be erased. In addition, they had both witnessed something neither of them understood. The boy knew that they, too, had to decide what to believe.

Once that messy task of caulking the timbers was finished and everything was cleaned up, Papa gathered the remaining edible fish that Fishel pulled out of the net. "I'm taking these home to cook up right now. Your grandfather will help me."

The boy remained on the beach to help Fishel remove the mainsail and stretch it out on the sand for thorough examination. Fishel cut canvas as a patch to sew on top of the large tear near the top of the sail. In addition, he discovered some smaller tears that didn't need a patch. He decided to stitch those tightly closed.

Meanwhile, Shai examined every rope and line for tears and wear. He set up a splicing kit on the bow of the fishing boat. Loosening the weave of each worn rope, he cut out the frayed thinness and wove in sections of new, strong hemp line to strengthen it.

Fishermen strewn out across the beach were busy with their own repairs. Last night's wind gusts had damaged more than one boat on the Galilee. As he worked, Shai imagined the fish resting. They, too, took a day off from using their sly wariness to avoid fishermen's nets.

A young boy, probably a son of one of the fishermen, sat down on a nearby log. He strummed a crude three-string lute. The music that the young one created had a beat that helped to pass the time completing the repairs. The young boy even sang some songs to some of the chords he strummed. Shai found himself softly humming with the singer as he spliced the lines. His own humming reminded himself of Mama's and he wondered how often he did that without realizing it.

After about an hour, he looked up to see a familiar sight. Simon's white-hulled boat grated onto the sandy beach. Shai surmised that his repairs were completed. With help, that boat was soon sitting on rollers beside *Ole Blue*.

~ 268 ~

The Whistling Galilean

Once beached, Ezra hopped out. Shai saw his brother lend a hand to assist another fisherman with some sort of chore. So, that was where his older brother had been.

Shai worked next to Fishel in mostly quiet companionship. His mentor chuckled and winked at a shared joke, "Look, I'm sewing like a woman…it is still a good thing."

Shai chuckled, too. He nodded with a better understanding of that wisdom.

Eventually Fishel talked about something bothering him, "Earlier this morning, I heard about your adventure last night. It's hard to believe that Yeshua walked on water to the boat."

"He did. I saw it."

"And Simon did, too? Walk on water? I can hardly believe Yeshua's ability to do that. As a result of all of the healings he has been able to perform, he continues to amaze us all. No person can walk on water. Surely not a large boned, heavy-weight like Simon."

"I had trouble believing that I saw Simon walk on water. I was there. As I watched him, I doubted what my eyes saw but -"

Andrew's familiar voice interrupted, "Ah, remember, Shai, Simon had much trouble. He sunk to his thighs."

The fisherman had slipped up behind them without their knowledge.

Fishel asked, "What? Tell me more. I have not heard about him sinking."

Now, Andrew walked forward to face them both. Simon immediately joined his younger brother. The two popular fishermen were quickly surrounded. To everyone working on the beach, this was welcome entertainment, a break in their necessary repairs.

Simon said, "Ah, brother, I was the one brave enough to walk out to our master. You stayed in the boat. Why is that?"

Several observers clucked like chickens.

"Someone had to stay aboard to row over and pick you up when you sank," Andrew retorted.

Sticking his chest out in playful boasting, Simon responded, "Well, I did not fail. I actually walked on water."

~ 269 ~

Jennifer Bjork

Andrew gloated with a cheery smile while acting out his words, "No brother, you sank to your thighs. Your eyes looked straight at mine. They were full of terror. Once you realized that you were actually out of the boat and on the water, you realized your stupidity and became afraid. You instantly doubted that you could achieve the task you desired, to walk to Yeshua. You even thrust your hands back toward me with pleading eyes."

Shai did not remember that last part, but it was entertaining. Everyone surrounding the two brothers laughed long and hard. Simon huffed and balled his right hand into a fist. His face turned red with the effort it took him to keep from striking his brother. That was the appearance, anyway. His arm shook with the strain of being slowly lowered to his side. Shai was certain they were joking to amuse their friends – almost certain.

After all, the fishermen surrounding them were friends of the two brothers. The gathered group knew both of the men very well. They knew about Simon's pride but also about his quick temper. For decades, they had worked with both of them.

As the laughter died down, Shai asked, "So, did you sink underwater, Simon?"

Andrew answered before Simon could say anything, "First, Simon said, 'Lord, save me!' I even heard his words tremble with fear."

"No, not Simon. I've never seen him afraid of anything." Fishel could not believe that Simon had ever been afraid.

Simon's face took on a stern appearance. "Alright men. Let me be serious with you, my friends. You have probably already heard this tale several times, and I am sure you will hear it many times again. Some of you may even retell this story yourselves. Remember the words you hear out of my lips right now. What I tell you now is the truth. Do not alter this truth."

They recognized that Simon's face took on stern warning signs. They knew that he was requesting - no, demanding - their obedience. Most of the men in the large circle nodded their agreement with his demand.

~ 270 ~

The Whistling Galilean

Simon continued, "Yes, I was afraid when I realized how far from the boat I had walked. I did walk on water, on the actual surface of the sea we all know and love. I did start to sink. Andrew told the truth. Then, my eyes linked with Yeshua's and I felt the strength of his will. Calling upon his power, I stepped up to the surface again and stood beside him. My mind tells me that it was impossible. It is even hard for me to believe, but it is the truth. Together, we walked to Yona's fishing boat, *Ole Blue*. It was the most amazing thing that has ever happened to me. I have seen Yeshua perform incredible miracles, but this one happened to me."

He let that sink in before he spoke again, quiet enough that Shai and all of the others had to strain to hear him. In mass, Shai and the others leaned toward the large redhead. He held everyone's undivided attention.

"That is when I knew for sure. The mist lifted from my eyes like it lifted after the storm last night. Yeshua is the very Messiah that the prophets of old foretold. Yeshua is the Messiah. He can be nothing less. Tell that message to your friends."

Then the two brothers went over to Shai and thanked him for his help before heading down the beach. The fishermen dispersed, returning to their tasks. Some remained in deep discussion, probably debating the events and conclusions they had just been told by their respected leader.

That was when Ezra climbed into *Ole Blue*, "Hi, Shai-ooo. Everyone's hard at work today. Missed you and Papa at home last night. Mama was so grateful for your safe return."

Fishel stretched and picked up his mending bag. "Excuse me. I've got to get home now. Time to prepare our dinner. Like the others, I've got a lot to think about…Simon walking on water…." His voice faded as he walked away.

Ezra sat down beside Shai. "Earlier this morning, I heard the brothers retell what happened on the water last night. They must have been drinking heavily. Walking on water? Preposterous. What do you think happened?"

"You forget, I was there, too. I saw Yeshua and then both Yeshua and Simon standing on and walking on the surface of the Sea of Galilee. That's what I saw."

"Did you have your first drink with the men?"

"No. No one had anything to drink."

"Ghostly wisps are seen out there at night all of the time. I am sure that you were mistaken."

"Ezra, three men you respect, Simon, Andrew, and Papa, were all witnesses to this event, this miracle. Why don't you believe them?"

Ezra bowed his head. "It is hard to trust that they are not pulling my leg, Shai. I need to see something with my own eyes to believe it, not just hear about it. You experienced Yeshua's healing firsthand. Simon experienced Yeshua's will to have him join him on the water. I need that, too, Shai."

The pre-teen realized with shock that his brother was being honest, vulnerably honest with him. His older sibling was expressing his real feelings. Shai realized that he had indeed made so much headway in breaking down the barrier between them. Now, that barrier lay like rubble at his feet.

He did not want to make a mistake. He knew he needed to tread gently. "I do understand, Ezra. I have had the benefit of developing a relationship with the Nazarene physician, even friendship, definitely admiration, respect, and awe. I have been lucky to have witnessed and even participated in some of his miracles. Therefore, I do believe and trust him. If you would like, we can go together to listen to him during our next opportunity."

Ezra nodded with a smile. "I want to understand. Like Papa, I will have to make up my own mind."

"Agreed."

"Have you finished up your work here?"

"Almost. I haven't oiled the woodwork. It badly needs it." Shai ran his hand gently across the rough, dry wood.

"I'll help."

Shai quickly swallowed his sarcastic, *Really?* Ezra jumped off the boat. Shai was shocked that his bratty, bossy brother was willing

The Whistling Galilean

to work with him, even when Papa was not around to watch. This turn of events was fantastic.

Ezra quickly returned with the small, corked, clay jar of olive oil and clean rags. As they both rubbed the oil into the wood, they talked about girls, something they had started doing more frequently.

"Do you like Carmi's sister, Rachel, or the neighbor girl better?" Shai asked as he rubbed oil with the grain of wood to avoid getting a painful splinter.

"Both. It is hard to choose. The neighbor is prettier, but Rachel is nicer."

After discussing the merits of both girls, Shai discussed the girl of his dreams. "I still have eyes only for Carmi."

"No interest in anyone else?"

The vehement shake of his head in the negative almost caused the younger to fall off the bow onto the sand below. Ezra laughed so hard, he almost knocked over the jar of oil.

"Careful, boys. You will both end up down here with me."

Shai turned quickly toward the familiar voice coming from behind the stern. "Dov?"

"No other." Dov sauntered into view. "Shai, I just heard a retelling of your adventure last night. Do you seriously believe anyone could walk on water?"

If Shai told the truth, that would probably end their conversation right then. If he just recounted what he saw, maybe Dov would get curious. The third option was to lie and make something up. He knew he did not want to lie.

Therefore, he replied, "Yes I do believe that two men walked on the water of the Galilee. I saw it with my own eyes."

"Oooh, Mr. High and Mighty himself, all propped up on the bow."

"What do you believe, Dov?" Shai boldly threw the question back in the taller boy's face.

"Would you believe that I think it is all hogwash? I think Yeshua has the whole lot of you tricked into believing he is a miracle-worker. He must be a mass hypnotist. He is merely a man, just like us, muscle and bone. He's sneaky, I give him that. Maybe he faked somehow

~ 273 ~

Jennifer Bjork

and you believe his tricks. He is definitely not a true prophet and definitely not the Messiah, as Simon just professed."

Dov pointed at Shai, wagging his finger as if scolding him. "It's hard to imagine that I sought you ought to give you a chance to be friends again the day you got hurt at the Sukkoth. After that, you claimed Yeshua healed you. All of you who choose to believe that he is special are gullable, stupid, loony…blind. I wash my hands of the whole lot of you."

Shai watched his former best friend, Dov, wipe his hands together as if washing them. Then, he strode off the beach with urgency, as if he could not wait to get off of hot coals setting fire to the bottoms of his feet.

"I didn't know you had a falling out with your good friend over Yeshua. That must be hard." Ezra's voice was quiet and thoughtful.

"It hurt a lot at first. I missed having a best friend to confide in… to pal around with. He was the only person that knew I liked Carmi way back when. I just cannot choose Dov over Yeshua. We both made our choice about what to believe about a year ago. Neither of us has budged from that position since then."

"All this time…I had no clue. Now that we talk about girls, maybe we can spend more time together. You are almost a teenager. The older guys that I used to hang around have moved on to more dangerous activities like heavy drinking and thievery. I just don't want to do that. I don't want to dishonor Papa in that way."

"That's good to hear. I would like to spend more time with you."

Ezra reached around his waist and pulled out grandpa's fillet knife, "If you would still like to have it, I can ask Papa if I can give it to you as your apprenticeship gift next year."

"Really?"

Shai reached out and touched the knife. That black and silvery swirled metal blade was still so beautiful. It was obvious that Ezra was taking good care of it. Shai had not touched the fillet knife for a long time. He suddenly had mixed feelings. Should he take up Ezra's generous offer?

The Whistling Galilean

After a few moments of indecision, Shai decided. "No, you should keep it, Ezra. Grandpa gave it to you."

"I requested that specific gift. I asked him to give it to me to spite you."

Today was certainly a day of speaking truths. His brother did not apologize, but he did acknowledge how he became the recipient of that famous knife.

"That is an incredibly generous offer, Ezra. Thank you for telling me the truth. Let me think about it." Shai drummed his fingers on *Ole Blue*. "You deserve it and use it very well. I see that Papa and Grandpa are so proud of you when they watch you expertly using the knife to fillet fish. I am, too. No, I don't need time to consider your offer. The knife should stay in your hands."

27

Sabbath Revelation

SHAI GAZED AT THE ELDER'S CROOKED FINGERS AS HIS GRANDFATHER carefully smoothed his robe. Then the Elder rubbed the knuckles of one hand with the other. Was it just a nervous movement, or did they hurt? They looked painfully swollen, but the beloved man rarely complained. Shai wondered how the old man controlled his pain while seeming so cheery.

It was the Sabbath again. Mama had already scurried out the door with Adi. Papa walked the rambunctious Sim up the path. Earlier, Shai and Ezra had decided to follow the foursome with the Elder.

The white-haired man cleared his throat. "Grandsons, I appreciate your willingness to walk at my pace, but I do not think I can walk all the way to Capernaum today. We have no donkey to ride, and you certainly cannot carry me. Even if you could, that would constitute work and be forbidden. I have decided to stay here and sit in the sunshine. I will try to still my mind... concentrate on being thankful."

Shai worried. "Are you sure? With Ezra on one side and me on your other, our locked arms can support most of your weight. It

The Whistling Galilean

won't appear as work. We have already used that technique to help you around the yard."

"I know, grandson. I am certain. I am staying home today."

"What is bothering you, Grandpa? Your hands haven't stopped moving since you awoke this morning. Are you worried?" Shai's concern was evident in his voice.

"Yes, I am. I feel that I have unfinished business but I don't know what it is."

Ezra patted the Elder's shoulder. "I am sorry, Grandfather. We will honor your decision to stay, but we will miss your company. Let us make you comfortable before we depart. I will set up the small table by your stool in the sunshine and get you some cool water." Ezra departed after another loving pat on the old man's shoulder.

"Thank you, Number One." With a grin, he said to Shai, "It makes my heart glad to see you two as friends again."

Shai liked that, too. He saddened when he realized that this was the first time that the old man would not get to the synagogue on the Sabbath. The Elder took that responsibility seriously. It hurt the lad to think that his grandfather was getting so old, too old to do things that gave him pleasure, like honoring the Lord of Israel.

Despite Yeshua's visit and a brief respite in his decline, the Elder had aged considerably over the last few months. He now had trouble eating and remembering things that happened earlier in the day. He ached somewhere all of the time. Shai hated that there was nothing he could do to stop the approach to the end. All he could do was to be a companion, to listen, and to make the old man as comfortable as possible.

With help, Grandpa sat on the three-legged stool. He leaned back against the exterior house wall for support. "This is not going to work. I will be more comfortable on the ground with the cushions Mama made."

After a change in position, with help from Shai, he nodded, "This is better."

Ezra placed the gourd full of cool well water on the stool next to the Elder. Now the aged fisherman appeared to be comfortable. Shai held his own knees as he squatted in front of his grandfather and sat on his heels to keep his bottom clean.

"Grandpa, I have a question." Shai started. "Yesterday Ezra offered me the incredible fillet knife that you gave him when he became an apprentice fisherman. Did you know that he would do this?" He wondered if this generous act had really been his grandfather's idea.

"No, it is a surprise to me. It shows Ezra's maturity and change of heart."

"Yes. I have seen the transformation, too."

"You both realize that I am standing here." Ezra reminded them, since they appeared to have started a private conversation.

"Listen away, brother. What do you think, Grandpa? Should I accept it?"

"Number One has been an expert at using that blade. Remember, I obtained it in Jerusalem from my cousin. I have watched Ezra fillet fish. I think he should keep it. You have a gift from me already, my love."

Shai liked hearing Grandpa call him, *my love*, not *Number Two*. The pre-teen replied, "I agree that Ezra is an expert with your blade. I agree that he deserves to keep it. I thanked him for the offer and told him to keep the fine knife. I wanted you to know."

Shai paused, thinking hard. What gift was grandfather referring to? What gift did Grandpa give him? Was it the small carving knife?

As if the old man could read his thoughts, he spoke, "Shai, I have given you the gift of learning a skill with me, sharing time with me, hearing my stories. I loved that time with you." He grinned his still-toothy grin, "We carved wood and gourds. I have also given you the gift of my small carving knife. Granted, it is not as elegant and showy as the one that Ezra received, but it has more talents. It can whittle and carve many surfaces, deep or shallow etches. Together, we created a beautifully carved bowl following your design. You, my grandson, might not be a fisherman all your life. I think that you have need of the knife I gave you. I feel in these achy bones that as an adult you are destined to do something important."

The Whistling Galilean

That was quite a speech. They were eye-to-eye, brown eye to fading blue eye. Shai felt the deep love and his strong connection with this old man. His eyes teared up. So did his grandfather's.

"Grandfather? What about me?" Ezra wondered aloud.

"We have talked, too, Ezra. I love that I taught you to use the fillet knife and that you have become a very skillful carver. You bring the family, me, and that famous blade great honor. You have become a talented fisherman and a valuable member of the community. I am proud of you and sense that you will follow in your respected father's footsteps."

The Elder gestured with a point of his chin. "Now, go Shai. Go Ezra. Trot to get to the Sabbath service, then you can tell me all about it when you return. I feel curiously refreshed...as if I have completed something that has been on my mind. Go." Raising his palm-down hand from his leg, the old man dismissed his grandsons with a few flicks of his bent fingers.

Shai stood, patted the old man's knees, and kissed his wrinkled cheek. "I love you so much. Thank you for my gifts, especially the time you carved out for me. I treasure them all - especially your love."

Ezra did the same. "Thank you for your high praise. It gives me pleasure to follow in your footsteps. Enjoy the warm sunshine. We will return shortly."

Quickly, the brothers hurried down the familiar, weathered path. Shai enjoyed their relaxed, friendly companionship. Neither of them felt the need to talk. Their conversations with Grandfather had left them both feeling content. Since they were late, they picked up the pace to a trot.

Shai knew that the Elder was right. He felt it in his bones, too. He loved holding and handling his grandfather's small carving blade. He loved his memories of all of the time the two of them had spent together. He was satisfied. It was enough. It was more than sufficient.

When the two brothers arrived in Capernaum, there was a large crowd gathered around the synagogue.

A man wearing a faded robe with pale brown stripes suddenly

took hold of Shai's arm, whispering urgently, "Our Yeshua is in trouble today. A few days ago, he sharply criticized a small group of traveling Pharisees and scribes, spies from the Jerusalem Temple powers."

A tall man holding a shepherd's cane with a crook on top stepped in front of Ezra and grabbed Shai's other arm.

"Let go of my brother." Ezra tried to pull him off.

The man with the cane pushed the taller brother behind him. Leaning forward, the man spoke across Shai's chest, "I thought that the Nazarene merely chastised them in public. Wasn't the issue over the Laws of purification, the cleansing of the hands before handling food?"

The man in the brown-striped robe answered, "Yes. They believed that Yeshua and his followers did not wash their hands before breaking bread." Shaking Shai's arm to draw the lad's complete attention, the man asked, "Were you there son?"

"If you are speaking of the hillside east of the Jordan a few days ago, yes. I was there that day, but I am unaware of the events to which you refer." That was a partial lie because Shai remembered all of it very well.

The man wearing stripes described, "I saw the face of one of the robed ones flushed red in anger. I'm not sure that their criticism was true. They may have made it up. On that day in the grassy desert near Bethsaida, I saw Yeshua pray before breaking bread. Therefore, he appropriately blessed that meal. He raised his hands skyward to Heaven. The Law states that raising one's hands skyward is a symbol for the purification, if the meal isn't a sacrifice to the Lord of Israel. Since it wasn't a sacrifice, he met the letter of the Law."

Shai added, "I saw Yeshua do that, also."

The man with the crooked cane continued, unfazed, "As the old saying goes, 'bread eaten with unwashed hands is as if it has been filth.'" The man's chuckle seemed forced out from his rounded gut, as if he didn't want to share it with anyone else.

Shai felt that the man wearing the striped robe was explaining the events of a few days ago for Shai's ears alone as he continued in

The Whistling Galilean

a quiet tone, "The spies claim he broke the tradition of the Elders. In order to abide by the Law for purification under King Solomon, the Temple priests had to totally immerse their hands in clean water before they handled food that was sacrificed to Elohim. Now it is common for a man to just uplift his hands toward the heavens before handling common food prior to a meal."

Shai nodded. "Yes, that is what I have been taught."

"I remember learning that, too." Shai was surprised to hear Ezra's voice behind him. He had forgotten that they had walked - no, trotted - together that morning.

He noticed that their progress toward the doorway of his destination was very slow. He heard Rabbi Selig's prayers that started the Sabbath service. He wiggled to get away from the two men. However, their grasps around his arms tightened.

The man with the cane accused, "The Pharisees and scribes discovered Yeshua and his disciples at rest on the hillside. The disciples did not partake in the earlier feast but had busily collected baskets of uneaten fish and bread. I watched them. They did not wash their hands with water, dip their hands in water, or at the least, raise their hands to the heavens. Therefore, they were caught. They broke the Law."

The man in stripes showed his disagreement by wagging his finger. "Oh, but you are wrong. The meal that they ate had already been consecrated. Yeshua acted as head of household and blessed the meal early that evening, his arms raised to the heavens."

"That is what I observed," Shai added, hoping to end the debate and soon pass through the doorway into the synagogue.

"Well, that may be technically correct, but the appearance seemed to be improper."

"Did Yeshua apologize to them for breaking the Law?" Shai asked.

The man wearing stripes answered, "No he did not. I have not myself seen Yeshua break any of the Laws."

"Did he defend his actions as appropriate?" Shai continued to press.

~ 281 ~

Jennifer Bjork

The man with the cane ignored the question. "The Nazarene accused the Pharisees of making their traditions more precious and binding than the Law of Moses that came directly from Elohim. He claimed that their teachings condemned them and were incompatible with the very words of Elohim."

The man in the striped robe worried, "Those accusations are harsh. Are you siding with the plot underfoot to disprove the healer. You know that it comes from the Jerusalem Temple crowd, the know-it-alls. I hear that they claim he does the work of Satan."

Shai felt emboldened since he had an ally beside him, so he defended Yeshua also, "That is ridiculous. Alter, the former paralyzed man here in Capernaum, was healed by the Nazarene physician. The change from lame to walking was immediate. Alter even ran around with his friends that evening. Only Elohim has the power to let the lame walk. Yeshua prays to Elohim first. I have heard him pray, 'in the power and glory of Elohim.' Yeshua does not do evil work, the work of Satan."

The man wearing stripes spoke softly, "You are a convincing witness, son. Be careful. The powers from the south have spies here in Galilee today. I have seen them. These spies are trying to catch the Nazarene in a lie. I overheard them say that if they can prove that he blasphemies and lies, they feel that they can discredit all of his teachings."

Both men finally released him and Shai eagerly slipped into the synagogue. Ezra followed closely. "What was that all about?"

By then, the service was already underway. Shai pushed Ezra gently towards the men's side of the synagogue. In a hushed voice, Shai whispered, "We will speak about it later."

The pre-teen still had to stand on the side with the women and children because he had not yet come of age into manhood. He was not yet thirteen years old.

The previous conversations upset the lad. He was not in his usual, calm, worshipful mood in this holy room. Instead, he was irritated that some people misunderstood and opposed his caring adult friend. How could he warn the Nazarene?

~ 282 ~

The Whistling Galilean

It was now the time in the service for a guest to speak. Rabbi Selig nodded to some robed visitors from the south. When they nodded in return, the rabbi beckoned to someone out of Shai's view.

Yeshua walked to the center of the room. To Shai, the Nazarene looked well-rested despite his endless, frantic schedule of late. He looked well groomed, with his short beard cropped and tamed. The last time Shai had seen him, the teacher was tired, damp, and disheveled in *Ole Blue*.

Shai was surprised that Rabbi Selig stood aside for a man he did not respect nor welcome. He did not have time to ponder that mystery. Feeling anticipation build in the small, packed room, Shai watched his adult friend nod to some and smile at others. There was quiet verbal recognition in return:

"Yeshua, good to see you..."

"I look forward to hearing your sermon..."

"Thank you for healing my son..."

There were also whispers:

"It is Yeshua..."

"He came..."

"He is not afraid..."

"Heal me, oh great one...."

Yeshua straightened his tan robe and cleared his voice. He included them all by raising his arms straight upward above his head making a V-shape and turning in a circle.

As the master teacher did this, Shai guessed that Yeshua's popularity created a demand that was impossible for Rabbi Selig to ignore or deny.

His adult friend began calmly stating what many in the room wondered, "I tell you the truth." He paused for emphasis. "You are looking for me because you ate the fish and loaves a few days ago and had your fill."

The Nazarene reminded his listeners about the manna from heaven that the Lord of Israel had provided to their ancestors when led by Moses towards the promised land. "The manna arrived each morning from the heavenly skies, appearing with the morning dew.

Jennifer Bjork

The white flakes lay delicately on top of the ground. The travelers, your ancestors, had to collect it immediately and had to eat it that very day or it would spoil. For forty years, this manna sustained their journey throughout the deep desert to the south. It gave them life. Without it they would have died."

While he spoke, Shai nodded in agreement for he had heard this story many times, ever since he was young.

Then Yeshua told them. "Do not work for food that spoils, but for food that endures to eternal life."

As usual, the teacher added something new. The boy heard murmurs around the room. He wondered what his friend would explain next.

First, Yeshua reminded his listeners, "Even though the manna from Heaven sustained the Israelites, it had to be provided every day. It did not last forever. Even those who ate the manna from Heaven eventually died in the wilderness. Their carcasses fell in the desert. The manna did not sustain them forever, just long enough for a remnant of their young to enter the land promised to them."

He continued in his patient, calm manner, "*I tell you the truth, it is not Moses who has given you the bread from Heaven, but it is my Father who gives you the true bread from Heaven. For the bread of Elohim is* the one *who comes down from Heaven and gives life to the world. I am that bread of life.*"

There was a united gasp. Then, shocked stillness descended into the room like a heavy curtain blocking out the light. The shock of this statement silenced them all, even the spies from the south with their undercurrent of hissing.

If Shai understood the Nazarene's words correctly, he recognized that Yeshua first reminded them that only Elohim - the Lord of Israel, their powerful God - only He could provide the manna, the bread from Heaven. Yeshua said that he was the bread of life, the new manna. What did that mean?

Secondly, Yeshua had identified Elohim as his Father. That meant that he had claimed that his father was God. Every local knew

The Whistling Galilean

that Joseph and Mary were his parents. Many in the room knew them personally. Is that what Shai had heard? Oh, my. How could that be? That wasn't possible. Was it?

Shai wanted - no, needed - to hear more. He didn't understand. He needed clarification. He knew this man from Nazareth. They were friends. He knew him to be truthful. Shai needed ammunition to dispute the plot of opposition that was growing against the Nazarene. Right before his eyes, the Galilee that he knew and loved was becoming a war-ground of suspicion.

That is when a gray-haired man bolted forward, disturbing the sermon and shouting, "You are in a holy place. You claim to speak the truth, but you do not. You speak blasphemy against the Lord of Israel. I cannot stay and listen to YOU!"

The man stomped out of the synagogue, leaving everyone unsettled and wondering.

Yeshua remained calm, "I paused to let you reflect. It was intentional. I want my words to sink into your hearts. I repeat, *I am the bread of life.* The person *who comes to me will never go hungry, and* the person *who believes in me will never be thirsty. But... you have seen me and still you do not believe.... For I have come down from Heaven not to do my will but to do the will of Him who sent me.*"

The boy heard a growing mutter around him stir up the silence like a wooden spoon in a mixing bowl. One disgruntled man muttered under his breath, "Is this not Yeshua, the son of Joseph, whose father and mother we know? How can he say, 'I came down from Heaven'? He was born here among us."

The tall Nazarene replied, "*Stop grumbling among yourselves.* I was raised by Joseph and Mary, whom you know. I was sent by my Father in Heaven and have been teaching you for over two years, as was prophesied long ago.

"It is written by the prophet Isaiah, 'They will all be taught by God'. Over several years, you have come to hear my words. *Everyone who listens to the Father and learns from Him* is invited to *come to me.* I invite you to listen to these words. I invite you to seek and learn.

"Over the past years, some of you have listened to my words

~ 285 ~

about prayer. I pray to Elohim every day. I hope that you do, too. In these daily prayers, you can tell Elohim about your worries and concerns, as I do. You can share gladness and good deeds with your Creator, as I do. Tell the Ultimate Judge on high about your shortcomings and the apologies and actions you are taking to make amends. Thank the Great Sustainer for His many blessings. Ask for healing, wisdom, peace, and joy. Ask the All Knowing to remove the barriers to your understanding. And, yes, even ask for your daily bread, as I did not too long ago near Bethsaida. You know me and my body of work.

"Now, I ask you to use that body of work and stretch that knowledge into the truth. My personality and character are your bread of life, from which you have drawn sustenance - knowledge about the true Kingdom, physical cures and care, and spiritual comfort. I have provided for your deepest need and for the hunger of your soul.

"I repeat, *I am the bread of life. Your forefathers ate the manna in the desert, yet they died. But here, standing before you today, is the bread that comes down from Heaven, which a man may eat and not die.* By 'eating this bread' I mean chew on my words like you do with the teachings of Rabbi Selig. Think and discuss my words and the ideas behind them. Chew on them to understand them.

"But I mean even more. Eating this bread means taking my words into your very hearts and believing that I am the one that I claim to be. The faith that you have in me to heal your loved ones is the very same faith that you need in order to recognize me as the one sent from Heaven. Believing in me as your heavenly bread and spiritual sustenance will truly give you everlasting life.

"*I am the living bread come down from Heaven. If anyone eats of this bread, he will live forever. This bread is my flesh, which I will give for the life of the world.* All you have to do is to believe and to trust. I ask you today, believe in me. Believe that I am who I say I am."

With those last words, his sermon was over. With a quick prayer

The Whistling Galilean

to the Lord of Israel, Yeshua departed. His disciples quickly moved out of the synagogue and disappeared with their teacher.

People around Shai stood. After a smattering of "Amen's," they departed, also. As Shai searched for Ezra, several disgruntled men pushed past the pre-teen in an angry rush, saying things like:

"...thinking he is equal to Elohim. Preposterous!"

"Bread of life...that is not possible."

"I know his father, Joseph...."

Another man nudged Shai. As the adult passed beside him, Shai saw tears on the man's cheeks and collecting on his beard. The man departed with a wail of despair, "Noooo! I considered him a prophet. Not anymore. No man is equal to the Lord of Israel!"

A few, like Shai, stood in wonderment, remaining rooted in place.

Eventually, Shai heard one lone voice break his reverie, "Hallelujah. He has come. The Messiah is here!"

Soon, other voices joined the first in praise, "Hallelujah." The people remaining in the synagogue seemed to have enough proof to decide. They chose to believe, like the disciples before them.

Not, Shai. Despite Simon's profession of belief, Shai had to chew on the new thoughts, digest today's events. In his sermon, the Nazarene openly identified himself. He claimed to be the son of God, the son of their very Lord of Israel. At the end of the sermon, Yeshua gave each of his listeners a choice. They either could believe in him as the promised one, the Messiah, or they could choose not to believe. There was no longer any neutral ground.

28

Shai's Tale

THE PRE-TEEN WOVE HIS WAY THROUGH THE CROWD STILL DISPERSING from the synagogue in Capernaum, moving like a stream with very little current. Like Shai, many were still confused and unsure.

A man in front of him muttered, "Manna was the bread of life. Yeshua fed us bread in the desert. Is that what he means by the new manna? When will he feed us again?"

Many gray-beards wearing phylacteries on their foreheads were sprinkled throughout the slow-moving crowd. Shai had noticed their growing presence and interest. He knew that some religious lawmakers were actually clever watchers, spies, trying to trip Yeshua into doing something wrong. Other spies appearing as common travelers were probably sprinkled around, too. The opposition toward the Nazarene had grown. Yeshua's shocking message admitting to being the long-awaited Messiah had given them plenty of fuel to stoke their fires.

Shai knew that his parents wanted him to become a proper Hebrew man. To honor them, he continued to go to school despite Rabbi Selig's growing open opposition to Yeshua. Shai knew that

The Whistling Galilean

Rabbi Selig still stressed the many Hebrew laws governing their lives, as he was taught to do in Jerusalem. In addition, the rabbi boldly spoke specifically against Yeshua for wanting to modify or transform some of them. Shai felt that he could not defend his friend in that classroom setting. It was frustrating.

Going to school made him feel like a traitor. He believed Yeshua's sincerity and honesty. For example, by accepting the one unpleasant thing about Ezra as the Nazarene had suggested, the barrier between the brothers eventually crumbled. The skilled teaching, even though it had seemed counterintuitive, had been a successful path of action.

Where was Ezra, anyhow? Shai had searched for his older brother but had not seen him in the crowd. Instead of continuing to wait, he decided to head for home. That path took him through the marketplace. That path took him right to Carmi. He was not aware if it was intentional or not, but there she stood, right in front of him.

In surprise, Shai exclaimed, "Carmi, it's you!" He peered into those deep brown eyes and long eyelashes. "What a nice surprise. I think about you all of the time."

She grinned. "Imagine that. What do you think about?"

He felt hot as his checks reddened. He knew that she noticed because of her coy smile - one side of her cute lips curled higher than the other.

He stammered, "Uhhh...I can't tell you. I mean...nothing really...just about being together...you know...friends."

She let his words lamely peter out before replying, "It's good to see you, too. As you know, my family is not selling anything on the Sabbath. I am merely on my way home from the synagogue."

"Me, too. You look wonderful."

Today, she wore a pretty, pale yellow fabric with some bright yellow and green flowers stamped on it. He had seen his sister, Adi, cut the flat of a raw tuber into a shape, then dip it into a bowl holding a plant-based dye, and finally, stamp the dye onto the fabric. That made it unique. He guessed that Carmi had done the same thing.

"Thank you. It is good to see you, too. Let's walk and talk. We have a lot to talk about."

~ 289 ~

Jennifer Bjork

As they walked, Shai noticed that his freckled friend had pulled her wavy, light-brown hair away from her face. The resulting braid hung gracefully down her neck and back. At nearly thirteen, she was developing into an attractive woman. *Oops.* He better not have thoughts like that, or he would blush again.

"Occasionally I see your brother, Ezra, visiting Rachel. You should come with him someday. Then we could see each other, too."

"Is he secretive, like just happening to find her in the orchard? Or does he come formally with an adult chaperone?"

"I guess they meet by accident, like us. She wonders if he likes her."

"He does. He talks about her a lot. He also likes a neighbor girl. I'm not sure that he has selected a favorite yet. That makes me wonder. Does another boy come looking for you?"

"Oh, there are a few that act interested."

"Really? I mean…you are certainly pretty enough to attract attention. You also have a friendly, happy personality. I can see that there would be many boys attracted to you, just like I am. I just didn't know if I needed to worry about that."

"You worry too much, Shai."

"Should I be worried? Do you have a boyfriend?"

"Yes, I do."

"Oh, no." Now he was really worried. "Do I still have a chance with you…to become your boyfriend?"

"Quit your worrying and listen. It is you. I like you better than anyone else."

"Me?" The pre-teen exhaled, "Ooooh, goooood…that's a relief."

"Are you still worried?"

"I guess so. Carmi, there is no other girl that I like. I do not go seeking anyone else."

"I am glad to hear that."

"Since neither of us officially have a boyfriend, or a girlfriend, would you be my girlfriend?"

She laughed so hard that she stopped walking. Shai just stood there looking down at his feet. Her laughter at him hurt his feelings.

The Whistling Galilean

Was she rejecting him? He could not tell from her joyous face and demeanor.

She finally responded using words, "Silly. I have been your girlfriend for years. Don't you already know that? I cannot imagine liking anyone else."

Shai was elated. Now he, too, burst into laughter. "You just made my heart glad!"

She did like him best. He was surrounding himself with joyous people, just like Yeshua had suggested. Her mere presence made his head swim and his heart happy. Yeshua was right...again.

That reminded him of something, "Yeshua! You were in the synagogue, too, so you heard him claim to be the 'bread of life that came down from Heaven.' What do you make of his sermon?"

"It was a shock to everyone. I noticed that even his disciples were surprised."

"Not too many days ago, Simon and Andrew professed their belief that Yeshua is indeed the Messiah, the one that the prophesies of old said would come, the new King of Israel."

"Oh? I had not heard they believed. I heard some of them debating about it."

"The night he escaped the growing crowd wanting to crown him "king", after he fed them the loaves and fish...that day in the desert meadow near Bethsaida, 'Fisherton'..."

"Yes, I was there with Rachel. I saw you give Yeshua the fish and barley loaves. How many did you give him?"

"I gave him five barley loaves and two sardines. They were for my afternoon snack."

"Oh, my. Yeshua stretched that meager offering to feed thousands of us. It was another miracle, Shai."

"Yes, it was. I gave him all I had. I apologized that it wasn't more. Yeshua thanked me. He told me that my gift was sufficient. Yeshua, through the power of Elohim, made it so. I was amazed, too."

"I am not surprised, but I am so impressed - proud of you."

Shai felt taller. He felt so glad to hear the cute girl beside him

Jennifer Bjork

think highly of him. It meant a lot, more than anyone could ever guess.

"That was not all. Papa and I took many of Yeshua's disciples out into the Galilee while the teacher slipped up into the hills to pray and refresh. That night - you won't believe what I tell you, so just listen - that night, we returned to Capernaum to pick him up. In the misty rain after the storm, we saw an apparition standing on the water. It was Yeshua - standing on the waters of the Galilee. After he called to Simon, that giant fisherman we all know well, stepped out onto the Galilee, also. Together they walked on the water back to *Old Blue*. That's the summary of what happened. I can tell you more details if you would like."

"Did you just tell me that they both walked on the sea...on water?"

"Yes. When Simon's attention was diverted from Yeshua, when his trust wavered, he started to sink, but Yeshua reached out and refocused Simon's attention and trust."

"Oh, my. That is hard to believe. No man - no person - can walk on top of water."

"You are right. It is hard to believe that even the miracle-worker, Yeshua, did it. It is even harder to believe that Simon walked on water, too."

Carmi drew an interesting conclusion. "So, I infer that if we believe in Yeshua, we can do miracles, too?"

"I had not thought of that. I guess so, but the power must still come from Elohim. Is that what you understand?"

"Yes. So today, Yeshua talked about the manna from Heaven and caring for us when we need him - like feeding thousands of people bread and fish as an example. He admitted that he could only do these things through the power of Elohim."

"Yes, that is what I heard and believe, too."

"But Yeshua also said that Elohim is his father. Do you believe that can be true? I have never heard Yeshua tell a lie."

Shai agreed with her. "I haven't either. That is the issue that I am wrestling with, chewing on mentally. How can Yeshua, the man

The Whistling Galilean

I know as my friend...how can he be the son of Elohim, the very Lord of Israel?"

"Isn't that what the word '*Messiah*' means? The *Christ*?"

"Carmi, Rabbi Selig taught us that '*Messiah*' means the expected King and deliverer."

"Alright. I understand that the Messiah will be more powerful than Moses or any of the prophets."

"Yeshua seems to have drawn on and used that type of power."

They reached the outskirts of Capernaum, where Shai's trail branched off to the right. Together, they stepped off the path.

"This has been nice, Shai, but I must go left to get home, and you must go right." The back of Carmi's soft hand brushed his.

Shai's insides trembled with delight. "We must continue this discussion, Carmi. There are so few, only Grandpa and you, with whom I can talk about my faith, religious beliefs, and Yeshua so openly."

"I have only two confidants, too - you and Rachel. I hope to see you again...soon."

"Me, too. Take care. Keep that dinar close." Shai grinned at the girl he really, really, really liked.

"I do. It travels with me every day. You be careful, too. Don't try to walk on the water." With a grin and a wave, Carmi left with a chuckle.

29

Yona the Elder

Confused, Shai stopped at the edge of the clearing with a jolt. No one seemed to be acting normally and they were still wearing their best clothing. He sensed that something was wrong.

Mama paced in front of their home, wringing her hands and humming nervously. Adi and Sim sat on the ground pretending to be chickens. He could hear their *peeps*. Strangely, both kids were covered in dirt. Papa absently moved pieces of wood from one side of the woodpile to the other. Ezra and Grandpa were not in sight.

Mama spotted him and rushed over, surrounding him with her slight arms. She gave him a tight squeeze with a sigh. She buried her head in his chest and wailed, "Shai, my son…oh, Shai…."

Shai had never heard her sob before and did not know how to react. She continued after a big sigh, "He is gone to rest, my son. He is gone…." And she sobbed some more.

Shai had already been dealt several shocks that day. Now what? Mama had never reacted in this manner, at least not in his presence. He worried about her. Out of concern, he gently patted her back,

The Whistling Galilean

mumbling, "There, there...there, there...there, there...." He had experienced that type of comfort and hoped it would help.

They remained rooted in that spot repeating the same sounds and actions. Finally, she pushed away from him, wiping moisture from her reddened cheeks and blue eyes. Instinctively, Shai knew she was struggling to pull herself together, so he gave her additional time.

Finally, he asked timidly, "Are you alright?"

She drew in a deep breath and steadied her nervous hands. She nodded in affirmation, then patted his shoulders. "Oh, Shai. Even though we expected it, we didn't know it would happen today."

Now, Shai was really concerned. "What happened?"

"The Elder went to rest. He is now hidden from us."

Now, Shai was even more concerned. He readied himself to go and search for the old man. "Hidden? Where?"

"He died, Shai. He has been gathered by the Angel of Death." In disbelief, Shai watched his pillar of inner power, his mother, shudder as she gathered herself into temporary control. "We are all surprised. We knew it would eventually happen but were surprised anyway. I am sorry I got so emotional and could not tell you calmly. You two were so close. It hurts me deeply to have to tell you this sad news."

"But we had such a wonderful talk this morning. How can it be?"

Then Shai felt his father's strong arms around him, pulling Shai toward his strong body. "I am sorry, Shai. You will miss him deeply. We will all miss him." Shai felt his father tremble with emotion. "I will miss my father...."

His father's sudden release of tightly held emotion helped Shai release his own. They stood in a hug, heaving and sobbing together. Mama joined them. The immediate release of a passionate longing to undo the separation - the living from the dead - was intense. It tore a hole in his heart. Shai was shocked to hear his voice join Mama's in a high-pitched, keening wail. He had no idea that he could even make that sound.

Shai had never wanted anything with more desire, not even Carmi's friendship, than he wanted to retain the presence, the

Jennifer Bjork

essence of the old fisherman that he loved so much. But grandfather was gone. His time on earth had been completed.

Eventually, Shai separated from his parents and breathed deeply, wiping his cheeks in an attempt to erase and hide his emotional release. "I could not find Ezra. Has he come home? Does he know?" His voice sounded weird - husky and gravely.

Papas voice was like that, too. "Yes, Shai. Ezra is with the Elder now."

"Where are they?"

Mama responded this time. "They are both in the house. He needed to say a private farewell and did not want to wait. Do you want a turn, too? Next?"

Shai felt an inward bravery and urgency. "Yes. I must see for myself that he has departed this life. Yes, I must say goodbye, too."

"Wait until Ezra comes out, then you can go in. We will all remain outside." Papa, in control again, directed the proceedings. Shai watched his father gently request, "Anat, this is a hard task. Please, go tell the neighbors and ask for their help after sunset, after the Sabbath has passed."

"I will, my love." They embraced and kissed. "I will take Adi and Sim next door. They need to be fed." After a lingering pat on his bearded cheek, she gathered the kids and departed into the forest.

Papa turned his attention to Shai. "You have not seen death yet, my son. It will be hard. Take as long as you need. After sunset, when we can again go to work, we will do what is necessary to honor my father, your grandfather. You, Ezra, and I will notify the other fishermen about his death and obtain what is necessary for the funeral. We must display our love and respect for the Elder and honor him properly."

"I will be glad to do whatever task necessary, Papa. I am glad that the Elder spent years with us. I am grateful to get to know him. I have grown to love him deeply." Before Shai could control himself, he was sobbing again.

His father hugged him again, whispering, "And, he loved you deeply, too. He felt closer to you than to Ezra, or even to me. It was a

The Whistling Galilean

wonderful, special connection. Draw on your memories of him, my son. They will help sustain you."

Shai was surprised by his father's tenderness and advice. That was a side to the man that the boy did not know - yet. "Is there something specific that I can do?"

"Yes, I will outline our needs when you have finished your private farewell."

After a gentle squeeze of Shai's shoulder, Papa disappeared into the forest. The boy suspected that his father needed time to gather himself together.

It was Shai's turn to pace alone. His thoughts were in turmoil. His mind flashed with glimpses of his grandfather. A few seconds later, other scenes involving the wonderful old man appeared. He could not concentrate on any one thought for long. His rapid breathing was driven by these memories. When he realized he was panting, as if in a long-distance race, he tried to slow down his breathing. He hoped that would calm his emotional upheaval.

Shai heard the enormous sigh before seeing his brother appear at the doorway. All Shai noticed at first was matted brown hair. Ezra's head drooped downward, and one hand was wiping his nose. In a daze, Ezra glanced around and motioned for Shai to go in. That was the cue. Shai squeezed Ezra's shoulder to acknowledge the invitation. Many unspoken thoughts passed between them before the eldest brother headed to the fire pit.

Shai did not want to face what awaited him on the other side of the door, but he was drawn, compelled forward. He felt his legs walk his body into the dark interior. As his eyes adjusted to the darkness, Shai saw Grandpa's body. The only light in the room came from the doorway and from one large, lit candle that sat on the old man's three-legged stool at his head. His grandfather's body was laid out flat on his back in the center of the bare floor on top of his sleeping mat. He was still dressed in the clothing he had donned to go to the synagogue that early morning. Shai relaxed a little bit when he realized that the Elder appeared as if he was taking a peaceful nap and was not in a gruesome, tortured configuration.

~ 297 ~

Jennifer Bjork

He slowly approached and knelt at Grandpa's side one last time. The Elder's wrinkled face looked relaxed. At least he was no longer in pain, aching in all of his joints. Shai laid a hand on the stiff chest and let his tears flow at will. With no one to watch him, he released his love through his hand into the old man, willing him to smile that crooked smile, cock his head, and wink with that pale blue eye one more time. He laid his head on Grandpa's chest and cried inconsolably:

"Oh, Grandpa…don't go…I love you…stay…."

"Oh, Grandpa…how can I live without you?

"Oh, Grandpa…how can I go on without your laughter…without your wise humor…without your companionship…without you?

"Oh, Grandpa…I love you so much…I will miss you so much…I love you so much…."

Shai rambled about their times together, his thoughts flowing out as freely as his tears. He was in free-fall. He felt lost, like he was falling in a deep, bottomless abyss. He verbalized as many memories as he could recall. When he had exhausted his memories, he just lay there to remain in touch with a man that had meant so much to him.

It took a considerable amount of time, but it finally sunk in - his grandfather was no more, he had died. What was left was just the shell of the man he loved.

With a deep, shaky sigh, Shai unfolded himself from his grandfather's body and sat up. The boy took several deep breaths before he opened his eyes and gazed lovingly at the beloved fisherman's face, trying to memorize every fold and wrinkle.

Then Shai smoothed the crinkled fabric where he had lain. "Oh, Grandpa…I am glad you are at peace…I am glad you are no longer in pain…but I am sorry that your time with me has ended. I will miss you more than anyone can imagine. Thank you for your companionship and for guiding me into manhood. I will complete my journey with the memories that you etched in my mind, as the etchings on the food bowl. Thank you, O Lord of Israel, for providing me with the most marvelous gift - the best grandfather that a boy could ever have. Thank you, Elohim."

The Whistling Galilean

He was spent, totally exhausted. Shai stood on shaky legs, blew the body of the old man on the floor a kiss, and walked out of the door into the sunlight.

A different arrangement of people met him at the door. First, Mama gave him another hug. "Are you alright, Shai?"

"Yes, Mama. I am alright. I had the time I needed for my farewell."

"Good, I know that was difficult." She patted Shai lovingly on the cheek like she had done with Papa earlier that day.

Moving into the doorway, she beckoned the ladies behind her to enter also. Mama paused and explained to her son, "Since the sun has set, it is time to prepare the body. Two neighbor women will help me wash his body, anoint it with olive oil, trim his hair and nails, and wrap him in the linen burial cloth I purchased only weeks ago. It will take us several hours."

Now her words came to him from over her shoulder, "Go, find your father and Ezra. Adi and Sim are with a neighbor."

So, he searched the gathered group of people outside of his home for his remaining family. Someone offered him some cheese and bread. He ate a little but was not really hungry. He heard his father's voice and headed toward it.

"Now that we have the musicians for the procession, we need the orator for the funeral. I had hoped Simon would be available."

"I am available." Simon's deep, gravelly voice seemed to boom out of the gathering. "I want to honor my friend, your family, and your father, Yona. I am here to be your orator, if that is your desire."

"It is."

"I have already asked several of the fishermen to dig the burial shaft next to the Elder's wife. Is that acceptable?"

"Yes, thank you." Papa was surprised. "That was going to be my request."

"Good. It is done. We have already taken care of the wickerwork box to carry his body. It is beside the house. Do not fret about anything else, my friend. You rest up. Say your necessary farewells. What time do you want us to gather tomorrow?"

~ 299 ~

"The Elder was an early riser. He would appreciate a sunrise burial. Sunrise represents hope. It unfolds the day to come."

"I will spread the word, Yona. We will be here just before sunrise to start the procession."

"I will help spread the word," another voice said.

The gathered people quickly dispersed, leaving Shai alone with Papa and Ezra.

"It is done." Papa looked exhausted. The color seemed to have left his face, and he looked like he had aged several years. "I thought we would be quite busy. Why don't you boys start a small fire in the pit? Our family has spent many good times together out here. This would be a good place to spend the night, get some needed rest. We cannot sleep inside next to the Elder's body. We will stay out here under the heavenly stars."

And they did.

By sunrise, many neighbors and families of the fishermen gathered in front of the house. Shai, Ezra, and Papa had not slept very much but had talked quietly into the night. It was a bonding experience to share memories, laughter, and even tears. They had each washed, donned clean tunics, and brushed off their nice robes. Shai gathered every detail of this sad process into his memories.

The trio had entered the house before anyone else arrived to place grandfather's body in the wicker bier. The Elder was so light that Shai could have lifted him all by himself. Mama and the ladies had done a masterful job. The Elder looked good, truly at rest. Shai and his brother had returned to the fire pit to give their father some extra time alone with Papa's own father.

The family was ready to start the funeral procession. The last arrivals were the three musicians - two flutists from Capernaum and a cymbalist, the son of a guild fishermen. He was the young boy who drummed rhythms on palm trunks or played a lute to make their tasks easier. The boy was a nice touch. The Elder would have liked that.

In a loud voice, Simon, the official funeral orator, started the

The Whistling Galilean

proceedings. "Alas, Yona the Elder is at rest. O, Lord of Israel, accept Yona the Elder into your great eternity. Alas, Yona the Elder, the great fisherman of the Galilee, is at rest. We honor his memory."

Simon led the procession from the house. He was barefoot. So was everyone else. During the night, Papa explained the traditions of reverence in honor of the dead. Simon was followed by the musicians and then the women, many of whom wailed openly. Shai and the family immediately followed the wicker basket bier carrying the Elder. The family was followed by friends.

It was an honor to carry the bier holding the body. The Elder lay tightly wrapped in cloth, face upwards. The old man's face remained uncovered. Shai knew the Elder would have wanted the breeze on his cheeks one last time. Four men, all friends of the Elder, carried the bier. The procession occasionally stopped so that another four friends could relieve them. Shai knew it wasn't because the Elder was heavy; he himself had nearly carried the old man while helping him change locations. Shai had learned that this task was one of the highest forms of a good deed because it was done without the expectation of a favor in return. Many men wanted to carry the Elder's body to his gravesite in order to share the good work, to help their friend reach his final rest. It was done out of reverence and love.

At these stops, Simon would say something glowing, praising Yona the Elder. Then the women led a chant: "Weep with him, all ye who are bitter of heart." It was repeated by all in attendance. By the time they reached the dry, rocky knoll within sight of the fisherman's beach, Shai knew that this chant would echo in his memories for a long time.

Since Shai had never been to the community burial grounds before, Papa had explained to him that it would dishonor the deceased to stand on or walk over a grave. Therefore, Shai was careful to follow in his father's footsteps. Thankfully, tufts of wildflowers and unshaped large rocks acted as markers for the graves.

Shai was surprised that the grave was actually a shaft. It was deeper than it was wide - about three and a half cubits deep by less than one cubit wide. Only Simon and the family of four - Shai,

Mama, Papa, and Ezra - stood around the grave shaft. The body of his grandfather was placed into the shaft feet first, after his exposed face was covered with a cloth. Despite thinking he had no more tears left, Shai wept again. It was final - Grandfather was no more.

He and his family placed a few ceremonial shovels of dirt on top on this *'place of silence'*. He vowed to return soon and place one of the smooth skipping stones next to the stone marker. He vowed to carve something for his grandfather.

The burial ceremony ended with a few words. It was all surreal to Shai. His emotions were drained. Having had little sleep, he felt as if this was all happening in a dream. But...it was real.

Simon said a prayer, "May you, O Lord of Israel and the source of mercy, pardon all of Yona the Elder's transgressions. Purify them so he may enter your eternal light. Shelter his soul beneath your wings for eternity. Make known to Yona the path of true life so he may rest in your peace."

Out of his daze, Shai noticed that Simon could vocalize spiritual comforts. He must have learned these skills under Yeshua's tutelage. Simon had become not just a leader of men, but a spiritual leader as well. Simon gave a short, touching, personal eulogy of praise about Shai's grandfather. No one had a dry eye.

A few other men spoke, too. Shai appreciated the quote from Ecclesiastes given by the closest friend of the Elder, who explained that the words had been passed down from King Solomon's time and revealed that God was at the center of every human endeavor:

"There is a time for everything, and a season for every activity under heaven:

- a time to be born and a time to die,
- a time to plant and a time to uproot,
- a time to kill and a time to heal,
- a time to tear down and a time to build,
- a time to weep and a time to laugh,
- a time to mourn and a time to dance,

The Whistling Galilean

- a time to scatter stones and a time to gather them,
- a time to embrace and a time to refrain,
- a time to search and a time to give up,
- a time to keep and a time to throw away,
- a time to tear and a time to mend,
- a time to be silent and a time to speak,
- a time to love and a time to hate,
- a time for war and a time for peace...

Friends, (we) have seen the burden Elohim laid on men. The Lord of Israel has made everything beautiful in its time. He set eternity in the hearts of men. There is nothing better for men than to be happy and do good while they live. That everyone may eat and drink and find satisfaction in all his toil - this is the gift of Elohim. I know that everything Elohim does will endure forever."

Simon added, "We are fishermen. We work hard and long. Through our labor and experiences with living, we have learned the seasons that Elohim has charted for us. We have learned that we are not in control - the Lord of Eternity is. Yona the Elder reached his season of old age. It was his time to die and our time to mourn the loss of his presence in our life. Farewell Yona the Elder. We will keep the memory of you alive in our hearts and our tales of your good deeds."

One last friend of the Elder spoke the final farewell. His familiar musical voice filled Shai's broken heart with immediate gladness. It was Yeshua. The Nazarene was Grandfather's friend, too. Shai felt that this man's presence and words were the equivalent of the '*there, there*' pats on his back that had comforted him years ago. The boy needed that comfort and was grateful.

Yeshua ended the ceremony with the following:

"In order for the memory of a loved one at rest to remain in our hearts, we must keep their name alive. It is our tradition. When

~ 303 ~

Jennifer Bjork

something reminds us of Yona the Elder, speak his name aloud or, at the least, silently in your heart. For example," and he paused between each statement to let the gathered absorb each thought:

> "I remember my friend, Yona the Elder, with the rising of the sun,
> I remember my father, Yona the Elder, with the blowing of the wind,
> I remember my grandfather, Yona the Elder, with the blueness of the sky and his eyes,
> I remember Yona the Elder with the vastness of the Galilee where he worked, and
> I remember Yona the fisherman with each catch of bounteous fish the Galilee provides.

"Remember Yona the Elder not only in your own memories. That can get lonely. Emulate Yona's goodness and acts of kindness by doing them yourself. He was a generous man. You cannot go wrong if you try to imitate the type of man that the special old fisherman became. If you strive to be like him, you, too, can receive respect and the love felt for that good soul. In the end, the greatest reminder of the life that anyone - that Yona the Elder, specifically, lived - are the actions that each of us chooses to show to others.

> "I will teach others the skills I learned from Yona the Elder,
> "I will share my friend's many tales with laughter,
> "I will share the wisdom of Yona's short quips, and
> "I will share the guidance he taught me through stories and examples.

"Remember the love that Yona the Elder shared with you. His love had great depth. Don't be afraid to share the kind, caring respect he shared with others. Remember, love does not die. Elohim is the source of love. Elohim is always close to the brokenhearted with a

The Whistling Galilean

peaceful comfort. As you mourn the passing of Yona, ask your Lord to mend your heart, to guide your path, and to restore a healing wholeness to your life. Elohim will guard your soul and your going and your coming, now and forever, as He guards the soul of Yona the Elder. Say not in grief - 'he is no more'. Instead say in thankfulness - 'he was.'

Now, go in peace. Go in remembrance of Yona the Elder."

The rest of the day was a blur. Shai was drained by his emotional upheaval and subsequent release. He was also exhausted from a lack of sleep. He felt he experienced the comfort from neighbors and friends through a fog, as if he himself had departed into another world.

Shai wasn't really hungry, but he ate some food to be polite. While he ate, Shai absorbed only a few of the many stories about Yona the Elder that people eagerly shared. Despite trying to acknowledge the kind words said to comfort him, he knew he fell short of appreciation.

"The Elder was a wise mentor," One fisherman said, recounting a tale.

"I will miss a talented fisherman. He could find fish better than anyone I knew. I will miss your grandfather," an older man said with misty eyes.

"May the Lord of Israel repair and restore your soul." Many neighbors hoped it would be soon.

Only one visitor made a really strong impression. At some point, Shai was startled out of his stupor by the familiar, fresh, intoxicating odor of clean hair. A person leaned over and touched the top of his hand, drawing his attention. Even in his funky fog, his insides jolted with a shock of recognition - Carmi!

"It is you! You came." Shai quickly tried to pull himself together as he straightened his robe.

"Of course, I came. I am your friend." Carmi spoke softly, for his ears only.

"Thank you, Carmi. That means a lot to me."

"Oh, Shai, I know that the Elder was very important to you. I

Jennifer Bjork

know that his death hurts you deeply and that it will take a long time for you to recover. After all, you were with him every day."

"That is true. I don't know what to say...I don't quite feel like myself. It hurts so much."

"I am sorry that you have to walk this path, Shai. He lived with you for several years, and you grew very close. I know that you will miss the sharing of feelings, experiences, skills, and ideas. I know that you will miss him very much and need a friend. I am your friend. I wish I could see you daily, as the Elder did, but I will see you as often as I can."

"I believe you. And I would like that."

"We still have a lot to talk about. Just the other day, you told me that your grandfather was one of two people with whom you could speak about anything, especially your growing belief in Yeshua as the Messiah. Please remember that I am the other one."

Her smile filled his world. "I remember." He sighed. She brought a temporary reprieve. "We wanted to talk about something specific... but I can't remember what."

"When you are ready, it will come to you."

Shai nodded and wondered aloud with a concerned edge to his voice, "Did you come alone?"

"No, I came with my family. My parents are speaking to yours right now and I can just make out Rachel with Ezra."

"Oh. Good. I didn't want you to have to walk home alone."

They sat side by side for a little while on the edge of the fire pit. He was content to just be with her. He was beyond holding a thought or conversation.

"I hope to see you again soon, Shai. My family is gathering to return home." Carmi patted the back of his hand. Her presence and touch were the best comforts he received on that difficult day.

30

Shai's Choice

THROUGHOUT THE WEEK, MANY FROM THE FISHING COMMUNITY continued to drop by to cook, clean, take care of the children or the garden, and do chores. This provided some needed time for every family member to rest and recover their energy. Shai slept more than ever before, so he wasn't aware of very much else. In wakefulness, he reviewed memories of the Elder.

Eventually, routines returned to normal. Papa and Ezra went fishing again. Mama took over the running of the household. Shai returned to learning his trade and Hebrew Laws.

One afternoon, he slipped down to his favorite private beach, his place of security and solace. There he swam and had a solitary place to reflect. As usual on this sliver of sanity, he wondered how his friend, Yeshua, was doing and where his travels had taken him.

Shai had not seen Nazarene since Grandpa's funeral and that Sabbath when the master teacher announced that he was the bread of life, equating himself to heavenly manna and even to Elohim Himself. Over the past weeks, the twelve-year-old had occasionally taken time to reflect on this. He had missed discussing it with his grandfather. Alone, he had chewed on the words that Yeshua had spoken, especially those about being the 'bread of life'.

Shai realized that Yeshua's identity had never been hidden. Over the last year, it had been revealed over and over again. Yeshua had given everyone, including himself, a choice to make - believe what he claimed or not. The twelve disciples had made their choice first. Shai knew it was his turn to decide.

As he sat on the palm log, he reached into his robe and pulled out the bird whistle that Yeshua had hand carved and given him as a gift. He turned it over and over in his palm, examining every detail delicately carved by the experienced carpenter. It was truly a most treasured possession.

He blew into the whistle, *Joy,* hoping to attract the group of songbirds just above his head. Through practice and breath control, he had taught himself how to change the sound emerging out of the wooden bird's mouth. It never failed to relax him to blow this whistle. It also made him remember and appreciate Yeshua, the man he'd befriended over two years ago.

In response, he heard the song of a beach wren just behind him and turned slowly toward the trill. He didn't want to startle the bird and send it flitting away. To his surprise, he faced Yeshua, the very person in his thoughts.

"It is you!" The obvious burst from his startled lips.

"Shalom, Shai. It is good to see you. I heard *Joy,* the whistle. The sounds that you create are much improved, even realistic."

Shai was thrilled. "I always think of you when I hold her. I was just thinking about you when I *tweeted.* And you appeared, standing behind me - as if I called you with the whistle, as if by magic. I wish it could always be that way."

"No, Shai. You know that it won't. Magic is not real."

"I just would like to see you more often. I miss you when you are gone so long, especially since grandfather is no longer with me daily."

Yeshua sat on the log beside Shai and pulled something from his own sleeve. "I want to show you something. I carry a flattened river

The Whistling Galilean

stone, one of the ones that we collected together the day that you taught me to skip stones on top of the water. I, too, carry something with which to remember a favorite friend."

Shai was surprised that his friend had a token, too. He quickly wished he had thought to give Yeshua this gift himself. It was just like the Nazarene to be so thoughtful.

"You look better than the last time I saw you, at Yona the Elder's funeral."

"I do feel better, but I still miss him. It is a jagged, deep wound, but I have an appetite again. It is hard to fill up with food. Mama says that I eat as much as two boys."

"It does look like you are taller."

"Perhaps."

"I know you miss the Elder, as do I. He was my friend, too."

"Yeshua, thank you for coming to the funeral. You reminded me that my actions emulating Grandpa show others what I learned from the Elder. It also demonstrates the importance of the Elder to me and it helps me keep his memory alive. It reminded me of a lesson that you taught me, several times now - actions speak louder than words. It was a comfort."

Yeshua patted the lad on the back. "You have learned very much, Shai. I see your grandfather's wisdom growing in you. Do you have time to visit for a moment?"

"Yes, of course. I would like that very much. What have you been doing?"

"My twelve helpers and I have been traveling throughout the north and east. It seems that my reputation for healing still precedes our travels. As soon as people recognize me, they bring their sick to be healed. When one of the twelve goes ahead to procure lodging, the sick quickly gather in the marketplace."

"In the Galilee, we get some word of your movements and miracles. I heard that you even healed someone who touched the edge of your cloak. Is that true?"

"Yes, true faith and trust were displayed that day."

"You are an incredible healer, Yeshua. There is no one

~ 309 ~

comparable. I witnessed so many...the paralyzed man, the man with leprous skin, and even me, remember?"

"How could I ever forget being able to use Elohim's power to help my joyous friend? Now, it is your turn to tell me how you are faring. How is your relationship with Ezra? Better?"

"Much better...repaired. Ezra even offered me that fillet knife. The knife grandfather gave him as an apprenticeship gift. Remember how jealous I was that day on this beach a few years ago?"

Yeshua merely nodded with a smile.

"When he showed it to me, I did momentarily desire that beautiful, sharp, marbled blade. I decided to let Ezra keep it and told him so. I spoke with its original owner, Grandpa.... Oh, my, I just realized that was the day Grandpa died...."

Yeshua gave Shai a moment to compose himself.

The pre-teen continued, "Grandpa agreed with me that Ezra should rightfully keep it. I realized that I have sufficient gifts and memories from the Elder. I have also seen Ezra use it to very skillfully fillet fish. I have seen the pleasure and pride that gives Papa...and gave Grandpa. I feel that way, too. My brother deserves the knife."

"That was a wise, mature decision. I see that you are blossoming into an adult. I bet your father is proud."

"He is. He changed, too. Now, he is no longer ashamed to express his pride and caring for me in public. That makes me feel good, included. The Sabbath that Grandfather died, Papa, Ezra, and I sat up all night talking. We have become very close."

"That is wonderful news." Yeshua chuckled at that image. "It may have all started when you accepted one unpleasant thing."

"It was difficult to do. You were right, as usual. I am glad I took the first step. Now I have a brother who I am growing to respect. We have become friends again."

"That is good news."

"Did you know that Dov and I are no longer friends?"

"I suspected there would be a falling out. I knew you would both be making hard decisions. Tell me about it."

"Dov washed his hands of anyone who believes your teachings.

The Whistling Galilean

That was directed at me specifically, of course. He even tried to get me to disavow seeing you walk on water."

Yeshua nodded. "While I was busy elsewhere, I see that serious decisions were made. One of your choices reconciled you to your brother. A second choice lost you a friendship. I am sorry that choice caused you to experience firsthand one of the consequences of defending me."

"Yes, losing my best friend did hurt. Now, though, I am glad I made that choice to tell him what I truly saw. Dov also made a choice. He chose not to believe me...or you."

"That is true."

Now seemed a good time and opportunity to warn his friend. "Yeshua, I am worried for you. I am concerned for your safety."

Yeshua nodded and patted Shai's knee. "Thank you for your concern. Despite dissenters and spies, I will continue to speak out. I have an obligation to speak the truth wherever I go. I must spread my message whatever the consequences may be. My friend, I warn you, too. Be careful. The opposition will worsen."

"Will you be alright? You are my friend. You are a man of peace."

"I am safely in the hands of my Father, Elohim, Shai. It is not yet my time. As you already know, I am here to do His bidding. His work took me away from our visits, and I need to stay away for longer still."

"I wish that wasn't so."

"I miss you, too, but I must continue to reveal that I am the Messiah, the Son of God. As you know, I give a choice to those to whom I reveal myself. It is difficult for some. Have you made your choice, Shai?"

"I have grown to know you well. In our conversations, I am able to have more honest and revealing conversations with you than with anyone else in my life. You address my spiritual nature. You point out Elohim's desires and character." Deflecting his eminent decision, Shai splashed his toes in the pool of water at his feet.

Yeshua nodded affirmatively. "Yes, we are speaking about the nature of God."

Jennifer Bjork

"Often, we discuss love. You have consistently reflected what you teach through your caring, loving actions, Yeshua. To me, your actions reveal your true character. You have taught me that actions speak louder than words since that day when we first met. It made a big impression on me."

"I am glad. I cannot stay much longer, Shai. Please tell me what you have decided. Do you believe that I am the Messiah?"

It was time to declare his heart. Shai took a calming breath and looked into Yeshua's hazel eyes, those that seemed to reflect all colors and were so unfathomably deep that they seemed to contain the universe of stars.

"Yeshua, I thought my decision was obvious and would be easy, but it has not. On the one hand, I have witnessed so much. From your many miracles and teaching, I know that you cannot be a mere man, like Papa and Simon and Andrew. If I were merely a witness, I would have admitted that you are the Messiah much earlier. But, on the other hand, you are my friend. How can you be the powerful Messiah and spend so much time with a mere child...with me? How can the Son of God befriend the son of a fisherman...me? That is the part that I have trouble with."

"I understand. It is straightforward, Shai. Elohim is the God of love. He loves you so much. Elohim chose to place me in this part of the world. He planned for us to be together. I have been glad - even more, grateful - to share my time, peace, and wisdom with you. Shai, you also chose to share your time with me. You have shared your curiosity, wonder, playfulness, honesty, and especially your joy. I told you a long time ago that you were Elohim's gift to me, remember?"

Shai felt Yeshua clasp both of his hands. He felt his bearded friend's warm love pulse through him. He felt his own heart expand to fullness. Shai whispered, "Yes, I do."

"You have been my special Galilean friend, Shai. I love you. Do you believe that I speak the truth?"

"Yes."

"Then, believe who I say I am."

The Whistling Galilean

The boy could not stop staring into Yeshua's eyes. He had seen, participated in, and experienced so many of Yeshua's miracles firsthand. Quick memories flashed through his head - teaching him to swim, helping Alter get to the healer, seeing the trust of the leprous man, watching Yeshua skip a stone twelve times, overlooking thousands of people eat from the few fish and barley loaves, feeling the sudden calming of a storm at sea, and witnessing Simon's profession of faith after walking on water. Most importantly, he remembered feeling warmth from this healer's hands on his torso as his own small, broken body was healed. Yeshua had to be who he claimed to be!

"Yeshua," Shai's voice shook with emotion. "I believe that you are the Messiah. You cannot be anything less. I believe you, too."

APPENDIX 1

Characters, Definitions, and References

CHARACTERS

THE CHARACTERS IN THIS STORY ARE GROUPED BY RELATIONSHIP TO Shai, the protagonist. The Hebrew meaning of the name appears in parentheses.

Main characters
Shai (gift), nickname for Isaiah. Son of fisherman on the Sea of Galilee. Age 10-12
Yeshua (Jesus), first century name for Jesus. Also known as the Nazarene, the "rabbi of Nazareth," the Nazarene physician, Messiah (the Christ). Age 30-32 during this story.

Shai's family
Adina or **Adi** (gentle), younger sister. Age 7-9
Anat (to sing), mother. Also known as Mama Anat.

Ezra (helper), older brother. Age 14-16 (four years older than Shai).

Simcha or **Sim** (joy), younger brother. Age 5-7.

Yona (dove), a variation of prophet Jonah:

Yona the Elder, grandfather. Also known as the Elder. A former fisherman.

Yona the Younger, father. Also known as Papa Yona. A fisherman on the Sea of Galilee

Shai's friends and schoolmates

Carmi or **Carm** (vineyard), desired girlfriend. Family grows grapes, olives, lemons. Ezra knows her sister, Rachel. Age 10-12.

Dov (bear or strength), best friend. Family are fishermen to the south. Age 10-12.

Gil (joy), schoolmate and twin of Gal. Father is Capernaum's fishmonger.

Oz (strength), school bully. Farm boy. Age 11-13.

Shai's Teachers

Fishel (fish), mentor teaching Shai fishing trade. Age 19-21 (9 years older than Shai).

Rabbi (teacher) **Selig** (blessed or happy), spiritual leader in Capernaum.

Disciples of Yeshua

Andrew. Brother of Simon. Fisherman, lives in Capernaum. (Matthew 4:18-20)

Levi-Matthew, later called **Matthew**. Tax collector; lives in Capernaum. (Mark 2:14)

Simon (hear), later named **Peter**. Brother of Andrew. Fisherman, lives in Capernaum.

HEBREW TERMS

Elohim = the only name of God that first century Israelites could say out loud

Phylactery = black box worn on rabbi's forehead containing two scriptural passages

Shabbat = to detest from work; Sabbath or Saturday; day of rest in honor of God

Shalom = peace be to you

Sukkoth = booths, canvas tents; a ceremonial holiday in remembrance of Israelites forty-days in the desert

REFERENCES

Some passages in this story were quoted directly from the Bible. The author assessed several Bibles to expand her understanding of specific events for this book. She settled on <u>The Holy Bible, New International Version Study Bible</u>, 2008, published by Zondervan, as the source for the passages spoken by characters in this historical fiction. Phrases spoken by Yeshua that are exact quotes from this Bible appear in italics.

Chapter 2 - Yeshua told Shai a fisherman's version of the parable of the two sons, Matthew 21:28-31. "To us a child is born...." came from Isaiah 9:1.

Chapter 4 - Yeshua taught in a synagogue using Deuteronomy 6:4-9 and 11:13-14

Chapter 8 – Rabbi Selig taught his students from Leviticus 19:3 and 20:9. Students were taught to respect their father and mother from the Ten Commandments – Exodus 20:12 and 20:4-6. Rabbi Selig stressed the consequences of failure to honor them - Leviticus 19:13 and 20:9. Yeshua fondly referred to the sentiments of King David in Psalm 145:8 and 32:10.

Chapter 14 - Yeshua healed the paralytic, Matthew 9:2-8; two other disciples also reported these events - Mark 2:3-12 and Luke

5:18-25. "Praise the Lord, O my soul...." came from Psalm 103:1-5, 20-22.

Chapter 18 - Three of the Beatitudes from the Sermon on the Mount:
"Blessed are the poor in spirit, for theirs is the kingdom of heaven." Matthew 5:3
"Blessed are those that mourn, for they will be comforted." Matthew 5:4
"Blessed are the peacemakers, for they will be called the sons of God." Matthew 5:9

Chapter 19 - Yeshua healed the Leper, Matthew 8:1-4. Two other disciples also witnessed and recorded this event - Mark 1:40-42, Luke 5:12-13.

Chapter 20 - Yeshua calmed the Storm, Mark 4:36-41. Two other disciples reported this event as well - Matthew 8:23-27 and Luke 8:22-25.

Chapter 21 - Yeshua had so much work, that he called his twelve disciples and gave them authority to drive out evil spirits and to heal every disease and sickness.". Three disciples report his actions: Matthew 9:35-11:1.; also in Mark 6:6-11; and Luke 9:1-6
"I praise you, Father...because you have hidden these things from the wise and learned, and revealed them to little children." Matthew 11:25-26 and Luke 10:21.
"May the God of hope fill you with all joy and peace as you trust in him, so that you may overflow with hope by the power of the Holy Spirit." Romans 15:13

Chapter 24 - Yeshua fed the five thousand, Matthew 14:13-21. This event is reported in all four gospels - Mark 6:30-44, Luke 9:10-17, and John 6:1-14, 29. Yeshua's baptism is reported in John 1:19-34.

Chapter 25 - Yeshua walked on water, Matthew 14:22-33. This event is also covered in two other gospels - Mark 6:45-52, John 6:16-21.

Chapter 27 - Yeshua claimed to be the bread of life. This event is only covered by the disciple John. The entire event is found in 6:35-51:

Chapter 29 - "There is a time for everything...." Ecclesiastes 3:1-14

In addition to the Bible, the following were used as the primary sources to provide context for life in first-century Israel and the events surrounding Yeshua's ministry:

Edersheim, Alfred. 2014. The Life and Times of Jesus the Messiah: New Updated Edition, Complete and Unabridged in One Volume. Hendrickson Publishers Marketing, LLC. 1,109 pp.

Edersheim, Alfred. 1996. Sketches of Jewish Social Life in the Days of Christ. Hendrickson Publishers, Inc., Massachusetts. 342 pp.

All course materials provided by the Bible Study Fellowship during five years of study by the author: Genesis, the Books of Moses, Isaiah, Matthew, and John.

Vamosh, Miriam Feinberg. Daily Life at the Time of Jesus. Palphot, Ltd, Israel. 104 pp.

APPENDIX 2

Weights and Measures

THE AUTHOR CHOSE TO USE ROMAN WEIGHTS AND MEASURES TO STAY within the historical context of first-century way of life in Israel. The reader can convert those Roman terms to those with which they are familiar.

Weight
The Hebrew coin and weight, the **shekel**, had its origins in Babylonia and was carried throughout the Middle East. It was gradually adopted by other countries. In 268 BC, Rome standardized weights based on a silver **denarius**.

Capacity, liquid (volume)
The Roman capacity measurement was based on the **sextarius**. Since no two sextarii were identical, a mean general capacity was agreed upon.

Length
The royal cubit was standardized by a piece of black granite in Egypt. It was developed around 3,000 BC based on the length of

the arm from the elbow to the extended fingertips. The cubit stick was used in building the Great Pyramid of Giza. The Roman linear measurement was based on the Roman standard foot (**pes**).

	1st Century system	British/ United States system	Metric system
Weight			
Shekel (Hebrew)	1 shekel	40 chickpeas or 180 barleycorn	11.5 grams
Mina (Hebrew)	60 shekels		
Talent (Hebrew)	3,000 shekels		
Denarius (Roman)	1 denarius	0.167 ounce	4.57 grams
	6 denarii	1 ounce	27.41 grams
Capacity, liquid (Volume)			
Sextarius	1 sextarius	35.4 cubic inches or 1 pint	0.58 liters
Bath	6.5 sextarii	6.073 gallons or 4 quarts	3.785 liters
Amphora	48 sextarii	1,699.2 cubic inches	27.84 liters
Length			
Cubit (Egyptian/Hebrew)	1 royal cubit	1.718 feet	52.4 centimeters
Digit or finger (Roman)		0.062 (1/16) foot	5.55 centimeters
Palm width (Roman)		0.25 (1/4) foot	7.4 centimeters
Pes (Roman)	1 pes	0.971 feet	29.6 centimeters
Stadia (Roman)	625 pes	625 feet or 0.12 mile	185 meters
Mil (Roman)	8 stadia or 5,000 pes	0.72 mile	1.48 kilomets
Mil (Roman)	1.527 mil	1 mile or 5,280 feet or 10 minute walk	1.609 kilometers
Area			
Pes quadratus (Roman)	1 pes quadratus	1 square foot	0.088 square meters
Jugerum (Roman)	1 jugerum	1 square mile or 640 acres	2.59 square kilometers

Calendar

The Julian calendar in 45 BC was 365 days long. Starting in the year 4 AD, leap years occurred regularly every four years, adding an extra day. Romans grouped days into an eight-day cycle with every eighth day being a market day.

Astrologers kept a seven-day cycle naming the days after planets: Saturn-day, Sun-day, Moon-day, Mars-day, Mercury-day, Venus-day, Jove-day, and Venus-day.

The Hebrews also used a seven-day week. Their day began at sunset, not at sunrise. Their days were numbered rather than named except for two of the days. Friday could be called either the Prasceve or the sixth day. On Saturday or seventh day, the Sabbath or the holy day of rest began at sunset and ended at sunset the following day.

Time

The Romans divided the daytime into twelve hours, starting in the morning and ending in the evening. The night was divided into four watches. The duration of these hours and watches varied with the seasons. During the winter when nights were longer, each watch had a longer duration. Astrologers divided each day into twenty-four equal hours which became the basis for our modern days.

APPENDIX 3

Images

SINCE WE LIVE IN A VISUAL SOCIETY, THE AUTHOR SOUGHT HISTORIC photographs to help her set the scene. Those provided through the Library of Congress, Prints and Photographs Division were invaluable. The G. Eric and Edith Matson Photograph Collection were the primary source of digital images for landscapes and people around Palestine, now known as Israel and the West Bank.

Photographs in this collection were taken from 1898 to 1954 by unknown photographers with the American Colony (Jerusalem) Photo Department, a Christian colony of Americans and Swedes, and its successor firm, the Matson Photo Service. The Kensington Episcopal Home obtained exclusive rights for use of the Matson Photo collection and conveyed the images to the Library of Congress in 1978. In 2003, they transferred the rights for use of the collection to the American public.

The Detroit Publishing Company acquired exclusive rights to a form of photography that allowed them to mass produce color post cards and materials from 1905 to 1932. Their collection contained several early images documenting life in Puerto Rico. The author created portions of her story from several of these images also.

1. **Shoreline near Bethsaida.** The beach and trees in the distance of this historic image provided the idea for the fishermen's beach. The author imagined Shai's family and the fishing guild living nearby, utilizing the forest and hillside, and launching their boats from the beach. The photograph was taken in 1945 by a photographer associated with the Matson Photo Service.

2. **Fisherman throwing a cast net**. Shai tediously tied knots to make this type of net and Fishel taught him to cast it. In the late 1950's while living in Colombia, South America, the author's father purchased a similar cast net. She watched a fisherman teach her father how to throw it. Even though this photograph was taken at Caesarea in 1938 by a photographer with the American Colony Photo Department, this type of net was also used by fishermen on the Sea of Galilee.

3. **Boys in an olive grove**. This image helped create the scene in which Shai and his best friend throw stones and other objects at their girlfriends. As sixth graders, the author's class got into a similar rock throwing contest. In the author's mind, the olive trees were older and larger. This image was taken in a grove near Bethlehem, Israel, sometime between 1900 and 1934 credited to the Matson Photo Service. It was published in G. Eric Matson's <u>The Middle East in Pictures</u> in 1980.

4. **Five boys climb coconut palms**. Even though this stereoscopic photograph was not taken in Palestine, but in Puerto Rico in 1899, it illustrated Shai and other boys collecting palm leaves for the Sukkoth festival. As a child, the author watched young boys climb and harvest coconuts from palm trees on the coast of Colombia, South America. This image was made available to the Library of Congress by Strohmeyer and Wyman Publishing through the Detroit Publishing Company.

5. **Interior of a synagogue**. In 2014, the author visited the Nazareth Village site in Israel. This Village was developed for visitors to experience first-century life. She used the smoothed stone-hewn synagogue as her imagined interior of Capernaum's synagogue. Other aspects of the recreated village were also helpful, including residences and costumed Arabs using tools typical of that period of time.

6. **Model of a first-century fishing boat.** A boat was discovered in 1986 near Nof Ginosar in the mudbank of the northwestern shore of the lake. The twenty-eight-foot-long boat was only four feet wide. It was built of cedar and oak using mortise and tenon joints. It had only one mast and a cloth sail made of flax. Archeologists dug it out of the muddy sand. Carbon-14 dating on selected wood slivers dated the vessel to the first century. This boat has been preserved and available for study in the Yigal Alon Museum north of Tiberias. It is thought to be typical of the kind of fishing boat used by the fishermen in this story. The model was used to describe *Ole Blue*, Papa Yona's fishing boat.

7. **Carved food bowl.** This is actually a Caribbean calabash gourd, a useful container for food and drink carved by the talented wandering sea gypsy, Daniel Mead. Its outer hard shell lends itself to decorative carving. The author purchased this bowl during a visit to the US Virgin Islands. This design became her guide in describing Shai's idea for his own wooden food bowl.

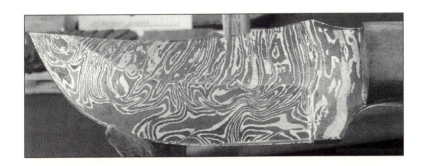

8. **Damascus steel-forged knife blade**. The first Damascus steel blade the author ever saw was designed and forged by the exceptional artisan, Ron Ganiero aka Buffalo Prairie Knives. The unique marbled appearance of the steel was created by melding carbon steel (shiny silver) and nickel steel (black). Even though the blade in this image is not a thin fillet knife, it was used to describe Yona the Elder's famous and coveted knife.

AUTHOR'S NOTE

A conversation with Jennifer Bjork...

Why did you choose to write this historical fiction? What inspired you?
Inspiration for this book arrived suddenly during a trip to Israel where I walked in Christ's footsteps with my husband. That trip not only brought the Bible to life, but it charged me with a special task. While riding on a touring boat on the Sea of Galilee with fellow pilgrims, my spirit was charged with the idea to write a story about Jesus from the unique point of view of a child.

My walk with God was slow. It began with learning to value, appreciate, and protect His creation. Over time, I sporadically learned stories about Jesus. Curiosity led me to in-depth study in the Bible Study Fellowship (BSF) and joyful singing of Christian music. Adding sermons and occasional mission trips, I grew into a different person. Through writing this book, I developed an even deeper relationship with and dependence on God. It took decades, but I now recognize that this was His plan all along.

What challenges did you face in writing this historical fiction?

My challenge was to select portions of the life of Jesus that could have been experienced and understood by a child. Once the decision to place the protagonist in a Galilean fishing community near Capernaum was made, the setting became the northern Sea of Galilee. Research took over a year. The Bible was my primary reference, especially the four Gospels. I only selected events that the boy may have heard about or witnessed. Then I turned to writings of Josephus, Alfred Edersheim, and study material from BSF to provide valuable insights into historic events revolving around Jesus. This material served as the backbone of this story.

Using my imagination, the ten-year old son of a fisherman, became a playful, active, joyful, deep thinker who imitated bird songs. Endowed with the personality of innocence, openness, and curiosity, I hoped Shai would provide a gentle filter through which to explore your own feelings about those ancient times.

Using life experiences, I created the boy's family, friends, their relationships and lifestyle. Inventing this world was easier. My childhood was filled with fabricated people, stories, and games, since there was no radio or television in my home. Parts of the story were based on experiences in coastal Colombia, work in marine environments for thirty years, life and struggles living in the third world, and sailing.

My focus was to show the character's reactions to what he learned from Jesus. His choices have consequences not just to him, but to those around him. In this coming-of-age story, the poor Hebrew subject of Rome dealt with jealousy, sibling rivalry, bullies, budding romance, and his desire for his father's respect and love.

Who helped you create this story?
My seed of knowledge sprouted in Bible Study Fellowship. This international, nondenominational organization focused on reading the Bible. The study questions assisted each of us relate the Bible message to our lives. I not only learned about Jesus and the time he spent on earth, but I also learned about myself and my beliefs.

Thanks also to the pastors who led the journey to Israel in 2014, especially Bill Carmichael and the tour guides who informed, guided, and created moving experiences among the hordes of other visitors to the historical geography we visited. It was there that God called me to do what was beyond my natural ability so that I would have to rely on Him to get it done.

Early readers of parts of the budding manuscript offered helpful suggestions which changed it considerably. Fia Cronin and Jill Fernandez come to mind. I especially valued the guidance and feedback from a retired pastor, Paul Wrenn.

When I needed an editor, John Fox was available and quickly provided incredibly useful developmental recommendations and final polishing. Many thanks to Ruth Mull, a valued sounding board throughout and helpmate during the tedious proofing phase.

My greatest thanks to my husband, Doug Deese. Our in-depth discussions were treasured as was the loving gift of time for this huge endeavor. The book would not exist without these people or my publisher, WestBow Press. My thanks to all.

Do you have a hope or desire through this novel?
I hope that you, the reader, allow this story to create a yearning to get to know Jesus. If you could spend time with Him like Shai did, what would you ask? What would you want to know?

There have been varied reactions toward the Nazarene and his radically different teachings, both then and now. Shai and other characters reflected many of those reactions. I pray that you get curious, like I did. Be bold! Explore your own knowledge and beliefs. Welcome to the journey! Mine is not over yet either.

Printed in the United States
by Baker & Taylor Publisher Services